Triple CROSS

In 1993, James Patterson wrote *Along Came a Spider*, which introduced the world to Alex Cross, a young detective working out of Washington, DC. Idealistic and courageous, Cross's deep love for his family gives him the strength to overcome the many forms of evil he confronts in his life and work. Since then, every Alex Cross thriller has been an international bestseller. *Triple Cross* is the thirtieth novel in this extraordinary series.

James Patterson is the author of other bestselling series, including the Women's Murder Club, Detective Michael Bennett and Private novels. His books have sold in excess of 400 million copies worldwide. Passionate about encouraging children to read, he also writes a range of books specifically for young readers. James has donated millions in grants to independent bookshops and has been the most borrowed adult author in UK libraries for the past thirteen years in a row. He lives in Florida with his family.

Why everyone loves
James Patterson and Alex Cross

'It's no mystery why James Patterson is the world's most popular thriller writer. Simply put: **nobody does it better**.'

Jeffery Deaver

'No one gets this big without **amazing natural storytelling** talent – which is what Jim has, in spades. The Alex Cross series proves it.'

Lee Child

'James Patterson is the **gold standard** by which all others are judged.'

Steve Berry

'Alex Cross is one of the **best-written heroes** in American fiction.'

Lisa Scottoline

'Twenty years after the first Alex Cross story, he has become one of the **greatest fictional detectives** of all time, a character for the ages.'

Douglas Preston & Lincoln Child

'Alex Cross is a **legend**.'

Harlan Coben

'Patterson boils a scene down to the single, telling detail, the element that **defines a character** or moves a plot along. It's what fires off the movie projector in the reader's mind.'

Michael Connelly

'James Patterson is **The Boss**. End of.'

Ian Rankin

WHO IS ALEX CROSS?

PHYSICAL DESCRIPTION:
==================

Alex Cross is 6 foot 3 inches (190cm), and weighs 196 lbs (89 kg).
He is African American, with an athletic build.

FAMILY HISTORY:
================

Cross was raised by his grandmother, Regina Cross Hope - known as Nana
Mama - following the death of his mother and his father's subsequent
descent into alcoholism. He moved to D.C. from Winston-Salem, North
Carolina, to live with Nana Mama when he was ten.

RELATIONSHIP HISTORY:
======================

Cross was previously married to Maria, mother to his children Damon and
Janelle, however she was tragically killed in a drive-by shooting. Cross
has another son, Alex Jr., with Christine Johnson.

EDUCATION:
=========

Cross has a PhD in psychology from Johns Hopkins University in Baltimore,
Maryland, with a special concentration in the field of abnormal
psychology and forensic psychology.

EMPLOYMENT:
==========

Cross works as a psychologist in a private practice, based in his home. He
also consults for the Major Case Squad of the Metro Police Department,
where he previously worked as a psychologist for the Homicide and Major
Crimes team.

PROFILE

A loving father, Cross is never happier than when spending time with
his family. He is also a dedicated member of his community and often
volunteers at his local parish and soup kitchen. When not working
in the practice or consulting for MPD, he enjoys playing classical
music on the piano, reading, and teaching his children how to box.

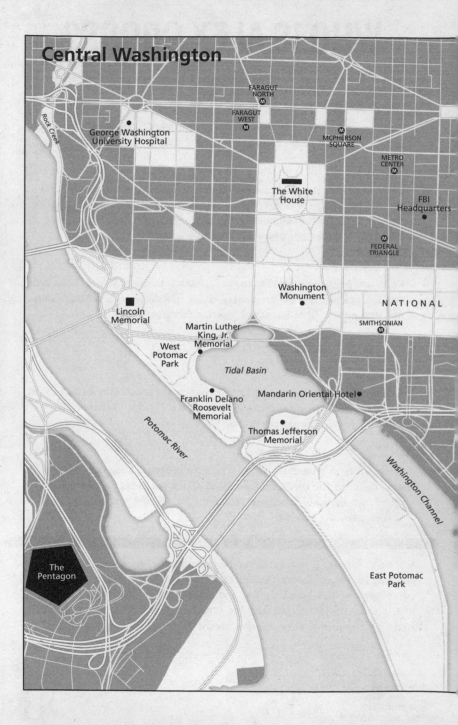

Verizon
Center

Metropolitan P.D.
Headquarters

MALL

L'ENFANT
PLAZA
Smithsonian
Institution

FEDERAL CENTER
SW STATION

NASA
Headquarters

WATERFRONT-
SEU STATION

WASHINGTON
UNION
Union
Station

United States
Supreme Court

United States
Capitol

Library of
Congress

CAPITOL
SOUTH

Garfield
Park

CAPITOL

HILL

5th Street Southeast

Cross family
home

EASTERN
MARKET

Lincoln
Park

NAVY YARD-
BALLPARK

Anacostia River

1000 yards

1000 metres

CIA Headquarters,
Langley

Hyattsville   495

WASHINGTON

Arlington
National
Cemetery

66

Fairfax

495

Annandale

Springfield

95

395

495

Alexandria

Joint Base
Andrews

495

Clinton

95

Accokeek

Waldorf

Potomac River

95

Quantico

5 miles

10 kilometres

A list of titles by James Patterson appears
at the back of this book

Triple
CROSS

JAMES
PATTERSON

PENGUIN BOOKS

PENGUIN BOOKS

UK | USA | Canada | Ireland | Australia
India | New Zealand | South Africa

Penguin Books is part of the Penguin Random House group of companies
whose addresses can be found at global.penguinrandomhouse.com

First published in the UK by Century in 2022
Published in Penguin Books 2023
001

Printed and bound in Great Britain by Clays Ltd, Elcograf S.p.A.

The authorised representative in the EEA is Penguin Random House Ireland,
Morrison Chambers, 32 Nassau Street, Dublin D02 YH68

A CIP catalogue record for this book is available from the British Library

ISBN: 978–1–529–15960–8
ISBN: 978–1–529–15961–5 (export edition)

www.greenpenguin.co.uk

MIX
Paper from
responsible sources
FSC® C018179

Penguin Random House is committed to a
sustainable future for our business, our readers
and our planet. This book is made from Forest
Stewardship Council® certified paper.

Triple
CROSS

PROLOGUE

ONE

SUZANNE LIU LIVED FOR days like this, days when her world seemed like a great game and the sweet smell of opportunity and cash hung in the air like lavender and sage.

In her late thirties, stylishly dressed, attractive, and very tall, Liu arrived at work in Lower Manhattan two hours before her crucial first appointment. She opened the door to a corner office with dramatic views of the Hudson River, stepped inside, shut the door, and paused a moment to take it all in.

On the inner wall to Liu's left hung her diploma from Yale and a photograph of herself playing Lady Macbeth in her first and only year in the graduate program at that university's fabled drama school. She did not give them a glance.

Her attention was drawn instead to the wall to her immediate right and three framed jackets of books by mega-bestselling nonfiction writer Thomas Tull.

Liu took a step closer to the framed jacket of Tull's most recent work, *Doctor's Orders*, which had been on the bestseller list for sixty-three weeks and showed no sign of fading anytime soon.

Liu studied Tull's author photo, and despite herself, she felt her breath and heart quicken. God, he was handsome and photogenic. His charisma seemed to jump out at you.

In his early forties, with chiseled facial features and built like a brick, Tull sported an unruly shock of sandy-brown hair. He also had piercing gray-blue eyes and a smile so easy and dazzling, it had played a big part in attracting female readers. Tull's natural good looks tended to disarm people, and Liu could not afford to be disarmed.

Not today. Not with so much at stake. My entire career, really.

That last thought almost triggered a panic attack, so Liu went quickly to her desk and put down her purse, her grande latte, and the canvas bag she used to carry manuscripts. She sat and forced herself to close her eyes and breathe deeply.

After fifteen minutes of meditating, Liu had calmed enough to focus on her intention for how the day would go.

"I made Thomas Tull," she muttered to herself. "He's mine. Tull is still mine. And no one is taking him from me."

Liu said it five times before opening her eyes and smiling. This *was* her day. She could feel it in her bones.

She took out a legal pad, and for the next hour, the editor in chief of Alabaster Publishing sipped her latte and wrote out four negotiating scenarios, every one of them involving a ridiculous number. That was what it was going to take, wasn't it? A ridiculous number. Liu was sure of that. There was no way around a ridiculous number, given Tull's repeated monstrous successes. And he'd made it clear he would entertain other offers.

How could he not?

At eight fifteen, Bill Hardaway, the founder and publisher of Alabaster, knocked on her door and entered.

"Ready for battle?" Hardaway asked as he took a seat opposite her.

"Always, Bill," Liu said. "When have I not been a fighter?"

"Just don't bankrupt us, Suzanne."

Hardaway was in his early fifties and people tended to underestimate him because he dressed like a stodgy college professor. But while other publishing firms crashed and burned around him, he had managed to build a thriving company. Hardaway had a keen understanding of what books could touch a nerve and reach blockbuster status, but he also ran a tight ship when it came to expenses.

"What's our top number?" she asked.

Hardaway shrugged. "I haven't decided yet. But we can't afford to lose him."

"We won't, Bill," she said. "I promise you that."

TWO

BILL HARDAWAY STOOD UP. "I'm holding you to that promise, Suzanne. Sorry I can't be here for all the horse-trading. Cynthia's got tests and I need to be there."

Hardaway's third wife was carrying twins. She was in her second trimester, and the pregnancy was considered high risk.

"Of course, Bill," Liu said. "And don't worry. I've got everything under control. You just do what you need to do, and we'll celebrate with champagne when you get back."

Hardaway left and she tried to return her focus to her legal pad. Fifteen minutes later, Liu was interrupted by another knock at the door.

Thomas Tull stuck his head in and threw a thousand-watt smile at her. "How's my favorite editor?" he asked in a teasing voice.

Feeling a little rattled, Liu got to her feet. "You're forty minutes early, Thomas."

"Because I knew you'd be here already, and as you might imagine, my day's full as well," Tull said. He came over to her, took her hands, and blew a Euro-kiss past each cheek. "You look stunning as always, Suzanne."

Liu tried to ignore the little thrill that went through her and said, "And you're looking better than ever. How often do you bleach those teeth?"

He grinned. "No need. Good genes."

"Something to drink?" she asked as they both sat down.

"I'm fine," he said. "Bill going to join us?"

"Cynthia's going in for tests. He left me to deal with you."

Tull laughed. "Okay, then. As soon as we finish here, I'll e-mail you a detailed proposal for the next book. But it's about the Family Man murders going on down in the Washington, DC, area."

Liu had heard of them, of course. Who hadn't? "You on the inside?" she asked.

"I will be shortly," he said. "I've already been down there several times doing research. Every time I leave, I wonder why. The story's gotten hold of me, Suzanne, and you know what that means."

She did. Tull favored total immersion in his subjects. When he got into that kind of all-encompassing state, he came up with a remarkable story, the kind that few readers ever forgot.

"I do," Liu said. "I've been with you all the way, haven't I?"

"Not all the way," he said.

"No one else would give you an offer on *Electric*, Thomas."

He chuckled. "Look who benefited from one of the all-time-lowball advances."

"We all benefited," Liu said, shifting in her chair. "As I remember, you bought a Tesla with the first royalties. The fact remains that we stepped up. We made you."

Tull's good cheer faded. "*I* made me, Suzanne. You and Bill helped. And I'm forever grateful. But your offer has to reflect the market and the interest in my work. I'll expect your best offer for world rights by five."

"World rights?" she said. "Best offer?"

"No negotiations; I want it to be clean," he said, getting to his feet. "I want a home and a partner and clear income for the next few years. And I want it to be simple."

"This is simple, and you've got a partner," she said, feeling anxious as she followed him to the door.

"We'll see," he said, blowing a kiss past each cheek again. "May the best editor and publishing house win. And remember, this isn't personal. It's business. I love you and Bill no matter what."

"Of course," she said, putting on a brave smile. "Good luck."

Tull grinned and walked off, looking at his phone. "I'm sending you that proposal now. I'd read it soon if I were you," he called over his shoulder.

"Right away," she said and hurried to her desk.

An hour later, Liu shook her head in admiration and a little awe. How did Tull always manage to find the powerful angle? How did he get so many people to speak to him? Even the people with something to lose!

Her cell rang.

"Sorry I didn't call earlier," Hardaway said. "Cynthia's been admitted and the wing she's in at Lenox Hill has zero service."

"Admitted? I thought she was just getting some tests."

"She was until she started bleeding." The publisher sighed. "Right there in the ob-gyn's office. It's touch and go."

"Oh God," Liu said. "I'm so sorry, Bill. I'm praying for her and you."

"I'll take the prayers," he said. "How was Tull?"

"Smug," she said. "But he has a right to be. The proposal is dynamite, blockbuster material as strong as the others. Maybe stronger."

"I wish we could clone him," he said and then paused. "Hold on."

The editor waited, tapping her pencil, looking at her legal pad and her negotiating strategies. They would have to be adjusted in light of—

"Suzanne, I have to go," Bill said. "It's not good."

"I'm sorry, Bill," she said. "But I need some guidance here. He wants—"

"I trust you," he said. "Make your best call and keep him in the fold."

He hung up.

THREE

AT SIX THAT EVENING, Liu kicked off her heels and began pacing again.

She'd been doing it off and on since sending Tull Alabaster's formal offer, which she'd made without Hardaway's final approval because she hadn't heard from the publisher since that morning.

Even her texts had gone unanswered.

It's a good offer, the editor thought, ignoring the beautiful sunset over the Hudson. *No, it's a great offer for world rights. And we made him. I made him. Rescued him when there were no other offers. He'll take that into account, won't he?*

An hour passed. It was dark. She could hear other employees calling it a day and leaving.

Liu looked at Tull's framed book covers once again: *Electric, Noon in Berlin, Doctor's Orders.*

Every one of them had sold millions of copies, even *Electric*, which he'd written while an older undergraduate student at Harvard after a stint as a military police investigator with the Marines and NCIS.

"I was the only one who saw your talent back then," Liu whispered to Tull's most recent author photo. "You owe me, Thomas. You owe me big-time. And it's a great offer. No one will be more generous than me. You know that. I've given you everything, haven't I? You know I—"

Her cell phone buzzed. She walked over, saw a message from Tull.

"You're mine, Thomas," she said, opening the text.

Liu's stomach began to drop even before he'd stated it plainly.

"No," she whispered. "That's not right."

Anger surged up through her and she punched in Tull's number. The call went straight to voice mail. "Call me," she said. "You've got to allow me some time to counter. I can't—"

The line went dead. The editor stared at her phone, her anger turning to the kind of rage only a scorned woman knows.

"No, no, no," she said, punching in the number again. The line disconnected after one ring.

Liu grabbed her coat and shoes. "This is not happening! You are not ghosting me, Thomas Tull! You owe me!"

The editor charged out her door and down the hall, muttering, "He's at the Ritz. Thomas always stays at the Ritz. He'll be at the bar and—"

Glass shattered. A voice roared in pain from the office on the opposite corner of the building, near the elevators.

Liu stopped and stared; she heard choking noises coming through the open door. She hurried over and saw Hardaway sitting at his desk, hunched over and sobbing.

"Bill?" she said, the bad feeling in the pit of her stomach growing. "What's happened?"

The publisher looked up at her, ruin in his face and rheumy eyes. "They're gone," he said hoarsely. "Both stillborn."

"No," she moaned, stepping into his office. "You must be crushed. Cynthia?"

"In shock," he said. "We're both in shock. It was our last chance to have kids and...she's sedated. I want to be."

Liu swallowed. "Bill, I know this isn't the time to talk about the offer I made."

Hardaway stared at her blankly. "How much?"

"It doesn't matter," Liu said. "He didn't take it."

He blinked. "Tell me that's not true."

"He took a higher offer. One book. Eleven point two million for world rights."

"Eleven point two?" the publisher said, sounding stunned. "Well, that's...why didn't you offer twelve?"

"Twelve million?" she said angrily. "We'd have to sell almost a million and a half copies in hardcover to make that—"

"So what?" Hardaway snapped, red-faced. He got to his feet. "You should have counteroffered it."

"There were no counteroffers heard, Bill," she said. "His terms. Make the best offer by five, that's it, winner takes all. I tried to tell you that this morning and—"

"What was your best offer?"

"Ten."

"Ten?" he shouted and then shot her a disgusted look. "Were you trying to insult him? Drive him out? The man who made your career and this house? The man you still have—"

"No, I don't," Liu shouted back, cutting him off. "And *we*

made *him,* Bill. Not the other way around. I thought ten million was insanely generous. I thought—"

"You thought wrong," Hardaway roared. "You lost the golden goose on the worst day of my life, Suzanne! For that, you're fired!"

"Fired?" she said, shocked into a whisper. "Bill, you can't—"

"I just did," he said coldly. "Get your things and clear out. I need new blood in here before everything around me dies."

Triple
CROSS

CHAPTER

A WALL OF RHODODENDRON bushes prevented anyone in the neighborhood from seeing the interior of the compound: a rambling
white Cape with dark green shutters and a four-bay carriage
house set on three landscaped acres.

Though it was dark now, the killer the media had recently dubbed "the Family Man" knew everything beyond
the rhododendrons was picture-perfect. The lawns were lush
and cut so precisely, they looked like green jigsaw-puzzle
pieces set amid flower gardens ablaze with spring glory and
color.

The sprinkler system goes on at four, Family Man thought, glancing at the phone. Two a.m. *More than enough time.*

With latex-gloved hands, the killer started the book-size
Ozonics ozone machine attached to a belt, tugged up the hood
of the black hazmat suit, and donned a respirator mask and

night-vision goggles. Family Man padded across one piece of jigsaw lawn to a walkway and the junction box of the alarm system.

It was disabled in six minutes.

Around the back, by the pool, the killer went to a bulkhead. It opened on well-oiled hinges.

The Schlage dead bolt on the basement door was no match for the technician's skills. It turned in under a minute.

After two careful steps, then three, Family Man halted inside and listened a moment before peering around the basement. The floor was bare. The wall cubbies and shelves, however, were filled with artifacts of a suburban family, stacked and organized like a Martha Stewart dream.

The killer started up the stairs, knowing that on the other side of the door lay a short hall and the kitchen. And a dog, an aging Labrador retriever named Mike.

At the door, Family Man reached through a Velcro slit in the hazmat suit, took out a baggie containing a cheese-and-anchovy ball, opened the door, tossed in the bait, and closed the door with a loud click.

The killer stood there, taking slow breaths with long pauses and listening to the sound of dog nails clicking on hardwood floors. The ozone machine purred, destroying all human odor.

Mike snuffled at the door, clicked over, and slurped down the treat.

Fifteen minutes later, Family Man eased open the door and stepped into the main house, hearing the loud ticking of the grandfather clock in the front hall and the snoring of the dog lying just a few feet away. Swinging the night-vision goggles around, the killer took in the particulars of the kitchen.

Huge stainless-steel Coldspot fridge and freezer. Six-burner Aga stove. Double sink on the prep island. Copper pots hanging from the ceiling. Italian espresso machine.

These details counted, didn't they? Of course they did. They were the essence of it all.

Satisfied that things were going according to plan, Family Man shrugged off a small pack, retrieved a pistol, and began the evening's real work.

CHAPTER

2

THE PISTOL, A GLOCK, was chambered in .40 caliber and fitted with a sound suppressor. Family Man liked the balance it gave the weapon.

The master suite, which lay beyond the kitchen and the great room, was so neat it looked like a crew of maids had just finished cleaning. The leather furniture was showroom new. The rows of books on the shelves appeared unread.

It could be a stage set, the killer thought, easing open another door to reveal an anteroom and a huge walk-in closet.

To the right of the anteroom lay the bathroom. Beyond a pocket door to the left, Family Man knew, Roger and Sue Carpenter were deep asleep, aided by the hissing of a white-noise app.

The couple didn't hear the pocket door sliding back or the Family Man slipping across the carpet to the right side of a four-poster bed. Mr. Carpenter, an attorney with boyish good looks, lay on his back with his forearm across his eyes, which made things easier.

Once, long ago, the killer had heard a Navy SEAL commander describe the perfect up-close execution with the word *canoe*. It meant shooting someone high in the head so that the bullet left the shape of a canoe bottom as it passed through the top of the skull.

Family Man canoed Carpenter through the forehead. His wife stirred at the thud of the silenced shot.

By the time the killer got around the bed to a WASPish-looking blonde in her thirties, she was half awake, her eyes open but puzzled.

"Roger?" she asked sleepily.

"Shhh," Family Man said and shot her from two feet away.

She died instantly, but blood splashed off the headboard and spattered the upper chest and arms of the killer's hazmat suit. A few drops hit the night-vision goggles.

Family Man plucked a tissue from the box beside the dead housewife and dabbed at the goggles until the view was clear again. The tissue fell on the bloody pillow next to Mrs. Carpenter.

The killer slid the pocket door back into place, walked through the great room and kitchen, stepped over the snoring Mike, and found the door to the mother-in-law apartment.

Pearl Naylor, Mrs. Carpenter's mother, was a light sleeper and spry for seventy-eight. She rolled in bed and almost got her bony finger on the light switch, which would have sent blinding light through the goggles and might have changed the course of the night.

But before the old woman could flip the switch, Family Man

shot her through the upper left side of her skull. She sagged off the bed, her legs caught in the sheets and blankets.

A few moments later, the killer exited Mrs. Naylor's apartment and paused a moment before climbing the stairs.

Despite the Family Man's training and experience, children were always the hardest.

CHAPTER

3

MY NAME IS ALEX CROSS. I am an investigative consultant for the Washington, DC, Metro Police, where I was a homicide detective for many years, and for the FBI, where I was once a member of the Bureau's Behavioral Science Unit, the team that hunts serial killers and other bringers of doom and mayhem.

I felt like I was tracking one of those dark beings when I got out of my car in a swank neighborhood in Chevy Chase, Maryland, not far from the nation's capital. Blue lights flashed on two state police cruisers blocking the road.

John Sampson pulled in behind me in an unmarked squad car. A first-rate detective in Metro PD homicide, Sampson was also my oldest friend.

"I thought this was over," he said.

"Dreams dashed," I replied.

An FBI forensics van arrived before we even got to the yellow tape and the cruisers. A hundred yards ahead, two more cruisers were parked, lights flashing, cutting off traffic from that direction. Beyond them, the first satellite-news van was pulling in.

"And the games begin again," Sampson said.

"This is the sickest game I've ever heard of," I said angrily, showing my identification to the troopers.

Once we were beyond the police barrier, Sampson said, "We know numbers?"

I shook my head. "The maid saw the grandmother and backed out."

A short man in his mid-forties with sandy hair and wearing a blue FBI windbreaker came down the driveway toward us.

"You been inside?" Sampson asked.

"Waiting for you," said Ned Mahoney, FBI special agent in charge. "You're the only ones who've been to all the earlier crime scenes, and I wanted your eyes on the place first. See if Family Man has finally made a mistake."

"Hope springs eternal," I said. We walked up the driveway and saw a white Porsche Cayenne in one bay of the carriage house and a red Corvette in another.

"Big money?" Sampson said.

"The whole neighborhood is big money," Mahoney said.

"What's the maid's story?" I asked.

Mahoney said she'd arrived at six a.m., her normal time, and came in through the kitchen door to find the family dog whining. After feeding the dog, she went into the mother-in-law's apartment, also her routine.

"The maid saw grandma and got so upset, she had chest pain and couldn't breathe after she called 911," Ned said. "She's in the ER with a uniformed officer now."

We put on hazmat suits, blue booties, latex gloves, surgical masks, and hairnets so as not to contaminate the house with our own DNA.

The assassin the media had dubbed "the Family Man" had attacked twice before in the DC area, and twice before, we and a great team of forensic investigators had scoured the crime scenes top to bottom and did not come up with a single strand of DNA that did not belong to the victims or their immediate families or friends.

There had been no unidentified fingerprints either. And no footprints. No alarms triggered. No signs of tinkering at the locks. And the killer had left no witnesses and no suspicious footage of any kind on the security cameras in the surrounding areas.

Mahoney adjusted his mask and said, "Let's go catch the perfect killer."

"There's no such thing," I said.

"I don't know, Alex," Sampson said. "He hasn't thrown a ball off the plate yet."

CHAPTER

4

I HAD GROWN TO hate entering the Family Man's crime scenes.

In my line of work, it was normal to come upon a murdered adult. It was all too common to encounter multiple victims. And while it was always shocking and disheartening to face slain children, it wasn't unusual.

But it was almost unheard of to find three and sometimes four generations of a single family murdered, one after another, in the same house over the course of the same night. So far, the killer had given no reason, left no note, offered no insight whatsoever into his mind.

It enraged me and everyone else assigned to the case. Indeed, as we went into the house, I could see grim anger in the faces of every agent, detective, and forensics expert on hand.

Who shoots old people and children like that? With no emotion? And why? Goddamn it, why?

I had never seen anything like this case. The killings were all cold, technical, no signs of passion or obsession.

The seven newest victims—Mr. and Mrs. Carpenter, Granny Pearl, twelve-year-old twins Alice and Mary, nine-year-old Nick, and five-year-old Alan—had all been executed the same way the others had: shot at close range through the upper part of the skull.

Seeing the victims angered me even more, especially the kids, particularly the boys. Nick was a year younger than my son Ali, and Nick's younger brother, Alan, had cerebral palsy. Mahoney and Sampson were equally shocked.

"What kind of sick, unfeeling bastard executes a special-needs kid?" Ned said.

"Or the grandmother of a special-needs kid?" Sampson said.

Those questions spun in my mind as I tried to suppress my anger and see the crime scene on its own and in relation to the others.

"A careful, sick, unfeeling bastard," I replied. "I think he did it bottom to top—mom and dad first, grandma second, the four kids last."

"Makes sense," Mahoney said. "Biggest threats first."

I nodded. "And he polices his brass as he goes."

Sampson said, "The more I think about the lack of DNA evidence in the other cases and probably here, the more I figure he's got to be dressed like us."

"You mean in PPE?" I said.

"It's the only explanation I can come up with," he said. "I mean, we're seeing no signs of recent cleaning up here."

Mahoney said, "The maid says Mrs. Carpenter was a neat freak, so we might not know if he cleaned anything."

"PPE, I'm telling you," Sampson said. "Gloves plus gown plus hairnet plus mask plus eye protection equals no DNA."

"I think we should operate on that assumption until proven otherwise," I said. "And I need to get out of this gear for a bit. I'm getting claustrophobic."

"Let's take a break," Mahoney said. "Get forensics in here."

We left by the back door and stood by the pool stripping off our protective equipment, feeling renewed outrage at these deaths and a little defeated by the lack of evidence around them.

"However he's dressed, he's a pro," I said. "Gotta be."

"Hundred percent trained assassin," Mahoney said, nodding.

"I agree," Sampson said. "If he were an ordinary sicko, he might have done it in a different way each time and then hung around to play a little. This guy is on a mission, in and out. Absolutely ruthless. I mean, again, who shoots a special-needs kid?"

"Someone who's getting his own needs met," Ned said as he waved to a crew of FBI techs waiting to enter the house.

I said, "Sure, but what needs? What does he get out of this? He's certainly not doing it for jollies."

Sampson shrugged. "Money? Power? Revenge?"

"Maybe," I said. "But there were no connections whatsoever between the Hodges family and the Landau family, and I doubt the Carpenter family will break that pattern. What links them? How does he choose his victims? What's his motivation? We're no closer to knowing that than we were a year ago when these killings started."

"Then we need to work harder," Sampson said, looking down the driveway at a growing crowd of neighbors across the street. "Go back to basics. Pound some shoe leather until something gives."

"I'm with you," I said. "Let's go."

Mahoney said, "I'm staying put. Let me know what the locals say."

We walked down the driveway and across the street to the police tape, behind which about twenty people were gathered. The media was being kept off to the left.

Sampson and I knew several of the reporters, and they began shouting at us. But we ignored them, split up, and tried to talk to the neighbors, who were upset and firing more questions at us than we were at them.

When we informed them that the entire Carpenter family was gone, several of the women broke down sobbing. Carrie Baldwin, who lived up the street and claimed she and Sue Carpenter had been BFFs, almost fainted in her husband's arms when we confirmed that Alan had also been murdered in cold blood.

"Our son's going to be devastated," Carrie said when she'd calmed down enough to talk. "Stuart has special needs too. They…they were the best of pals."

"Any reason someone would target the family for murder like this?" I asked.

"Sue was a saint," Carrie said, genuinely bewildered. "When my Stuart was born, she was the first one who reached out. She was always like that, looking out for others. People loved that family, all of them."

Baldwin's husband, Max, tilted his head and said, "Well, for the most part."

I looked at him. He was dressed for a tennis outing. "How's that?"

"Roger was a high-dollar divorce attorney," Max said. "Super-nice dude here at home, but he had a reputation for tearing husbands' throats out in family court."

"Max!" his wife said. "Don't speak ill of the dead!"

"Hey, it's true, Carrie," Max said. "Two guys in my office?

Their ex-wives hired Roger. They said dealing with him was like being examined by an angry proctologist."

"What?" his wife said.

"Think about it a little, Carrie," Max said. He turned to me. "You want a list of suspects? Start looking at all the poor bastards Carpenter took to the cleaners."

5

THE WEATHER COULD NOT have been more perfect for a mid-April evening: temperature in the mid-seventies, low humidity. My wife, Bree Stone, and I decided to sit out on the front porch until dinner.

Bree used to be the chief of detectives for Metro PD and now worked for a private security company. Along with Sampson and Mahoney, Bree was who I went to when I was trying to figure out a case or when I wanted a different perspective on things.

After I'd described the investigation's initial findings, Bree said, "It's a little extreme to kill an entire family because of a lousy divorce settlement, don't you think?"

"More than extreme," I said. "And my gut says that's not the motive for these killings. There's no link that I know of to a bad divorce or divorce attorney in the Hodges or the Landau cases. Hodges was a petroleum lobbyist. Landau was a pilot for Delta."

"What about the wives?" Bree asked.

"Mrs. Carpenter was evidently devoted to her children and did volunteer work, a pillar of the community. Mrs. Hodges taught school in Falls Church. Mrs. Landau was a CPA in DC. If there's a common link, I'm not seeing it."

From behind the blooming vines that shielded one end of the porch, a voice called out, "Maybe it's their kids, Dad."

Bree moaned her displeasure.

"Ali?" I said, crossing my arms.

My youngest came around where we could see him. Smiling, his dirty hands chopping the air, he said, "Think about it! They probably went to the same summer camp or had swimming lessons together, or maybe they were in the same Sunday school. I'm telling you, it's the kids."

Bree, who did not approve of Ali's obsessive interest in our cases, said, "How long have you been eavesdropping, young man?"

Ali's face fell. "I wasn't eavesdropping."

"What would you call it?" I asked.

"Weeding Nana Mama's herb garden like she asked me to?"

I looked at Bree, who sighed.

I said, "You know the cases we work on are confidential."

Ali nodded. "I'm not telling anyone anything."

"That's not really the point, pal," I said. "I'd be in a heap of trouble if it got out at the Bureau or inside Metro that I shared information about an ongoing case with a ten-year-old, even one as sharp as you."

He frowned. "I'm almost eleven. And you're saying I shouldn't weed for Nana?"

"No, we're not," Bree said. "But if you hear us talking in the future, do the right thing and let us know you're there, please."

Ali brightened a little. "I can do that."

Before we could add anything, the front door opened, and my ninety-something grandmother peered out at us.

"Dinner's ready," Nana Mama said. "Spicy salmon-and-sweet-potato cakes, homemade tartar sauce, baby asparagus, and bow-tie pasta with garlic and butter."

There was no argument from any of us, and we followed Nana back into her beloved kitchen, where the woman who'd spent many years as the vice principal of a tough inner-city school performed culinary magic every day. We sat at the table, said grace, and dug in.

After her first bite of the fish cake, Bree closed her eyes with pleasure. "Oh, Nana, that's so good. Where did you get this recipe?"

My grandmother pushed her glasses higher up on the bridge of her nose. "I made it up."

"C'mon," I said. "This tastes like something you'd get in a restaurant."

She grinned. "Except you can only get it here, tonight, for the first time ever."

"So good," Ali said. "The homemade tartar sauce too."

"What's in the cakes besides salmon and sweet potatoes?" Bree asked.

Nana Mama hesitated. "Green onions, some sriracha sauce, a little of this and a little of that. I'm still experimenting."

"Make them exactly this way again next time," Ali gushed. "You can't make them any better than this!"

My grandmother laughed and said, "Want to bet?"

6

BEFORE ALI COULD ANSWER, we heard the front door open and shut. My seventeen-year-old daughter, Jannie, came in a few moments later dressed in a blue tracksuit, her skin glowing, her eyes and smile wide.

"It smells so good," Jannie said. "Sorry I'm late, Nana."

"Everything's still warm, child," Nana Mama said. "You must be hungry."

"I need a shower first."

Bree waved at the food with her fork. "Take it after. Better sit down and have a few of these salmon cakes before we devour them all."

Jannie took off her warm-up jacket, sat down, and heaped food on her plate. After several bites, she groaned and said, "These are incredible! Can you try them with crabmeat?"

"I can," Nana Mama said.

"No," Ali said. "Just like this."

"I'll make them both ways," Nana promised, then looked at Bree. "You've been home quite a while, haven't you? What exotic city are you off to next?"

Bree smiled. "I don't know, Nana. I wrapped up a project last week and my boss is keeping my next assignment a secret until our meeting tomorrow morning."

"Just as long as it's not Paris again," my grandmother said. "That was too dangerous, if you ask me."

Bree and I exchanged glances, and I knew to change the subject. "I'm sure it will be a domestic deal, Nana," I said, then I looked to Jannie. "How did practice go?"

Jannie was chewing, but she beamed and clapped until she finally swallowed. "Coach said it was my best workout of the season. I'm fast, hundredths off my best, consistently."

Jannie had grown seven inches in eighth grade and four more in ninth, so she was taller, longer, and lankier than most girls her age. She was also stronger, with tremendous lung capacity and a God-given talent for running the grueling four-hundred-meter race.

Jannie was so good at the event, she'd attracted the attention of coaches at Division 1 schools as well as private coaches. She had already been offered scholarships to several colleges, including the University of Oregon and the University of Texas. But the coaches who'd talked to her and us had been split on whether she should focus solely on the four-hundred-meter or broaden her horizons to the multi-event heptathlon, where her natural overall athleticism shined.

"Are you training for any of the field events these days?" Bree asked.

"Not this week," Jannie said, taking another salmon cake.

"I'm running in that regional invitational Saturday at Howard University, and Coach wants me to focus on the four-hundred. He said a lot of college coaches will be there."

"There's always some college coach at your meets," Ali said. "When are you going to make up your mind and choose?"

"I was kind of wondering the same thing," I said.

"Take the best track program," Bree said. "The one that will take you the farthest toward your Olympic dream."

"The best academics," Nana Mama said, shaking her fork. "Sports are fleeting."

For a few moments, Jannie didn't say anything, just gave us all a cryptic smile. Then she said, "After this race, if it goes the way Coach says it could go, I think I'll know exactly where I'm supposed to be."

CHAPTER

7

BREE LEFT THE HOUSE first the following morning, heading off to her meeting at the Bluestone Group's headquarters across the Potomac in Arlington, Virginia.

Sampson and I were not far behind her.

We drove back to Chevy Chase and the Carpenters' neighborhood and knocked on the door of many a small mansion. We got very little. Either the residents had not known the Carpenters or they had known them so well that they were too devastated to talk.

Again and again, we were told how wonderful Sue and Roger Carpenter had been as neighbors, friends, and fellow worshippers at the nearby Episcopal church. And again and again, we saw the evidence of the strange, terrible fascination and fear that the Family Man killings had ingrained in the public mind.

"I haven't seen it like this since the Beltway sniper attacks when I was a kid," said one neighbor, a man named Chuck Reed. He lived around the corner from the Carpenters. "Everyone's scared to go out or is talking about putting in better alarm systems. But it doesn't matter, does it? The killer has to be an expert on those systems because Roger Carpenter had one. Am I right? He disables them and goes right on in, doesn't he?"

"We think so, Mr. Reed," I said, giving him my card.

Elaine Parsons lived up the street from Reed in a large Tudor-style home with a For Sale sign out front. She opened her door on a chain and peered out at us with bloodshot eyes.

We held up our identification. "We're with Metro Police," I began.

"I figured," Parsons said. "I don't know anything. If I did, I'd tell you."

"Can we talk anyway, ma'am?" Sampson said.

She hesitated, then drew back the chain and stepped out onto the porch. "Place is a mess inside. I've been…packing."

She was in her late thirties, I guessed, and quite pretty, with long, wavy auburn hair. She wore yoga gear and her body looked fit, but her face was a different story. Her skin was sallow. She had bags under her eyes. Her breath and the coffee she carried smelled of vodka.

"Did you know the Carpenters?" I asked.

"Sue was the salt of the earth," Parsons said. "And Roger was the best divorce attorney in the business. Got me this house and half of everything Hank had."

"Hank's your ex-husband?"

"As of last month, you betcha," she said and sipped on the coffee and vodka.

"Did Hank know the Carpenters?"

She snorted. "He and Roger were big golfing buddies until

Roger told him I'd given him a five-dollar retainer fee years ago in case Hank and I ever got on the outs."

Sampson asked, "When did Hank learn this?"

"When he tried to hire Roger to divorce me so he could marry Sally the Ice Queen," she said, smiling and enjoying the memory. "Hank flipped and broke a nine iron because he knew what Roger could do to him. He called Roger a traitor even though I retained Roger the very first time I met him. I'd heard what a tiger he was and just handed him the five bucks. Turns out he *was* a tiger, a kind—"

Parsons stopped talking, her jaw quivering. Tears began to roll down her cheeks. She looked up at us. "Roger was one of the good guys. Even though Hank hated him after that, he did right by me. I…I can't believe he's gone."

Sampson said, "When did you last see Roger or Sue?"

She thought for a moment. "I saw Sue jog by last week. Roger I saw maybe two days ago?"

"Where was that?"

She appeared confused. She squinted and said, "At his mailbox."

"At the bottom of the driveway?" I asked.

Parsons looked down and nodded. "I was late for a spa appointment. I didn't stop. We just waved at each other. I…I didn't know I would never see him again."

She put her face in her hands and broke down sobbing. "So many things are ending on me, I can't stand it half the time."

8

THAT MORNING, BREE WALKED into the corporate offices of the Blue-stone Group in Arlington, Virginia, greeted the receptionist, and was told that Elena Martin was awaiting her in the conference room.

Bree had been in law enforcement for nearly twenty years and had worked every kind of case people could imagine and a few no one could. But she still felt the familiar thrill of anticipation as she headed to the conference room.

The last time she'd come in for a secret assignment like this, she'd ended up in Paris in a firefight with modern vigilantes associated with a mysterious organization known as Maestro and its even more mysterious leader, a man who called himself M.

Maestro and M had come into Bree's life through Alex. One day about five years ago, out of the blue, Alex and John Sampson began getting texts from M. At times, M's texts were taunting, criticizing her husband and his partner. But occasionally, M gave Alex information that resulted in big arrests.

But that all changed when M sent ex–Special Forces commandos to ferret out and kill U.S. federal law enforcement officers and agents corrupted by the Mexico-based Alejandro drug cartel. After Bree survived the firefight in Paris, Alex and Sampson got in the middle of the Maestro investigation and were caught in the Montana wilderness in open combat between M's forces and the Alejandro cartel's soldiers.

The experience had almost cost them their lives.

But now, the Alejandro cartel was no more. And M had been silent ever since the cartel's leader had been killed when her private jet was blown up as it was taxiing down the runway.

Elena Martin waved at Bree from the other side of a glass wall. The founder and CEO of the Bluestone Group was talking on her phone and nodding. Two large cardboard boxes rested on the table in front of her.

Martin, wearing a sharply cut gray pantsuit, had shoulder-length light brown hair and a no-nonsense style that Bree loved. A former investigator with the Defense Intelligence Agency, Martin was also an entrepreneurial visionary who, after leaving the military and her marriage, had built Bluestone into one of the top private security firms in the country by aggressively recruiting top law enforcement professionals like Bree.

Martin was demanding but generous. What more could you want in a boss?

She ended her phone call as Bree pushed open the door and said, "Hello, Elena. Am I early?"

Martin smiled, stood, and extended her hand. "Bree," she said. "How good to see you." The two shook, and Martin gestured for Bree to sit. "I saw there's been another Family Man killing. Alex must be busy."

"Up to his eyeballs, as our boys, Ali and Damon, like to say," Bree said, sitting.

"Any leads?"

"None that I've heard," she said, feeling slightly uncomfortable. "Because he doesn't share much with me about the case. He can't."

"Understood," Martin said, also sitting down. "The whole thing's just wrong. On another, happier note, I read your report on the Wallace Industries investigation. Well done."

"Thank you. It didn't take me long to figure out who was embezzling from their research fund."

"Well, *they* couldn't figure it out, and Ken Wallace himself called yesterday to say how pleased they were with the results of your work," Martin said. "He also gave us a hefty contract to examine his company's security protocol worldwide, which I believe calls for a hefty bonus for you in your next paycheck, Ms. Stone."

Bree was happily surprised. "Thank you, Elena. I didn't expect that, but I'm not going to turn it down if you're offering."

"Who would? And I'm insisting," Martin said. She steepled her fingers. "You were the one."

Raising her eyebrows, Bree said, "The one?"

Martin pointed to the two boxes on the conference table. "The first and only one I thought of when this delicate case came our way. We have a client with very deep pockets who wishes to remain deeply anonymous."

"Do you know the client?"

"I know the client's representative but not the client, no."

"What am I doing?" Bree said, reaching for the boxes. "Where am I going?"

Martin put her hand on Bree's. "You need to sign a nondisclosure agreement."

"Isn't nondisclosure boilerplate in our contracts?"

"Not in this case," Martin said. "The client's nondisclosure agreement is punitive."

"Punitive?"

"If anything leaks, you and I and the firm could be sued for damages."

Bree frowned at that. "Elena, I'm not saying anything is going to leak, but—"

"Don't worry," Martin said. "I'm taking out an insurance policy to cover any damages we might incur from this case."

"Is the contract worth it?"

"Yes, and you have no idea what it might mean down the road for you, for me, and for Bluestone if we can prove ourselves with this case." Martin slid three documents across the table to Bree. "Sign if you're in. If not, no problem, I can find someone less talented to do the job for a smaller piece of the company's future."

Bree hesitated for a moment, then smiled as she found a pen in her purse. "Well done yourself, Elena. You got me hook, line, and sinker."

"Thank you, Bree," Martin said. "I'd hoped that would work."

9

AFTER BREE SIGNED THE NDA, Elena Martin left for another meeting. Bree took the two cardboard boxes into her office and locked the door behind her.

She removed her jacket and got out a pad of paper and her phone in case she wanted to take photographs for later reference. Bree opened the first file and was intrigued to see it held the records of a lawsuit from several years before; the file was stamped DISMISSED and SEALED in red letters.

The case had been brought in Raleigh, North Carolina, by two women and a man she'd never heard of against a defendant whose name was instantly recognizable. It shocked her.

"Frances Duchaine," she whispered. "*The* Frances Duchaine? Really?"

Bree read the first few sentences of the dismissed suit and her free hand traveled to her mouth. By the time she was halfway through the document, she was not only thoroughly engrossed but also angry. When she finished, she was furious and wanted to throw the file away. But then she went back to the start of the complaint and that stamped word DISMISSED and wondered how much, if anything, she'd read was true.

Bree forced herself to withhold judgment, calm down, and be open-minded. She set that file to one side and chose another from the box.

Before Bree opened it, though, she thought: *What if it is true? But how could it be? Wouldn't someone have known? Duchaine is not exactly a secretive billionaire. A billionaire, yes, but not some secretive financier. She's a marketer at heart. She's her own brand. In the public eye all the time. Someone should have known. But again, why would a woman as successful as Frances Duchaine take the risks alleged in the suit?*

Bree looked back at the first suit and the date of its dismissal, then wrote down the name of the plaintiffs' attorney—Nora Jessup—and her address. She also noted the superior court judge's name—Eloise Carmichael. Only then did she open the second file.

It contained a stapled sheaf of photocopied press clippings about Frances Duchaine and her meteoric rise and sustained position in the world of high fashion. Bree knew some of her history, but she spent the next hour studying the woman in greater depth.

Duchaine had suddenly appeared twenty-five years earlier, plucked from New York's Fashion Institute of Technology by no less an icon than Tess Jackson.

At that time, Tess Jackson's eponymous brand was growing so fast, she couldn't keep up with design demands. Jackson had graduated from FIT herself and was a generous alum. She'd called the president of the school and asked to see the portfolios of the three senior students the faculty believed showed the most promise.

Jackson was scheduled to give a lecture at FIT a few days later. Of course, word of the three chosen students got out. Duchaine, at that time a sophomore, was not among them. But she heard Jackson was looking for a young designer and ambushed her near her car when she arrived at the school.

"Frances looked like a model then too," Jackson told *New York* magazine ten years later. "In fact, that's what I thought she had in her portfolio, headshots and such. And when she told me she was a sophomore in the design program, I said I was interested only in the most experienced students. Frances would not take no for an answer and said I should at least look at her drawings. So I did. Right there in the parking lot."

Jackson was floored by what she saw, and on the spot, she offered Duchaine a job as her personal assistant to learn the business while she coached her on her designs. Not long after that, Duchaine's fashion started to appear under Jackson's label.

And not long after *that*, Duchaine became Jackson's sometime lover.

It worked until it didn't. For almost seven years, Jackson's brand and its subsidiaries grew and prospered. At age twenty-seven, however, and with Jackson in her late forties, Duchaine left the company and the relationship and started her own brand.

"It was inevitable, but it still broke my heart," Jackson said in the article. "Now we are friends and I know it was the right choice for Frances. She is not the kind of woman who likes to be contained by any sort of convention. That's what I loved and still love about her."

Duchaine's brand exploded because she aimed at the finer ready-to-wear market before going wide.

On the notepad, Bree wrote, *She followed Jackson's business model. Worked even better for her than it did for Jackson. When Duchaine sold part of her company to a hedge fund, it made her a legit billionaire. Why would she do the things the women allege in the lawsuit? Why jeopardize the empire?*

Bree kept turning the pages in the press packet and saw pictures of Duchaine with one handsome man or beautiful woman after another. Now forty-eight, Duchaine had been romantically linked to a number of people of both sexes over the years.

But she had never married, never even gotten engaged. Whenever Duchaine was asked about that, she laughed and said she was simply one of those people not meant to settle down for long.

"I work hard, and I want to satisfy my whims when I like," she said in an interview with the *New York Times*. "Go to my ski house in British Columbia when the powder's deep or my island in Fiji when I long for solitude. Whatever. Whenever. A marriage, a family, kids—they're not conducive to the lifestyle of a female knight that I cherish."

Bree thought about that last statement—*the lifestyle of a female knight that I cherish*—and realized Duchaine was revealing a deep inner truth about herself.

She wrote, *Frances is a queen any way you look at her. But she views herself as a female knight. Not a queen. Not a princess. A female knight.*

Tapping her pen on the legal pad, Bree reread her note and thought about that. She was about to push on when it all clicked in her mind.

Bree scribbled, *What does a female knight do? What all knights do. She goes out and slays dragons. When she's back at the castle, she's wooing fair maidens or handsome men. Think of all the fair maidens and handsome men in her business. They're everywhere.*

But she never forms a deep relationship with any of them. In a sense, Duchaine conquers her partners, beds them, and moves on. At some level, partners could be objects to her. Like mannequins to use and discard at will.

Bree again looked at the dismissed lawsuit before writing one last note to herself:

From that perspective, it is plausible that she might have done the things alleged in the lawsuit. The victims would not be humans to Duchaine. Just pretty dolls to be used and set aside when they're broken.

CHAPTER

10

THOMAS TULL STEPPED BACK from a wall in one of the two bedrooms of a luxury town house in Georgetown he'd rented for the duration of his research and writing. This bedroom had already been transformed into an office for the bestselling author and his longtime researcher, Lisa Moore.

A sturdily built, fair-skinned woman with short black hair, Moore looked at the wall and said, "That's a good visual representation, I think. Enough to get the imagination going."

"It's a start," Tull agreed.

A few hours before, Tull and Moore had finished hanging custom-built pegboards and whiteboards that covered the entire wall, from the floor to the nine-foot-high ceiling. Since then, they'd been organizing the information from the three Family Man murders.

The Hodges family, the first to die, was on the left. In the middle of the crime scene photos and notes, they'd arranged recent pictures of the victims so they would not lose track of who was most important in the story they would tell in Tull's next book.

Information about the Landau family, the second to die, was represented on the right side of the wall and arranged in a similar fashion. In the considerable free space between those two families, they'd put up that morning's *Washington Post* articles about the Carpenter killings as well as the latest photographs of that family.

"I'm amazed you got the pictures that fast," Tull said.

"The kids were on Instagram," Moore said, sitting down at a new laptop computer. "The mom, dad, and grandmother were on Facebook. Password?"

"*FamilyMan*. One word. Capital *F*, capital *M*."

His researcher typed the password.

Tull stepped forward to study the photo of seventy-eight-year-old Pearl Naylor; in it, she was standing on a tennis court, the picture of health. Then he trained his eyes on Roger Carpenter's photo. He was in a suit and tie outside a courtroom. In her picture, his wife, Sue, was wearing a heavy pack and beaming atop a mountain. "Prime of their lives," Tull said into his phone's recording app and tried to feel whatever emotions the victims conjured up in him as he looked at their faces. "Tragic, yes, but more. These were shining lights, snuffed out. The world is a lesser place without them."

This was all part of the writer's method, part of the way he was able to bring characters alive on the pages of his books. Tull believed that if he understood the emotional center of a person and, in turn, the emotions that person stirred in other people, he would be able to depict him or her in a much more three-dimensional manner.

He moved a few feet and steeled himself to look at the children's pictures. The twin twelve-year-old girls, Alice and Mary Carpenter, were on skis out west somewhere with their goggles up and their arms thrown high over their heads.

"The Carpenter girls, so privileged and yet so innocent," he said into the recording app. "Their lives cut short. Buds before they could blossom. We need to hear from their teachers," he told Moore. "Their friends too. And coaches if they had them."

Moore said, "I'm always five steps ahead of you, Thomas. I'm sending a list of names, numbers, and relationships your way."

"Do me a favor and prioritize them first," he said, looking at the images of nine-year-old Nick Carpenter in a Little League uniform and his brother, five-year-old Alan, who was sitting in a wheelchair at an amusement park somewhere and grinning like he was having the time of his life.

Tull felt a surge of emotion—grief over the senseless loss melded with pity—and had to fight the ball of pain filling his throat.

"Alan. That poor kid is one of the heavyweights of this story," he murmured into the recorder. "Born into terrible circumstances beyond his control and then dying the same way. But in the years between, there was love. Deep love for and from Alan."

Tull paused and shook his head before speaking again. "Need scientific background on cerebral palsy. Talk to Alan's therapists. His friends. His doctors."

He stopped, rubbed his eyes, and sat at his desk.

"Do you like them?" Moore asked. "As subjects?"

"I do," Tull said. "I'm sad, of course, but these were good people caught up in events beyond their understanding. I need to explore that theme, I think. Readers will relate to that. They love it when the victims have good souls."

"No doubt," Moore said. "What about law enforcement?"

"I'll take the local crime-beat reporters out to lunch, begin building our sources for the nitty-gritty to come."

"Alex Cross?"

"Dr. Cross is near the bottom of the list for the moment," he said. "Along with the other two detectives quoted in today's articles, Mahoney at the FBI and Sampson with Metro Homicide."

"Why so low?"

"Because we're conducting our own extensive investigation first and in parallel."

"You believe they've already made mistakes?"

"I do. A couple of big ones."

11

THE FAMILY MAN SENSED the time was ripe to increase the pressure and make the critical next move in the promotion of general hysteria.

Up to this point, the killer had focused primarily on white suburban families. Now that had to change.

The Elliott family of Alexandria, Virginia, would do nicely, thank you. A family selected to change the popular buzz about the killings, broaden and deepen it, spread the fear far and wide.

With the floor plan of their Craftsman bungalow memorized, the night-vision goggles ready, and happy that there was no canine to contend with, the Family Man eased down an alley behind the house, finished putting on the hazmat gear, and vaulted the rear gate.

The killer landed and trained a laser pointer on the wide-angle security camera high above the rear door, effectively blinding it to the backyard.

There was no camera above the concrete steps that led to the basement door, a steel-clad affair with double dead bolts. With the help of a pair of stainless-steel picks and a small electromagnet, the Family Man had the bolts turned and the door open in under ten minutes.

The bungalow design presented an interesting challenge. The members of the Carpenter family had slept on different levels of their house, but the Elliotts were all clustered upstairs in three bedrooms around a common area and a bath.

The house was nearly sixty years old. A creak in a floorboard or a stair riser could alert one of them and make life and death messier than it had to be.

The Family Man got out the pistol with the sound suppressor, climbed the steep stairs out of the musty basement, and slipped into the kitchen. The night-vision goggles revealed a living room on the right and a dining room and stairs to the second floor on the left.

The killer took several breaths with closed eyes, rehearsing, before moving to the staircase and, with near robotic precision, settling each foot on the side of the risers, not in the middle, where they might squeak or squeal in protest.

The Family Man made no detectable sound the entire climb but paused at the last step anyway to listen for movement. Hearing nothing, the killer stepped up onto the landing and then slid along the wall, head up, intent on the master bedroom's door, which was ajar.

The Family Man's soft-soled boot accidentally kicked a wineglass on the wood floor. It hit a second wineglass, which tipped over an empty bottle, which hit the wood and rolled. It might have given another intruder a heart attack.

But, adapting, the killer just pushed up the goggles and aimed the pistol at the bedroom door.

"Tristan?" a woman said groggily on the other side. A light went on.

Then a light went on in the bathroom; the door opened and Tristan Elliott, a massive Black man who'd played lineman at Georgia Tech, stepped out. He saw the Family Man aiming the gun at him. Elliott raised his huge hands, sudden terror in his eyes, and whispered, "No, please. I know who you are. I know what you're here to do. Don't do it!"

"That's not possible," the killer said and shot him, then pushed open the master bedroom's door to find Elliott's wife on the edge of her bed, just about to scream.

CHAPTER

12

BREE AND I WERE up and out of our house to run at six on Thursday morning.

We usually put in five miles every other day. It was not only a chance to exercise; it was also a chance to connect and talk about the work to come.

"I'm having a tough time with my new assignment," Bree said as we ran downhill on the south side of Capitol Hill and onto the sidewalk along Independence Avenue, headed toward the National Mall.

The spring morning was beautiful. Flowering trees and shrubs were in full bloom everywhere you looked on the Capitol grounds.

"This is the assignment you can't talk about?" I said, trying to ignore the way my knees protested the steep descent.

"That's the one," she said. "But I think I can do it without naming names."

"Handy skill to have."

"Took years to develop."

Bree told me she and Bluestone were working for an anonymous client who'd dug up dirt on a major player in the fashion industry.

"What kind of dirt?" I asked.

"I can't say," Bree said. "But it's rough."

"Why would a major hitter in fashion be involved with something rough?"

"Exactly my reaction," she said, puffing as we reached the bottom of Capitol Hill and started down the Mall toward the Washington Monument. "But there's enough on paper to suggest it may be real. There was a lawsuit filed in North Carolina, but it was dismissed and sealed before depositions took place."

I wiped the sweat off my brow and I thought about that for a few moments. "Why North Carolina?"

"The hitter evidently has relationships with multiple textile and clothing manufacturers there. The two women and one man claim they were coerced with promises that the hitter and friends would help them get a foothold in the modeling or fashion industry. But they said it was a lie, a pretext for the roughness."

"Reasons for dismissal and seal?"

"That's unclear and part of why the anonymous client has asked us to investigate. I'll put in calls this morning to the attorney who sued and see what she remembers about the case."

"At least you'll have a better idea of what to believe," I said. "What else?"

"I'm going up to New York this evening," Bree said as we took a right on Fourth Street and looped toward the north side of Capitol Hill. "I figure five days to do what I need to do, which means I'll probably miss Jannie's big race."

"I'll film it," I said. "Or I can FaceTime you and you can see the whole thing."

She grinned. "I like that idea better. Ready?"

"Never," I said, seeing the sidewalk starting to climb ahead of us.

We've been doing this route for years, and Capitol Hill still beats me up. My calves were screaming, and I had a stitch in my side when we crested the hill and slowed to a walk at First Street.

"God, that's steep." I groaned.

"Never gets easier," Bree said, panting.

We walked to Second Street and had just started to jog home slowly when my cell rang. Ned Mahoney. We slowed to a walk again.

"We're out for a run and almost home, Ned," I said. "Can I call you back in ten?"

"Afraid not, Alex," Mahoney said. "Family Man struck last night in Alexandria. I need you there, pronto."

My stomach soured as it had before I'd entered the Carpenters' home. I hated going into the Family Man's crime scenes—I feared the multiple victims would be too much for me to process, which meant they'd soon haunt my daydreams and my nightmares.

But I said, "I'll be there in forty."

"Make it thirty. I'm calling Sampson," Ned said and hung up.

"Another one?" Bree asked in concern as I lowered the phone from my ear.

"In Alexandria," I said, and we broke into a run toward home.

CHAPTER

13

THE FOLLOWING MORNING AROUND ten, I was at the desk I use when I'm working at Metro PD, forcing myself to study the crime scene photographs from the Elliott family home. Sampson sat at the desk opposite me, writing up the case for the murder book that would help us in our part of the overall investigation.

I was able to look at the pictures of forty-three-year-old Tristan Elliott and his thirty-nine-year-old wife, Madonna, with relative dispassion. But those of the children made me want to close my eyes and banish them from my memory.

It was clear from my first moments inside the Elliott house that the crime scene was different. Not only were the Elliotts the first family of color to die by the Family Man's hand, but these murders had not gone as smoothly as the others.

In the first three cases, the Family Man had managed to sneak in and execute his victims as they slept. But not at the Elliotts', where we'd found lights on and bodies strewn about the second floor. After Ned, John, and I thoroughly inspected the scene, we came to believe that Tristan Elliott had been in the main bathroom and had surprised the Family Man, who shot him from across the landing, probably right next to the staircase.

Madonna must have heard something because she had turned on the lights in the master bedroom and seemed to have been getting out of bed when she was shot. She'd thrown up her right hand; the bullet that killed her had gone through her palm before hitting her high in the forehead.

We believed the Elliott kids, fourteen-year-old Marisa and eleven-year-old Zach, who slept in adjoining rooms, must have heard their father fall or their mother scream, because they were both out of bed.

Marisa had opened her door and been shot at near point-blank range. We found her lying on her back staring upward with unseeing eyes.

Her younger brother seemed to have tried to hide. We found him dead in his closet, curled up. That was the one that really got me, the one that had festered in my brain as I slept the night before, the one driving me to action now.

"Remember Paladin?" I said to Sampson.

"The needle-in-a-haystack people?"

"The same. They pulled it off for us in the Alejandro and Maestro killings. Let's see what they can do with this case."

"Worth a try. But you'll probably have to do the formal request through Mahoney and the FBI director's office."

"I'll alert Paladin that a request is coming," I said; I found the main phone number in my list of contacts and called.

A receptionist answered. I identified myself and asked to speak with Steven Vance, the CEO of Paladin Inc. Vance had been our point person the year before.

"I'm sorry," the receptionist said. "Mr. Vance is in Italy on vacation and won't be back until early next week."

"What about Mr. Malcomb? This is a big murder investigation."

"I'll see if he's available."

A few moments later, there was a click. The cofounder of and coding genius behind Paladin said in a soft voice, "Dr. Cross, what a pleasure. This is Ryan Malcomb. Steven speaks highly of you."

"And we speak highly of him and your company. Paladin was a big help to us last year, and I wanted to tell you I'm going through formal channels to get approval for one of your precision data sifts."

Don't ask me to explain exactly how these sifts worked. But the results were sometimes remarkable. Paladin's search algorithms had laser-focused our investigation into the Alejandro cartel the year before, and the director of Homeland Security had recently stated that the company had helped identify multiple terrorist plots that were thwarted as a result.

There was a pause. "Of course we'd love to help. What are you looking to sift?"

"Any data generated around the murders of three families down here."

"I heard about that on NPR yesterday. The killer sounds insane."

"At some level, I agree."

"You'll need federal wiretap approval on all cellular, GPS, video, and computer data you provide us. Then the algorithms will do the grunt work, and we'll let you know what we've found when we find it."

"Sounds like a plan," I said. "And thanks."

"We're here to help."

He hung up. I felt like we were going to get a break and fast. Paladin's strong suit was its ability to use supercomputers and artificial intelligence to identify similarities and anomalies in given sets of data. They might find, for example, that one cell phone was active near all three crime scenes. Or that there were similar messages going out over computers active in the area. In essence, Paladin's unique methods identified needles in the haystack of data that surrounds modern life.

I called Ned Mahoney over at Bureau headquarters and asked him to start the request process; he said it would take several hours to get to the attention of the right people at the highest levels of the agency.

"I've got something coming your way in the meantime," Mahoney said. "Footage from the Elliotts' backyard security camera."

"Got it," Sampson said a second after I hung up.

I came around the desk and stood behind him, watching a dark figure climb over the Elliotts' back fence, land in a crouch, then aim a laser pointer at the camera, blinding it.

"Back up. I want to see that moment when he lands, just before—"

Mahoney was ahead of us because the video ended with a magnified and enhanced still from the video showing us the killer for the first time. He was crouched at the moment of landing and dressed in black hazmat gear head to toe, including a hood, an industrial respirator mask with dual filters, and night-vision goggles.

"No identifying features whatsoever," Sampson said.

"But it's him," I said. "And we were right. He's using hazmat gear to keep his DNA closely contained."

"He's wearing the night-vision goggles, and he uses the laser to blind the camera," Sampson said. "Wouldn't it blind him?"

"If he had the goggles turned on, but he doesn't," I said. "Otherwise we'd see a smoky green in the lenses."

John nodded. "He comes over the fence prepared. Goggles off. Laser in hand."

"And he knows right where that camera is," I said. "Which means he's scouted the place before, which means he may be on other cameras in the vicinity earlier."

"I'll start looking for any footage in the area for the three days prior."

The phone on my desk rang. I'm not often in the downtown office, so most people know to call me on my cell.

I went around and answered. "Alex Cross."

"This is Sergeant Baker at the front desk, Dr. Cross."

I'd known Baker for ten years. "Hello, Leslie. Missed you this morning. How are you?"

"I just started my shift and I'm fine," she said, sounding happy that I'd asked. "Say, there's a lady in the lobby here who'd like to talk to you or Detective Sampson."

"If you've seen the news, you know we're pretty swamped."

"I told her that, but she's insistent, says she thinks she knows who the killer is."

I closed my eyes a moment and moaned because the more high profile a case was, the more crazies with crackpot theories we had coming at us.

"I know," Baker said. "But she's convinced."

"Are we talking nutcase?"

"No, she's sharp upstairs. And dressed to kill."

14

A FEW MINUTES LATER, the elevator opened, and I agreed with Sergeant Baker's fashion assessment. The woman before me was slim, tall, and beautiful in tight black leather pants, purple stiletto heels, a black blouse with a diving neckline, and pearls.

My first guess was that she was a model of some sort. Or had been. She smiled and stuck out her hand. "Thank you for agreeing to see me, Dr. Cross. I'm Suzanne Liu."

I shook her hand. "You have information about the family killings, Ms. Liu?"

"Suzanne, please, and I do," she said, staring at me evenly. "I also have three other big cases you should be looking at. Or the FBI should."

"Three?" I said. "We've run the MO of the killer through databases around the world and have not—"

"These are completely different," she said. "But I believe that the various killings are ultimately the work of one person."

I took in her body language, her tone of voice, and her confident posture and decided she did not seem crazy. "Who?"

Liu looked around at the police officers and detectives streaming by us, going to the elevators and the bullpen. "Isn't there somewhere quieter so I can explain fully? This is sensitive. I believe the killer is someone in the public eye—a celebrity, you could say."

Inwardly, I groaned. It sounded nuts. But I saw the same confidence, the same even gaze and authority in her voice.

"Follow me," I said and led her back to our desks, introduced her to Sampson, and asked him to join us in a conference room.

When I closed the door, I said, "Suzanne thinks she knows the identity of the Family Man. She believes he's a celebrity and that he has also murdered other people."

I could see John struggling not to roll his eyes.

Liu seemed not to notice as she took a seat and put down her sleek silver briefcase. "It just makes too much sense when I think about it and I wanted you both to know."

Sampson growled, "Time out. Who are you exactly, ma'am, and how did you find all this information?"

She seemed a bit taken aback by John's rough demeanor but said, "I'm a book editor in New York. You can Google me. I was recently fired from my job at Alabaster Publishing for not keeping a superstar writer in the fold. He went free agent and found a better offer, and now I'm out of a job, which has given me lots of time to think about things."

Sampson and I traded glances. He played bad cop better than I did.

He leaned across the table. "Suzanne, can you please get to the point and tell us who you believe the killer is?"

Liu looked at her lap a moment and swallowed. Her voice was shaky when she said, "I think the killer is my former superstar writer Thomas Tull."

Our reaction was clear and the same.

"I knew you'd be shocked," she said.

"Thomas Tull?" I said. "The guy who writes the crime books?"

"I've seen him a bunch of times on television," Sampson said. "Always comes across as a straight shooter to me."

"To me too," Liu replied. "And we worked together for ten years. I was his editor. You heard about the size of the deal for his next book?"

"We've been kind of busy to keep up on things like that," I said.

"Well, it hasn't been formally announced, but I know for certain that the advance was huge, and the book is about this case—your case, the Family Man case. He's doing research here in Washington, DC, now."

"Tull is?"

"That's what I'm telling you," she said. "He was here in DC last night. He's rented a town house in Georgetown. Don't you see? He had the opportunity and the motive."

Her voice had gotten higher, her delivery quicker, and her eyes just a little wilder.

"To kill the Elliotts?" Sampson asked, incredulous.

"Yes," she snapped. "That's what I'm telling you."

"What's the motive?" I asked.

The editor flipped open her briefcase and came out with three thick paperbacks, all by Thomas Tull: *Electric, Noon in*

Berlin, and *Doctor's Orders.* Liu tapped them with her fingernails. "Here's your motive."

"I'm not following you," Sampson said.

"You've read them, of course."

"Can't say I have."

I shook my head.

"They are all great, different, and intricate stories in their own right," she said. "But in some ways, they are the same. There's a series of baffling murders. Intrigue. Drama. Very little evidence. The police are getting nowhere, and suddenly the author insinuates himself into the investigation, helps the cops, gets crazy access, then writes a blockbuster."

Sampson said, "He helped in the investigations?"

Liu lifted her chin. "Thomas's role is debatable. Some say he was involved in framing and railroading the men who were convicted."

15

SAMPSON SEEMED AMUSED. "THOSE are some strong accusations you're throwing around about the author whose books you edited."

Liu sat back. "Don't you think I've thought about that? I haven't talked to a lawyer, but does that make me an accessory after the fact?"

"You're getting ahead of yourself by a mile, Suzanne," I said, gesturing at the three paperbacks. "Why do you think he's the real killer in these books?"

She'd obviously been thinking about this. But from the way Liu stared at the table, as if seeing long-ago events spin by, I could tell she was still confused, still not quite convinced herself.

"It helps to start at the beginning," I said.

"Maybe it started in the Marines," Liu said at last. "After high school, Thomas enlisted as shore police. The end of his second tour, he joined the Naval Criminal Investigative Service. Did you know that?"

I shrugged. "I may have read it somewhere."

"Anyway, while Thomas was posted at Camp Pendleton, north of San Diego, there were several prostitutes murdered in northern San Diego County. You can look it up. Anyway, the San Diego sheriff's investigators had no clues. The killer was that good, that clean."

Sampson checked his watch. "Where's this going, Suzanne?"

That irritated her. "To Thomas Tull, if you'll be patient a moment. Most of northern San Diego County borders the Marine base. The second body was found in a canyon area about a hundred yards inside the boundary of Camp Pendleton, which got Thomas involved."

"Okay. Did he solve the murders?" I asked.

"He did indeed," she said. "The case made him. Writing about it in his admission essay is what got him into Harvard when he finally left the Marines and NCIS."

"How old was he at that point?" Sampson asked, picking up a pen.

Liu thought about that. "Thirty?"

"Kind of late to be starting college," I said.

The editor said Thomas had been a mediocre student in high school with little or no desire for higher education. Eight years in the Marines changed his mind. He wanted to study writing at Harvard because he thought the prestige of having a degree from that college would help his career in the long run.

"Did it?" Sampson asked.

Liu tapped the book on the left, *Electric*.

"Harvard helped Thomas long before he got his degree. He

was able to get inside the investigation while he was living in Cambridge and attending classes."

She said Tull was a sophomore when he got interested in the murders, all of which involved electrocutions. He started going around Cambridge and the surrounding towns asking questions.

"He's good at that, I have to tell you," Liu said. "Thomas has this ability to disarm people and get them to tell him things. Do you know that the three killers he wrote about in these books all love Thomas? They do. They consider him a friend, a good one, someone who's on their side, even if he had a role in their convictions."

"C'mon," I said.

"It's true," she insisted. "They all say they were framed. They all maintain their innocence to this day. They say the police, the prosecutors, and the book had it wrong. And yet they consider Thomas their buddy. And to a man, they expect he will prove their innocence someday and rewrite their stories to reflect it."

That was unusual and I said so, adding, "I'm still not seeing the basis for you thinking Tull is a killer."

The editor hesitated before returning to her briefcase and coming out with a sheaf of paper about an inch thick. She set it on the table in front of us. "This is a copy of the book proposal he circulated in New York recently."

In the middle of the first page were the words *Family Man, by Thomas Tull*. At the bottom was *NDA in effect*, followed by Suzanne Liu's name, initials, and a date.

"Nondisclosure agreement?" I said. "You're breaking it?"

"I'm here, aren't I?" Liu said. "Look at the last two pages. Forty and forty-one. There are things there about the case that he could not have known when he wrote them. Things about the Carpenters and the Elliotts. See the date? He wrote this *before* they were killed."

I picked up the document and flipped through it to page 40, which was headed "The Future." Sampson moved closer to read.

Up to that point, the book proposal had focused on the Landau killings, which had taken place six months ago, and the Hodges killings, which occurred eight months before that. There seemed no doubt in Tull's mind that the killer would strike again and at shorter and shorter intervals.

I looked up at Liu. "If you're talking about Tull predicting a shortening of the cycle, we predicted the same thing. Most serial killers follow this trend over time."

"They do," Sampson said.

"Keep reading," the editor said. "Last paragraph on page forty, first paragraph on forty one."

16

I READ THE PARAGRAPHS out loud. "'No one can say who the next victims will be, what family will be chosen, and how many generations will be wiped out. We don't know if the killer will stick to the pattern or change. Will he shut down his operations in the DC area and move to other hunting grounds? We don't know. And we don't know if he'll keep shooting his victims execution-style, high through the head. And what links the targets? What's the connection? Will he continue to kill only white families? Or will he change his racial profile and attack Black families? Hispanics? Asian-Americans?'"

I turned the page and kept reading. "'As I conclude this proposal, we just don't know the answers to these questions and many others. But no matter who the Family Man targets or where and how he kills them, I will leave no stone un-turned, no angle unpursued. I will go where the police fear to tread, without friend or favor, in pursuit of this story and the killer, who I believe wears hazmat clothing of some type. After all, who doesn't leave DNA behind them these days?'"

"See?" Liu said when I finished. "He predicted the change in racial target and the hazmat suit. Is that what you believe the killer's wearing?"

I nodded. "But we've suspected that for a while. Since the Landau case. He could have talked to someone in the department about it."

"Or he was being logical," Sampson said. "I mean, how else would you do it?"

Liu turned frustrated. "What about the Elliotts? Black dad. Hispanic wife. Blended kids? That fits."

"I suppose," I said, unconvinced. "The way I read it, Tull has no idea what the future holds, which is where we are as well. He's speculating here so editors like you will cut him some slack if his theories about the case fall apart."

"I agree," Sampson said. "It reads like the man knows he's selling something that might not pan out the way this proposal suggests."

"It's more than that," Liu said, her voice rising. "Do you know he owns guns? Lots of them? He almost always carries one."

"He was a Marine and an NCIS investigator," I said. "I can't imagine him not carrying a weapon."

"But—"

"Hear me out, Suzanne. I appreciate you coming all this way to talk to us, but I'm not seeing a shred of evidence to back up your suspicions."

"They're not suspicions!"

"They are," Sampson said. "I'm sorry, but you sound like a

former editor who is pissed at Tull because he took a bigger offer than yours and it got you fired."

"That has nothing to do with it!" she said, standing up, slamming the lid of her briefcase down, and locking it.

"I think it has more than a little bit to do with it," I said.

She gestured at the paperbacks angrily. "If you don't believe me, read the books. Ask yourself how Thomas Tull could have known all these things. How could he have seen what no one else did? I was his editor and I always wondered. So did our legal department. Thomas had answers for every question we threw at him, but to be honest, I always came away feeling like there was more to his part in the story than he was letting on."

We said nothing. Liu shook her finger at the three paperbacks. "My gut says there are things in those books that are not right, Dr. Cross. Maybe I don't know enough about criminal investigation, or maybe I'm too close to the narrative to see them. But someone like you, an even better investigator than Thomas—you just might spot the holes in his books when you read them for the first time."

CHAPTER

17

Manhattan

BREE STONE STROLLED UP Fifth Avenue around four Friday afternoon, killing time. She'd spent the train ride up from Washington the evening before studying the contents of several more of the Frances Duchaine files.

In them, she'd seen many references to possible quashing of a search-warrant request on Duchaine's homes and offices; there was also a list of the times the fashion designer had been visited by police.

One detective, Rosella Salazar, had paid at least three visits to Duchaine's pied-à-terre in the Dakota, the famed apartment building on the Upper West Side. Bree wanted to know why and had called Salazar.

Luckily, the detective answered, and luckier still, she had a cousin who had worked for DC Metro when Bree was the chief of detectives. Still, Salazar was a little hesitant to meet

Bree when she found out she was now working as a private investigator.

But when Bree told her she was looking into Frances Duchaine on behalf of a very wealthy client, the detective immediately agreed to see her. They arranged to meet at the Lombard Lamp on the southeast corner of Central Park around five.

Six blocks south of the park, Bree realized she was approaching Duchaine's flagship store. Since she was wearing her nicest blue suit with a cream-colored blouse and a fine red and gold silk scarf she'd bought in Paris, she decided to go in for a look.

The store oozed elegance, Bree had to admit, with its black marble floors, gold walls, and black marble spiral staircases with polished bronze railings. There were three floors altogether. The ground level featured Duchaine-designed accessories: purses, jewelry, scarves, hats, gloves, and shoes. Bree noticed that there were fewer shoppers than she would have expected for a famous store like this.

Many of the salesclerks, men and women wearing all white, were standing around chatting or looking at their phones. Bree walked by them without arousing their interest and climbed to the second floor, which was devoted to Duchaine's ready-to-wear business and leisure fashions.

There were a handful of shoppers browsing the aisles there, but no one seemed to be buying much. She had not seen a customer at a cash register yet.

The third floor featured Duchaine's evening wear, from daring black cocktail dresses to sequined ball gowns. There was no one there other than a pale, freckled clerk in her twenties who marched up to Bree, gave her a forced smile, and asked if she was on the correct floor.

Bree got the subtext, smiled sweetly, and glanced at the girl's name tag. "Marjorie, I've been invited to a dinner at the White House in a couple of months," Bree said. "I'm looking for an appropriate gown to wear. If you don't mind."

Marjorie seemed so shocked by this that she didn't know what to do or say for a moment. Then she nodded and said, "Of course. What an honor for you, Ms...."

"It doesn't matter," Bree said, walking past her to a rack of gowns. She ignored the lower-priced items and went straight to the most elegant and ornate dresses, the ones that reeked of cash.

Apparently realizing that she might be in for a decent commission, Marjorie bustled over and said, "There are three or four there that would look beautiful on you."

"You think?" Bree said, pausing at a black one that featured a plunging neckline and intricate brocade across the bodice.

"That's almost one of a kind," Marjorie said. "Frances had only ten made."

"Unfortunately, I don't think it will fit me."

"It might. But I can check the computer and see if we have a larger size somewhere."

Bree made a noncommittal noise and went to another dress, this one with an Indian influence. "Not many customers here today. I'm surprised," she said.

She glanced at the clerk, who pursed her lips. "Yes, well," Marjorie said. "The economy's a little off, and it is shoulder season."

Cocking her head, Bree said, "Shoulder season?"

"Too late for winter, too early for summer. Give it a week or two and we'll be slammed again."

That did not sound right to Bree. New York had more than enough wealthy women who traveled to different climates and could afford to shop at Duchaine even in an economic downturn.

So what was going on?

Bree glanced at her watch and realized she needed to head to Central Park. She turned away from the gowns to find Marjorie looking at her expectantly.

"None you want to try on?"

"Afraid not," Bree said. "Nothing that screams White House, anyway. And now I must be going. I have a meeting at five."

The clerk's face fell in a way that told Bree it had been a while since someone wandered in off the street looking to spend thousands on a gown. Marjorie stood aside, saying, "Where else are you looking, if you don't mind me asking?"

"I was thinking Chanel, Saint Laurent, and Tess Jackson if I have enough time before my flight back to Atlanta," Bree said.

"I hear that a lot," the clerk said. "Everyone's going back to Tess."

"That's unfortunate for you, Marjorie," Bree said and left.

18

AS BREE HURRIED NORTH, she kept thinking that the shine seemed to have gone off Frances Duchaine's name; the brand was no longer attracting flocks of customers eager to open their purses or wallets for anything that had the famous FD logo on it.

When had that happened? For years, all you heard about was the Duchaine brand getting bigger, broader, deeper.

Bree crossed West Fifty-Ninth and started up the sidewalk along East Drive toward the Lombard Lamp, making a mental note to get in touch with some of the financial analysts that covered Duchaine's companies.

When Bree reached the meeting place, she noticed a short woman who appeared to be very pregnant leaning against the ornate lamp.

"My cousin Pablo, he raves about you, Chief Stone," she said, reaching out to shake Bree's hand. "He says Metro PD is lost without you."

"Pablo has always flattered me, Detective Salazar."

Salazar laughed. "Call me Rosella, and yes, Pablo is an expert at flattery. Shall we walk?"

"If you're okay with it?"

"The doctors tell me I need to," Salazar said, pitching a plastic water bottle into a trash can. "I've got gestational diabetes and they said a little exercise every day will help lower my numbers."

"How far along are you?"

"Almost eight months," the detective said, smiling. "It's going to be a boy this time. I told the ob-gyn not to tell me if it was a boy or a girl, but I can feel it. A brother to my little Elaina. You got kids?"

"Three stepchildren who I love to pieces."

"You're married to Dr. Cross, right?"

Bree nodded as they walked into the park. "Last time I looked."

"I heard him lecture when I took a class at Quantico a few years back."

"He's a talker."

Salazar laughed. "He is. And it's fascinating how his mind works."

"There's no one like him," Bree said. "So, tell me what you think about Duchaine."

Detective Salazar said, "You really don't know who you're working for, huh?"

"All I was told was that the client has very deep pockets and wants us to follow the trail wherever it goes."

"To find out what?"

"I don't know," Bree admitted. "I'm just supposed to listen

to my instincts based on information I was given about Frances Duchaine."

"What kind of info?"

Bree hesitated, then decided she needed an ally. "Some financials, some personal info, press clippings, and some information about a few run-ins with the law she's squirmed out of, including a civil suit in North Carolina filed by three young wannabe models—two females, one male—that was dismissed and sealed."

"Of course it was," Salazar said. "That has Frances Duchaine written all over it."

Over the next hour, they walked north through Central Park as Bree listened closely to the detective's take on the fashion icon. Salazar said that she'd known of no complaints against Duchaine whatsoever until four years ago when a young woman who said her name was Molly contacted the vice squad, where Salazar was working at the time. Molly said she had been lured from North Carolina to New York by Duchaine's representatives with promises that she would be considered for modeling jobs.

"Molly had to pay her own way up here and get a place to live," Salazar said. "Duchaine's people provided her with a photographer for headshots, and they paid to put her in mockups for possible advertising campaigns. Molly's life went well for a minute."

The detective said Molly was called in by Duchaine and another woman who worked for her, Paula Watkins. They told Molly that the market testing on her was lower than they'd expected and that she should get plastic surgery to fix some of her flaws so she could be considered for future campaigns.

"This sounds somewhat similar to the allegations in the

dismissed lawsuit," Bree said. "Keep going. What were they recommending?"

"Bigger boobs, porcelain veneers, a nose job," Salazar said. "Molly told them that she could not afford any of that, and they offered her a company loan that they said she could pay back over time once the work was done."

"Let me guess. She takes the loan, has the surgeries and cosmetic enhancements with doctors and dentists they recommend, and they still don't give her any work."

"Yes. And now she's twenty-one and owes them like seventy grand."

Molly had asked Paula Watkins if the company could forgive the loan; Watkins said no. Molly found a few jobs, but she earned nowhere near enough to pay off the loan.

Desperate, Molly feared becoming homeless and she wondered whether to return to her abusive family. One night, she went to her favorite bar around the corner from where she lived and started drinking.

"A woman named Katherine, early forties, pretty, put together, slides onto the stool next to Molly," Detective Salazar said. "Katherine's outgoing, sharp, easy to talk to. She picks up on Molly's sadness, gets her to open up. She buys Molly a few drinks, gives her a shoulder to cry on. And then Katherine tells Molly she might be able to help her make real money, certainly enough to pay off her debt in a couple of years."

"Katherine's a madam," Bree said.

"More like a scout," Salazar said.

Two days later, with no luck on the job front, Molly called Katherine. They met at a coffee shop. Katherine told Molly there were many men and women who would pay well to sleep with her.

Molly was horrified; she was about to leave until Katherine said that with her looks and figure, she'd get two thousand an hour and as much as ten thousand for an overnighter.

"Lot of money," Bree said. "Did she take the offer?"

Salazar nodded. "Three years ago. Long story short, they used her. Katherine's 'friends' took a serious cut of Molly's fees, so she never made quite enough money to pay off the loan, which carried a ridiculous interest rate. When she got close to getting all the money she needed, one of Katherine's friends, a guy Molly knew as Candy, introduced her to cocaine and then oxy."

"Get her hooked. Keep her working. Sounds like sexual slavery to me."

"It did and does to me too. Interestingly enough, Molly did not come to me with her story until she happened to see Katherine one day in a different part of the city. Got a guess who Katherine was with?"

19

Washington, DC

I DECIDED TO CALL it a day around six o'clock Friday evening. Sampson, a recent widower, had already left to spend time with his young daughter, Willow.

And I wanted to get home to see where my daughter Jannie's head was the night before her big race and the decision about college. But before I left, the three paperbacks by Thomas Tull caught my attention. Each one was over five hundred pages.

A lazy part of my brain tried to convince me that Suzanne Liu was what Sampson had said she was: an editor scorned who was out for payback.

There's nothing to it, I thought and almost walked out. But the obsessive-compulsive part of my personality wouldn't let me. *Shouldn't you at least make sure?*

I scooped the books up, dropped them in a day pack, and

headed for the exit. On the Uber ride home, I read the back cover and the preface to *Electric*.

Set in metro Boston, Tull's first book was about a series of electrocution deaths that police in separate jurisdictions had initially thought were unlinked accidents. The first three victims all worked at various high-end stores in and around the city.

The fourth victim, Emily Maxwell, attracted Tull's attention because he'd met her several times at the Harvard Book Store, where she worked. Tull was a sophomore at Harvard, but he had a background as an NCIS investigator, and aspects of the bookstore clerk's "accidental" death had not made sense to him.

He began to dig into the case and was soon convinced that Emily Maxwell and several others in the greater Boston area had been electrocuted on purpose. About the same time, Jane Hale, a young Boston police detective, also became suspicious about the electrocution deaths.

Hale ultimately let Tull shadow her during the investigation, giving him an inside look at the probe that proved riveting, especially when suspicions turned toward an unlikely serial killer operating in the open.

I had to admit, the back cover and the opening had me intrigued enough that I didn't realize I was home until the Uber driver pulled over and told me.

My phone rang as I shut the car door. Caller ID said Paladin Inc. "This is Cross," I said.

Ryan Malcomb said, "I just wanted you to know that your request came through with all the correct permissions. The data is being loaded onto our supercomputers."

"And then what? You start looking for the needle in the haystack?"

"First thing in the morning. I like to write the codes after a good night's sleep."

"You're the expert."

"We will let you know," Malcomb said and hung up.

Inside, I found Ali engrossed by something on his laptop; he barely waved when I said hello.

Nana Mama was almost done with a shrimp and pasta dish with basil and garlic, and it smelled fantastic. Jannie was setting the table.

"How did practice go?" I asked.

"Light jog and stretching," Jannie said.

My grandmother said, "She came in beaming with confidence."

Jannie smiled. "I'll do my best, but I honestly have no expectations. Whatever happens, I'll be fine. Whichever school I decide on, I'll find a home there."

"Gotta like that attitude," I said.

Bringing the steaming bowls of food to the table, Nana Mama said, "It's the best attitude I can imagine. What time does your race start?"

"Around eleven, Nana."

"Oh, good. Damon called. He's got a week free before finals and he's coming up for the race. He'll get to Howard around ten thirty."

I grinned. I hadn't seen my oldest child in several months.

"How's he getting here all the way from Davidson?" Ali asked.

Nana Mama started laughing. "Some college friend's mother is turning fifty, and there's a surprise birthday party in Chevy Chase tomorrow night, so the girl's father is flying her home on the family jet."

"And Damon is hitching a ride?"

"La-di-da," my grandmother said and cackled. "I could never have imagined such a thing when I was his age."

We were all laughing as we sat down to eat. It was pretty remarkable to think about my twenty-year-old in a private jet.

Ali said, "I've been looking at the girls you'll be racing against, Jannie. There are some really fast—"

"I don't care who they are or how fast they are," Jannie said, scooping pasta from the bowl onto her plate.

"But—"

"But nothing," my daughter said firmly. "Coach says I'm not racing them."

Ali frowned. "Then who are you racing?"

"Me," she said. "My best."

"Oh," my youngest child said, brightening. "I like that. You think you're going to break your personal record?"

"I think I'm going to run like I know I can and I'll see what happens," Jannie said.

Ali was very goal-oriented for his age and I could tell her answer bothered him, but he sighed and said, "I hope you crush it."

"I know she will," I said and winked at Jannie, who smiled back.

The meal was delicious as usual, and hardly anyone spoke for several minutes. Then Nana Mama yawned and put her fork down. "Where did you say Bree went off to?"

"New York," I said.

"What's she doing there?" Ali asked.

I shrugged and told him the truth. "Your guess is as good as mine."

20

Manhattan

"YOU WANT ME TO guess who Katherine was with?" Bree said to Detective Salazar, her eyebrows knitting. "I don't know. Frances Duchaine?"

"She's too smart for that," Salazar said, going to a park bench and taking a seat. "Sorry, my dogs are killing me."

"No problem," Bree said, also taking a seat. "So who was it?"

"Molly said she was sure it was Paula Watkins."

"Who works for Duchaine."

"Correct," the detective said. "You don't have to look at the story too long to figure out that it could all have been a setup, a bait and switch. They lure the young men and women in with promises of fame and fortune, get them in debt, then put them to work."

Bree thought about that. "Any idea how much Molly made in those three years?"

"More like two and a half years," Salazar said. "But I know she did roughly a hundred overnighters the first year. That's a million right there. I'm thinking she might have pulled in two to two and a half million by the time she wanted out."

Shocked, Bree said, "That's real money."

The detective agreed and said it was what had gotten her interested in the case. She'd gone to Paula Watkins, who denied knowing anyone named Katherine and said that Molly had just not worked out. How Molly had paid off her loan was anyone's guess, she said.

Salazar visited Duchaine and asked the same questions. The fashion designer acted as if she had no idea who Molly was when the detective showed her a recent picture. When Salazar showed her one from Molly's modeling portfolio, Duchaine recognized her and was dismissive, said she'd hoped a little nip and tuck and some pearly whites would have changed things for her.

"She told me, 'Marketing tests don't lie,'" the detective said. "Then she cut our meeting short. I tried to get Molly to set up a meeting with Katherine, but Katherine's line was suddenly disconnected. And then Molly started ducking my calls."

"Bought off?" Bree asked.

"That's my suspicion," Salazar said. "I never got to ask her."

"Why not?"

The detective groaned and struggled to her feet. "She took off, went back to North Carolina. Her family said she was flush with cash and acting wild. It's probably what got her killed."

Bree had feared that possibility. "Murdered?"

"Three months after she got home," Salazar said as she started to waddle again. "Shot at two in the morning outside her apartment building. Police down there have no witnesses and no leads. And here we are. Tell me about this lawsuit that was dismissed and sealed."

Bree gave her the highlights. The two young women and the young man had been lured to New York the same way Molly had, with promises of modeling jobs. Once there, they were told they needed to get plastic surgery and see a cosmetic dentist. After the procedures, they still weren't hired for modeling jobs, and so, saddled with debt and alone, they were leveraged into the sex ring.

"But the young man was lucky," Bree said. "A Russian named Victor offered him work as a gay prostitute, and he was about to say yes when a relative died and left him a lot of money, enough to pay off his debt. But he was still angry and joined the suit."

"You talk to the attorney?"

"I've got calls in to her," Bree said.

"Let me know what she says," Salazar said. "I suspect there may be a lot of others like him and Molly."

"I agree, but I'm still confused about the why, you know?" Bree said. "Why would someone like Duchaine get involved in a racket like this? She's a billionaire."

"Unless she isn't," the detective said. "Lots of rich people claim they are, but who can really check unless they own a publicly traded company? Duchaine's brand has always been privately held."

Bree thought for several moments. "I went to her flagship store on Fifth today and there were not a lot of customers."

"That right?" Salazar said. "Well, there you go, then. Cash flow may not be what it used to be. Think about it: If Duchaine needs cash and can make a million a year off Molly, why wouldn't she want fifty or a hundred girls just like her?"

21

Washington, DC

AFTER DINNER, NANA MAMA went up to her room to read and I told Jannie I'd do the dishes so she could chill and rest before her big race tomorrow. When I finished in the kitchen, I found Jannie and Ali in the front room engrossed in a show about doctors.

"What's this?" I asked.

Jannie looked up in awe and said, "It's a documentary series called *Lenox Hill,* about a hospital in New York where they deliver babies and operate on brain tumors."

Ali said, "And they really show the brain operations, Dad!"

"Really?" I said, wondering if it was appropriate for him.

Ali nodded. "Not everyone makes it, which is sad."

"I'm sure," I said. "Listen, I've got to get some work done tonight, so you're on your own for bedtime. Jannie?"

"Ten sharp," she said. "And don't worry, Dad, I've got this."

"I have no doubt. See you both in the morning. Love you."

"Love you too, Dad," they both said, their eyes back on their show.

I climbed up to the attic, which I'd long ago converted into a small office. I often went up there just to think, but that night, when I flipped on the light and weaved around stacks of old case files, I was on a mission.

I sat down at my desk and picked up *Electric* by Thomas Tull. My plan was to skim through the book, looking for the kinds of discrepancies or holes his editor said I might spot.

Except Tull had this compelling, propulsive narrative style that sucked me in and made the story come alive with three-dimensional characters who were constantly surprising me and twists I never saw coming. He also had a knack for interpreting the evidence and describing the way each of the murders must have happened.

Tull opened the book with the fourth victim, the one he'd known personally.

A year after an unwanted divorce had left her heartbroken and alone, Emily Maxwell was looking forward to her customary hot bath after a day on her feet seeing to the needs of Boston readers. She was usually home in her apartment in Cambridge's Ward Two neighborhood by six thirty in the evening, and after she fed her Siamese cat, Jimbo, and ate, she'd take her bath.

That evening, Emily picked up a Caesar salad with salmon at the Whole Foods near work. After feeding the cat, she ate the salad and had a glass of white wine before filling the tub. She checked the locks on her doors and then the thirty-nine-year-old felt safe enough to pour herself a second glass of wine and go to her bathroom for what she called a "full decompression session."

The music went on first, a playlist on her iPod that featured soft-rock hits by bands like the Eagles and Fleetwood

Mac, tastes she'd inherited from her parents. She connected the iPod to a black JBL portable speaker plugged into the wall about two feet from the tub and sang, *"You can go your own way!"* as she climbed into the hot water.

Poor Emily Maxwell would not get out of the tub alive. Somewhere between seven thirty and nine o'clock that evening, the plugged-in speaker entered the tub water and sent one hundred and ten volts of electricity shooting through the bookstore clerk.

As the speaker dropped, Emily must have had a moment of clarity and horror before the current blazed through the electrochemical machine that was her body, short-circuiting her broken heart.

"The Boston PD said Emily's death was an accident," Tull wrote, "but my gut said it was murder."

My cell phone rang. Bree.

"How's New York?" I asked.

"Making headway, actually," she said. I heard the sounds of a restaurant in the background. "But having a dinner here isn't half the fun it would be with you."

"Well, I wish I were there," I said. "Where are you eating?"

"La Grenouille," she said. "My target often eats here, but not tonight."

"What are you having?"

"Haven't ordered yet, but I'm thinking the saffron lobster bisque to start, then the oxtail in burgundy sauce, and a lemon tart with meringue for dessert."

"You're liking this whole expense-account thing."

"I am." She laughed. "One of the best perks of this job. How was your day?"

I told her in general terms about the visit from Thomas Tull's editor and her contentions about the author and his previous three books.

"You're going to read them all?" Bree said. "They're door-stops, aren't they?"

"Close," I replied.

"Anything jump out at you yet?"

I looked at the cover of *Electric*. "Maybe. He sells it as pure nonfiction, but some of the details and the way he describes the murders seem fictionalized to me, or at least speculative."

"How so?"

"At times, he kind of zooms in and puts you right there in the scene as the crime unfolds. But of course, that can't be an exact replication."

"I wouldn't think so," Bree said. "He's probably extrapolating from the available evidence, and that's always a somewhat subjective call."

"I'm going to take a look at the other books before I snooze. Got to be up early for Jannie's race."

"She excited?"

"Actually, she's calm, cool," I said. "Nana, Ali, and I will be nervous wrecks. And Damon's coming!"

"Oh, a family reunion without me."

"I'm FaceTiming you the race."

"Not the same, but it will have to do."

"I'll call you when they're heading to the blocks," I promised. "Around eleven a.m."

"Oh, here comes my waiter. Love you."

"Love you too," I said. I hung up and glanced at the wall clock before picking up Tull's second book.

CHAPTER

22

CERTAIN ASPECTS OF *Noon in Berlin* echoed *Electric*.

Early on, for example, the killer left little or no evidence at the scenes. And the police bungled the initial investigations before Tull entered the picture, retraced their steps, and found previously unknown clues or hidden aspects of the victims' lives that opened up a new avenue for the probe and gained him insider status.

Noon in Berlin, however, was written in a completely different tone than the first book. And the story was an unexpected tale of eroticism and savagery that shocked me again and again in the hundred pages I read that night.

Tull wrote that he'd learned of the story while he was on tour for the German-language debut of *Electric*.

The Berlin victims had all died as couples—illicit lovers, in fact, some straight and some gay, all of whom had had their trysts at noon in various hotels and pieds-à-terre around the German capital.

The first couple was discovered in a one-bedroom apartment in southeast Berlin not far from Treptower Park. Edgar Bruner was found naked, gagged, and tied to the four posts of the bed. His Russian mistress, Katya Dubosholva, was collapsed on top of him and also naked. Each had been shot in the neck with a tranquilizer dart from a gun normally used by veterinarians, wild-game biologists, and the like to subdue dangerous animals. Tull wrote that "each dart at that crime scene contained enough tranquilizer to take down a bull elephant."

Apparently, within a second of being shot, the mistress had fallen on top of her lover, pinning him, before she died of a heart attack. Then her lover was shot. At close range.

The second couple in the series, both suburban women, were married to men and had children. They were killed in an apartment in west Berlin, not far from Tiergarten and the zoo, shot with the same kind of tranquilizer dart as the first couple as they lay beneath the sheets.

Tull was allowed to observe the investigation in part because of the success of *Electric*. He learned that the Berlin police had focused heavily on CCTV cameras, trying to spot the killer on the way to and from each apartment. When that proved fruitless, the lead investigator, Inspector Ava Firsching, began to focus on the tranquilizer and its origin.

Her rationale was simple and smart. Inspector Firsching figured the killer had to have access to drugs normally used to tranquilize large animals. She and Tull went to the Berlin Zoo and talked to veterinarians and handlers. They learned that tranquilizer darts often contain benzodiazepines, a class of drugs that depress the nervous system.

"Administered at proper doses," Tull wrote, "these drugs will not kill humans or animals. But increase the doses or combine them with alcohol or opiates, and the risk of death rises dramatically. In toxicology screens that Inspector Firsching ordered, the German national crime lab found high doses of the benzodiazepine midazolam mixed with higher doses of the opiate fentanyl. The lethal cocktail caused almost immediate cardiac and respiratory failure."

Firsching and Tull believed the killer might be someone who had access to the drugs—a zoo worker, perhaps. That accusation caused an uproar, and the zoo administrators denied that any of their drugs had gone missing.

Two weeks passed with no additional murders. Then a heterosexual couple was found dead in an empty farmhouse in a rural area south of Berlin. The victims were both naked with plastic bags over their heads and cords around their necks. German investigators at first announced that the divorced housewife and her married lover had died of hypoxia during a bout of mutual "autoerotic asphyxiation."

Even though there was no sign of struggle and the deaths did not involve tranquilizer darts, Inspector Firsching and Tull did not believe these two deaths were accidental.

"The different method of death was less important," Tull wrote. "It was the time frame and motive that mattered. The noon hour. The illicit trysts."

Firsching and Tull turned out to be correct, of course. But was this one of those illogical leaps that Suzanne Liu had described to me?

I made a note of it and glanced at the clock—it was close to midnight. I yawned and set the book down, figuring I'd continue reading in the morning. But as I shut off the light and started down the stairs, I admitted that I would get little, if anything, done until after Jannie's big race was over.

I climbed into bed, reached out to shut off the light, and saw I'd received a text from Bree. It kept me smiling long after the room went dark.

I love you, baby. Wish you were here in my nice five-star hotel bed!

CHAPTER

23

Manhattan

BREE SLEPT IN A little that Saturday morning. Around eight, she went out for a run in Central Park, where she followed much the same route she'd taken the afternoon before with Detective Salazar.

After a shower, she ordered a room-service breakfast, sat at the desk, and wrote down the different angles she wanted to explore in the Duchaine case. Bree still had not received a return call from the attorney in North Carolina, and she made a note to try again before she left the hotel.

She also wanted to know what Wall Street analysts could tell her about the true financial health of Frances Duchaine's companies, but she realized most analysts did not work weekends. Bree decided to go down that road first thing Monday morning. In the meantime, what about the people around Duchaine? People like Paula Watkins, the fashion designer's close business associate, who Salazar said lured young, attractive people with dreams of model superstardom to New York. And the mysterious Katherine and Victor, who lured them with promises of rescue from disappointment and economic ruin—who were they? How had the fashion designer found them?

What were the traits of someone like Katherine or Victor? Bree wondered. She jotted down several that came to mind.

Cold, she wrote. *Calculating. High emotional intelligence. Amoral. Narcissist.*

A knock came at her door. Room service.

Bree waited as her breakfast was wheeled over to the desk, then ate an excellent cheese omelet with roasted peppers and onions on the side. She was pouring herself a second cup of coffee when her personal cell phone rang. She glanced at it, expecting Alex, only to see it was her boss, Elena Martin.

"Elena," Bree said. "I was going to call. I made some headway yesterday."

"Good," Martin said. "I'll let you make a little more. Frances Duchaine is hosting a black-tie fundraiser tonight at her estate in Greenwich, Connecticut. I've finagled you a ticket. I trust you have a gown with you?"

Bree laughed. "Uh, no, I was trying to travel light."

"Then go get yourself one and rent a limousine to take you there," Martin said. "Don't scrimp. You need to fit in with the kind of people who will be there, and the client is paying all your expenses."

"Okay. What do you expect me to do at this fundraiser?"

"Mingle. Talk a little. Listen a lot. Observe the women in her world."

"I can do that," Bree said.

"I know," Martin said. "We're sending you new identity

documents by courier. They'll be at the front desk of your hotel by noon. The event starts at seven thirty. You want to be there at seven forty-five."

"With the main flow of arriving guests," Bree said.

"When you'll get less scrutiny," her boss agreed. "Good luck. Keep me posted."

Bree hung up and looked at her watch. It was nearly ten fifteen. She had fewer than ten hours to get a dress, get her hair done, and get to Greenwich before the crush of partygoers reached Duchaine's estate.

Bree grabbed her purse and her phone, put on her shoes, went downstairs, and asked the doorman to hail her a cab.

"Destination, ma'am?"

"Frances Duchaine's store on Fifth Avenue," she said and was soon on her way.

It was raining lightly, which kept the crowds and traffic away. Ten minutes later, she was climbing out of the taxi in heavier rainfall.

Inside the store, Bree saw many more customers browsing than she had the day before. *Maybe the lack of customers yesterday was a onetime thing?*

But then Bree noticed that the flowers in the vase by the staircase looked a little droopy. So did the other flower arrangements positioned artfully throughout the store. *Someone's definitely cutting back,* she thought, climbing past the second floor to the third and wishing she could find an analyst to talk to about Duchaine's finances on a rainy Saturday morning in New York City.

Bree had taken no more than three steps onto the floor where the fashion designer displayed her wedding dresses, ball gowns, and big-ticket limited-run creations when she heard a squeal of delight.

"I knew you loved that dress with the brocade!" Marjorie cried, almost skipping to her side. "I'm right, aren't I?"

Bree smiled at the eager young woman. "You're almost right. I have a sudden need for a gown immediately. As in tonight."

Marjorie's face fell. "Tonight? That's going to be tough if alterations are needed."

"Money is no object," Bree said.

"Oh," Marjorie said, grinning now. "Then we can make this happen."

"Excellent," Bree said and followed her to the rack where the gorgeous black ball gown with the exquisite brocade work on the bodice hung.

Marjorie pulled it off the rack and held it up against Bree. "So dramatic. I think it'll fit, and if not, we'll make it fit."

"How much?"

"Fifty-five hundred," Marjorie said.

Bree hesitated, then said, "That works."

"Let's see what we're dealing with," Marjorie said, taking charge. "The fitting rooms are this way."

Marjorie was standing in front of several mirrors and holding open the fitting-room door for her when Bree's personal cell phone rang. She dug it out of her purse and saw Alex was trying to FaceTime her.

"I'm going to need a minute, Marjorie," Bree said. "I have to watch my stepdaughter's big track race."

"I used to run track," Marjorie said brightly. "The eight-hundred."

"Jannie's in the four-hundred," Bree said, answering the video call.

24

I CALLED BREE AS I was standing in the bleachers by the track at Howard University between Nana Mama and my son Damon, who had just regaled us with the story of his ride in the private jet. Ali was sitting behind us, absorbed in a book.

Bree's face appeared on my phone.

"Still want to watch?" I said, seeing that she was in a store of some kind.

"Definitely," Bree said. "Is she getting ready?"

I glanced at the track. Jannie was doing a few loose practice starts out of her blocks, which were in lane three on a stagger of six.

"She is ready," I said.

Damon leaned over. "She was in the zone when we got here."

"Hi, Damon!" Bree called.

"Good to see you! Wish you were here!"

"Next best thing."

Ali set his book aside, grabbed my wrist, and pulled the phone down so Bree could see his face. "I think she's going to blow people's doors in, Bree," Ali said. "Where are you?"

"A store in New York," she said. "Let me talk to your dad again."

I raised the phone to my face. "Shopping?"

She grinned a little naughtily. "I am. On an expense account. For a black-tie affair."

"Well, la-di-da," I said, and laughed. "You and Damon!"

"I know, right? Do you want to see the dress?"

"Sure."

Bree looked away. "Marjorie, can you bring the dress over so my husband can take a look?"

She turned the camera and I saw a slight, pretty blonde come toward the lens carrying one of the most beautiful dresses I had ever seen.

"Wowzah," I said.

"Wowzah if I can fit into it," Bree said.

"You absolutely will," Marjorie said, sounding insistent.

Nana Mama pulled on my left sleeve. "Jannie's getting ready to go."

"C'mon, sis," Damon said. "Show 'em how."

Out on the track, the official was calling the girls to race. This was an invitation-only event, which meant the competition would be fierce. Indeed, four girls in the field were already committed on scholarship to Division 1 NCAA programs. Only Jannie and a young woman from Richmond had not yet completed their dance cards.

"What's happening?" Bree asked.

"Sorry," I said and I aimed the phone camera at the track. "Can you see?"

"Now I can," Bree said. "And Marjorie says turn your phone sideways so we can see in full screen."

I complied. Looking around at the people getting to their feet, I saw eight or nine coaches I recognized from past recruiting visits. Shortly after we'd arrived today, several of them had come up to me, including the coaches from the Universities of Oregon and Texas. I had to tell them that I honestly had no idea where Jannie would decide to go to school.

"On your marks," the official called out.

The athletes went to their blocks, some appearing confident and some who struck me as tense. Several of them glanced at Jannie, who settled into her blocks, loose, ignoring them and everything else but the lane before her.

"Set."

My daughter coiled like a big cat about to spring.

The starting gun cracked.

Jannie burst out of the blocks low and charging, her hands open and slicing upward like blades. Twenty yards out, she began to lift her torso inch by inch with each stride. Her legs and arms were chopping as she ran the first curve. But by the time Jannie exited the turn, her shoulders and head were nearly upright, and her stride and arm pumps had become longer, easier.

As the athletes came down the backstretch, battling the stagger, the two women to Jannie's inside were falling off the pace. But a young woman committed to Syracuse University was way out to Jannie's right in lane six and looking strong.

In lane five, and also running well, was a girl pledged to the University of Florida. The uncommitted athlete from Richmond was in lane four.

"Why's Jannie so far behind?" my grandmother asked.

Damon said, "They're fighting the stagger, Nana. We won't see where she really is in the race until they come out of the second turn."

Ali said, "That's when she'll kick in the afterburners."

As the four athletes still in contention entered the far turn, I made sure the camera was still on them. Then I noticed that the coaches below us were all on their feet, watching the race and taking quick glances at their stopwatches.

I could see now that Jannie was gaining on the girl from Richmond, who was running hard herself. So were the athletes committed to Florida and Syracuse. Then my daughter did something I'd seen her do multiple times but that was still breathtaking to witness. Midway through the final turn, Jannie tapped into some God-given reservoir of energy and athleticism deep within herself.

She hit another gear.

Her stride lengthened, causing her to bound more than run as she finished the curve and blew past the girl committed to Syracuse. In the far outside lane, the young lady set to attend Florida was flying. So was the girl from Richmond. They were all neck and neck entering the homestretch.

The crowd in the stands roared louder when Jannie hit yet another gear and swiftly opened up a ten- and then twenty-yard margin before blazing through the finish leaning forward. The high-schooler from Richmond finished second and the Florida-bound recruit a winded third.

Jannie took her foot off the gas, slowed to a jog, and turned.

The Florida athlete appeared astonished. The Richmond girl had her arms overhead. The coaches were going wild.

But my focus was on Jannie. One of the track officials had run out and was saying something to her. My daughter looked at the man incredulously before she fell to the track, sobbing.

CHAPTER

25

"WHAT IN GOD'S NAME just happened?" Nana Mama demanded.

"Did they disqualify her, Dad?" Damon said.

Ali cried, "No, she was in her lane!"

"I thought so too. I'll go see," I said, my stomach souring as I tried to get down through the crowd in the stands and onto the track.

Disqualified? She's going to be heartbroken.

I passed the women's coach from the University of Texas, who slapped me on the back and said, "How does that one feel, Dr. Cross?"

I thought that was an odd thing to say, and I turned to look at her. "That Jannie was disqualified?"

"Disqualified?" the coach said, and she threw her head back and laughed. "She wasn't disqualified! Jannie just ran fifty point seventy-four!"

"That's good, I think," I said, relieved.

"Good? Your daughter just tied the national high-school record in the four-hundred, Dr. Cross!"

My jaw dropped. "What? No."

The coach had tears in her eyes before I did. "Yes! And I know I told you she should be a heptathlete, but I would be absolutely honored if she came to Texas to run the four-hundred for the Longhorns."

"Not if she comes northwest to the land of Nike," said the coach from the University of Oregon, a long, lanky guy who was now standing beside the Texas coach.

Several other coaches I recognized were all looking at me for hope.

I wiped away my tears, threw up my hands. "Your guess is as good as mine!"

After yelling the news up to Ali and Nana Mama, I got down on the track and ran to Jannie, who was back on her feet and surrounded by athletes, coaches, officials, and spectators, all clapping and congratulating her. She saw me, burst into tears again, and ran into my arms.

"Tell me," she said, trembling against me. "Fifty point seventy-four seconds. Tell me I just did that, Dad."

"You did. I saw it. We all saw it."

"I just ran my race," she said, weeping. "I just stuck with the plan and believed."

"And a miracle happened," I said, only then realizing I was still holding my phone. I lifted it off Jannie's back and peered through my tears at the screen.

Bree was gaping at me. "Is this for real?"

I nodded at her. "Can you believe it?"

Behind my wife, Marjorie, the store clerk, started jumping up and down and pumping her fists, cheering.

"That was the greatest thing I've ever seen on a phone!" Marjorie yelled.

In my arms, Jannie started to laugh. She turned to look at my phone.

"Unbelievable," Bree said, tears flowing. "I'm so proud of you, Jannie."

"I am too!" Marjorie yelled.

"Who is that behind you, Bree?" Jannie asked, still laughing.

"Oh," Bree said. "That's Marjorie, my personal shopper!"

"Woot!" Marjorie cried. "You're a rock star, Jannie!"

My daughter thought it was hilarious when the young lady came closer, waving. She waved back and then left to take a urine drug test because she'd been invited to a national development camp in June and the U.S. Track and Field Association required it.

"And I have to get fitted for my gown," Bree said. "Thank you for filming that, Alex. I'll never forget it."

"I don't think any of us will," I said. "Have fun with the dress."

Her face disappeared from the screen.

Ali and Nana Mama came down to the field after the eight-hundred-meter race ended. Jannie returned from taking her drug test and there were more hugs and congratulations.

A photographer and a reporter from the *Washington Post* appeared and spoke to Jannie and her coach and me. Many of the coaches who had recruited Jannie were watching from the perimeter. Then Gail Andrews, a popular local television sports reporter, and her cameraman came onto the scene, and we had to do it all over again.

As that interview wound down, Andrews gestured at the pack of coaches still standing off to the side and then looked directly into the camera. "Jannie Cross is one of the most heavily recruited track athletes in the nation," Andrews said. "Fifteen top Division One schools have offered her full scholarships."

She turned back to my daughter. "Jannie, a whole lot of folks are interested in knowing where you are planning to run in college next year. Can you give me an exclusive and put these poor coaches out of their misery?"

Jannie's smile faded a little. She glanced over at the coaches, then back at the sports broadcaster, emotion making her cheeks quiver. "I can do that. I know where I want to be next year."

"Really?" Andrews said, thrilled and grinning. "Well, okay, where does your future lie? Which one of the fifteen colleges dying to have you will you choose, Jannie Cross? Texas? Oregon? University of Southern California?"

Jannie glanced at me and Nana and Ali before looking back to the reporter.

"Here," she said, beaming. "I want to run here, on this track. This magical track."

Andrews looked a little puzzled. "You want to run for Howard University?"

Jannie nodded and looked over at the pack of coaches, many of whose faces had fallen. "I want to run here if Coach Oliver's offer is still good, yes."

David Oliver, the track coach at Howard, wasn't even in the front row. He came around ten or twelve other coaches with a stunned and then joyous expression on his face. He pumped his fist at the sky and went over to Jannie. "Of course the offer's still good," Coach Oliver said, putting his hand over his heart. "Do you really want to run for me, Jannie? With all these other powerhouse offers?"

"Yes," Jannie said firmly. "I want to run for you and for Howard, Coach. You won the world championship from here. You made it to an Olympic podium from Howard. And I want to run as a Bison, right here where my family can watch me."

26

Greenwich, Connecticut

BREE FELT ALMOST SEWN into the gorgeous black dress with the brocade bodice. She put some arch in her spine so she could breathe a little better in the back seat of the town car she'd hired to take her to Frances Duchaine's fundraising soiree.

At first, Bree thought it would be impossible to fit into the dress. But Marjorie and the tailor she brought in had been insistent, and with the help of an industrial-strength pair of Spanx tights, they finally coaxed and squished Bree into it.

Marjorie said she looked incredible. And with the stiletto heels, earrings, and necklace Marjorie picked out, Bree admitted she looked beyond stunning in the dress.

Beyond stunning or not, Bree thought, shifting again to get air, *if I'm not careful, I could pass out or break a rib before this night's over.*

They pulled up to a gate behind two limousines. A guard checked Bree's invitation against the guest list.

"Okay, Ms. Carlisle," the guard said, handing it back to her. "Enjoy the evening."

"Thank you," she said brightly.

The town car wound up a serpentine drive through well-tended grounds to a two-story white brick mansion built in the 1920s. It had a beautifully lit fountain in the turnaround courtyard; a valet came to Bree's door and opened it.

She blew out all the air in her lungs, smiled, squirmed out, and straightened, which made the dress looser and her next breath easier to take. Soft jazz came through the open front door to Duchaine's home. It was a warm evening.

Bree followed several other couples spilling from the limos up the stairs and into a grand foyer with dual spiral staircases rising at the back to a landing where a quartet played. She showed her invitation to a woman, who checked Bree off under the name Evelyn Carlisle, gave her a bidding paddle for the live auction, and directed her to the rear terrace for drinks and hors d'oeuvres.

"That's a beautiful dress, by the way," the woman said.

"I can barely breathe in it, but thank you," Bree said.

Moving with the equally well-dressed crowd, Bree went down a hall to the left of one staircase, passing a library and a dining room and seeing art nearly everywhere, which reminded her of an article on Duchaine in *Vanity Fair*. The writer had noted that the fashion designer was no bleak modernist. Duchaine lived with as many textures and beautiful things around her as possible.

Bree entered a huge ballroom decorated for a party, with tables set with white linen, fine china, and crystal. The French doors on the far end were flung open, revealing a large blue-slate terrace decorated with bare white branches and webs of tiny lights that blinked every so often, like fireflies.

Perhaps a hundred of the seriously well-heeled were already on the terrace, sipping champagne and munching beluga caviar on toast. Bree joined them.

Most of the people near the doors were deep in conversation with friends and acquaintances. As she passed them, she heard yacht chat and golf chat and reviews of Caribbean hot spots.

The rich are different than you and I, Bree thought, snagging a flute of champagne as a waiter passed with a tray.

She moved toward the perimeter of the terrace and a table that featured sushi, cooked shrimp on ice, and a slab of smoked Scottish salmon. Filling his plate high was a rail-thin man in his fifties with stretched-looking skin. He wore black pants, a black T-shirt, a black jacket, and red high-top sneakers.

He looked up at her. "I'm on a diet, but I can't resist."

"Neither can I," Bree said and picked up a plate.

"My, my, that's a dress to die for," he said, eyeing her up and down. "It's one of Frances's pieces, isn't it?"

"Yes," she said. "I picked it up today at the store on Fifth."

"Lucky you," he said and held out his hand. "Phillip Henry Luster."

Bree took it. "Nice to meet you, Phillip Henry Luster. I'm Evelyn Carlisle. Do you work for Frances?"

"I have, twice, briefly both times," Luster said. "Two brazen egos always clashing. It was never functional."

"But you remain friends?"

"Of a sort. Frances still invites me when it's time to raise money for one of her causes. I like this cause, so I'm here."

"Scholarships for minorities and LGBTQ students in fashion," Bree said, putting shrimp on her plate. "I like the cause too."

"So does my boss," Luster said. "Tess Jackson."

"Lucky you," Bree said. "What do you do for Tess?"

"I draw and … well, here's our hostess, the woman of the hour."

27

FOLLOWING LUSTER'S LINE OF sight, Bree saw Frances Duchaine coming through the French doors and greeting several people on the terrace as dear friends. Bree had to admit that the fashion designer was a presence—tall, Pilates-slim, and devastatingly chic, with short auburn hair that set off the turquoise of her flowing gown.

Other people on the terrace sensed Duchaine's arrival and turned to see her.

"'Walk into my parlor,' said the spider to the fly," Luster said and laughed a little bitterly to himself.

"What do you mean by that?" Bree asked and sipped from her champagne.

"Frances is too energetic and charismatic for her own good. Always has been. But when she wants money, she can sure turn on the femininity and the charm. What do you do, Evelyn?"

"Whatever I want, whenever I want," Bree said.

"Cheers to that," Luster said, raising his glass. "Live local?"

"Newport Beach, California, but I'm considering a move east. Long Island."

"Are you in desperate need of Lyme disease or something?"

Bree laughed. "No. Just a change."

"Recently divorced?"

"Recently widowed," Bree said, sticking to her cover story.

"I'm sorry," Luster said.

"So am I."

He ate one of his shrimp before saying, "How was business at Frances's Fifth Avenue store?"

"You know, that's funny—"

"Oh God, here she comes already," Luster muttered, setting down his plate on a table as the fashion designer approached.

"Phil-lip," Duchaine said in a throaty, ironic voice. "Nice sneaks. Anything creative coming out of that pencil these days?"

"Every moment of every day, darling," Luster said. "Have you met Evelyn?"

The famous designer looked to Bree with all the force of her nature, blue-green eyes wide, beckoning, her face so...interesting. Bree found herself dazzled when the designer held out her hand and said, "Hello, Evelyn. I'm Frances Duchaine."

"Evelyn Carlisle," Bree said, feeling flustered as she briefly took Duchaine's hand. "From Newport Beach."

"You have great taste in dresses, Evelyn. It's one of my favorites."

"Thank you, I love it," Bree said, then blurted out something she didn't know if she believed. "And it's a real honor to meet you."

Duchaine put her hand over her heart. "Bless you for that, and I hope you help us with your paddle this evening."

"That's why I'm here," Bree said.

"Excellent. Where did you get the dress? In our Santa Monica store?"

"Fifth Avenue."

"Oh, that worked well, then," Duchaine said, smiling and putting her hand gently on Bree's forearm. "Nice to meet you, Evelyn, and please spend freely."

With that she was gone, swirling off into the crowd of well-wishers, and Bree felt like a spell had been broken.

"Is she always like that?" she asked Luster. "Overwhelming?"

"Always," Luster said, seeming amused by her reaction. "It is why ordinary people can't see the cracks in the empress's armor. So, you were saying something about business at the store on Fifth? Something funny?"

Bree studied him a moment. "I don't know. There just weren't as many customers as I'd thought there would be in her flagship store."

Luster smiled. "Because all the customers are over at Tess's new flagship store on Lexington, putting on dresses of our design."

All right, she thought. *Mr. Luster is a constant surprise. Keep the man talking.* She said, "The flower arrangements were a little wilted too."

Luster sniffed. "Not surprising, given Frances's ballooning debt."

Someone rang a bell, calling the crowd to dinner.

"She's in trouble financially?" Bree said.

Now Luster studied her. "That's the rumor."

"Do you have plans to sit with anyone for dinner, Phillip?" Bree asked.

He paused and then smiled. "You are more than you seem, I think, Evelyn Carlisle. I would love to break bread with you. And I just might know where some of the skeletons are alleged to hang in dear Frances's closet."

Washington, DC

EARLY SATURDAY EVENING, NANA MAMA, Ali, John Sampson, Willow, and I were watching Jannie fidget as she stared at her laptop; on the big screen across the room, the weekend anchors of ESPN's *SportsCenter* were engaged in witty banter about the unfolding baseball season.

Lucille Jones, one of the anchors, shifted in her chair, looked to another camera, and said, "But enough about baseball. Let's talk a little track-and-field, shall we?"

Evan Kincaid, her partner, adjusted his glasses and said, "She's so fast."

"So fast," Jones said, admiring.

"How fast is seventeen-year-old Jannie Cross of Washington, DC?" Kincaid said to the camera.

Jones said, "We thought we had a sense when we featured this film three years ago, when Jannie was fourteen and a freshman in high school."

The screen cut to a much thinner and smaller version of my daughter in the blocks against much older girls. She rocketed out of them at the crack of the gun but stumbled and fell while her competition roared off into the first curve.

Instead of giving up, Jannie jumped back to her feet and took off. She didn't win, but she caught up to and passed every competitor but one.

"I don't care who you are, that was fast," Kincaid said when the camera returned to him. "But you ain't seen nothing yet."

The screen jumped to today's race. Jannie exploded from the blocks while the anchors kept talking.

Jones said, "For ten years, the record stood. A decade passed after a San Diego runner shattered the women's U.S. national high-school record in the four-hundred-meter track event by two seconds, breaking the tape at fifty point seventy-four seconds."

Kincaid picked up the narrative as the racers ran the first curve and into the backstretch, saying, "For ten years, that record was considered unassailable. For a decade, no U.S. female high-school athlete came close to that blistering time. Until Jannie Cross ran today in an invitational meet on the track at Howard University."

On-screen, Jannie and the other athletes were close to the far turn.

Jones said, "The rest of the field is looking competitive at this point in the race. But watch what happens when Jannie Cross enters that turn."

The screen showed Jannie hitting fourth gear and going into her bounding gait, then hitting fifth gear and running down the straightaway and through the tape.

Kincaid said, "How fast was Jannie Cross today?"

The camera showed the timing box flashing: *50.74.*

Jones returned to the screen. "Fast enough to tie the national record. She tied the national record and she looked like she still had a lot left in the tank at the finish!"

"Fast, fast, fast," Kincaid said, "and we've got Jannie Cross live here tonight from her home in DC. Hi there, speedster."

The big screen across the room showed Jannie smiling nervously into the camera. "Hi."

"Hi back," Jones said. "Young lady, you are something."

"Thank you," Jannie said.

"How does it feel to be co-holder of a national record?"

Jannie's mouth hung open a second, then she said, "At first, I could not believe it. I mean, I did not go out there today trying to do that. I just ran like I know I can. I was as shocked as everyone else was."

"Tell us how you did it while we show the race in split screen."

"Okay," Jannie said, watching the screen and seeing the race again. "I felt solid about my start, which gave me confidence through the first curve and down the back straight. I felt like I was flowing, easy, and I was ready to attack coming into the final turn. Then I just let it go when Coach said to let it go."

"You did indeed," Kincaid said. "I heard you picked Howard University over six or seven top track programs. Why was that?"

Jannie looked at Nana Mama and then back at the camera. "My great-grandmother lives here with us. She used to be a teacher and told me education should come first even if I am fast. And Howard has such a great reputation academically and in track. And Coach Oliver is an inspiration to me."

Jones said, "Smart great-grandmother, and good for Howard and Coach Oliver."

Kincaid said, "And good on you, Jannie Cross, and thank you for coming on *SportsCenter*. I don't think it will be the last time. I expect we'll be able to play our little shtick about your achievements in the future."

"Thanks for having me," Jannie said.

Her face disappeared from the big screen, leaving the anchors shaking their heads and arranging papers on their desk.

"Jannie's so fast," Kincaid said.

"So, so fast," Jones said.

The show went to commercial and we all started cheering.

"How does it feel to be one of the fastest young runners of all time?" I asked, giving Jannie a hug.

"Honestly, Dad?" Jannie said, snuggling into my chest. "It's like a dream I never want to end."

CHAPTER

29

Greenwich, Connecticut

BREE AND PHILLIP HENRY LUSTER found seats at a table for eight some distance from the small stage where musicians were playing softly for the patrons gathering to dine in Frances Duchaine's ballroom.

Bree settled into her chair and immediately felt constricted.

Luster noticed and said, "Spanx?"

"How did you guess?"

"The Heimlich maneuver expression on your face."

Bree laughed and rubbed her stomach. "Funny but true. I feel like I'm wearing a medieval corset with whalebones."

Luster chuckled. "Can I give you advice so you can actually enjoy the meal?"

"I'm not taking this dress or the Spanx off," she said. "I'll never get back in it."

"No, no," Luster said, and he chuckled again. "Just do the broadcaster-on-a-couch sit."

Bree knit her brows until the fashion designer scooted forward to the edge of his chair and spread his legs. "There. My belly is free to hang now. My diaphragm becomes less restricted. The breath comes easier. Try."

Bree scooted forward, hesitated, then spread her thighs wide. With the snugness of the dress, it put a strain on her neck and back, but she found it was much easier to breathe.

"Okay," she said, smiling. "Thank you. That does help."

"I'm here to serve." Tess Jackson's chief fashion designer looked away for a moment. "Well, it's a boy toy this evening."

Bree followed Luster's amused gaze and spotted Frances Duchaine being escorted to her table by a tall strapping blond man twenty years her junior.

"He's right out of central casting, isn't he?" Luster said. "It's a shame he's straighter than an arrow."

"Who is he?"

Luster shrugged. "This one is a Burt or something like that. But it could be a Greg or a Tony or even a Karen if Frances is feeling a little exotic and…oh, the black widow makes an early appearance. Imagine that."

Bree looked over and saw a pretty, petite brunette in her forties wearing a simple black dress talking intently to Frances Duchaine.

"Who's that?" Bree asked.

"Paula Watkins," Luster said. "Frances's dark shadow."

"Her dark shadow?" Bree asked.

"It's an accurate description," Luster said. "Oh God, here she comes. Decide for yourself. It's like I'm a magnet or something."

Indeed, Watkins had left Duchaine's table and was now making a beeline straight for their table.

"Hello, Phillip," Watkins said, her smile a little forced. "I hope you brought your checkbook."

"A black card," Luster said. "Paula Watkins, have you met Evelyn Carlisle?"

"I haven't had the pleasure," Watkins said, locking eyes with Bree as she moved around Luster with her hand extended. "But in fact, I came over more to talk with you, Evelyn, than Phillip. That dress looks stunning on you, by the way."

"Well, thank you," Bree said, standing to shake her hand. "And talk to me?"

Watkins smiled, said, "Yes, I wondered if I might have a quick moment in private to chat with you about the particulars of tonight's charity in hopes that you might be overly generous during the auction. You don't mind, do you, Phillip?"

"As long as it's quick," Luster said. "Evelyn's wonderful company."

"We won't be long," Watkins promised.

CHAPTER

30

BREE SET DOWN HER napkin and followed Paula Watkins, breathing almost normally by the time they got well down the hallway. Duchaine's dark shadow stood aside and gestured Bree into the library, where she was surprised to see Frances's escort of the moment.

Burt, the buff, blond guy, stood with his arms crossed beside a formidable Black man in his thirties. Watkins shut the doors and turned, still smiling.

"That dress is magnificent on you," she said.

"I don't think I've ever owned one as beautiful."

"Very few women can wear that kind of dress, much less afford it."

Bree thought that was an odd comment. "Yes, well, let me hear about the charity and what I can do—"

Watkins's smile vanished as she cut Bree off. "Frances being

Frances, she was interested in who sold you the dress and she discovered it was Marjorie Mayhew, her cousin's daughter, who works at our Fifth Avenue store. Is that who you bought the dress from?"

Bree's stomach dropped, but she said, "Marjorie was a great help. But she never mentioned she was Frances's cousin's daughter."

"And you never mentioned the name Evelyn Carlisle. Who are you working for? Why are you here, Bree Stone?"

"I honestly don't know what you're talking about. Bree Stone is a name I use when I don't want people to know who I am."

"We know exactly who you are," Watkins shot back. "You are the former chief of detectives of the Washington, DC, Metro Police force and you now work for the Bluestone Group, which, ironically, has done some work for us in the past. So again, why are you here and who hired you?"

Bree saw the jig was up. "I was sent to soak up the world of Frances Duchaine, and I honestly have no idea who hired me. You could ask my boss, Elena Martin, but I don't think she knows either."

"Oh, I will ask Elena. Just before I inform her that Frances will no longer do business with her. And now, please leave, Ms. Stone, or I'll have these men drag you out in your once-in-a-lifetime dress. Which doesn't fit you well, by the way."

Bree put her hands up and opened the door to the chattering and clattering of fifty wealthy people dining. She looked over her shoulder at Burt, who was following her, and then Watkins.

"Send my regards to Katherine and Victor, won't you?" Bree said.

The face of Duchaine's second in command lost all its color.

31

Takoma Park, Maryland

LISA MOORE LOVED THE night, loved the cloak of anonymity it gave her as she eased down a dark alley around eight thirty in the evening, trying to see over an ivy-covered chain-link fence into the small backyard of a gray-and-white two-story house not far from Maryland's border with the District of Columbia.

The house itself was dark, but a small floodlight on the right rear corner allowed Thomas Tull's chief researcher to make mental notes and take pictures of the tricycle by the back stairs and the swing set and the sandbox with two large Tonka trucks in it.

Moore walked past another few houses before opening the recording app on her phone. "It's a place of hopefulness," she said. "Of young, innocent children and parents who genuinely care. And maybe the threat to their lives will fade, no match for the love they nurture and share."

Tull's researcher turned off the app, thinking that sounded pretty good, poetic even. She exited the alley and turned left. Though she'd already seen the front of the house virtually, Moore wanted a real look at it, just for reference.

A bald, forty-something man in running gear jogged down the sidewalk toward her, holding the leash to a Jack Russell terrier that yapped with excitement.

"Happy little guy," she said.

"Happy little girl," the man said, puffing and smiling as he passed.

Tull's researcher wore a plain ball cap that she'd kept low over her eyes, and her pants and windbreaker were intentionally dark and logo-less. The jogger with the terrier might remember the brief conversation, but he would never be able to identify her.

Never in a million years, Moore thought as she crossed the street and took another left on the sidewalk. The house of interest was roughly halfway down the block and across the street from a two-story brick house that had a For Sale sign out front. According to the listing Moore had found on Zillow, it was newly remodeled and empty. The empty house was one of the reasons Moore had chosen the home opposite it for more detailed scrutiny. When the street was quiet on both sides, she crossed the driveway and took a hard right at the For Sale sign.

She went up the stairs to the porch, which lay in shadows. Tull's researcher went to the far left corner, where the shadows were darkest.

She straddled the porch rail. To break up her silhouette, she leaned back against the house next to a tall, thick lilac bush that was blooming to her immediate right.

As long as I stay still, quiet, and phone-free, I can be here for hours.

It was a pleasant, balmy night, and the lilacs smelled delightful, which combined to keep Moore still for a good twenty minutes, even when a young couple with a basset hound puppy passed by on the sidewalk.

Two minutes later, a late-model silver Toyota minivan pulled into the driveway across the street. Both rear doors slid back and a burly Asian-American man in a red tracksuit climbed out of the driver's side. A petite blonde in charcoal-gray yoga pants and a yellow hoodie got out of the front passenger side.

The Pan family, Moore thought. *George and Angela. What a love story there is to tell about those two, huh?*

The Pans were reaching into the back seat of the minivan. With the interior lights on, Tull's researcher could see they were fumbling with car seats. Angela came out with one of their sons first. His twin came out in George's arms a few moments later. Both looked sound asleep.

A long day for three-year-old Derek and Miles, Moore thought. *I wonder how the Pans tell the boys apart. I can't tell who's who from the pictures Angela posts on Instagram.*

The Pan family entered their front door and soon there were lights on downstairs and up. Moore wondered whether she should shut down this observation post for the evening and pay a short visit to the secondary one before calling it a night. Then her phone buzzed in her pocket.

Feeling like a decision was being made for her, she got off the porch rail, fished out her phone, looked at the caller ID, and saw TT. Tull's researcher declined the call and texted the author that she would phone when she got to her car.

After checking both ways, Moore moved out of the shadows and down the street with only a glance back at the Pans' bungalow before she turned the corner. Three blocks on, she opened the door of a black Prius and climbed in.

After she'd gone several more blocks, she called Tull.

"How's it going, Lisa?" the author asked.

"Solid foundational work, T," she replied. "The surveillance site on the Pans is good. And I've got pictures of their house, front and back, as well as copies of their recent renovation blueprints. I think they are a go if there's ginning to be done."

"Excellent," he said. "And the Allisons?"

"I'm heading in their direction now," Moore said. "You shouldn't wait up."

"I will anyway," Tull said. "I want to see those pictures and the blueprints."

32

AROUND ELEVEN SATURDAY EVENING, I was alone in the front room watching the local news when my cell phone buzzed with a text.

Bravo, Cross, you must be one happy pappy now that Jannie has shown the world her true mettle. A stunning achievement. Congrats to all. Your faithful servant—M

My stomach turned at the text's end and that single letter *M.*

I had been getting these kinds of texts and messages on and off for years, and I was still no closer to identifying M or Maestro, the group of ruthless vigilantes M controlled.

Before that evening's text, M had been silent for nearly seven months, ever since the explosion that took the life of Emmanuella Alejandro, last of that drug cartel's leaders. I stared at this latest message, frustrated all over again at my inability to nail M. I wanted to reply to the text, but M always used dark web filters and routing systems to scrub all identifying information, making it impossible to answer.

I had tried changing my phone number several times, to no avail. If M wanted to message me, he always found a way.

Before my irritation could turn to anger, my phone rang. Bree.

"How was your grand evening?" I asked.

"Grand until my cover got blown," Bree said.

"Ouch."

"Big ouch and my own fault," she replied. "I was buying a dress and watching Jannie's race with Marjorie, the clerk who was helping me."

"I remember her."

"She's related to the target and knew my real name from the credit cards."

"What happened?"

"I got tossed from the gala."

"Escorted out?"

"To my town car, and they watched as I was driven away."

"You tell Elena Martin yet?"

Bree sighed. "She's my next phone call."

"Did you find anything useful before you got the heave-ho? Any positives you can report to her?"

After a long pause, she said, "I believe the target is having serious cash-flow problems."

"Is that the motive to sexually exploit?"

"I think so. But I have to get it nailed down as fact," Bree said. "The target's business is privately and hedge fund–held, so there aren't the kind of declaratory documents a public company has to file with the Securities and Exchange Commission."

"Anything else?"

"As I was being led out, I purposefully mentioned the first names of two people allegedly involved in the sex ring."

"You get a reaction?"

"Lost color. Big glare. Fists clenched. Dead silent."

"Sounds like you should tell Elena that good news first."

"Maybe I'll give her the choice."

"Coming home tomorrow?"

"I think I'm going to stay through Monday, see if I can salvage this. How about you? What was your day like?"

"Exciting, to say the least. Jannie was on *SportsCenter* live again."

"Live! Did you record it?"

"Ali did," I said. "Jannie did great. Acted like an old pro."

Bree laughed softly. "God, that's so great for her, Alex!"

"And for us. She's decided to go to Howard because of Coach Oliver and so we can watch her run."

"Howard! That's fantastic too—you know, choosing a historically all-Black school right here rather than going across the country. Are you beside yourself?"

"As a dad, I think *ecstatic* is the right word," I said, deciding not to mention the text from M. "In fact, I'm exhausted from being ecstatic for so many hours in a row."

"Then you better get some sleep," Bree said, her voice softening. "I love you."

"Love you too. Good luck with all of it."

"Thanks," she said, and hung up.

Upstairs in bed, I decided I would go back and finish *Noon in Berlin* after I skimmed Thomas Tull's third book, *Doctor's Orders,* which was set in South Carolina. But after reading the same paragraph three times and grasping little of it, I knew I was too far gone; I set the book down and turned off the light.

I fell into dreamless oblivion in seconds and slept so soundly I did not hear my phone ringing until it vibrated off my nightstand and hit the floor with a crack.

The phone stopped ringing and buzzing, but I'd been startled awake enough to peer blearily at my nightstand clock. It was six thirty Sunday morning.

I groaned, knowing I should either check the phone or ignore it, get up, and go for a run. But then it started ringing again.

I leaned over, picked up the phone, and saw that, fortunately, the screen wasn't broken. The caller ID showed a 212 area code—New York City. Was Bree calling on the hotel phone?

I answered. "This is Alex."

"Dr. Cross, it's Suzanne Liu," she said breathlessly. "I need to speak with you in person as soon as possible."

"Well, I can't come to New York, if that's what you're asking."

"No, no, I'm still here in DC. I'm staying at the Watergate and doing research on Thomas. I came across something I was going to call you about, but he found out and is threatening me. I desperately need your help, Dr. Cross."

33

I LEFT A NOTE for Nana Mama, Jannie, and Ali, all of whom were still sleeping, telling them that I was meeting someone for an early breakfast and that I'd be back soon.

It was a spectacular day in the nation's capital—not a cloud in the sky, low humidity. I saw spring flowers blooming every-where as the Uber took me to the Watergate Hotel. I had suggested we meet at one of its restaurants.

But when I phoned to say I was almost there, Tull's former editor sounded shaky.

"I know it's probably irrational, but I never knew what Thomas was capable of, and I still don't. I'm sorry, but could you come upstairs? The management comped me one of the ambassador suites. It has a kitchen and a balcony where we can eat."

I said, "I try not to be in a woman's hotel room if it's not my wife's."

"Perfectly understandable," she said, though her voice sounded strained. "But this is a huge suite. We'd be nowhere near the bedroom and I've already taken the liberty of ordering room service."

Against my better judgment, I sighed and said, "What's the suite number?"

She gave it to me along with a code I had to put into an elevator reserved for suite holders. When the elevator doors opened, Liu was standing there barefoot in black pants and a black top; her hair was pulled back, and she had dark circles under her eyes.

"I so appreciate you coming over on such short notice, Dr. Cross," she said. "This has all been nerve-racking beyond my wildest imagination. And now I'm being threatened. I mean, these things don't normally happen in a book editor's world."

"I expect they don't," I said.

"I hope you're hungry."

"I could eat something."

"It just arrived," she said and led the way into a beautiful suite with dark wood floors, custom Italian leather furniture, and a sweeping view of the Potomac River.

A room-service cart was parked in front of the open sliding doors. On the balcony was a small table with two place settings.

"I ordered scrambled eggs, toast, bacon, fruit, coffee, and juice. Does that work?"

"Sounds good," I said.

Liu began lifting stainless-steel lids, and the aromas quickly had my stomach growling. After she'd served herself and sat down, I spooned eggs, bacon, and fruit onto my plate and poured a cup of coffee.

I carried it out onto the balcony where a breeze blew and made conversation a little difficult. The book editor had put on sunglasses. She smiled.

"I really appreciate you coming, Dr. Cross."

"It's my job," I said as I took a seat opposite her. "But honestly, I'd appreciate you getting to the point. I'm missing time with my kids."

Liu's smile faded a little and she busied herself with her napkin. "Oh, of course. I'm sorry. Okay, where to begin?"

"You said Tull threatened you after you found out something about him."

"Yes," she said emphatically. "You can hear the threat for yourself. But let me tell you what made him so angry first."

"Okay," I said, taking a bite of delicious scrambled eggs made with melted Boursin cheese.

"Remember when I told you and Detective Sampson that there were things that seemed off during the writing of all three of his books?"

"I do, but you gave no specifics."

"I admit I blocked the details from my mind because the books were doing so well," Liu said, and she sipped from her cup.

"And now you've recalled the details?"

"And more from my old notes," she said. "Did you know that Thomas was the one who first told the police that the accidental electrocutions of shop clerks around metro Boston might be the work of one murderer?"

I blinked and shook my head. "That's not the way it reads in the book. He said he and a detective with the Boston police came to that conclusion about the same time."

"I know it reads that way, but it turns out it's not true. Jane Hale, the Boston detective, went to one of Thomas's book signings when *Electric* hit the hardcover bestseller list. Hale comes across like a rock star in the book, and she was grateful for Thomas's depiction. She'd not only become semi-famous; she'd received a big promotion after the killer was caught and convicted. But we all went out after the book signing and had many drinks to celebrate, and that's when Hale told me that she'd had no idea the electrocutions were connected until Thomas brought the possibility to her attention."

That *was* a different story, and Tull's revision did cause me to pause. "Why would he have done that?"

"I asked Thomas that same question," Liu said. "He said he remembered things differently. But then again, he was sleeping with Hale for most of the investigation."

"Is that true?"

"It's a fact," she said. "She left her husband for Thomas and they were together for almost a year after the book came out. But by then he was in Germany, working on *Noon in Berlin* and sleeping with Inspector Ava Firsching of the Berlin criminal police."

I frowned. "He didn't mention that relationship in the parts I read."

"He doesn't talk about his relationships with female detectives in any of the books," Liu said. "And I didn't find out about Inspector Firsching until I was over there for the German-language launch of *Noon*. You'll never guess what else the inspector told me."

34

I WAS LISTENING CLOSELY by that point. I pulled out a notepad and began jotting down some of her assertions. "It would help if you just laid it out."

Liu seemed irritated. She took off her sunglasses, looked straight at me, and said, "Did you know Thomas speaks perfect German? His mother was from Munich and he spent many of his summers at a lake in Bavaria."

"I don't remember that from the book."

"Because it's not mentioned," she said. "He portrays himself as being out of the loop half the time because of the language barrier."

"Why would he do that?"

"Exactly. I asked and he said it made him more sympathetic, as lost in the investigation as the reader."

I said, "It's odd, but not a crime."

"There are other inconsistencies, Dr. Cross," she said. "In *Noon,* for example, Thomas depicts Inspector Firsching as the one who comes up with the idea of focusing on Berlin Zoo employees because the initial victims were all killed with darts loaded with animal tranquilizer."

"I remember that."

"Except that's not exactly correct," Liu said. "Ava told me she and Thomas were sleeping together by that point and he was the one who came up with the logic of focusing on the zookeepers."

I held up my hands. "I apologize because I've read only the first hundred pages. Was the zoo really involved?"

"Ultimately, yes. But Firsching did not find that damning evidence until very late in the investigation, after she'd dropped the zoo angle and taken the probe in a different direction, arresting two suspects only to release them."

"I'll bite. Who ended up being the killer?"

"A large-animal veterinarian who was an outside contractor. He came to the zoo occasionally to treat elephants, rhinos, and the like. The vet's wife had cheated on him with various men over the years, all during the noon hour. When she divorced him and took half his money, he got obsessive and then turned homicidal."

Liu put her sunglasses on again and said that in the book, Tull claimed he was only tangentially involved in the big break in the *Noon* case. But Firsching told her that it was Tull's idea to focus on the zoo again, not on staff but on the vendors and consultants.

"Do you see the pattern?" she asked. "Thomas underplays his role when in truth he has a great deal of influence over these investigations."

"And the investigators," I said.

"Exactly," she said.

"What about the third book? I haven't gotten to it. Female investigator?"

"Heidi Parks with the South Carolina State Bureau of Investigation," Liu said. "She and Thomas were shacking up within a week of his arrival on the scene, which was shortly after the body of the second doctor was found. Again, I think he downplays his role in the book and gives all the light and praise to Parks."

"You think?"

"Okay, I have strong suspicions based on the way Detective Parks reacted when I called her yesterday and asked several pointed questions about that investigation. She got quite hostile, so hostile she called Thomas and told him what I was up to."

"Which led to the threat?"

"Yes," she said. "Are you finished with breakfast? With this wind, you'll be able to hear what he said better inside."

"I'm good, thanks," I said, putting my napkin on the table and standing up in the stiffening breeze. "Let's go hear it."

We left the dishes on the table and went inside. Liu crossed to the suite's bar and retrieved her phone.

As she did, I looked around, seeing through the open bedroom door two of the hotel's robes lying on the bed.

"It's a little garbled," Liu said, returning. "And I didn't start recording until Thomas turned abusive. But you'll get the gist of it."

The book editor pushed a button and there was a static hiss through which a male said, "Suzanne, what the hell are you doing? Are you trying to gut me? Get revenge? Grow up! You lost out after making big money off me for years. Live with it and don't be a crazy bitch. I'm telling you, I won't take this lying down. If you keep trying to smear me, Suzanne, you'll pay for it. One way or another, you will pay for it."

Liu turned it off. "Believe me now?"

Tull had not suggested he'd physically harm her, but the tone *was* threatening. "I do."

Without warning, the book editor threw her arms around me. "Thank you, Dr. Cross," she said. "I've been so alone, so in my head, I needed someone to believe me, and here you are."

I was uncomfortable at that point. It got even more creepy when she tried to kiss me.

"Whoa, whoa," I said, backing up and extricating myself from her arms. "What's this all about? I'm married. See the ring?"

Liu looked a little angry, then chagrined, and she blushed and turned away. "I don't know what came over me. I'm so sorry. I...I sometimes misinterpret things, and like I said, I've been so lonely and in my head. I honestly don't know why I did that."

"I don't know either, and I think it is time I leave."

As I turned to go, she said frantically, "You won't look into what I've told you?"

"I didn't say that, Ms. Liu. Goodbye and don't call me again. If I need to talk to you, I know how to find you."

35

AROUND FOUR THAT AFTERNOON, I climbed off an Amtrak Acela train in New York's Penn Station and got a cab to the Langham, a five-star hotel on Fifth Avenue not far from Central Park. After showing my FBI and DC Metro credentials to the assistant manager, I was given an electronic key to Bree's room on the sixth floor.

When I knocked, I heard her yell that she did not want turn-down service this evening. I waited and then knocked again, lowered my voice, and said, "Sorry, ma'am, special delivery for Bree Stone?"

I could hear her footsteps coming; the door was wrenched open on the chain and she glared out and said, "What—"

Then her face brightened, and she shut the door to remove the chain, squealing happily, "What are you doing here, Alex?" She pulled open the door and came into my arms.

I squeezed her back. "I'm on my way to Boston to check on a few things. I figured I'd surprise you and catch the first train up in the morning."

"Mmm," she said. "Best idea I've heard all day."

Bree led me into a big room with a large desk that she'd pulled over beside a king-size bed that was covered with piles of manila folders. Her laptop was open and glowing, revealing the picture of a woman I almost recognized.

"Give me a second to get things organized," she said as she closed the laptop.

"I wasn't thinking of looking," I said, taking a seat on the couch.

"I know," she said. "And I want to be sure everything's secure." Bree took the files and her laptop and locked them in the hotel room's safe, then returned and sat on the bed. "How is Jannie doing the day after?"

"Still on a magic-carpet ride," I said. "You should see the picture and headline they had in the *Post*'s sports section."

"I saw it online. What a great action shot of her."

"Isn't it?" I said, unable to control the grin on my face. "And the piece said that more girls will commit to Howard now that Jannie has made her decision."

"Phenomenal. What's in Boston?"

"An outside shot on the family killings. I don't think there's much there, but I feel obligated to try. Also, I need to report a pass a woman made at me."

Bree's right eyebrow rose. "A pass?"

"Hug and attempted smooch on her part. It came out of nowhere with zero provocation from me."

She watched me closely. "Who was this woman?"

"Suzanne Liu," I said. "She used to be Thomas Tull's book editor. She called me this morning to say Tull had been threatening her. She claims there is more to the author than meets the eye."

"Did he threaten her?"

I nodded.

"And what happened then?"

Bree has always been a thorough investigator, so I expected no mercy until she was done with her questions.

"We were supposed to meet for breakfast in a restaurant at the Watergate Hotel," I said. "But when I got there, she said she was terrified of Tull and wanted me to meet her in her suite for breakfast on the balcony. I said okay."

Giving me a look, Bree said, "Well, that was dumb."

I held up my palms. "In the extreme."

"And what preceded the hug and attempted smooch?"

"She was amped up, said she was spending too much time in her head and was afraid no one would believe her about Tull. After hearing a recording of the threats, I said I believed her. The pass ensued, and I shut her down hard, said I was deeply in love with my wife."

"Good response," Bree said, getting up.

"Thank you. She apologized. End of story."

"End of story," she said, smiling as she crossed the room to me. "Do you have plans for dinner?"

"Reservations at Gramercy Tavern at seven thirty," she said, sitting on my lap.

"Nice," I said, kissing her. "And in the meantime?"

"Well, I was wondering about that special delivery you promised at the door."

CHAPTER

36

AS I WALKED THROUGH Boston's South Station around eleven o'clock the next morning, the pleasant aftereffects of an incredible dinner and a special delivery were still lingering in my mind and making me smile.

Outside, a raw, dank, late-April wind cut through my sport coat and open rain jacket. Shivering, I zipped it up and then ordered an Uber to take me to Cambridge and the Harvard Book Store.

"You work there or something? Harvard?" asked Vic Daloia, the driver, a nice guy in his forties with a thick Boston accent. He had an all-news station playing softly on his radio.

"Just visiting the area," I said. "You remember the electrocution killings in Boston years ago?"

Daloia sat up straighter. "Sure, I followed that one. And I

149

read that book about it, *Electric*. Great book. I'm a true-crime buff and he nailed it."

"Thomas Tull."

"That's him. Stickler for details. I like that."

"I do too," I said. "I work with the FBI."

Daloia looked over his shoulder. "I knew you were something like that."

That made me laugh a little. "Nice to know. Say, is there a way to hire you for the day? Have you drive me around a few places?"

In the rearview mirror, I could see Daloia beaming. "You bet. You pay Uber for this leg. Then I'll sign out of Uber and you can pay me in cash for the rest of the day."

"Deal. How much?"

"How far are you going?"

"Around the city. And MCI–Cedar Junction."

"You mean the Walpole prison? That's a cruise. How's two hundred sound?"

"Like a plan," I said.

Daloia dropped me at the Harvard Book Store and went to a nearby Dunkin' to await my call. I entered the store, imagining Tull wandering the aisles, dreaming of being a writer and pulling book after book from the shelves.

Then I thought about Tull becoming aware of Emily Maxwell, one of the store clerks, a recent divorcée and the fourth victim in his first book, *Electric*.

How often had they spoken before she died? Did he know Emily had a broken heart before she was murdered?

These questions and others swirled in my mind as I sought out Martine Harris, the store manager. She remembered Maxwell and was saddened.

"Emily was a special, special person," Harris said. "Customers were constantly asking her what they should read next."

"She had a broken heart."

Harris nodded. "She did, but she was coming out of it. I mean, getting over a divorce takes time, especially when you didn't see it coming. I told her that a lot."

"Was Emily friends with Thomas Tull?"

She hesitated and looked at the ceiling. "I've thought about that. I mean, how well he knew Emily. He says they spoke three or four times, just exchanging pleasantries when he was checking out. But I think he was shaken by her death and that triggered his interest and everything else—the book, the television series, all of it."

"And yet I sense a little conflict in you."

"Well, I've always wondered if there was more to their relationship than Tull let on. Something that would have explained the passion he brought to that case and to his book. What's this all about, anyway?"

"Just wrapping up some loose ends for the Bureau," I said. "Thanks for your time, Martine. I think I'll walk around town and try to orient myself to where it all happened."

"Do you have the map with you?"

"Map?"

"It's in the back of the paperback edition of *Electric*. Shows where everything happened and when. People come here just to walk around and see it all. Like a tour, you know?"

"I have the book with me, and I'll look at that map," I said. "But I can't imagine Herman Foster's old haunt is hard to find."

"No," she said. "It's where most people either start or end their tour."

I thanked her again for her time and left, digging in my roller bag for my copy of *Electric*. Sure enough, there was a map at the back showing Cambridge and the surrounding towns and cities involved in the case.

I was interested to see that, with the exception of Emily Maxwell, all the victims lived outside of but close to Cambridge: in Boston's Back Bay, Watertown, Somerville, Newton. With the electrocution scenes all identified on the map, I could immediately see a rough oval pattern with Cambridge and Harvard University slightly left of center.

Maxwell had lived seven blocks from the university. I decided to see a few places on campus and then walk to her old apartment before getting driven to the prison.

The wind had slowed but it was drizzling when I left the store and I hurried toward Harvard Yard, glad for the umbrella I'd thought to pack. I found a security guard and asked the way to Lyman Laboratory.

He showed me on a map where I'd find the physics research lab. I walked north through Harvard Yard, which was crowded with students hurrying through the light rain to their next classes or chatting about their looming final exams.

I crossed Cambridge Street and passed the university's music hall on my way to the brick-faced laboratory on 17 Oxford Street. Remembering how Tull had described the place, I looked up at the window of the second-floor office on the right, where acclaimed theoretical physicist and Harvard professor Herman Foster had gone mad and plotted the electrocution deaths of seven innocent women.

CHAPTER

37

I GAZED AT THAT window for four or five minutes, wondering what had set Professor Foster off on a homicidal spree and what he'd gotten from electrocuting the women.

Tull claimed in *Electric* that Foster as a young boy had seen his mixed-race mother treated terribly by a white female clerk in a high-end store on Newbury Street. Foster also had a history of train-wreck relationships where he so alienated his girlfriends, they dumped him, often in a humiliating fashion.

Police had discovered damning evidence in the professor's office. They found Foster's diary, which contained glued-in photos of the victims he'd taken without their knowledge, unaware of the camera and the danger of the man behind it.

They also discovered e-mails and writings on Foster's computer that were deeply and violently misogynistic. In one of those writings, the professor fantasized about kidnapping women, bringing them to his lab at night, stripping them, then shooting them with the proton-beam machine that had made his academic reputation.

I tried to go inside the laboratory, but a security guard turned me away due to an experiment going on in the lab. I wanted to ask if it involved kidnapped women and a proton beam, but I held my tongue and left.

It began to rain. I walked to Cambridge Street and called Vic Daloia, who found me and drove me to Perry Street in Ward Two and the triple-decker building where Emily Maxwell had lived in an apartment that took up half the second floor. He pulled over opposite the house.

"How did Tull think Foster got up to her floor?" I asked.

"Picked that door there, the middle one," Daloia said. "All triple-deckers have them, you know, a door to the upstairs?"

"Picking it is a brazen act," I said. "He could have been spotted by all sorts of people, and yet he wasn't."

"The professor was kind of a nondescript dude, remember?" Daloia said. "Not handsome, but not butt-ugly either. Tull described Foster as the kind of guy no one notices unless he's at work in his lab."

"Let's go see if that's true," I said.

"Walpole?"

"Walpole."

Around forty minutes later, Daloia parked near a low white building set near the high wall of the maximum-security facility. On the arch above the blue front doors were the words MASSACHUSETTS STATE PRISON.

FBI special agent in charge Ned Mahoney had called ahead to alert the warden that I was coming to talk to Herman Foster.

After the guard checked my identification and credentials, I surrendered my phone, pistol, waist holster, and belt.

I passed through a metal detector and two hydraulic stainless-steel gates, then crossed an inner yard to the cell blocks. Ten minutes later, I was sitting before a pane of bulletproof glass in a small room set aside for police and legal visitors.

The door in the identical room on the other side of the glass opened and Herman Foster shuffled in. Even in his orange jumpsuit, the medium-height, medium-weight former physics professor was indeed rather nondescript.

With his dull brown eyes, thinning gray hair, and prison-issue glasses, Foster was the kind of man who could easily be overlooked outside of a laboratory setting. The physicist's face displayed neither interest nor fear as he picked up the phone.

"Who are you? And what does the FBI want from me?"

"Hello, Dr. Foster. My name is Dr. Alex Cross. I'm a psychological and investigative consultant to the Bureau. And I'm just interested in talking to you."

"About what? My inner noggin? Theoretical physics? This hellhole?"

"Thomas Tull," I said.

The prisoner's face softened. "Ahh, Thomas. Where is he these days?"

"Right now he's in Washington, DC, researching a series of murders down there."

"It's what he does so well," Foster said. He looked at his lap and then stared at me, hard. "Wait, why are you here? What's Thomas done?"

"As far as I know, he's done nothing," I said. "But there have been allegations made against him by his former editor."

His expression soured. "Suzanne Liu. I've talked to her.

Well, over the phone, anyway, when she was fact-checking. She struck me as vindictive and opportunistic. What does she claim Thomas did to her?"

"Not to her, and I can't get into details. What's your take on Tull?"

"Thomas is a friend, a dear one," Foster said. "One of the few I have left. He has treated me decently from the start and never wavered in his support. He just wanted to know me and my side of things."

"You think the way he portrayed you in the book was fair?"

"Fair? Yes, I suppose so. I mean, Thomas doesn't really tell you what he thinks. He lets other people take all the shots at you. But he did quote me accurately more than ninety percent of the time. And if he comes across evidence that exonerates me, I know he will do the right thing and fight to free me."

I cocked my head, studying the scientific genius. "You still maintain someone else electrocuted those women?"

"I do, Dr. Cross," Foster said, gazing at me again with no hint of his emotional landscape. "I'm innocent. I may have fantasized about doing harm to women, but I never had the guts to follow through."

CHAPTER

38

Manhattan

MONDAY AFTERNOON, BREE WAS in a coffee shop having an espresso before returning to the courthouse in Lower Manhattan to look through more legal filings involving Frances Duchaine and her business empire.

Bree had found records of a few recent lawsuits by former employees seeking back wages and bonuses and several liens on her company for failure to pay rent on various stores, but other than that, not much that could be described as damaging. Then again, the index of the various filings against or by the fashion designer was nine pages long. *I probably still have one or two more days of looking at records before—*

Her phone rang. A number she did not recognize. Bree almost declined the call, but something told her to answer.

"Bree Stone," she said.

"This is Nora Jessup," a woman with a soft Southern accent said. "You called me about the lawsuit I filed against Frances Duchaine in Raleigh a few years back?"

"Yes!" Bree said, fumbling for a notebook. "I'm so glad you returned my call!"

"I would have called you Friday, but my mother's in an Alzheimer's facility and she fell down and broke her hip."

"Oh God, I'm sorry to hear that," Bree said.

"Me too," Jessup said. "How can I help? You know that case is sealed, right?"

"I don't know where it came from, but I was given a copy. I know the facts you alleged, and they jibe with research I have been doing in Manhattan."

After a few moments, Jessup said, "Research for whom?"

"I honestly don't know the client," Bree said. "They've requested anonymity and told me to dig as deeply as I can into Frances Duchaine. That's what I'm doing. What can you tell me that I don't already know about her?"

"Tell me what you've found so far."

Bree gave the attorney a rundown of the information she'd been able to gather.

"Well," Jessup said, "some of that I did not know. But I've always wondered if there were limits to what they'd do. And here you say Frances may have had this other girl, Molly, killed?"

"I'm saying that's a possibility," Bree said.

"I'm betting Frances didn't do it. I'm betting Paula Watkins was the one who did it or at least arranged it. Frances doesn't like to get her hands dirty."

For the next hour, Bree listened as Jessup described the tentacles and intricacies of an operation that lured young women and men entranced by the dream of being supermodels and working for the great Frances Duchaine to New York.

Raleigh. Miami. Dallas. Houston. Phoenix. Los Angeles. San Francisco. Portland. Seattle. Salt Lake City. Denver. Minneapolis. Chicago. According to the attorney, Duchaine had stores in all those cities, and in all those stores, Watkins had scouts who were paid well to recruit new victims. Jessup believed almost five hundred young women and men might have been caught up in a scheme to saddle them with debt and ensnare them in sexual slavery so Duchaine could profit from their new and miserable existence.

Five hundred! Bree thought. If what Salazar believed was true—that each victim could generate as much as a million dollars a year—then the fashion designer could have pulled in several hundred million dollars in the past five years.

"How did they get your lawsuit squelched and sealed?" Bree asked.

Jessup said, "Bought off the judge, who, sickeningly enough, was a woman."

"I saw that."

"I can overnight you some of the other material we were able to dig up," the attorney said. "But I want no part of this. As far as I'm concerned, the seal stands. I will, however, give you some advice. Once you go down the rabbit hole into Frances's world, it's complicated, almost overwhelming. I suggest you find someone to guide you."

"Smart. But a whistleblower on the inside might be hard to come by."

Jessup said, "Then find one on the outside. Someone who knows how Frances and Watkins work. Even better, someone who holds a grudge. Or two. Or three."

Bree thought about that and smiled. "That's a really good idea."

"I have them now and then," Jessup said. "And you should know one more thing about this entire affair. Perhaps the most troubling aspect of all."

39

Walpole, Massachusetts

IT WAS ALMOST THREE P.M. when I left the prison, feeling more confused than I had when I'd entered it. After Herman Foster asserted his innocence, he grew irritable and increasingly unresponsive to my questions about the case.

About the only thing I could pin him down on was his beliefs about Thomas Tull.

"Thomas is a tough, fair guy with a cop's mind and a penchant for self-promotion," Foster said. "But he's no killer. I'd trust that man with my life."

"Looks like you already have," I said, which pretty much ended the conversation.

Vic Daloia was waiting by his car in the prison parking lot, drinking his fourth or fifth cup of Dunkin' coffee. "That was fast. You talk to him?"

"For a bit, then he went quiet on me," I said, climbing into the back seat.

Daloia got behind the wheel, started the car, and pulled out. "He give you anything good, Doc? Anything new?"

"I'm still trying to figure that out."

"Tull would have known if he said anything new."

Even though that annoyed me, I knew the Uber driver was right. "I should have brought Tull with me, I guess."

Daloia laughed. "Maybe next time, huh? Meantime, where to?"

"Head toward Boston," I said, picking up my phone and looking in my notes for a 617 area code number. I found it and called.

"Boston Homicide," a man growled.

"I'm looking for Detective Jane Hale."

"Good luck—she's on her honeymoon in Australia. Be back in three weeks."

Before I could say anything, the line went dead.

In the front seat, Daloia said, "No go on Hale? She would have been good. But you would probably have needed Tull there too."

"Right again," I said. "So I think I'm done here. Take me to Logan, please."

"Really?" the driver said, sounding disappointed. "Nowhere else?"

"Just the airport," I said. "I'm going to catch a late flight to Charleston."

Daloia waved one finger in the air as we pulled onto Route 128 heading north. "*Doctor's Orders,* am I right?"

"Can't get a thing past you, Vic," I said.

He shrugged and smiled. "Another crazy case courtesy of Thomas T., but you know I Googled you while you were in with Foster. You're no slouch yourself, Doc. Very impressive. And you're on those Family Man murders, so I figure that's why Tull's down in DC and why you're up here checking on him. Right?"

I had to admit that he was making substantive leaps with relative ease. "You missed your calling in life," I said.

That seemed to upset him. "I tell my girlfriend, Leigh, that all the—"

His phone rang. He glanced at it. "There she is, like she's clairvoyant." Daloia answered. He had a Bluetooth in his ear. "Leigh, what do you know?"

His girlfriend evidently knew a lot because he listened for quite a while as we drove toward the Massachusetts Turnpike. When we were within a half a mile, he said, "Hold on, pumpkin." He glanced over his shoulder at me. "You sure you got nothing else to do here?"

Before I could answer, my phone rang. Paladin.

"Dr. Cross, how are you?" Ryan Malcomb said.

"Excellent, and you?"

"Excellent as always," he said. "I wanted to tell you that the search is going on as we speak."

"Even better. Any commonalities come up?"

"Several."

I glanced at my watch, saw I had nearly five hours before my flight.

"I'm not thirty miles from you," I said. "Can I come see for myself?"

After a pause, Malcomb said, "It would be wonderful to meet you, and what we do is better explained in person anyway."

CHAPTER

40

Manhattan

WHEN BREE WALKED THROUGH the front door of Tess Jackson's store on Lexington Avenue, she was startled.

Just two days before and three blocks away in Frances Duchaine's flagship store, she'd seen few shoppers and fewer customers waiting to pay for purchases. But here there were scores of eager shoppers jamming the aisles and the checkout queues of Tess Jackson's new flagship store, which was remarkably designed.

The interior lines of the store were simple, almost industrial, but overhead hung a colorful and whimsical depiction of hundreds of small fairies with gossamer wings flying among treetops laced in fog. Bree could not help grinning as she looked up, seeing how each of the fairies was unique, almost magical.

Remembering something she'd heard two evenings before, Bree climbed the stairs to a mezzanine, where shoes and accessories were on display, and then continued up a third flight.

At the top, behind a desk, Ella Martin, a female security guard with linebacker shoulders, said, "The store stops down on the second floor, ma'am. These are corporate and design offices."

"I know," Bree replied. "I'm looking for a friend who works behind those double doors. I wanted to surprise him."

"Who's your friend?"

"Phillip Henry Luster," Bree said.

That changed the guard's attitude. "And how do you know Mr. Luster?"

"We had dinner together the other night at a fundraiser at Frances Duchaine's home in Greenwich."

"Okay," Martin said, picking up her phone. "Who should I say is here?"

"Evelyn Carlisle," Bree said. "From Newport Beach."

The security guard made a call. A few minutes later, the doors opened and Luster emerged, giving her a look that mixed amusement with disappointment.

"My dear Evelyn," Luster said, taking her hands. "Wherever did you get to the other night? Paula said you had terrible news and had to leave but she wouldn't be specific."

"I'm sure she wouldn't," Bree said. "Is there somewhere we can talk in private? Where I can explain what really happened?"

"What really happened? Oh God, you had me at hello. As I told you, I love mysteries and secrets."

"I remember," Bree said. "And I'm full of both."

The fashion designer seemed to take great pleasure in that and asked the security guard to open the doors. Martin winked at her as she followed Luster through the doors into a short hallway that ended in a large open room surrounded by smaller rooms with glass walls.

The center room housed the design team of one of the top fashion brands in the world. Artists, designers, cutters, and seamstresses all created a happy buzz of creativity; Bree and Luster walked through to a small office in the corner with a workbench, a drafting table, and a mannequin wearing a flowing lavender dress.

"It's gorgeous," Bree said as he closed the door.

"Do you think so?" Luster said, pleased, and gestured her to a couch.

"I love it," Bree said, sitting. "Whose idea was it to have the fairies downstairs?"

"That was Tess's four-year-old granddaughter, Eliza."

"I think it's enchanting. I've never seen anything like it."

"I'll tell Eliza that the next time she's in," Luster said, taking a seat at the other end of the couch and shifting to face her. "So? What's the dish?"

Bree said, "The main dish is that I am not Evelyn Carlisle, newly widowed gazillionaire from Newport Beach. My name is Bree Stone. Until quite recently, I was chief of detectives for the DC Metro Police."

41

LUSTER ACTED TAKEN ABACK and then fascinated. "My, my, you are like an onion, aren't you? What's the next layer you'll peel back?"

"I currently work for an international security and investigations firm in Virginia called the Bluestone Group."

"You're some high-dollar private investigator?"

"I am," Bree said.

The fashion designer's eyes shifted left and down slightly before returning to Bree. "You're investigating Frances Duchaine."

"And Paula Watkins."

"For whom? I hope you're not going to say Tess."

"No. I mean, I have no reason to believe so. It's complicated."

"Entertain me."

Bree explained about the deep-pockets anonymous client who'd provided her with public, private, and sealed documents that hinted at Duchaine's involvement in criminal activity.

Luster studied her intently, his fist at his lips, his eyes revealing little.

"What kind of criminal activity?" he asked.

"Human trafficking."

The fashion designer's shock was complete. "What? No. That can't be true. I know her and—"

"You mentioned she might have cash-flow issues."

"I did, but—"

"When was the last time you worked for Frances?"

"Seven years ago?"

"You should know that there is a detective here with NYPD who believes Frances might have generated several hundred million dollars through the trafficking, cash that has allowed her to stay afloat despite the debts."

"Several hundred million?" Luster said. "How can that be?"

Bree laid it out for him in detail, describing the lawsuits and the allegations made by multiple young men and women who'd managed to escape the clutches of the prostitution ring but were bought off before cases could go to trial.

"This is terrible," the fashion designer said, shaking his head.

"It gets worse," she said. "An attorney in North Carolina told me she believes that some of the victims were never exploited as high-dollar escorts. They were sold off to buyers in the Middle East and taken out of this country."

Luster's lips curled in disgust. "You're saying sexual slavery?"

"That's exactly what I'm saying, Phillip, and I need your help to end it and free those young men and women who might have been sold."

Luster looked down at the couch for several long moments before shaking his head. When he raised his chin, his eyes were wet.

"I have always prided myself on my instincts and my understanding of human nature," he said. "But I never thought Frances could ever be so ruthless and callous. If it's true, Paula Watkins had a big hand in it."

"I agree. And maybe someone with that hedge fund she's involved in."

The fashion designer's features shifted, as if he'd whiffed something foul.

"Ari Bernstein runs it. I can't stand that sanctimonious ass."

"Then help me shine a light on Mr. Bernstein and Frances and Watkins and what they may have done in the name of business."

Luster paused and then squeezed his hand into a fist again. "What do you need, Bree? I'll help in any way I can."

CHAPTER

42

Haverhill, Massachusetts

PALADIN'S FACILITIES WERE AS I remembered them—spread out through a quiet, wooded campus with plain concrete-and-glass buildings a few miles off I-495.

Vic Daloia parked in the visitor lot and I went to the largest of the buildings, which sat at the center of the campus by a small pond where ducks swam.

I entered a tight lobby with concrete walls. Behind a desk surrounded by bulletproof glass sat a woman in her forties with impressive biceps. A name tag on her blue polo shirt read RIGGS.

"Welcome back, Dr. Cross," Riggs said, smiling.

"Thank you for remembering," I said, passing her my credentials through a drawer.

"You and your colleagues were memorable," Riggs said. "My day-to-day job is actually quite boring, so I notice people like you."

"Good to know," I said. "I believe Mr. Malcomb is going to see me today."

She nodded and began copying my credentials. "Ryan's office just called down."

"Can I ask you something?"

"You can. Don't know if I'll answer," she said, waiting for the copying to finish.

I pointed at the bulletproof glass. "Why the security box?"

"I'll answer that one," Riggs said, putting my credentials back in the drawer. "Mr. Vance says it's probably overkill, but we handle sensitive information here and the company is getting known for its role helping law enforcement and Homeland Security. From a terrorist perspective, I guess we would be what you'd call a soft target."

"Makes sense," I said, taking my credentials from the drawer.

Riggs buzzed me into a larger, more welcoming reception area with a stacked-granite weeping wall. Beside the seeping fountain hung an understated logo, the word PALADIN superimposed over a faint number 12.

From my prior visit, I knew the company's name and logo were references to French literature, where the twelve paladins, or "twelve peers," were said to be the elite protectors and agents of King Charlemagne, comparable to the Knights of the Round Table in the Arthurian legends.

Paladin had been launched five years before by Steven Vance, a Silicon Valley CEO, and Ryan Malcomb, a brilliant tech guy who'd started and sold four companies before he turned forty. Vance and Malcomb's most recent venture involved deep data mining using artificial intelligence.

Paladin's ingenious algorithms, written by Malcomb, allowed the company to scour and sift through monstrous amounts of information with astonishing speed. The system had yielded investigative targets of interest to various U.S. law enforcement agencies that increasingly looked to Paladin's unique and accurate product.

A door opened on the other side of the weeping wall.

Sheila Farr, a short redheaded woman with a bowl haircut, exited wearing a blue puffy coat, jeans, and low hiking shoes. I'd met her on my last visit. She was the company's chief legal counsel.

She smiled perfunctorily. "Dr. Cross, how good to see you again."

"You as well, Ms. Farr," I said.

The attorney led me back through the door into a series of familiar hallways kept cold enough to see your breath because of the huge banks of supercomputers that Paladin had churning day and night. We climbed three flights of an unfamiliar steel staircase to a nondescript door; Farr knocked and opened it.

The office we entered was almost identical to the one Steven Vance had received us in the year before, with glass walls, floors, and ceilings—a block of glass, really, suspended above a much larger workspace that teemed with activity. The bigger space was set up with clusters of desks and computers interspersed with screens hanging from steel cables.

The people down there ranged from the seriously buff to the somewhat nerdy, like Ryan Malcomb, who sat behind a glass desk in the sleekest, coolest wheelchair I'd ever seen. A lanky man with longish graying hair and a salt-and-pepper goatee, Malcomb wore a look of genuine interest as he used a joystick to bring the silver wheelchair around the desk to me.

"So interesting to meet you at last, Dr. Cross," Malcomb said, brushing his hair back and giving me an elbow bump. "Steven was so impressed when he worked with you last year. He will be disappointed to learn he missed you."

"Vacations are important."

"So they are," Malcomb said, gesturing me toward a couch and two chairs arranged around a glass coffee table with cups and a pot of steaming coffee waiting.

CHAPTER

43

THE COFOUNDER OF PALADIN brought his chair forward while his corporate counsel and I sat on the couch.

"I've never seen a wheelchair like that," I said.

"Because it's a prototype built for me by an old friend. Six independent wheels, remarkable suspension—it can do three-sixties in the parking lot." Malcomb laughed and then leaned forward to pour our coffee with a slight awkwardness to his shoulder and arm movements and a tremor to his hands. But he performed the feat without spilling a drop.

"I still got the knack," he said and laughed again. "You're thinking, *What exactly is wrong with him?* Aren't you, Dr. Cross?"

"Yes," I said.

Malcomb smiled. "Muscular dystrophy. I was lucky and did not begin to develop symptoms until I was in my teens, because it is degenerative. I get very, very slowly worse."

"I'm sorry to hear that," I said.

He shrugged. "Everyone has challenges. I fight mine every bit of the way and remain happy because my mind is completely unaffected."

"You wrote the algorithms that the supercomputers run?"

"I had a lot of help to get them where I wanted them," he said with a slight wave at the bustling floors below and behind him. "Most of my engineers are far more sophisticated at the intricacies of looking for a needle in a haystack than I am. Steven and I had the vision, but they really wrote most of the code to achieve that vision."

"The vision of finding commonalities and anomalies?"

"Among other purposes, that is correct," he said, leaning forward again and tapping on the glass tabletop, which lit up like a large computer screen.

A bewildering stream of numbers, text, and images flooded the screen until Malcomb stopped it. "That's what a huge data dump looks like when we get it," he explained. "But then we pour it through our filters—our algorithms. Our digital sieves, if you will. We're looking for crossovers and singularities, commonalities and anomalies, as you said, in the data we're searching. In this case, the data is everything we could get on the six-block area surrounding each of the Family Man crime scenes."

Malcomb tapped the tabletop once more and the data stream began again. A holographic keyboard appeared; he gave a command, and the avalanche of information spewing across the rest of the table became a series of thin trickles that entwined in several places.

Gesturing to those knots, Malcomb said, "There is your first commonality. In the hour surrounding each attack, cell phone and mobile data service was spotty or interrupted in the six-block area."

"How's that possible?"

"A jammer of some kind, we believe," he said.

"Could the jamming have come from the cell service itself?"

"We don't think so. This appears to be aggressive outside interference directed at the cell towers most likely to carry calls and data into and out of those six-block areas."

He typed on the keyboard again. The waterfall of data again covered the tabletop for a moment before it filtered down to thin entwined streams.

"Here's the second commonality," Malcomb said. "Once the jamming begins, satellite phones are used."

I sat forward. "Really? How many?"

"At least two, maybe three."

I felt a ripple of excitement. "You have the phone numbers?"

"We do, but they're worthless," he said. "They belong to SIM cards that anyone can buy loaded with minutes on the satellite. The sat phones themselves are neutral nodes. It's the disposable cards that talk to the satellites, and that's what keeps the users anonymous for the time being."

"Time being?"

Malcomb held up one slightly tremoring hand. "I'm not promising anything, but I asked several of my smartest people to design a new kind of search, one that might at least give you a direction to move in."

"How would that work?"

"We'll look for electronic signatures that we did not pick up the first time through, something that might indicate the manufacturer of the satellite phone chips being used and perhaps their points of purchase. And the signature of the jammer."

I thought both angles were something of a long shot but nodded. My focus turned elsewhere.

Satellite phones and jammed cell towers. So this is a conspiracy of some kind. We are facing more than a lone wolf.

"What time is your flight?" Farr, the company's counsel, asked.

"Eight?" I said, looking at my watch. It was a quarter to five.

Malcomb said, "There's been endless construction slowing traffic going out to Logan, but you should make it in time. Where are you off to now?"

"Charleston, South Carolina," I said. "Can I get your bright minds to sift for anything tied to Thomas Tull in those areas?"

Malcomb frowned. "The writer?"

I nodded. "The crime writer."

CHAPTER

44

BREE LEFT PHILLIP HENRY LUSTER'S office feeling as if she'd taken a crash course in the business of fashion and the hidden life of Frances Duchaine, the stuff that never made the news stories or official biographies of the icon.

Perhaps more important, Luster had called two friends in investment banking to suss out Duchaine's current balance sheet. Barry, the first of them, had no clue, but he asked the designer to dinner, which Luster accepted for later in the month.

"For a moneyman, he's a hunk," Luster had told Bree.

The second investment banker, Sammy, was a different tale altogether. When asked about Duchaine, he had gone conspiratorial. He whispered that he had to close his door, then returned and asked, "What are you hearing? Is she going down? Chapter Eleven? We have a big position in Crescent Partners, Ari Bernstein's hedge fund, and he's got her leveraged out the wazoo. If Duchaine's going under, I could really use a heads-up here, Phillip."

"And here I came to you for the same reason, Sammy," Luster replied. "And you're doing business with a snake like Ari Bernstein? Since when?"

"Since he started crowing about his ten percent annual return."

"Tell me, what would Frances crashing and burning do to Bernstein's fund and his vaunted annual return?"

"We'd be hurt, but Bernstein would take a biblical hit. Maybe enough to take him out. So is Duchaine going down?"

"How much debt do you think she's carrying?"

Sammy hesitated. "That's private."

"Until she's in court."

After another pause, the investment banker said, "You don't know where you got this, Phillip, but her company's awash in debt and she's personally on the hook for four hundred and twenty-five million with balloon payments coming due in three months."

Luster whistled. "Four hundred and twenty-five million!"

Bree's heart had pounded. There it was. Frances Duchaine was under big-time financial pressure. It could explain the human-trafficking allegations. It could explain why she'd take the risk.

By the time she reached her hotel, Bree believed in her gut that it was all real, that the instincts of whoever was paying her were dead on, that Duchaine was the worst kind of criminal, a creature who ruthlessly preyed on human foibles, desires, and weaknesses.

But who is paying me? And why?

She put those questions aside as she changed her clothes,

ordered room service, and settled down at her laptop to write her report for Elena Martin's eyes only. Bree forced herself to be cold while she wrote; she noted which statements were facts supported by documents and which were conjecture, and she was succinct in her conclusions.

"While I have no concrete proof yet of Duchaine's ties to sex and human trafficking," she wrote, "it is clear now that her personal and business lives are indeed threatened by crushing debt and looming payments due, which could easily have created the need for her secret life of crime."

Bree marked the report *Urgent* and e-mailed it to her boss just as her dinner arrived: a medium rare New York strip steak, steamed broccoli and mushrooms, sweet potato fries, and a glass of red wine. She finished her meal and was carrying the rest of her wine back to the desk when her phone rang.

Phillip Henry Luster.

"Hello, Phillip," she said.

"I hope you believe in the law of attraction because it has just been proven once again," he said, the din of a bar in the background.

"Okay?"

"I just met one of Frances's victims, though he doesn't know he's her victim, of course. His name is Brad Jenkins and he's from Louisville, Tennessee. He's twenty-three and very sweet and handsome but not handsome enough, you know?"

"You're saying he fits the pattern."

"Plus or minus," Luster said. Jenkins had been spotted by a Duchaine representative in Nashville three years ago. Like the others, he had been lured to New York with vague promises of a modeling career with the fashion designer, only to be told that his looks weren't quite up to snuff. They recommended a lower-jaw advancement, a nose job, and veneers, for which he now owed close to one hundred thousand dollars.

"Let me guess," Bree said. "He was approached by someone named Victor after Frances left him hanging."

"You're clairvoyant," Luster said. "Brad now works for Victor as a gigolo."

"Can he give me Victor?"

"Better than that. Brad said Victor has been working on Brad's behalf with none other than Paula Watkins, who has agreed to reconsider his portfolio at a special gathering Wednesday evening at Paula's place on the Upper East Side."

"Define *special gathering*."

"Victor, who will be there, told Brad that the gathering will include other aspiring models whom Paula and Frances are considering for international work. And there will be talent agents from overseas."

"International work. Talent agents from overseas."

"Exactly my thinking," Luster said. "This could be it, Bree. The sex-slave auction."

CHAPTER

45

BREE FELT AS JITTERY and excited as she used to when a big case came together and the possibility of arrests was visible on the horizon.

Would Watkins be this bold? Have a sex-slave auction right in her own home? "How big is this place?" she asked Luster.

"Two adjoining brownstones Paula opened up and renovated—quite a space," he said. The noise of the bar in the background diminished.

"How many people can it hold?"

"I was there once for a party of fifty and it felt roomy."

"So the place could accommodate more," Bree said.

"You can't get in there," Luster said. "They'd turn you away at the door."

"But not you," Bree said. "You could get in. Be my fly on the wall."

"Not without an invitation, I couldn't."

"You'll be Brad's date. Someone in the biz looking out for his well-being, eager to meet Victor, perhaps as a customer."

"I don't—"

"You got Brad's phone number, I assume?"

"Well, yes."

"You'll ask him, then?"

The fashion designer hesitated, then said, "Oh, why not?"

"Last question: Would you wear a wire?"

"A wire?" Luster said and chuckled. "Bree, you just gave me goose bumps."

Luster said he'd text Bree if his young friend agreed to bring him along to Paula Watkins's special gathering. Bree figured the odds were against Luster getting inside. But you never knew unless you tried.

After they hung up, Bree stood and paced the hotel room. She glanced at her watch. Eight thirty. Alex's flight had left Boston at eight, which meant they couldn't talk until at least eleven.

She was thumbing through her contacts, looking for Detective Salazar's number, when the phone rang. Bluestone Group. A number she recognized. "Elena," Bree said.

"That was quite the impressive report. Do you believe it?"

"Wasn't I convincing?"

"Well, to be honest, from the thirty-thousand-foot perspective, I'm still skeptical because you don't have witnesses willing to go on the record. And this banker, Sammy, he knows for certain Duchaine is carrying that kind of personal debt?"

"He has a financial position that will be negatively affected by that debt if she goes bankrupt," Bree said. "So, yes, he sounded upset enough to know. And don't forget Detective Salazar has heard the same kinds of stories about money pressures."

"And she has been unable to get a search warrant because none of the stories came with hard evidence or a group willing to step forward and speak against Duchaine."

Bree took a deep breath, actually glad for the challenge. "Elena, I agree there's a long way to go to get it nailed down, but just in the half an hour since I submitted my report, I got the kind of break that could flip things. Paula Watkins is having a party the day after tomorrow, in the evening."

"Okay…"

Bree explained and Martin was quiet for a long time. Finally, she said, "I wore Frances Duchaine clothes for more than a decade. They make my skin crawl now. Be careful, and I'll send your report to our client to get approval for you staying on up there. Have you told the NYPD detective?"

"She's my next call," Bree said.

"Really impressive work, Bree," Elena said.

"Thank you, and you still have no idea who we're working for?"

"An attorney in Cleveland who represents other parties. That's as far as I've gotten. But Tess Jackson is originally from Cleveland. Maybe she knows more than she's letting on. Maybe that's why Luster's been helping you."

"To end competition from Frances once and for all?"

"I've heard worse motives in my time."

46

Charleston, South Carolina

DUE TO A FLIGHT delay, I didn't get into Charleston until one a.m. on Tuesday. The desk clerk at my hotel in the French Quarter could not find my reservation until nearly two. My luck finally changed around ten that morning.

After six hours of sleep and a breakfast heavy on the creole coffee, I'd gone to the Charleston police headquarters on Lockwood Drive, presented my credentials to the desk sergeant, and asked to speak with Detective Heidi Parks of the violent crimes unit.

Before he could answer, a woman behind me said, "I'm Detective Parks."

I turned to find a tall, attractive brunette dressed in a black polo shirt, jeans, and running shoes and wearing a gold badge on a chain around her neck.

"Alex Cross," I said. "I work as an investigative consultant for the FBI and the DC Metro Police."

Detective Parks cocked her head, smiled, and shook my hand, oozing Southern warmth. "I know you, Dr. Cross. Back in the day, I attended several lectures you gave on criminal psychology during a six-week investigative course I took at Quantico."

"I hope my talks were helpful?"

"Very much so," she said. "To what do I owe this honor?"

"I wanted to talk to you about the *Doctor's Orders* murders."

Parks frowned. "I closed the file on them a long time ago. The right man is sitting on death row in Kirkland."

I held up my hands. "I'm not here to reopen your case, Detective Parks. I just want to talk."

"About what, exactly?"

"Well, among other things, Thomas Tull."

The detective stiffened, looked past me at the desk sergeant, who was filling out paperwork, and blew out her breath in resignation. "I figured someone official would come sniffing around about Thomas eventually. I'm actually glad it's someone of your caliber, Dr. Cross."

"Okay," I said, a bit surprised by her answer. "Is there somewhere we can talk?"

Parks hesitated. "This is supposed to be my day off. But sure, just not here."

She gestured toward the doors. We walked outside. It was gorgeous weather, low eighties with a light breeze that caused the palm trees to sway.

"How much do you know about the case?" Parks asked.

"I read the first hundred and fifty pages of *Doctor's Orders* last night on the flight down from Boston."

She gave me a sidelong glance. "You were up there looking into the *Electric* murders?"

I nodded.

"Well," Parks said and cleared her throat. "That is interesting."

"Can you bring me up to speed on this case? From your perspective?"

Parks thought about that and then shrugged. "Why not? Let's take my car."

For the next few hours, the detective drove me around old and new Charleston, showing me the locations of the pivotal scenes in the murders of five prominent physicians. All of the victims had lived in gated communities.

"The first two were out on Johns Island," Parks said. "The last three were up on Daniel Island, facing the Wando River."

Dr. Carl Jameson was the first to die. A divorced surgeon with a thriving practice who was part owner of a private surgical center, Jameson had lived in a big home on the eighteenth fairway of a golf course in Kiawah River Estates.

The detective stopped her car across the street from the house and said the killer had been meticulous in the Jameson case. Parks had been the first detective on the scene after a housekeeper discovered the surgeon dead on his kitchen table, his throat cut with a razor.

"Blood all over," she said. "Which was amazing because there was no sign of the killer walking away through it and very little forensic evidence other than the body and the box cutter."

The early investigation had focused on Jameson's ex-wife, Claudia, and their tempestuous marriage and acrimonious divorce. Claudia had recently petitioned the court to increase her alimony payments, which the surgeon had opposed.

"She seemed like the obvious choice," Parks said. "Or her

live-in boyfriend, the top tennis pro on Kiawah. But both Claudia and the pro had ironclad alibis for the evening of Jameson's murder."

Parks started driving again. The second killing, she told me, came five weeks later, when Dr. Sandra Handle, an ob-gyn, was strangled in her home across the street from the seventh tee in another golf-course community on Johns Island. Her husband found her corpse upon his return from a fishing trip.

We pulled up in front of the Handles' former home.

"Different method but the same attention to detail," the detective said. "Even though it was a violent death, we found no DNA under Dr. Handle's fingernails or on her body or anywhere, for that matter."

"Enter Thomas Tull," I said.

Parks's jaw shifted a little. She put the car in drive and headed for Daniel Island. "That's right. Within a week of Handle's murder, he showed up, said he felt in his bones that this was going to be his next book."

"You just let him into the investigation?"

She did that thing with her jaw again. "Thomas sort of slid in after sweet-talking the police chief and the mayor. I mean, he was kind of a celebrity. Everybody I knew read his books, including me."

I waited until we were on Daniel Island and approaching the third murder scene before I said, "When did you start sleeping with the writer?"

CHAPTER

47

DETECTIVE PARKS'S JAW STAYED set as she pulled over onto the shoulder of a road.

"Suzanne Liu tell you that?" she demanded.

"She told me she called you the other day and you hung up on her," I said.

"Damn straight I hung up on her. She all but called me a whore. I mean, talk about the pot calling the kettle black. She slept with the guy all the time!"

I held up both hands. "I didn't know that and I'm not making any judgments here."

"Well, I hope the hell you do, Dr. Cross! My reputation is at stake!"

"I'm just running down leads, same as you would do in this situation. Did you sleep with him?"

Parks took a deep breath. "For almost two years. Thomas

has…he has a way of making you fall in love with him and not think too badly of him when he dumps you."

"You called Tull after Liu called you."

"First time in two years. But I thought he should know what his former editor was saying about him."

"He threatened her," I said. "I heard the recording."

"I certainly had nothing to do with it if he did."

"Tull never mentioned the affair in the book."

"Thank God. My mother would have been mortified."

"I'm sorry, but did you know Tull also had affairs with the female detectives in *Electric* and *Noon in Berlin*?"

Parks swallowed hard. "No, but it doesn't surprise me. Like I said, he has a way of making women fall in love with him."

After that, she took me to the site where the third Charleston doctor had been murdered, an area of big homes, all with docks that reached far out across the tidal flats to the Wando River.

"Peter Mason—an ear, nose, and throat specialist—died out there," Parks said, pointing to the T at the end of the nearest dock. "Beaten to death with an oar. The last two murder scenes are a few miles north. We believe the killer came in off the river via the docks."

"And Tull was here for all three of those investigations?"

"He was."

"In the book, Tull says it was your idea to change the course of the investigation and start looking into the doctors' medical-malpractice suits. Is that right? Or did *he* suggest it?"

Detective Parks stared into the middle distance for a long time before replying. "He did. It was his idea." Tull, she said, reasoned that the killings could all be revenge for shoddy medical work. Sure enough, they found that all five victims had been accused of medical malpractice on multiple occasions.

"How did you get from there to Walter Stevenson? Was that also Tull?"

Parks's face looked pained as she struggled internally. "I guess you could say it was Thomas who first brought Dr. Stevenson to our attention. But we were all instantly suspicious once we saw his depositions."

Dr. Walter Stevenson, also of Charleston, was in his late sixties, a retired physician who made extra money as an expert witness in medical-malpractice suits. In fact, Dr. Stevenson had testified against each of the five doctors, all of whom had been deemed justified in their actions at the end of court proceedings and suffered little or no penalties.

It turned out that Dr. Stevenson's beloved wife, Mirabelle, had died from a botched medical procedure, and he had not received a dime after he sued.

"There's a motive," I said.

"It was there all along, but only Thomas sensed it," Parks said. "You know, despite what happened between us, you have to give him credit. He saw it all."

"Which is why I'm here," I said. "What's the chance Tull was involved somehow?"

The detective frowned. "You mean, like aiding and abetting?"

"Or framing."

She snorted. "Well, Stevenson's still claiming he was framed. But he's also quick to condemn 'doctors who are all about business before patients and get away with it.' Look, the evidence was there. And I certainly saw no link between Thomas and the evidence we found in Stevenson's house."

I was quiet a moment. "Did you see any differences between what you know happened during the investigation and Tull's version? As you saw it, I mean?"

Parks thought about that. "Well, he did twist a few things and omit some others, I guess. And Thomas was always pushing the spotlight toward me."

"Did you ever call him on that? On not taking credit?"

"Once," she replied, looking into the distance again. "After the book was published and shortly before we broke up."

"And what did he say?"

"That it wasn't his job to shine, that he was supposed to let the characters shine. He said the writer's job was to disappear, to be an invisible hand at work."

Manhattan

IN THE REAR OF a black utility van parked down the street from Paula Watkins's fabulous double brownstone on the Upper East Side, NYPD Detective Rosella Salazar groaned and shifted uncomfortably on one of the metal folding chairs.

"I never should have let you talk me into this," Detective Salazar said, rubbing her stomach. "And I'm getting kicked in the ribs."

Bree felt bad. "What else can I do? The DA wouldn't give you the wiretap."

"Because there was not enough evidence."

"Well, in the end it doesn't matter. Luster gave his consent to the recording, volunteered to wear a wire for his own purposes. We're just listening in."

Salazar shrugged. "I don't know what you're hoping to hear."

"Something that proves there is sexual trafficking and maybe slavery going on in there tonight," Bree said.

"And then?"

"I haven't thought that far ahead."

Looking annoyed, the detective said, "I'm giving you an hour once your friend is inside. If he can *get* inside."

"My money's on Luster," Bree said, getting up and going to the tinted glass window at the back of the van.

She trained binoculars down the street toward the home of Frances Duchaine's second in command, saw town cars and limousines disgorging guests. There seemed to be several types in this crowd—men in their twenties, men in their fifties, and women in their twenties.

Soon enough, Phillip Henry Luster in a chic black suit climbed from a town car; he was followed by a tall, lanky, tawny-haired man in his twenties. Blessed with *GQ* looks, he was dressed in gray high-water slacks, no socks, black shoes, and a blue blazer with a starched white shirt, collar open.

"Luster's here with Brad Jenkins," Bree told Salazar. "We should be picking his audio up any—"

The closed-band receiver squawked. Over the sound of the breeze and other voices, they heard Luster say, "After you, Brad."

Bree made sure she was recording, returned to the rear window, and saw Luster and his date climb the stairs and disappear inside. The van was filled with the sounds of a cocktail party under way.

"My God, I didn't think Paula had so many friends," Luster said.

"Or enemies," Jenkins said. "She believes in keeping them close."

"Does she?"

"It's why she agreed to let you be my date, Phillip."

"Ha-ha."

Bree noticed a limo pulling up outside. A man in white robes and an Arab kaffiyeh headdress climbed out with two men who looked like bodyguards.

"Middle Eastern heavy hitter going in," Bree said.

Salazar rubbed her belly. "I've got a heavy hitter of my own right here."

Over the receiver, Luster said, "Gin and tonic, please. And a Shirley Temple for my young friend."

"You're such an amusing ass, Phillip," Jenkins said. "Sorry, make that an old-fashioned, please. A double."

"A double?" Luster said. "Are you compensating for something, Brad?"

"Fortifying something," his date said. "Victor says this night might make or break my career. Especially the after-party."

"What after-party?" Bree said.

The NYPD detective sat forward to listen.

"What after-party?" Luster asked.

"I don't know, but Victor said it's supposed to be intimate. A chance to connect."

"Like an orgy?"

"Oh God, I hope not," Jenkins said. "I'm not up for that kind of scene on a Wednesday night."

"Your drinks, gentlemen," someone said.

"Bless you," Jenkins said.

"Phillip?" A woman's voice.

The sound of ice tinkling against the side of a glass came over the receiver before Luster said, "Oh, hello, Paula. Nice gathering for midweek."

Watkins said, "I try to make my life a celebration no matter what day it is."

"I'm sure you've told that to Oprah on numerous occasions," Luster said. "I'm just happy to be in your presence again, Paula. Twice in one week. Imagine that."

"Yes," Watkins said slowly. "Lucky you for knowing Brad."

"Lucky me. He is a doll, isn't he?"

"If you like your dolls that young."

"And I do. Frances coming?"

"Frances is in bed in Greenwich, fighting a bug she picked up at the fundraiser."

"Poor dear," Luster said. "Send her my best, will you?"

"Of course," Watkins said. "Enjoy the party, Phillip, but don't forget that you have work tomorrow, and at your age you'll need a lot of sleep if you're going to try to keep up with a Ferrari like Brad. Ta-ta!"

49

"TA-TA," LUSTER REPLIED, THEN cleared his throat and said in a low voice, "Oh, the creative things I could call that woman. I hope you heard all that, Ms. Stone. I'm in and accepted, but I have not been invited to the after-party."

Bree wished she could respond to the fashion designer over the wire. She sent him a text: Hearing you loud and clear. Try to get an invite.

She and Salazar listened as Luster weaved through the crowd. "There's more beauty here than on South Beach. It's like a delicatessen for well-scrubbed skin." He paused. "What? No, I'm not going to try to get an invite to the after-party. You heard Paula's subtext. I'm expected to have two drinks, nibble some gourmet tasties, and be gone before the real fun begins."

Salazar said, "Tell Luster to take selfies around anyone he finds interesting so we can identify them later."

Bree texted him the orders.

"That I can do," Luster said.

For the next forty minutes, Bree and Salazar listened as the fashion designer mingled with people in the crowd, trying to engage in small talk with some of the older men and largely being rebuffed when he quizzed them about their backgrounds.

Luster said, "You're not picking this up, I suppose, but there's definitely a sense of lechery in the air in here."

Bree texted, What about Victor? Or Katherine?

After a few moments, he said, "I haven't met either of them yet, though Brad is engaged in a deep conversation with a thick-browed Russian sort at the moment. I'll wander over."

Salazar groaned, stood up, pushed her chair over by Bree, and sat by the rear window. "After-party or no after-party, ten minutes and I gotta go home, put my feet up."

"Understood," Bree said. "I'll get you a recording of whatever you miss."

Out the rear window, Bree saw two black Cadillac Escalades pull up in front of Watkins's house. A big muscular man climbed out from the front passenger side of each car, both with their hands in their black leather jackets.

"More guests. These are wearing body armor, I think," Bree said.

"Let me take a look," the detective said. Bree handed her the binoculars. Salazar peered through them as each bodyguard opened the rear passenger door of a vehicle. A man climbed out of each one.

"Holy Mother," Salazar said after a moment. "Will you look at that!"

"What? Who are they?"

The police detective did not reply, just kept studying the scene until the two men had gone inside and the bodyguards had been driven away. Then she lowered the binoculars in wonder.

"The guy from the first car? That's Petro Ivanovic, reputed head of a violent Russian crew based in New York. I learned about him when I was involved in an investigation of Russian organized crime in Queens. The brush-cut tough from the second car is Rory Flynn, runs the Irish mob out of Brooklyn."

Bree threw back her head and laughed. "Are you kidding me? Mobsters at Paula Watkins's house?"

"And maybe at an after-party at Paula's house," Salazar said. "God, I wish we'd known those two were going to be here. The DA would have been all over—"

The receiver squawked behind them. Luster said, "It's him—Victor. I'm sure of it. He and Brad are talking very, very intently."

Bree texted, About what?

Salazar, who was still watching the street, said, "Who's this now?"

Bree looked up in time to see a figure in a dark hoodie leave the sidewalk and jog up the stairs to Watkins's front door. The figure stood there a moment, pivoted, then jogged down the stairs, back up the sidewalk, and around the corner.

Salazar said, "What was that about?"

Before Bree could reply, Luster said, "How would I know what Brad and Victor are talking about? It's not like I can just worm my way in."

Why not? Bree texted.

As she was about to hit Send, Luster said, "What the hell? Oh my God, no!"

The lights in Paula Watkins's home died.

Nervous laughter poured from the radio receiver. Luster's voice shook as he said, "I think that guy had a—"

They heard a woman scream, four loud thuds, and more shouting and screaming.

"What the hell's going on in there?" Salazar said, lurching to her feet and grabbing the handles to the van's rear doors.

Luster bellowed over the mayhem, "They're shooting people in here! Help, Bree! Help, Detective Salazar! I'm calling Mayday, for God's sake!"

CHAPTER

50

BREE AND SALAZAR BURST out the rear of the van and raced to Paula Watkins's dark townhome. The detective lagged a little behind, holding her stomach with one hand and her police radio with the other.

"Shots fired!" she roared into the radio. "I repeat, shots fired at six East Sixty-Third, the residence of Paula Watkins. Need backup and ambulances at six East Sixty-Third! Now!"

Through the windows of Watkins's home, Bree saw the slashing of cell phone flashlights and heard more screaming and cries of terror. She bounded up the front stairs, drawing her pistol.

The door and handle were moving but the door wasn't opening; people were calling hysterically from the other side. She dug out her phone and shone the light into the locks, saw they were filled with some kind of glue or epoxy. "The door's locked from the outside!" Bree shouted. "We've got police on the way. Get to the front windows and open them if you can!"

Salazar reached the bottom of the staircase. She was gasping for air. Frenzied guests were at the windows, but the windows appeared locked as well.

Someone finally threw a table through a window to the right of the door. Detective Salazar shouted, "NYPD! Where are the shooters?"

A terrified Phillip Henry Luster stuck his head out the window and shouted, "We don't know! We couldn't see a damn thing!"

Sirens wailed at them from multiple directions and quickly after, patrol cars were skidding to a stop in front of 6 East Sixty-Third Street. Salazar ordered them to seal the perimeter of the town house. "No one leaves unless they need immediate medical help," the shaken detective said. "No one, not until we figure out who was shooting and who was shot. And get Con Edison on the line. I want the lights on in there before anyone enters."

Twenty minutes later, media trucks were lined up at the end of the block. The lights went on in Watkins's house and the screaming inside began all over again. Firemen broke down the front door with a battering ram.

Traumatized guests, many spattered with blood, streamed slowly from the residence. NYPD detectives and patrol officers began sorting and interviewing them.

Salazar looked at Bree. "I'm sorry, Chief, but I can't let you in there."

"I understand," Bree said. "Just tell me what you want me to do."

"Get the recording of Luster from the van. I want it in hand when I explain to my chief and the DA why I was first on the scene."

"Of course," Bree said.

The pregnant detective took a deep breath, climbed the stairs, and disappeared inside.

As Bree walked back toward the van she'd rented, she found herself suddenly trembling with adrenaline and on the verge of hyperventilating. *Who was shooting in there? The sheikh's bodyguards? The two mobsters?*

She sat in the back of the van, forcing herself to breathe deep and slow, until she heard Luster talking over the receiver again. She crossed to it as the fashion designer said, "Brad, I so need to get out of here. I'm feeling claustrophobic and nauseous."

Jenkins, sounding equally shaken, said, "You heard them, Phillip. Stay where we are until we're told we're good to leave."

"I'm good right now!" Luster shot back

Bree texted him: I'm in the van again. I can hear you. I know this is rough, but tell me what you see.

In a wavering voice a few moments later, Luster said, "There are at least nine people we can see dead in here. Paula's one of them. So is Ari Bernstein, the hedge-fund hack. They're on their backs about twenty feet from us. Both were shot between the eyes. And Brad's contact, Victor, is dead, along with a woman I don't know next to him. I don't recognize the others, but one looks like a sheikh of some sort. There are two men dead near him and two others by the bar that someone said were known mobsters."

Ivanovic and Flynn! Bree thought. She texted: Did you see the shooters?

"One," Luster said. "He was near Paula and Ari, wearing a

Saint Laurent tux from two seasons ago and a shirt with no bow tie. About five eight. Hundred and fifty pounds. Short, bristly, salt-and-pepper hair, unattractive face, unassuming manner. But he looked very fit, like a gymnast, so he held my attention more than several glances. Then I noticed he was playing with this metal cylinder thing in his left hand. It was maybe five inches long, two inches around, with buttons and glass lenses at both ends. Like a mini-telescope?"

"A mini-telescope?"

"Whatever," Luster said. "It doesn't matter what it was because Fit Guy closed his eyes then. His right hand went to his pants pocket and came out with a pistol so small, I wasn't sure if I was seeing things. Then the lights went out and everyone around me was groaning and laughing, even Brad, and I was thinking I was wrong about the gun. But then I saw this, like, green cyclops eye hovering near Paula and Ari, and the shooting and the screaming started."

51

Washington, DC

MY FLIGHT FROM CHARLESTON landed at Reagan National around midnight. I felt wrung out as I walked through the largely empty terminal, still trying to decide if there was enough evidence to warrant further investigation into Suzanne Liu's allegations against Thomas Tull.

Then I heard and saw CNN broadcasting on an overhead TV at one of the gates.

Footage showed cruisers with their lights flashing and crying people coming out of a huge brownstone; the banner read: DEADLY ATTACK AT FASHION EXEC'S MANHATTAN HOME. The words *fashion exec* stopped me in my tracks.

Bree's case is about some fashion bigwig, isn't it?

It was only then that I realized I'd been so tired, I had not turned on my phone after landing. I turned it on, half listening to a reporter saying that as many as eleven people might have died inside a home belonging to Paula Watkins, number two at fashion giant Duchaine.

My phone began to blow up with texts from Bree.

I needed to read only one: Call ASAP. All hell has broken loose and I may need an attorney.

Bree answered on the second ring. "Alex?"

"Right here, baby," I said. "Are you okay? Where are you?"

"I'm fine and I just got back to my hotel."

"Were you at the party that was attacked?"

"Outside it," she said and told me everything that had occurred that evening from her perspective as well as necessary background about the sex-trafficking and slavery allegations she'd been investigating along with NYPD detective Salazar.

"Is she keeping you in the loop?"

"As much as she can," Bree said. "Her superiors were not happy to hear she was listening in on a questionable wire-tap with a private detective who was thrown out of Frances Duchaine's house by Paula Watkins a few days before."

I started toward the airport exit again. "Which is why you need an attorney?"

"Just being cautious. Elena's working on retaining one for me as we speak. NYPD wants me in for questioning first thing in the morning."

"What's Elena saying?"

"She's as stunned as I am. But given the sex-trafficking allegations, the mobsters, and the sheikh, she also thinks it's not wildly out of the blue for there to have been an attack like this."

I exited the airport and got in a short line for a cab. "I kind of agree with her."

"Right?"

"Okay, what *has* Salazar told you?"

She said the detective told her there were indeed eleven dead, including the two bodyguards who had escorted Bree out of Duchaine's mansion, a man named Victor Roby, and a woman named Katherine Wise. Roby and Wise were believed to have been the main recruiters for the sex ring.

Salazar said the shooters appeared to have slipped into and out of the house through an old coal chute in the basement that was supposed to have been welded shut. The killers mingled with the guests, started shooting with night-vision monoculars once the lights died, and left quickly.

"How many wounded?"

"None."

"No wounded?" I said in surprise. "Hold on a sec." I climbed into a cab and gave the driver our home address. As we pulled away, I said, "So, eleven specific targets?"

"That's how we read it. Whoever the shooters were, they were disciplined assassins."

"Assassins with a tight, targeted agenda. What about Duchaine?"

"Evidently in shock but safe and under Greenwich Police protection. Why?"

"The intimate knowledge of the party. The layout of Watkins's home. The coal chute. The specific targets. The whole thing reeks of an inside job."

"It does, doesn't it," Bree said thoughtfully. "And there's no one more inside this stinking mess than Frances Duchaine herself."

"That's what it sounds like to me," I said and yawned. "Why don't you get some sleep and we'll talk in the morning?"

"First thing. I want my head on straight when I go in to make a statement."

"You always have your head on straight."

"Love you."

"Love you too, and I'm happy you're safe."

"Me too. Sleep well."

I ended the call as the cab was crossing the Fourteenth Street Bridge. I returned to my queue of unread texts. I was going to look at the others from Bree but then saw an area code and a phone number I did not recognize, and I thumbed the message open.

Dear Dr. Cross,

My name is Thomas Tull. As you may know, I am a bestselling true-crime writer. I have a contract to pen a book about the Family Man killings ongoing in the DC area and would very much like to talk to you about them. Also, I think some of the things you're being told about me and the way I work are completely off base. At the very least, I'd like the opportunity to set the record straight. Please call me at your earliest convenience.

All my best,
Thomas

CHAPTER

52

Manhattan

AT TEN THIRTY THE following morning, a Thursday, Bree followed a criminal defense attorney named Natalie Reed into an interrogation room in a midtown precinct.

Rosella Salazar and her partner, Simon Thompson, were waiting inside with their backs to the one-way mirror, behind which, no doubt, several of their superiors were watching. The killings had made national news and Bree knew from personal experience how much of a pressure cooker cases like these became.

"Chief Stone, Ms. Reed," Salazar said, gesturing to the chairs. "Please."

Reed took a seat, saying, "Is this a formal interrogation?"

Salazar rubbed her belly. "If it were, I wouldn't be here. We're just talking, catching up, and we need a bit more information."

"Such as?" Reed said.

"We need to know who Chief Stone's clients are and how much they knew about the sex-trafficking allegations before Bluestone Group got involved."

Bree said, "I still have no idea who they are beyond some attorney in Cleveland. But the attorney, or whoever his clients were, knew about the lawsuit in North Carolina and the various sealed complaints here in New York."

Detective Simon Thompson, Salazar's partner, spoke for the first time. "We need the name of the attorney in Cleveland."

"I don't know it."

"I do," Bree's attorney said. She removed a business card from her briefcase and pushed it across the table. "Gerald Rainy with Grady and Rainy. His phone number is there. He is expecting a call, and in light of what's happened, he has already given me his client's name. In return, he would appreciate it remaining out of the press."

Salazar shifted uncomfortably.

"We'll see," Thompson said. "Name?"

"Theresa May Alcott," Reed said. "As in the billionaire Theresa May Alcott. Since her husband's death, she is the majority shareholder in Alcott and Sayers, the big soap and household products company."

That came out of left field, Bree thought, annoyed that Reed had not informed her before the meeting. *What's the connection between Duchaine and Alcott?*

Thompson seemed impressed by Bree's client. "My girlfriend uses Alcott and Sayers organic soap. You have an address and phone number for Mrs. Alcott?"

"She splits her time between Cleveland and Jackson Hole, Wyoming," the attorney said. "She's in Ohio at the moment. I will track down a phone number for her."

Bree looked at the attorney. "Why exactly did she hire Bluestone?"

Salazar shifted in her chair. "I was wondering the same thing."

Reed cleared her throat and glanced at Bree. "I don't know all the sordid details, but evidently Mrs. Alcott's favorite grand-daughter got caught up in a sex-trafficking ring after being lured to New York to work as a model for Frances Duchaine. When the family found out, the young lady killed herself. Mrs. Alcott wanted the scheme exposed so it would never happen again."

That's odd, Bree thought. *I don't remember anything about a young girl from Ohio in the material I was given at the beginning. But maybe that was intentional?*

Thompson had a sour look on his face. "How was Mrs. Alcott going to expose the scheme?"

"She'd planned on going to the media, where she has con-siderable influence," Reed said.

"Not afraid she'd be sued by Duchaine?"

"From what I've been told, Mrs. Alcott has far deeper pockets than Frances Duchaine these days."

Bree looked at Salazar and Thompson. "Did you find evidence that there was going to be a sex-slave auction at Watkins's last night?"

Salazar said, "Nothing concrete yet, but the computers just got to our experts."

"What about the other people attending the party?"

Thompson said, "We can't talk about them at this point."

Salazar stared at her partner. "I would not have been there if it hadn't been for Chief Stone."

"*Former* chief Stone," Thompson said.

"Read up on her sometime—maybe you'll learn something," Salazar said. She looked at Bree. "Several of the younger members of the crowd copped to being there for a special party involving sex that was going to happen later in the evening, after most of the guests left. None of the older males in the crowd mentioned being there to buy sex slaves."

"Of course they didn't," Bree said. "I'd talk to the number-two guys in the Ivanovic and Flynn mobs, see what they know. And talk to the sheikh's embassy. And I'd be looking for money moving from any of the partygoers' bank accounts to Paula Watkins or Frances Duchaine. She's who I'd be leaning on right this minute, by the way. What did Frances know? And when did she know it?"

The pregnant detective squinted and put her hands on her stomach. "Well, Thompson and I are just about to ask her those same questions, Chief Stone. Would you care to observe and point out anything we might miss?"

"What?" Thompson said. "Why would we do that?"

Salazar suddenly looked exhausted. "Because she knows things we don't."

CHAPTER

53

Washington, DC

THURSDAY MORNING, JOHN SAMPSON and I entered an Au Bon Pain on Tenth Street, not far from Metro PD headquarters.

Thomas Tull shot to his feet and waved to us from beside a small booth near the rear of the establishment.

Tull had craggy good looks and a solidly muscled body. A sliver under six feet, he was dressed casually in denim, and he'd let his sandy-brown hair go a little grayer than it was in his recent publicity photos, giving him a middle-aged Robert Redford quality. The writer's steel-blue eyes danced over me as he smiled and stuck out a big hand.

"It's an honor to meet you, Dr. Cross," Tull said, fully engaging my eyes before turning to John. "And you too, Detective Sampson. A real honor."

I have an expert nose for someone blowing smoke at me. But

213

I didn't smell anything coming off Tull except goodwill and curiosity.

Sampson felt it as well and he smiled back. "You're the big-time writer, Mr. Tull."

"Thomas, please," he said and gestured to the booth, where a carafe of coffee, clean cups, and a plate of breakfast rolls awaited. He slid in, still smiling, looking at each of us in turn as if trying to burn our images into his mind. Then he knocked his knuckles against the tabletop twice and put his right hand over his heart.

"Dr. Cross, your lectures at the FBI Academy were a revelation to me. I first heard them when I was working for NCIS in San Diego," Tull said. "And Detective Sampson, several of your investigations should be taught in every police academy in the country."

"Nice of you to say so," I said.

Sampson nodded. "How can we help?"

Tull flashed a thousand-watt smile at us, then grew serious, putting the palms of both hands on the table.

"Let me explain how I work," he said. "First off, I am not here to second-guess you and I will never, ever reveal anything you might tell me about the Family Man murders without your explicit approval. Ever. I know how delicate an investigation like this is, and you don't need some clueless writer accidentally letting something critical slip."

"Comforting," I said. "You're saying that you'll say nothing about the case until your book is written?"

"And vetted by each of you before it's published," Tull said. "You may not like what I've written, but I will hide nothing from you."

For the next ten minutes, the writer described how he'd worked with investigators in the research of his previous three books. In each one, he had signed an agreement stating that he would not disclose anything about the probe until it was complete. In return, he asked to be a fly on the wall as the case unfolded.

"You mean, like, constantly?" Sampson asked. "That's not going to happen."

"No, of course not," Tull said. "Only in those instances where you think I need to be there in order to understand some new twist or breakthrough in the case."

"I need to ask you a couple of questions first," I said.

The writer sat up straighter and steepled his fingers. "Anything."

I asked him about the threat he'd made to Suzanne Liu. "She taped it," I said.

"So did I," Tull said. "She's been making false accusations against me and I wanted to let her know there would be financial repercussions if she continued."

"You deny you had relationships with the detectives running the investigations in your various books?"

"The detectives running them?" he said. "No. I had relationships with consenting adults who were part of those investigations. To my knowledge, no one ever complained about them."

"You don't mention the relationships in your books," I said.

"Because they're no one's business but mine and three wonderful women," Tull said, not batting an eye. "Do you have one of them on the record being critical of me?"

"I've only spoken to Heidi Parks," I said. "And no."

"There you go. Heidi and I parted on great terms," the writer said. "I'm sure you'll hear the same from Jane Hale in Boston and Ava Firsching in Berlin."

"Detective Hale is on her honeymoon."

"In Australia," he said. "I know because I attended her wedding. And I one hundred percent guarantee you that Ava will also speak well of me."

"Why wouldn't they?" I said. "You gave them the credit for making substantive breakthroughs in the investigations when you, in fact, made those logical leaps."

Tull's face screwed up. "Name one."

"You, not Jane Hale, first theorized that the electrocutions in the greater Boston area were connected."

"That's false," Tull said. "Jane came up with that theory the night of the retirement of her old partner. Jane got quite drunk on whiskey and told me she was going to look into other electrocutions in and around Boston. I just reminded her the next day."

"Why not just write that, then?" Sampson asked.

"Because Jane is ordinarily a teetotaler and would have been embarrassed if I'd described how plastered she was."

I said, "You told Ava Firsching to return the focus of her investigation to the Berlin Zoo, didn't you?"

"I may have suggested it," he said. "But isn't that a tried-and-true investigative method? Going back and looking again?"

There was no disputing that, so I said, "What about *Doctor's Orders*? I talked to Heidi Parks yesterday and she said it was your idea to look into malpractice suits."

The writer shrugged. "I don't remember it that way, but so what? Isn't it logical to look into the dark underbellies of the victims? Isn't that what you preached in one of your lectures at Quantico, Dr. Cross?"

That was true and it caused me to sit back. "Still doesn't explain why you kept yourself out of the narratives in three of the biggest breaks in the cases."

Tull sighed and for several moments watched me with no guile that I could see.

"I find it odd that you're, in a sense, criticizing me for being humble, for letting the spotlight shine where it should—on the detectives who drove the cases," he said at last. "But I'll tell you what, Dr. Cross. If you'll let me observe the investigation and I come up with an angle that you two had not considered and it turns out to be big, I'll take the credit. One hundred percent. Does that work for you?"

CHAPTER

54

Manhattan

BREE WATCHED FROM THE observation booth as Frances Duchaine entered the interrogation room with Katrina French, her young attorney. Wearing a widow-black pantsuit and dark sunglasses, Duchaine folded herself into a chair across the table from Detectives Salazar and Thompson.

Her attorney said, "We're here as a courtesy, Detectives."

Salazar was having none of it. "Did you want your client to come in under a subpoena? Or in handcuffs?"

French stiffened. "I'm saying that Ms. Duchaine is here to help in any way she can. She's devastated and horrified by what happened."

A tear trickled from under the fashion designer's glasses and dribbled down her cheek.

"No doubt," Thompson said. "And if your client won't mind taking off the shades?"

Though she appeared to be grieving, Duchaine had not lost her flair for the dramatic; she tore off the glasses and said in a hoarse voice, "What can you tell me? Did Paula suffer? Ari? Were they afraid before they passed?"

Salazar said, "Ms. Watkins was shot at close range between the eyes in the dark. I don't even think she felt fear before she died. Mr. Bernstein may have been frightened, but I do not believe he suffered."

Duchaine's lower lip trembled and more tears ran. Her attorney handed her a tissue, and she dabbed at her swollen eyes.

"Who would do such a thing to them?" she whispered. "And why?"

Detective Thompson said, "Who? We think they were professional killers. And why? We were hoping you could help us with that."

The fashion icon's lips drew back as she gazed wide-eyed at her hands, as if trying to see through them into some unknowable universe. "I have been asking myself why since I heard," she said quietly. "I can't come up with one good answer."

Salazar said, "Why weren't you at the party, Ms. Duchaine?"

Sounding bewildered, she said, "Can you imagine if I'd gone?"

"Why didn't you?"

Frances Duchaine shifted uncomfortably. "I'd rather not say."

"That won't work. This is an investigation into a mass murder, Ms. Duchaine. Why weren't you there?"

Duchaine's jaw tightened and she glanced at French, who nodded.

"I had hosted a large fundraiser at my estate in Greenwich and I was tired. But it was more than that. I...I was recently diagnosed with Crohn's disease and I was having a flare-up all yesterday afternoon."

In the observation booth, Bree studied the fashion icon, who seemed embarrassed. She glanced at the only other two people in the booth: Blaine Roy, chief of detectives for NYPD, and Ellen Larkin, Salazar's supervising lieutenant.

"My sister has it," Lieutenant Larkin said. "Times you can't drag her off the pot."

Chief Roy's nostrils flared. He asked Bree what she thought.

"Plausible but convenient," Bree said.

In the interrogation room, Salazar said, "We'd love to talk to the doc who diagnosed you."

"Dr. Leeann Webb at Lenox Hill," Duchaine said without hesitation. "I called her yesterday around five. She gave me a new prescription. I have it all documented."

"We'd like to see those documents," Salazar said. "Crohn's disease. That's brought on by stress, right?"

Duchaine shook her head. "The flare-ups can be, but not the disease itself."

"You were feeling stressed yesterday?"

The fashion icon nodded. "I had a ridiculous amount of design work due."

"Nothing to do with finances?"

She shrugged. "I don't think about finances. That was Paula's job. And Ari's."

In the observation booth, Bree said, "Don't let her have a pass on that."

As if hearing her through the mirror, Detective Salazar said, "You do grasp your financial situation, though, correct?"

The fashion icon looked at her attorney. "What's she asking?"

French looked at Salazar, seeming puzzled. "What financial situation is that?"

The detective rubbed her belly before saying, "By several

accounts, your company has experienced a seventeen percent decline in revenues in the aftermath of a massive expansion of your retail arm. Your company now carries a crushing debt load. You have balloon payments on over four hundred million dollars, which you are personally on the hook for, coming due in less than ninety days. Do you understand, Frances?"

It was the first time Salazar had addressed Duchaine by her first name. The fashion mogul tried to act imperious. "I don't have the foggiest what you're talking about, Detective…whatever your name is."

"With all due respect, Frances, you are either a liar or a fool."

Her attorney stood. "That's enough."

"Not by a long shot, Counselor," Salazar said firmly. "Sit down or we'll start looking into *your* role in all of this."

"My role in all of what?" French demanded.

"A criminal enterprise inside Duchaine Inc. that's engaged in human trafficking here in the city and over state lines to underpin the company's and Frances's rotting finances. Those are city, state, and federal offenses, Counselor, with extreme penalties."

CHAPTER

55

KATRINA FRENCH LOST MOST of her color and sank back into her seat.

"What?" the attorney said and glanced at Frances Duchaine, who seemed equally shocked.

Detective Thompson, who had been silent for several minutes, sat forward and jabbed a finger at Frances Duchaine. "Tell her."

"Tell her what?" the fashion icon demanded.

"That you lured young women and men to New York with promises of careers in modeling and fashion," he said. "Then you hoodwinked them into debt and gave them one way out— prostitution. All so you could go on making pretty dresses."

Duchaine had recoiled from the assault and looked to her attorney for support. "Katrina, I honestly have no idea what this is about."

In the observation booth, Bree said, "Sure you do."

In the interrogation room, Thompson said, "Don't lie, Ms. Duchaine. There are lawsuits over this that were sealed. I've interviewed young women and men who were caught up in your web. I believe them."

Salazar said, "We're searching Paula Watkins's computers, Ari Bernstein's computers, and the computers of everyone who died last night. We have also been granted a warrant to look at your personal and corporate computers, Frances. We're going to find evidence you were involved."

Duchaine lashed out. "You will not! I had nothing to do with whatever you are alleging. Nothing!"

"C'mon, Ms. Duchaine," Detective Thompson said wearily. "You had to have known what last night was about. The after-party? Paula's sex-slave auction?"

"What after-party?" she said, sounding bewildered. "What auction? No. Paula would never be involved in such a thing."

"Well, we believe she was involved up to her eyeballs," Salazar said. "Why else would she invite Russian and Irish mob bosses to her home? Why invite a sheikh known to traffic in underage sex slaves?"

In the observation booth, Bree shifted, thinking that last bit was a stretch.

But it got through to Duchaine, who looked rattled. "They were there?"

Thompson said, "They were, and they died. Maybe they got Paula killed. Maybe the whole sordid party and the sordid people involved got Paula and Ari and nine other people murdered by professionals."

Duchaine's attorney said, "I think we've heard enough. Ms. Duchaine says she had no knowledge of this crazy scheme you allege happened and she's confident you'll find no evidence of—"

Detective Salazar spoke right over the lawyer. "We think Paula crossed someone, Frances. Someone dangerous. Someone ruthless."

Duchaine seemed to shrink a little. "Like who?"

"Maybe a rival crime boss," Thompson said. "Maybe a Middle Eastern government."

He let that hang a moment before adding, "Or maybe someone less obvious. Maybe someone who thought things had gone too far. Someone who decided to end the sex ring and stop the slave auction before it could happen."

Bree could feel a crackling tension in the short silence that followed.

Then Salazar leaned forward in her chair and said, "Someone who wasn't at the party. Someone like you, Frances. Are you behind the killings? Did you order them?"

Katrina French threw an arm across Duchaine's chest and said, "Don't answer that question, Frances. Don't answer any of their questions. We are done here."

CHAPTER

56

Washington, DC

ALTHOUGH SAMPSON AND I had been impressed by Thomas Tull's calm, collected answers to our tougher questions, we'd given him a hard no on being a fly on the wall.

He'd wanted to know if we'd mind him asking the DC police chief, and we'd told him to go right ahead. Afterward, we spoke with Chief Michaels, who said he thought the exposure might be good for the department, especially if we caught the Family Man killer. But when we explained why Tull was a suspect, he agreed that until we cleared the writer, he would get no access whatsoever.

Which was why that Thursday evening we were hunkered down in an unmarked squad car up the street from the town house in Georgetown that Tull had leased.

A late-model midnight-blue Audi RS 7 was parked in front

of the town house's green door. The building was dark but for a single light shining in a second-floor window.

"How long are we going to give it?" Sampson asked.

It was a pleasant spring night. We had the windows open. I said, "Ordinarily, I'd be down for midnight at least, but Bree texted that she's on her way back from New York. I'd like to see her before she goes to sleep."

"And Willow's babysitter can only stay till ten thirty," Sampson said. "So, ten?"

"Ten it is," I said.

Fifteen minutes later, a fit woman in her forties with short dark hair walked up to Tull's place; she was wearing a worn leather jacket, jeans, and cowboy boots, and she carried a heavy messenger bag over one shoulder.

She dug in the bag, retrieved a large manila envelope, put it in Tull's mail slot, and continued on. She passed us without looking our way and disappeared around the corner.

"Who's she?" Sampson asked.

"No clue."

A few moments later, the light in Tull's second-story window went out.

The writer left the town house soon after; he climbed into his stylish four-door coupe and pulled out, heading north. Sampson put the squad car in gear and followed Tull at a comfortable distance.

"We have a license plate number?" I asked.

"New York plate S-C-R-B-L-R," Sampson said. "Like *scribbler*?"

"Got it," I said. He took a left and then another, heading south. Tull was soon on local-access K Street heading east. It was a moonless night, which somehow made the headlight glare worse as we approached Twenty-Seventh.

The writer put on his left blinker, indicating he was going to take the Rock Creek Parkway heading north. We were six cars back when the light changed.

Driving down the on-ramp at thirty miles an hour, Tull merged into light traffic on the parkway, a four-lane thorough-fare surrounded by woods and divided by a strip of trees and azalea bushes. Tull accelerated to fifty.

Sampson followed suit, passing two cars. Approaching the M Street exit, we were three cars behind him in the right lane.

Then the writer pulled over into the left lane and got up alongside a black Porsche 911 Turbo Carrera. I still had my window down, so I heard the roar of huge high-horsepower engines before both vehicles went screaming up the parkway.

"Stay with him!" I shouted, and Sampson stomped on the gas.

57

TULL'S STYLISH LITTLE GERMAN coupe turned out to be a wolf in sheep's clothing, a sleek but conservative-looking car with a raging monster of an engine.

The Porsche 911 tried to accelerate with the RS 7, but within the first three seconds, Tull opened a gap of twenty yards, then thirty. We were much farther behind when both high-performance vehicles hit the brakes and downshifted before the tight right and a sweeping left curve below Dupont Circle.

They vanished from sight.

"He had to have hit a hundred there," Sampson said. "I should put the bubble up and pull him over."

"Just keep him somewhere in range," I said, gritting my teeth as John hit the brakes and we went through the curves.

After we came out of the second one, the parkway straightened for more than a mile. We could see the rear lights of the Audi and the Porsche a good four hundred yards ahead, weaving in and out of traffic.

"He's nuts," Sampson said, pounding the gas pedal. "He's going to hit someone."

"Or they're going to hit him," I said as we sped forward, gaining some ground when both vehicles hit the brakes before a big right turn north of Montrose Park.

I caught only glimpses of what happened next.

The parkway ahead of the sports cars was near empty. Both drivers took advantage of that, the 911 in the right lane and the RS 7 in the left, burying their accelerators. The cars became a blur.

"That's it—they are going to kill people," I said. "Put the bubble up."

Sampson did as we entered the turn north of Montrose Park. He flipped on the siren and accelerated again.

"I don't know if I can catch up," Sampson said as I peered ahead, trying to pick out the rear lights of the Porsche and the Audi as we raced through the densest woods along the parkway.

We were going eighty when I caught sight of the split at the end of the road where Shoreham angles northwest and Beach Drive goes northeast. "That's the Porsche going up Beach," I said.

"Where's Tull?" Sampson said, hitting the brakes before the split.

I caught a glimpse of taillights on Shoreham.

"Cathedral Avenue," I said. "I think that's him."

Sampson took Shoreham and then Cathedral Avenue, a much narrower road that goes along the northwest side of Rock Creek Park. The road curves left entering the avenue, which features trees on the right and apartment buildings on the left.

When we came out of the curve, I expected to see taillights ahead. But there were none.

"Where the hell did he go?" Sampson demanded and slowed as we came up to Woodley Road, a left.

We both looked up Woodley and saw only a minivan pulling out of North Woodley Place, heading west toward Connecticut Avenue. Sampson turned off the siren and bubble and sped north on Cathedral Avenue to where it crossed Connecticut.

No Tull.

We backtracked. Sampson took us the length of Woodley Place and then up an alley between homes, apartment buildings, and small parking lots closer to Connecticut Avenue.

We shone police flashlights into every dark corner. Tull and his midnight-blue RS 7 were nowhere to be seen.

"We lost him," Sampson said, exasperated. "A goddamn writer at the wheel and we lost him."

CHAPTER

58

BREE LOOKED EXHAUSTED WHEN she finally came in the front door around eleven that evening. I'd been home less than twenty minutes and was still frustrated by our inability to stay with Tull.

We'd contacted our bosses and tried to have an APB put out on the writer, but since he hadn't done anything other than race the nameless Porsche driver, we were told we were on shaky grounds as far as cause.

"Hey, baby," I said, ditching my frustration and hugging her. "You look like you've been through a lot."

Bree hugged me tighter. "I feel like I'm back from another universe."

Between family and work, we'd had no time to talk and had communicated throughout the evening by text. I led her into the kitchen, where Nana Mama had left a pot of chicken stew warming for us. She and the kids had already gone to sleep.

I got Bree a bowl of stew and a cold beer.

"You're an angel," Bree said, sipping the beer and closing her eyes for a second.

"You want to tell me about your day?" I said after she'd taken a few spoonfuls and another swig of beer. "Your interrogation? Duchaine's?"

Bree looked relieved to be asked and recounted in full her discussion with Detective Salazar and her partner and then the interrogation of Frances Duchaine.

"Wow," I said. "I didn't see that coming. Do *you* think Duchaine ordered the hits?"

"It's almost all I've thought about since she stormed out of the interrogation room with her lawyer," Bree said. "She claims she knew nothing about the sex trafficking, but how is that possible? I mean, I suppose she could have been willfully ignorant."

I nodded. "Knew something was off but didn't want to put her nose in there and find out what Watkins was really up to."

"See no evil," Bree said. "But I'm not buying it. Not totally. She had to have known the financial hole she was in. Right?"

"I would think so. There's only so far you can go in business when you're a pure artist, not beholden to the market."

"Exactly. And look how huge she got. She knew."

"But did she order them killed?"

Bree took another swig of beer, set the bottle on the table, and dropped the tension from her shoulders. "My gut says no. If it's there, Salazar will find it. She's good. Real good. But my gut still says no."

"So who else could have ordered the killings? And why?"

After swallowing another spoonful of stew, she said, "I've got three possibles: Rivals of the two crime bosses who may have been cut out of the deal. Or rivals of that sheikh. I mean, if the

Saudis can murder and cut up a journalist in their embassy, a mass murder over sex trafficking is not out of the question."

I thought about that and nodded. "You have to keep it on the table. And number three?"

"The person who evidently hired me through that attorney in Cleveland," she said. "Theresa May Alcott. The heir to the Alcott and Sayers soap fortune. Her granddaughter got caught up in the modeling scheme and ended up killing herself."

That took me by surprise. "When did you find this out?"

"This morning," she said. "From an attorney Bluestone hired."

"Really. What does Elena say?"

"That she didn't know Alcott was our client. That she wished she'd known the motive, but ultimately our job is to investigate what clients want investigated and report back."

"And I can't imagine Theresa May Alcott is going to pay to have herself investigated by Bluestone."

"No," Bree said, brooding. "But look at the timeline, Alex. I submit my report to Elena Martin on Monday evening. She sends it to the attorney that night or the next morning, and he forwards it to Alcott. Wednesday evening the party is attacked and most of the major players in the sex ring are dead."

"But Salazar and NYPD know this," I said. "They're not going to look at Alcott?"

"For now, Salazar is convinced it's Duchaine and that's where her efforts are focused."

"If you're going head-hunting, why not go after the most high-profile head?"

"There's probably some of that involved too."

As Bree finished her stew, I put the rest in the fridge and cleaned up Nana Mama's kitchen, bringing it up to a standard that would make her smile in the morning.

"Bed?" I said when I finished.

Bree said, "We haven't talked about your day."

I gave her a quick rundown of our meeting with Thomas Tull, our subsequent surveillance of the writer, and the high-speed chase.

"Do you think he knew you were chasing him?"

"He had to have seen the bubble flashing."

"But he didn't know it was you and John."

I thought about that. "I don't see how he could have made us."

"No idea where he was going?"

"None."

"Then bed," Bree said and drained the rest of her beer.

Upstairs, after we'd brushed our teeth, gotten under the covers, and turned off the light, she snuggled into my arms and laid her head on my chest. I expected her to fall asleep immediately, but I could sense she was still on alert.

"What are you feeling?" I whispered.

After a pause, she said, "Like I've been used by someone with an agenda that I had a right to know about before I agreed to take the job."

"A valid emotion," I said. "What do you want to do about it?"

"Go to Cleveland with or without Elena's approval."

"Then you should."

"But on whose dime?"

"I think we can afford a trip to Cleveland."

She sighed and I felt the tension gradually leave her.

"I love you," she murmured.

"I love you too," I said, and drifted off.

CHAPTER

59

Potomac, Maryland

THE FAMILY MAN STOOD there in the shadows, highly aware of the respirator mask, which pushed against the goggles and the hood of the disposable jumpsuit. With latex gloves, the killer adjusted the goggles yet again before checking the time.

It was 2:45 a.m. More than a week since the last strike.

After a momentary thrill of anticipation, calmness settled over the Family Man, a mental and emotional cocoon that allowed near complete detachment.

That's the goal, isn't it? Full detachment from these necessary actions? Yes, and I have the right to a perfect life too. A dream life just like this.

The killer's eyes ran up the sweeping lawns to a neo-Georgian manor with English gardens on seven manicured acres. Five bedrooms. Two offices. A stable in the back with stalls for four horses. A garage with bays for five vehicles. An outdoor basketball court. An indoor lap pool. A sauna. A gym.

It defied belief that two people could amass this kind of wealth and prestige at such a young age. But here was the proof, right before any doubter's eyes.

Opportunity meets preparation, the killer thought, then lowered the night-vision goggles and left the shadows.

After padding quickly across the lawn, the Family Man reached a junction box through which the electric, telephone, and broadband lines connected to the residence. Quickly, the killer was tied into the house intranet and running a clever software program bought on the dark web that soon elicited the password for the alarm system.

With the system disarmed, the task ahead was easier. On a screened-in porch, the Family Man worked the lock to the sliding door of the kitchen and soon had it open.

Inside, the killer stood stock-still and listened. Elsie, the family's beloved eleven-year-old German shepherd, had passed nine days ago. The chances of them having gotten a new dog this quick were low, especially since there had been no mention of it on any of the four family members' social media accounts, which the Family Man had studied in detail.

Satisfied there was no new dog to make things complicated, the killer took in the kitchen. Even viewed in the dim light from a bulb over the red enamel six-burner stove, it was magnificent, with a long, stainless-steel sink with three different faucets and multiple cutting boards and racks. Pale gray quartz countertops, red cabinets to match the stove, and a dramatic island/bar.

Impressed, the Family Man made a mental note of that last feature, then left the kitchen, passed the small library and a larger office, and climbed the stairs to the second floor. The upstairs was as well-appointed as the lower floor, with four bedroom suites off a central hallway.

The killer crept to the only one with double doors, drew out a baggie, and shook free its contents, which vanished into the carpet pile. Drawing the pistol and turning the master suite's doorknob, the Family Man took courage from the belief that this was the logical next step.

We make them understand that no one is safe, no matter their wealth or race. That's the story we want them to hear. That's the story we want them telling over and over again to each other, undermining their certainty, building the collective terror.

That last thought caused the killer to smile beneath the black mask.

It was remarkable what a scary story could do, wasn't it?

60

SHORTLY BEFORE EIGHT THE next morning, just after Bree left to catch her flight to Cleveland, I got the call about the Kane family. Sampson and I soon arrived in one of the toniest neighborhoods in Potomac, Maryland, and found Ned Mahoney and his forensics team waiting for us.

"No one's been inside except the maternal grandmother, who came by to pick up her nine-year-old granddaughter for a trip to New York," Mahoney said, leading the way through the gates and up the slight rise in the driveway to a neo-Georgian manor. "Grandma was hysterical when I tried to talk to her. EMTs are giving her something to calm her down. Her husband is on the way."

"I gather the victims were big-time wealthy," Sampson said.

"And young," Mahoney said. "Irwin and Linda Kane, of Kane

Tech Advisers. They made a fortune doing consulting work for the government—Justice, Pentagon, and CIA."

"Any indication that that work is involved here?" I asked.

"As motive?" Ned said. "None so far. Sounds like Family Man all the way."

After donning blue booties, hairnets, and gloves, we went inside through the garage door, which Mrs. Kane's mother had opened with her key. The alarm system had been disarmed.

The lower floor looked untouched. The second floor was all crime scene.

The double doors to the master suite were open, revealing the Kanes dead in their bed. Irwin Kane had been shot through the temple with a small-caliber bullet. Linda Kane took one through the palm of her left hand and into her left eye and brain.

"She heard the first shot," Sampson said. "Held up her hand to protect herself."

"At this range, she couldn't have protected a thing," I said, feeling disgusted at the callousness of the act. There was no passion here. Quite the opposite.

We went into the other rooms and found Nate, age eleven, and Melissa, nine, dead in their beds. From a few feet away, you would have sworn they were sleeping.

I could not help but think of Ali. Almost the same age as Nate. They could have been classmates. Friends.

"Makes me want to punch a wall," I said. "It's just so…"

"Ruthless?" Mahoney said.

"I was thinking more like *cowardly*."

Sampson said, "In what way?"

"Shooting them as they sleep. Probably with a suppressor on the gun. He's unwilling to acknowledge the humanity of the targets. If they'd been awake, begging, he'd have to see them as fellow human beings. Executing them like this is a way of avoidance, a way to rationalize what is not rational. He doesn't have to think of them as a mom, a dad, and two children. They're just objects."

"Targets," Sampson said.

"But why?" Mahoney said. "What does he get out of this?"

I said, "Some thrill, no doubt. Other needs being met. And maybe…"

"What?"

"A means to an end," I said. "A more concrete end than what we're seeing here."

"You're saying these killings are part of a bigger picture?" Mahoney asked.

Before I could reply, Meagan McShane, a medical examiner, came to the doorway. "I've got a time of death on the mom and dad. Shortly before three a.m."

A sheriff's deputy in protective gear appeared in the hallway behind the ME. "I'm sorry to bother you," he said. "But there's some guy out at the yellow tape asking for you."

"Who's that?" Mahoney asked.

"He says he's Thomas Tull. You know, the writer?"

CHAPTER

61

THOMAS TULL HAD NERVE, I'd give him that.

Among fifteen lookie-loos and some camerapeople, the writer stood at the yellow tape, dressed to look dark and mysterious in black jeans, cowboy boots, shirt, and jacket. His sunglasses were black-framed wraparound reflectors. His hair was perfectly out of place. He smirked in reproach as Sampson, Mahoney, and I came near.

"I thought you might like to talk," he said.

Sampson said, "What are you doing here, Mr. Tull?"

"I'm assuming something happened."

The three of us ducked under the tape and surrounded him.

"I'm Edward Mahoney, FBI special agent in charge," Ned said quietly. "Walk with us, please, sir."

"What's going on?" the writer demanded.

I said softly, "We can get away from here and talk quietly, or we can put you in cuffs, make you look bad for television, and take you downtown to talk."

"I bet you make a lot of men shiver with that kind of chitchat."

I shrugged. "Your call, Thomas."

The writer took off his sunglasses and studied me. "Let's talk quietly."

"Good," Mahoney said. "We'll go up the street. My car."

We skirted the crowd and walked up the leafy road past the first satellite truck arriving on the scene, past our vehicle, and then past a midnight-blue Audi coupe.

"That's your car, right?" Sampson said.

Tull brightened. "All six-hundred-and-seventy-five horse-power."

"Rare car, I hear. An RS Seven."

"Especially that one," Tull said. "Audi built it for the car shows the year after they bought Lamborghini. The chassis, suspension, and engine block are all Audi, but every component after that is Lambo-made, from the transmission to the quad turbos. It's a true hybrid. A one-of-a-kind beast. But you wouldn't know it from the design. Sleek, but not outrageous. It's like a James Bond car in that respect."

When we reached Mahoney's gray squad car, I opened the back door. "After you."

Tull hesitated but got in. I shut the door, came around the other side, and climbed in beside him. Mahoney slid behind the wheel. Sampson took the passenger seat and swiveled around to look over his shoulder.

If the writer was nervous, he wasn't showing it in the least.

"Mind if I record this conversation?" Tull asked. "For posterity?"

"An excellent idea," Sampson said, getting out his phone. "We'll do the same."

Tull fumbled with his iPhone a moment, then nodded and said the date and time before continuing: "This is Thomas Tull with Edward Mahoney of the FBI, Detective John Sampson of Metro PD, and Dr. Alex Cross, a consultant to both agencies," he said, looking at each of us in turn. "Now, before we get into particulars, this is a Family Man crime scene, right? Yes or no?"

For a moment, I thought Mahoney was going to blow a fuse. "We're asking the questions, Mr. Tull."

I said, "Where were you earlier this morning? Like two thirty to three a.m.?"

Tull cocked his head. "Uh—sleeping?"

"You're unsure?" Sampson said.

"I'm something of an insomniac," Tull said. "Sometimes it's hard for me to tell if I'm sleeping or just kind of simmering there, hoping for unconsciousness. Why?"

"You can prove you were in bed?" Sampson asked.

"I...what's this about?"

"You were here in Potomac or in Chevy Chase last night, weren't you?" I asked.

The writer looked at me dumbly. "Maybe. Technically."

Sampson spun a bluff. "Not *maybe* or *technically*. We've got you on CCTV footage in that rare beast of a car you have there, racing a black Porsche Turbo Carrera up the Rock Creek Parkway at more than one hundred miles an hour."

Tull gazed at Mahoney. "And for that I get FBI attention?"

"You admit you were traveling in excess of one hundred heading toward Chevy Chase at roughly nine last evening?" Ned demanded.

He didn't seem to know how to reply. He sighed. "I read this interesting piece online about the culture of people in the DC area who have high-performance cars and do time trials up Rock Creek in the middle of the night. I found out on my own that there are also eager takers for a more adventurous kind of urban racing."

"You've done it before?" I asked.

"A few times, yes. Look, I know it's against the law, but it's just a way I blow off steam now and then."

Mahoney said, "You will kill someone."

"Or maybe you did," I said. "Last night. In the Kanes' house."

The writer went from surprised to stone-faced in two seconds. "That is nonsense. I have never been anywhere near this address in my entire life."

"And I suppose you can prove that?" Sampson said.

Tull thought about that. "That I have never been near here in my entire life? No. But last night? Absolutely. One hundred percent, I can prove I was nowhere near here between two thirty and three a.m."

CHAPTER

62

Cleveland, Ohio

BREE LANDED BEFORE TEN Friday morning. She'd spent the flight working on her laptop, researching the people who had hired her and the Bluestone Group to investigate Frances Duchaine.

Gerald Rainy, managing partner of the venerable firm of Grady and Rainy, was in his early sixties. According to an article in a Cleveland business journal, the attorney spent every lunch hour at a gym near his office. Bree got a rental car and used her phone to search for gyms around the law firm's downtown address; she found a high-end one within two blocks. She drove to the nearest parking lot, got out, and was on the sidewalk outside the gym when Rainy exited in a pale gray suit, crisp light pink shirt, no tie.

She recognized him from his pictures online: tall, lean, silver-haired, tanned, and with a patrician air about his handsome features.

The attorney gave her an appreciative glance and a nod as he passed, then stiffened and cocked his head when she called after him, "Mr. Rainy?"

The attorney pivoted and glared at her. "You're not serving me, are you?"

"No, sir. Do I look like a server?"

"One I used to know. In a way. You kind of stand like her. Who are you?"

"My name is Bree Stone," she said. "I work for—"

Several men in business suits left the gym. Rainy took a few steps toward her, glanced at them, smiling, and hissed to her softly after they'd moved on, "I know who you work for, Ms. Stone. What are you doing here?"

"Tying up loose ends," Bree said.

He gazed at her a moment, the barest of practiced smiles on his lips. "I told Elena that, given the terrible events in New York, we considered the private investigation complete. Let the police take it from here."

"You know I used to be police," Bree said.

"But you are no longer. You are a gun for hire. I hired you. You did your job. Events overtook things, resolved them. Now your job is done."

"*Is* everything resolved? Frances Duchaine is still alive."

"So she is," Rainy said.

"She claims she knew nothing about the sex trafficking."

The attorney wiggled his fingers while raising his hand dramatically. "Maybe she doesn't. Maybe she does. My client and I are sure, however, that our involvement is no longer needed. As I said, the police will take it from here."

Bree studied him. "What about going to *Sixty Minutes*?"

"What would be the point now? Whatever the truth is, it will come out in court. And, seeing that, my client has decided it would be in her best interest to keep her family's name out of it if possible."

"Why's that?"

Rainy's practiced smile disappeared. "Because the loss of her grandchild's life is enough pain. She doesn't have to drag the girl's memory through the mud if it isn't necessary. Are we done, Ms. Stone? I have an appointment."

"Just one more thing," Bree said. "How did you come to hire Bluestone and why did you ask for me in particular to work the case?"

For the first time, the attorney looked the slightest bit flustered. "Did I?"

"According to Elena."

"I don't know. I must have seen Bluestone and then your bio."

"We don't post bios."

"Google, then. I don't know."

"No outside referral?"

"No. Not that I recall."

"Not even from your client?"

The practiced smile returned to Rainy's lips. "I don't remember it that way, and in any case, that information would be privileged. Good day, Ms. Stone. Have a nice flight home. And give my best to Elena."

With that, the attorney pivoted again and strolled quickly off. She watched him until he'd rounded the corner and was out of sight.

For a moment, Bree thought of taking his advice and heading to the airport and a plane home. But given that she'd taken the time and spent the money to come all the way to Cleveland, she felt she should leave no stone unturned before her departure.

CHAPTER

63

Hunting Valley, Ohio

THE RICH ARE VERY *different from you and me,* Bree thought when, through a glen of budding hardwood trees, she caught sight of a sprawling mansion on a grassy knoll. She drove past the gate and around the perimeter of the twelve-acre estate off the Chagrin River Road, glimpsing a tennis court and then a pool still covered for winter.

Her cell rang. Elena Martin.

"Boss," Bree said.

"Explain why you are in Cleveland."

"Gerald Rainy called you."

"Uh-huh. And he was pissed."

"Can't help that, I'm afraid."

"Bree, he pulled the plug on us yesterday. I told you that."

"I know. After a mass murder that occurred after I wrote a report."

Martin paused, then said, "Meaning what?"

"Meaning that until I understand exactly how I'm involved with a billionaire and a fashion icon and eleven dead people, I am still looking into this case. On my own dime and my own time."

After a longer pause, her boss said, "I can understand that. But be discreet, Bree. Tread lightly. People with that kind of money can be terribly dangerous if provoked."

Elena hung up. Through a hedge of rhododendrons, Bree spotted the roof of a greenhouse and decided she had to take the chance.

On the plane, she'd read an article in *Architectural Digest* about Theresa May Alcott's renovation of her Hunting Valley home and a piece in *Better Homes and Gardens* featuring her Wyoming ranch house. According to the second article, Alcott was a die-hard horsewoman out west. According to the first article, she spent an equal amount of time tending her gardens back east.

"Gardening in Jackson is like doing combat with the elements," Mrs. Alcott was quoted as saying. "And you nearly always lose. If I want to see something grow out of the ground under my care, I retreat to my gardens in the humidity of Ohio."

Hunting Valley was one of the six wealthiest towns in the United States, a quiet, wooded village that billionaires and society matrons called home. Bree knew that leaving a rental car behind the property of one of the richest women in America was bound to attract attention.

Have to accept it, she thought, and pulled off the road by a thick grove of pine trees. She put on a tiny but sensitive Bluetooth microphone disguised as a small ebony carving hanging from a thin gold chain around her neck and connected it to her cell phone and a voice-activated recording app.

Bree tested the connection, then got out, crossed the street, and pushed through the rhododendrons. She emerged onto a wide lawn that felt like plush carpet beneath her feet and crossed to a wooden archway that led to a high-fenced garden that covered more than an acre.

Moving beneath the archway, she noticed the posts of it were wrapped in greening clematis vines, a few tentacles budding already. The walkway of crushed gray slate through the garden was bordered by five rows of raised beds on either side.

The rich soil in the far beds looked recently turned over and ready to be planted. In the near boxes, the annual flowers were already thriving. In another one, tulips and daffodils bloomed in full riot.

But Bree saw no sign of Theresa May Alcott anywhere in the garden. She caught movement in the greenhouse and walked to the door. Inside, a woman in her late sixties worked at a potting bench. She was tall, feline, with long pewter-colored hair in a braid, a classic beauty that put Bree in mind of the country star Emmylou Harris.

A big Polynesian guy was working beside her. He saw Bree, came up with a pistol, and walked toward her fast. "Who are you? What are you doing here? You do not have permission to be here."

Bree held up her hands but before she could identify herself and apologize for the intrusion, Theresa May Alcott said, "It's all right, Arthur." She gazed at him and then Bree. "You have exceeded my expectations, Chief Stone," Alcott said. "I predicted a phone call or a knock at my front door, not a barging into my greenhouse." The billionaire laughed. "But then I guess you are a barging-in kind of person, aren't you?"

Bree wanted not to like her, for some reason. But Alcott's smile and laugh were genuine and contagious.

"I guess I am," Bree said. "All elbows and knees."

64

IT TOOK THOMAS TULL an hour working with an FBI computer technician in a van outside the Kane crime scene, but using his cell phone and car GPS data, the writer began to convince us of where he'd gone after we'd lost him at the north end of Rock Creek Parkway the evening before.

Tull's data showed him bailing left off Cathedral Avenue and taking a quick right with his headlights off, which explained how he'd lost me and Sampson. From there, he'd zigzagged northwest through Chevy Chase back to Bethesda and close to Potomac, but he'd never come within six miles of the Kane home.

According to the data, at nine p.m., Tull was parking at an upscale Chinese restaurant in Bethesda. He used a phone app to pay for dinner a few minutes later.

"That was a quick eat," I said.

"Takeout," the writer said.

"But you didn't get back in the car for almost an hour," Sampson said. "What did you do? Go for a walk? Eat outside? Meet someone?"

Tull reacted awkwardly, then nodded. "I met someone. We ate outside."

"Who was that?"

After another awkward moment, he said, "Suzanne Liu. My former editor."

"Who you threatened with violence," I said.

"Who I promised financial repercussions if she continued to spread lies about me."

The writer said that the editor had messaged him earlier in the day, apologizing for her behavior and inviting him to meet her before she returned to New York.

"She said she wasn't angry anymore, but she had things to say to find closure," Tull said. "She told me she was going to change professions and work as a literary agent. She said she'd managed to find perspective and move on in the past few days, but deep down she loved me, and that had clouded her reactions to losing me as a writer and then losing her job."

Sampson said, "She'll back you up on all that?"

"Maybe not all of it. Women can be touchy about love. But the gist of it, I'm sure."

"Take us through the rest of your evening," I said.

"We hugged goodbye. She tried for a kiss, but I shut her down. She smiled, tears on her cheeks. And then she was gone. I took the leftover kung pao and drove home."

GPS data from the Audi and from his phone showed him back at his Georgetown rental at a little before eleven. The rest of the evening and until eight thirty the next morning, after he learned of the Kane killings, the Audi never moved.

Tull's phone was also largely stationary from eleven p.m. to eight thirty a.m.

Sampson leaned over and tapped the computer screen, said, "Except for this hour and twenty minutes, from two ten to three thirty. When the Kanes were killed."

"Wait, what?" Tull said, agitated and coming around behind the computer tech. "Show me moving. I defy you to show me moving anywhere."

"Not moving," the tech said. "Just not generating data between your phone, the cell tower, and the satellite. It was dead."

"You could have turned your electronics off," I said. "It's a stretch to make it from Georgetown to the Kanes and back in that time frame, but doable."

"Except I didn't do anything but sleep," the writer protested. "There must be a record of my phone turning off, right? Show me where it turns off and on."

The computer tech typed on his laptop. He looked at us. "You got me there. The phone was on the entire time, just not transmitting or receiving data."

"Is that possible in this day and age?" Mahoney said.

"If the cell tower or the satellite went down, sure, it could look like this."

"Perfect," Tull said. "Call Verizon. That's my carrier."

"We will," Sampson said. "Count on it."

"In the meantime, am I in or out of this investigation?" the writer asked me, John, and Ned.

"As far as the FBI is concerned, you are out," Mahoney said.

Tull looked like he wanted to argue but said, "Fine, I'm out for the time being. Am I free to go home and get some work done? You've got my phone and car signals. They're not electronic ankle bracelets, but then again, I'm not going anywhere."

Ned glanced at me and Sampson. I said, "We do know where to find him."

"Thank you, Dr. Cross," he said sourly. "Appreciate the support." He plucked his phone and car keys off the tech's bench, saying, "It would be easier if we cooperated, you know. I've written three books and worked with multiple police agencies, and this is the most static I have ever encountered."

I said, "We tend to keep people at arm's length until letting them in is warranted."

Tull paused at the rear of the van. "Suit yourself. I'll write the book one way or another."

With that, he jumped down and was gone. A few moments later, we heard the RS 7 fire up with a low-throated rumble and roar off.

Mahoney looked at me and Sampson. "What do you think? Is he our guy?"

I said, "I'm leaning that way, but let me call the folks at Paladin."

"Why?" John asked.

"In the data dumps from around every prior Family Man crime scene, the analysts at Paladin found localized blackouts of all digital information."

Mahoney said, "But Tull's blackout was not around the crime scene."

"I know," I said. "I'm interested in seeing if it happened other times around Tull's place in the past month or so."

"Preferably close to the times of death."

"Exactly," I said. "And if anyone can figure that out, it's Ryan Malcomb and his team at Paladin."

65

Hunting Valley, Ohio

THERESA MAY ALCOTT REMOVED the gardening apron she wore, went to a sink, and washed her hands.

"Can you finish up for me, Arthur?" she asked. "I'm going up to the house with Chief Stone for a cup of tea. Shall I send some down for you?"

Arthur was still regarding Bree suspiciously, but he nodded. "Tea would be nice. And don't worry, I'll have everything ready to put in the ground come morning."

"Seven sharp. I have meetings from nine on."

"Seven sharp, Terri."

Bree followed her out of the greenhouse and listened as Alcott chanted out the vegetables and herbs that would be "accepted into the ground" the following morning.

"How do you eat it all?" Bree asked.

Alcott led her out of the garden and up a short rise to the

house. "What we don't eat is donated to multiple food banks and school-lunch programs in the Cleveland area. Nothing goes to waste. And everything's organic."

"Was this always an interest of yours? Gardening?"

"My mother was a gardener, but I hated it as a girl. It was only over time that I came to appreciate the power and fulfillment of helping to nurture something to life." The billionaire said it was similar to her cattle ranch outside Jackson. "The ranch was my late husband's passion," she said, opening a rear door to the house. "He made me see the beauty in being part of the greater food cycle."

They entered a mudroom, where Alcott kicked off her rubber boots. Bree slipped off her sneakers and padded after her down a short hallway that emerged into a beautiful, immaculate, yellow-and-white kitchen.

A woman in her forties sat at the table. She put down her *People* magazine. "Terri?"

"Tea, please, Marie. In the office?"

"Coming up."

Alcott motioned for Bree to follow her down another short hall to an expansive office. The desk was huge and cluttered. Several computer screens glowed on and behind it.

"My reckless command center," Alcott said.

"Looks like you have a lot on your plate."

Alcott smiled and pointed her to one of two overstuffed chairs flanking a small cocktail table. "You have no idea."

"You're probably right."

The billionaire took the other chair, sighed. "You must think me cut off from the realities of life."

"Not at all, Mrs. Alcott. You seem surprisingly genuine."

"Call me Terri, and bless you for that. It took years in therapy and more than a few monthlong retreats in India after Gil—my husband—died for me to get to this point."

She chuckled wistfully. "And now to your loose ends," she said, sobering. "What has brought you to my greenhouse door, Chief Stone?"

"Tell me about your granddaughter."

Alcott's face fell. "Olivia. Olivia May. My younger daughter's second child."

The older woman proceeded to tell a story similar to the others Bree had heard: Duchaine scouts luring seventeen-year-old Olivia into a trap. The promises of fame. The excitement of moving to New York. The rejection. The plastic surgeries. The mounting debt. The sex trafficking.

"All the things you described in your report," Alcott said. "Olivia could have come to her mother or me for money. But by then, shame had set in and she was using drugs. When we found out what was happening, she could not face us. She intentionally overdosed, leaving us a letter that described her ordeal."

Marie came into the room carrying a tea service and a basket of cookies. When she'd gone and Bree had had a sip of tea, she said, "So you hired Bluestone and me to investigate at that point?"

"You were the second firm hired to investigate Olivia's death. The first dug up what was given to you when they reached a dead end."

"Why us? Your attorney indicated you had some sort of recommendation?"

CHAPTER

66

BREE HAD BLUFFED ABOUT the recommendation. Alcott seemed confused and looked into the middle distance.

"Yes," she said slowly. "That's right, from a small company I've invested in. Bluestone evidently worked on their internal security setup when they started doing some projects for the government."

Bree had not expected that, and Bluestone did do government IT security-compliance work. Quite a bit of it, in fact. She decided to move in another direction. "After you read my report, what was your reaction?"

Bree watched the older woman think back, her eyes softening a few seconds before sharpening. "I could not believe it was happening on that kind of scale."

"Did it make you angry?"

"Weren't you? Writing that report? I felt it."

"I was. I am."

"There you are, then," the billionaire said. "I was angry. Infuriated. Appalled."

"When did you hear about the killings at Paula Watkins's home?"

"The morning after, I believe. On the news."

"And what was your reaction to the murders?"

Alcott thought about that. "To be honest, I was horrified for maybe ten seconds, but then, as the names of the dead and their reputations came out, I felt less so."

"You didn't feel deprived of a chance to expose them, to get revenge?"

She curled her upper lip. "I admit that's been a bitter pill to swallow. But now I ask myself, what good is revenge? Will that bring back Olivia? No. Will it hurt my daughter Anna, Olivia's mother? Yes. And so, it is enough now. I can see that some kind of cosmic justice has been done. Powers greater than yours or mine were at play. And it is enough."

Bree said, "You won't go to the journalists with the evidence I dug up?"

"Again, will that bring back my granddaughter? The media will get its meat when Frances Duchaine goes on trial."

"She claims she's innocent."

Alcott turned colder. "So did Saddam Hussein."

A phone on the desk rang before Bree could respond.

"Can you hold on a moment?" the billionaire asked. "I rarely get calls on the landlines anymore." Alcott got up and went to her desk, picked up the receiver, and punched a button. "This is Terri."

She listened closely and then smiled, said, "Give me a minute, will you, Emma, dear? I'm with someone and I'll need to pick up in another room."

Alcott hit the Hold button and hung up. "I am sorry, Chief Stone. This won't take long, but it can't wait."

"Please. Take your time."

The older woman hurried from the room, closing the office door behind her. Bree got up and walked around, looking at the books and framed pictures on the shelves. Many featured Theresa May Alcott with her husband, Gil, at various places around the world. In others, the couple posed with various famous people: Presidents Bill Clinton, George W. Bush, and Barack Obama; LeBron James and Phil Mickelson; Meryl Streep, Denzel Washington, and Robert Redford. Jerry Lewis was featured in at least three of them.

The credenza behind Alcott's desk was crowded with photographs of large family gatherings, many taken with the Grand Tetons towering behind them. In each, you could see the family growing, evolving, the older generation gradually disappearing and the new gaining ground.

The most recent of those pictures showed the family and Alcott without her husband for the first time. Bree thought the widow looked stoic.

She turned and glanced at the messy desktop. One of the buttons on the multiline phone was still lit.

Caller ID was on as well, slowly streaming across the screen:

Paladin...Paladin...Paladin...

67

Washington, DC

"PALADIN," A WOMAN ANSWERED before the phone could ring a second time. "How may I direct your call?"

"Ryan Malcomb, please," I said. "Tell him Dr. Alex Cross needs a favor."

"I will, Dr. Cross. How are you?"

I flashed on the woman who worked at the company's front desk. "Riggs?"

"In the flesh," Riggs said, sounding pleased. "Hold on, Doc."

The line fell into a soft buzz. Several moments later, Riggs came back. "Dr. Cross, I'm afraid Mr. Malcomb's in the middle of a call he can't break. Can Steve Vance help you?"

"That works," I said.

There was a click and Vance came on. "Dr. Cross? How are you?"

"Fine," I said. "How was the Italy trip?"

"Too short. And I'm still a bit jet-lagged."

"I'm calling about something Ryan found in that first big data dump we gave him."

"Okay."

I described how Malcomb and his analysts had determined that cellular and data service had stopped for a brief period in the areas around each of the Family Man's crime scenes.

"We've had another incident and I'd like to see if there was a similar blackout around the Potomac address, which I can e-mail or text you."

"Text works. And since we've already received authorization for the Family Man case from the FBI director's office, I'm sure we can get right on it. Anything else?"

"Same thing around a Georgetown address. Seems like cell and data services were shut down in that area around the same time as the Potomac address." I also asked Paladin to see if there were similar black holes around Tull's rental home at the times of the other Family Man killings.

"Since we've already got the data loaded for those cases, this should go quickly," Vance said. "We'll get back to you ASAP."

"I appreciate it, Steve."

"Anything for law enforcement. And again, sorry I missed you last week."

"Next time."

"I look forward to it, sir," Vance said, and the line went dead.

I pocketed the phone and donned latex gloves, blue booties, and a hairnet before returning to the Kane crime scene. Bodies were being removed in black bags. Dozens of cameras were recording it. Reporters were yelling questions at me, all of which I ignored.

The fact of the matter was that we had no real suspect other than Tull. And I certainly was not going to mention his name to the media. Not without serious corroborating evidence, which, at the moment, we did not have.

Inside the house, the black bags containing the children were brought down the stairs amid a hushed silence. Anger appeared in the faces of every agent, detective, and forensics expert on hand, including me.

Who shoots children like that? Executes them? With no emotion? And why? Goddamn it, why?

I couldn't answer any of those questions and that made me even more frustrated.

"I feel like there's something we're missing," I told Sampson and Mahoney after the bodies of the Kane children had been taken outside. Before they could respond, Lara Mendelson, the FBI crime scene supervisor, came down the stairs. She held a small plastic evidence bag.

"We found these light brown hairs in the nap of the carpet on the landing," she said. "The Kanes all had black hair."

Sampson said, "Could belong to a friend? Their maid? Mrs. Kane's mother?"

"She has gray hair," Mahoney said. He returned his attention to the crime scene tech. "Thanks, Lara, let's get these out to Quantico for DNA analysis ASAP."

Mendelson nodded and went outside.

"What's the chance he's finally made a mistake?" I said, watching her go.

"Been sterile up to now," Sampson said. "But there's bound to be something at some point that will go in our favor."

Mahoney said, "Who knows? Maybe he had an itchy scalp and pulled back his hood to scratch it before he coldly executed a young family of four."

"Stranger things have put people behind bars," I said.

68

Hunting Valley, Ohio

BREE RETURNED TO HER seat in Theresa May Alcott's office when the light on the phone went out and the caller ID streaming on the screen ended.

Paladin. Is that someone's name? Or is it that data-mining company Alex has working on the Family Man cases?

The door opened and Alcott rushed in. "I'm sorry, Chief Stone, but I am informed that I have much to attend to in the next couple of hours. Have I answered all your questions? Do you understand why I wanted to keep Olivia's name out of it if I could?"

Bree wanted to ask a few more questions but she got to her feet and tried to be gracious. "Of course I understand. If there are other examples that can be used, why sully Olivia's reputation unnecessarily?"

The billionaire beamed with gratitude. "Bless you and thank you, Chief Stone. Where did you park your car?"

"Uh, on the road behind your house."

"On the lane beyond the back hedge?"

"Yes."

"Oh, dear. I hope it's there when you return. The local constable is quite zealous about towing away cars that are parked there."

"I'll be going, then."

Alcott stood aside.

Bree smiled and walked back down the short hall and through the kitchen, where Marie was listening to music and rinsing dishes. Before exiting, she glanced over her shoulder, saw Alcott standing at her office window, and waved. The billionaire smiled impatiently and returned the gesture.

It had started to drizzle. Bree hurried down the hill and past the garden, noticing Arthur standing in the door to the greenhouse, watching her go. Crossing the lawn toward the hedge, she fought the urge to look back and study the windows of the house to see if Theresa May Alcott was still watching her. But then it began to rain in earnest, and she ran to the hedge and found a way through onto the road. To her relief, her rental car was still there on the opposite shoulder, undisturbed.

After getting inside, starting the car, and cranking up the heat, Bree got out her phone, checked the forty-two-minute-long recording, and found much of it audible thanks to the little microphone necklace. Then she checked the time of the next flight to DC. Three hours.

After confirming a seat, she got out a notebook and started scribbling down her impressions, details she wanted to remember about her visit to the Alcott estate, certain things the billionaire had said to her, and questions she wanted answered. She would check it all against the recording later.

TMA is smooth, Bree wrote. *Polished. Pleasant, but hard to read. How old is she?*

Why did it feel a little creepy when I left? Like I was being watched?

Who is Arthur?

If the Paladin on her phone is the company Alex is dealing with, what is TMA's connection? Seems so random. Is it important?

Who was she talking to at the company? Who is Emma? Or do I have it wrong? Was she talking to Emma Paladin?

Sitting there as the rain beat down on the car roof, Bree did a series of internet searches on her phone based on the notes and questions she'd just written down. Within fifteen minutes, she found articles and filings that changed her view of Theresa May Alcott and her decision to hire Bree to investigate Frances Duchaine.

She put the rental car in gear and headed toward the Cleveland Airport, thinking, *Paladin may matter in this. But who is Emma?*

CHAPTER

69

Potomac, Maryland

WE SPENT SEVEN HOURS in total at the Kane family crime scene, watching as FBI forensic techs swarmed through the house, finding the four deadly slugs embedded in the floors and identifying where and how the killer had hacked the security system using override wires that were still in place.

We also helped canvass the neighborhood, which did us little good. The Kanes' house sat on seven wooded acres. So did the other nine houses in the area.

It was the kind of neighborhood where people valued isolation. Several of the neighbors had not yet met the Kanes, who'd moved in two years before.

Mahoney went to the Kanes' business to interview employees. Sampson and I took another course, trying to make some connection between the Kanes and the four other families executed in cold blood since the attacks began.

Using John's computer in the squad room at DC Metro PD, we tried common-word searches among the files, including schools attended, employment records, current and prior residences, ethnicities, religions, socioeconomic standards, even extended family trees. Then we mapped the killings, looking for overlapping travel routes the killer might have taken to and from the attacks.

But other than proximity to the Beltway—the band of freeways that loop the nation's capital—the attack sites appeared unrelated. Try as we might, we could not find the pattern, the motive, or the logic behind the killings. If there was a commonality among the victims, we weren't seeing it, and neither were our computers.

"Maybe that's the point," I said around six that evening.

"What is?"

"The randomness of the targets, the cold-bloodedness of the executions, the meticulousness of the killer," I said.

"Designed to throw us," Sampson said. "So we'll focus on his behavior instead?"

"That's right, though I'm too burned out at the moment to see how, and I have to get to National. Bree texted that she's coming in at seven."

"Then I'm on my way home too," Sampson said. "Willow and I are getting fried clams and French fries for dinner."

"Still running in the morning?"

"Every day." Sampson laughed and rubbed his lean belly. He headed outside to grab an Uber. I went to the garage and got the Jeep.

My cell phone rang as I exited the parking garage. I hit Answer on the Cherokee's navigation screen, turned into traffic, and said, "This is Alex Cross."

"Dr. Cross, it's Ryan Malcomb. How are you?"

"Stuck in traffic. You?"

"In possession of interesting ore, fresh from the mines."

"Already?"

"Frankly, you were lucky, Dr. Cross. As Steve may have told you, we had that first data loaded already. Your new request was merely a matter of changing filters."

"And what did you find?"

"Your instincts were correct. There was a cellular and data blackout around Thomas Tull's Georgetown address at roughly the same time another occurred in the Kanes' neighborhood."

"What about during the other family killings? Was Tull's place blacked out then?"

"No."

"No?" I said, disappointed because I was sure this blackout stuff was big, though I could not put my finger on why.

"Negative, correct," Malcomb said.

Traffic started to move, and I was soon crossing the Fourteenth Street Bridge toward Virginia and the airport. "How about his phone's GPS or his car's? Did you find data that put him in the vicinity of any of the killings?"

He sighed. "Afraid not. At the time of the first two attacks, he was in New York. The third time he was in Maine. The last two he was in DC, but his phone and car were nowhere near the victims at the time of their murders."

"Huh," I said. "What about a car we don't know about and a burner phone?"

"That's a different story," Malcomb said. "But we search for what we can't identify, if that makes any sense."

"It would help you to know more about the car or the burner going in."

"Exactly. Uh, sorry, Dr. Cross, but I have another call coming in. My…girlfriend."

"I make it a rule not to get between a man and his girlfriend. Thank you, Ryan, and have a nice evening."

Malcomb was chuckling. "You as well, and your wife and the entire family."

During the twelve minutes it took to reach the exit for Reagan National Airport, I kept thinking about the digital blackouts that had been engineered around every crime scene and, once, around Tull's house.

But why wasn't Tull blacked out every time? I had no answer, so I flipped the question. *Why was Tull's place blacked out just this one time?*

Immediately, I thought: *Because Tull sensed we were surveilling him. Then he covered himself in a cloak of cellular and data invisibility so we wouldn't know he'd left his home in the middle of the night.*

Maybe. But that didn't feel entirely right either.

Rain started to fall as I drove to passenger pickup and spotted Bree waving. She climbed in. We kissed and I pulled out.

"Productive trip?" I asked.

"Uh, yes," she said. "Absolutely."

When I glanced over at her, I could see her features were tight and she was studying the dash like it held mystic secrets.

"Why do I sense a *but* coming?"

Bree looked over. "I know things that I didn't this morning, but I haven't got them all straight in my mind yet. How they fit, I mean."

"I'm feeling kind of the same way," I said. "I'm sensing things in the Family Man case, but I've got nothing solid to back them up yet."

"*Yet.* That's the word we have to hold on to. *Yet.*"

I got us heading toward DC. "Did you talk to the attorney and the rich woman who hired you and Bluestone?"

"Both of them," Bree said. "But first, tell me about that data-mining company you've been working with."

"Paladin?"

She nodded. "Theresa May Alcott and her husband were some of the original investors in that company. They did it quietly, but I found the SEC filings online."

"She must know Ryan Malcomb, then. He's one of the founders. The brain behind the algorithms. An interesting, creative guy."

"Alcott is Malcomb's maternal aunt. She adopted him and his twin brother, Sean, after their mother—Alcott's sister—and father were murdered in a home invasion. The boys were nine. The killers were never caught."

"Jesus. I didn't know that. He's had a tough life, then. Did I tell you he was stricken with muscular dystrophy as a teenager?"

"No," Bree said. "But it makes sense. In her office, there are pictures of her and her husband with Jerry Lewis."

WE PULLED UP IN front of our house, still talking about the coincidence of Ryan Malcomb, the founder of Paladin, being Theresa May Alcott's nephew.

"What are you thinking?" I asked, climbing out.

"God, I don't know," Bree said, following me. "I just think it's odd that our two cases intersect with the presence of Paladin."

"It is odd," I said as we climbed the stairs to the porch. "I'll bring it up the next time I talk to Malcomb."

Our house was filled with wonderful aromas, all wafting from the kitchen. Ali and Jannie were watching a basketball game in the front room.

"Hey, guys," I said.

Ali twisted in his seat. "It's Atlanta versus Houston in the semifinals."

"Good game?"

Jannie nodded, taking her eyes off the screen. "Tied starting the second half."

"That's fun."

Bree said, "I'm starving."

"I am too," I said.

Jannie moaned. "It's so good. I don't know where Nana comes up with these dishes, but it's one of her best lately."

Ali said, "Chicken slow-cooked with onions, sweet potatoes, green olives, and some sauce she just invented!"

"On my way," Bree said and hustled toward the kitchen with me in tow.

My grandmother was in the great room beyond the kitchen, reading a book with oversize print.

"We've heard dinner is another original masterpiece, Nana Mama," I said, going straight to the lidded yellow ceramic casserole dish.

"Not all original," she said, putting her book down and struggling to get up. "I modified something I saw in one of my magazines the other day. There's rice in there too. And more hot sauce in the fridge if you want it."

Nana held her hip and limped toward us, looking frailer and more tired than I'd seen her in a long time.

Bree picked up on it as well. "Are you feeling okay, Nana?"

My grandmother said, "Just getting old. My sciatica's acting up."

"Well, sit down," I said. "We can get the food for ourselves."

"Sitting down is half the problem, my doctor says," Nana replied with a laugh and a flip of her hand. "I'll just go have Jannie help me stretch again while you eat."

The way she was moving had me concerned enough that I

made sure she did go out and have Jannie help her with her stretches before I started eating.

The dish was a masterpiece. The chicken practically fell off the bone. The green olives had become part of the sauce, which tasted a little sweet at first before the hint of fire crossed the lips and lit up the tongue.

Nana Mama came back into the kitchen after her stretches, moving much better. Bree moaned. "How did you get that sweet and hot taste in the sauce? It was so good!"

"Blackstrap molasses and cayenne pepper," Nana said, pleased. "Glad you liked it. Now that my back's feeling a bit better, I'm going up to my room to read a little more before I turn in. Can I leave the dishes for you?"

"Of course," I said, getting up to hug her. "Thank you for taking good care of us, old lady."

"It's an old lady's pleasure." She laughed. "And her purpose."

71

AFTER WE'D CLEANED THE dishes and put away the leftovers, Bree and I watched some of the game with Ali and Jannie. But then Atlanta pulled away and was up eighteen points in the middle of the fourth quarter.

Bree, drowsing on my shoulder, said, "I'm zonked. It's bedtime for this girl."

"I'm not long behind you," I said.

"Good night," Bree said; she kissed me and went up the stairs.

I yawned when the game ended and the kids went up to bed, but I knew I was still far too wound up to sleep. As I often did when I felt like this, I climbed up to my little attic office.

It had low ceilings and looked like a hoarder's paradise, but my best thinking took place in the old chair behind an older desk or on the ancient couch.

I'd no sooner sat down than my phone rang. "Suzanne Liu?" I groaned, seeing the caller ID. "I'm not taking this."

I thumbed Decline. Almost a minute later, the phone beeped to alert me to a voice mail. I ignored it.

Then the texting started. Seven messages, and all long. I scanned the first one, then read it and the six after it closely.

In each of the texts, Liu raised issues with the way Tull had written his second book, pointing out blatant errors and false statements. The editor finished by imploring me not to exclude the writer as a suspect in the murders.

Things are not as they seem, she wrote. Not with Thomas Tull, Dr. Cross.

I sighed. On the corner of my desk in a neat stack were Thomas Tull's three books. I picked up the only book of his I had not looked at in depth, *Noon in Berlin*.

Like the others, the writing pulled the reader in and did not let go. I think I'd read twenty pages before I picked my head up, realizing I'd been utterly fascinated with his description of the victims meeting for a noontime tryst at an apartment near the Tiergarten in Berlin only to be murdered while they made love, both struck with darts that contained powerful animal tranquilizers, enough to stop their hearts in seconds.

From there, Tull jumped to the point of view of Inspector Ava Firsching of the Berlin police, the female detective that the writer had gotten involved with on this case. As Tull depicted her, Firsching was in her early thirties, tough, dedicated, and in the midst of what would be the case of her career.

I read another two chapters and came across another name: Hauptkommissar Horst Martel. Tull portrayed Martel as Firsching's foil inside the department, a strictly by-the-book cop, too rigid to try creative ways to deal with the string of lovers being murdered at noon in the German capital.

I looked at my watch. It was nearly midnight in DC, nearly eight in the morning in Berlin.

On a whim, I Googled the phone number of the Berlin City Police and found it and something better, the number for the major-crimes unit. I called it and was not surprised that it was answered. Eight o'clock in the morning, cops answer. Later, when things get hectic or nuts, sometimes they don't.

Luckily, the detective I got spoke English, but he said he was sorry to inform me that Hauptkommissar Martel had retired the year before. When I asked where Martel had retired to, he said he thought he was still in Berlin.

It took me about ten more minutes to find a Horst Martel living in the Kreuzberg section of the German capital. A woman picked up on the third ring.

"Do you speak English?" I asked.

"Yes, of course," she said.

"My name is Alex Cross," I said. "I work as a psychological and investigative consultant to the FBI and the Washington, DC, police department. Is Horst Martel in? I would like to talk with him about a case I'm working on."

"Horst is retired," she said.

"I know," I said. "It's about a case he worked on. It became a book."

Noon in Berlin," she said sourly.

"That's right. I'd like to talk to him about it. Well, about Thomas Tull, really."

The line went silent.

CHAPTER

72

"HELLO?" I SAID AND was about to hang up when I heard muffled voices in the background. She had not hung up, just put the phone down.

A few moments later, I heard someone pick up the phone. In heavily accented English and with a suspicious tone, a man said, "I am Horst Martel. Who are you?"

I identified myself again and said, "If you're doubting my standing with the FBI or the Washington, DC, Metropolitan Police, Herr Martel, I can get my liaisons to call and vouch for me."

"Not necessary, Dr. Cross," Martel said. "My wife just Googled you. What do you want to know about Thomas Tull? And for what reasons?"

For the next ten minutes, I described the Family Man

murders. I told him that Tull was writing about the case and, largely due to his former editor, was also a suspect.

"*Ja, ja*, of course he is a suspect," said the former Berlin police inspector. "That is his pattern, I think. Well, I know here that was also true."

"Wait," I said. "You suspected Thomas Tull in the noontime murders?"

"*Ja, ja*," Martel said. "He was already in Berlin when the first killings occurred. Not far from where it happened."

Was that in the book? I didn't think so. I thought he'd written that the first murders took place before his arrival in Berlin. "Why did you consider him a suspect?"

"Because he tried to—how do you say it—insert himself into the investigation within two days of the first murders."

I was frowning so hard, my eyebrows hurt. That was definitely not in the book. In fact, he'd kept himself completely out of the narrative in the pages I'd read. "Let me understand," I said. "Tull decided to follow the case within forty-eight hours of the first murders?"

"Correct," Martel said. "He, uh—how do I say it?—claimed he had the extrasensory perception that the case might be important. You know, the feeling in the stomach?"

"I know that feeling."

"I had this same feeling about Tull. From the beginning, he made me feel this way, even after we cleared him."

"He had an alibi?"

"Cell phone records that showed him in another part of the city at noon," the retired police commissioner said. "And time-stamped credit card receipts."

I thought about the fact that Tull had used his cell phone data to prove he was nowhere near the Kane house the night that family was murdered. Was it a coincidence? Or was Tull gaming the system somehow?

Get away with it once, you'll definitely try again.

"So you let him into the investigation?" I asked.

A little bitterly, Martel said, "I was against it because we could not find CCTV footage of him to absolutely corroborate his whereabouts at the time of the killings. But my superiors said he was in a park having a beer, not many cameras, and they knew of his previous book and thought it might reflect well on the Berlin police department to have someone of Herr Tull's, uh, reputation to tell the story."

"Did Tull eventually solve the killings?"

He snorted. "Thomas Tull? No."

"The way he writes it, Ava Firsching decides on her own to go back to the zoo to look at vendors."

"You will have to ask her, but we were going back and looking at a lot of the evidence by then. The zoo would have been studied again by someone."

"What about the guy you ended up catching?"

"Dietrich Frommer."

"Any doubt it's him?"

"None."

"Could he have been framed?"

The retired police inspector made a dismissive noise in his throat. "Frommer believes so, but the evidence says it is him. Frommer had supplies of the tranquilizer. He knew the first woman to die from the gym where he exercised, Gerta Waldemar."

"Didn't you find the dart gun?" I asked.

"In a crawl space under his home, wiped clean. He claimed he had never seen the weapon before in his life."

"You said the evidence says it is Frommer. What does the sick feeling in your stomach say?"

Martel paused for several moments. "That if Frommer is telling the truth, Tull was somehow involved. At the very least, I feel Tull was pushing the investigation in directions he wanted it to go from very early on."

"Through his relationship with Inspector Firsching."

"*Ja, ja,*" he said and chuckled. "Tull left Ava the day after Frommer was convicted, and still she defends him every chance she gets. Tull will do the same with you this time. Has he become sleeping partners with anyone on the case yet?"

"Not to my knowledge."

"This is surprising," the retired commissioner said. "But give him time and—"

I could hear a woman talking in the background.

"*Ja, ja,*" he said. "I am sorry, Dr. Cross, but my wife reminds me I must go to the dentist. Can I give you my e-mail? You'll tell me what you find out about Tull?"

"I will," I said.

73

AFTER MY LATE-NIGHT conversation with retired Hauptkommissar Martel, I tried to read more of *Noon in Berlin,* but I soon got drowsy and stumbled over to the old couch to shut my eyes.

Less than two hours later, when I was dead asleep, my cell phone started ringing and buzzing. It startled me awake; I had no idea where I was for several seconds, then I stumbled to my phone on the desk.

"Cross," I said.

"Sampson's on the line as well," Mahoney said. "I'm in Baltimore and can't get there fast. But Family Man has made a mistake. We got a report from a residential security company that a silent alarm has gone off in the home of the Allison family in Falls Church, near Lake Barcroft. There is an intruder in the house as we speak. He is armed and wearing night-vision goggles."

"How do you know that? Where's the family?"

"In a safe room," Mahoney said. "They're watching the son of a bitch on a closed-circuit system."

"Get police there. And a chopper overhead. Surround the place. I'm on my way."

"Already gone," Sampson said.

I bolted out of the attic and down the stairs; grabbed my coat, service weapon, and the keys to the car. I put the address into my Waze app. Metro had given me a bubble that I could use in rare circumstances. This felt like one of those times, so I rolled down the window and slapped it on the roof.

It was two thirty-five in the morning when I squealed away from my house. With the early hour and the bubble, which let me run the red lights, I set some kind of land-speed record between Southeast DC and the wooded Lake Barcroft area, where I spotted a Fairfax County sheriff's cruiser parked sideways across the mouth of Dockser Terrace, its lights dark.

I pulled over behind him and got out, holding up my IDs and credentials. "FBI and DC Metro," I said. "When did you arrive, Deputy..."

"Conrad, and not five minutes ago, sir."

"Are we in contact with the family?"

"Yes, sir. I mean, I think so, sir."

"Let me talk to your dispatch."

He handed me a walkie-talkie. I took it and called for dispatch. A woman named Helena Rodriguez came on. I identified myself and asked about communications with the family.

"I was talking to Mr. Allison until four minutes ago, when his comm cut out."

Sampson pulled up and jumped from his car.

"I'm borrowing your radio, Deputy," I said. I looked at John. "We've lost contact with the family."

We both started to run toward the Allisons' house, which was on the left side of the road where Dockser Terrace split and looped back on itself.

"No way out of here in a car," Sampson said.

"Do you have eyes overhead?" I barked into the radio.

"Negative, Dr. Cross," Rodriguez said. "It's refueling. Two minutes to takeoff. Six minutes to you."

That made us run faster.

"I need two uniforms in the trees watching the back of the Allisons' house. Have them come in through the woods from the far side of the loop."

"Roger that."

We were less than two hundred yards from the Allisons' home by then, a big gray Colonial set back among pines and oaks. Even in the moonlight, it was one of the bigger structures in the neighborhood. The lights were off outside and in.

I slowed and stopped at the bottom of the driveway, gasping. "He's in there, John. He may have found the family already."

"How would he get into a safe room?" Sampson said, drawing his weapon.

"We're about to find out," I said, drawing mine as well, and we started to move forward, only to stop again.

A middle-aged man came jogging around the corner ahead of us on the opposite side of the street. He wore running pants, a white windbreaker, a headlamp, and a bright green reflective vest over a small knapsack with a water hose coming out of the top. A small red light blinked at his waist. A little dog on a leash ran at his side.

We went at him, guns drawn. The Jack Russell terrier growled.

Seeing us, he stopped and threw up his hands, frightened. "What is this?"

"Metropolitan Police," Sampson said. "Who are you? Why are you here?"

"Tim Boulter. I'm out for a run?"

"At three in the morning?"

"I own a bakery," Boulter said. "This is my six a.m."

"How did you get by the police cruiser blocking the road?" I demanded.

"I didn't see a cruiser. I came on the trail that comes into the far side of Dockser Terrace from closer to the lake. What's happening?"

"Where do you live?"

"Arcadia Road. Two miles from here."

I said, "Go straight to the cruiser behind us and give your contact information to the officer there. Sorry to have interrupted your run."

He nodded uncertainly. The terrier was still growling. "Thank you. What's going on?"

"Just checking a suspicious person seen in the area."

Boulter looked at our guns, nodded again, and turned.

"Hey," Sampson said. "What's the name of your bakery?"

"Sunrise," he said. "We're in the book."

"Go home, Mr. Boulter," I said and turned back toward the Allisons' house.

Boulter broke into a jog. As we started up the driveway, I glanced back, saw the silhouette of him and his dog stopping to talk to the officer blocking the road.

"I say we go inside before the uniforms," Sampson said.

It was somewhat against protocol, but we feared for the Allisons. If the killer had managed to shut down power or

287

communications from the safe room, he could have gotten inside. He could be executing them now or getting ready to.

"Dispatch, do we know the location of the safe room?" I asked.

"Center of the basement, behind the back wall of the wine cellar."

We went to the front door. I tried the knob.

Locked.

We moved fast around the house and found a screened-in side porch. A large piece of screen had been cut and folded down.

"Here we go," I whispered, crawling through on my hands and knees.

The porch had sliding glass doors. One was ajar.

74

THERE'S ALWAYS A SPLIT second of stiffness, of hesitation, before you go through a door seeking someone who's likely to try to kill you.

But then years of training take hold, and the shoulders relax and the mind focuses into an almost hyperalertness, attuned to any movement or sound. Sampson went into the house first, with me hard on his heels and covering our six.

We both turned on Maglite flashlights and held them in our left fists, our pistols braced on top across the backs of our hands. John stepped into a great room that ran the width of the house. We went toward the kitchen, clearing behind the sofas and the floor-length curtains.

We did not have a diagram of the house and were forced to bumble through, trying the lights unsuccessfully after we'd cleared the great room and entered the kitchen. We went to the first door off the kitchen, looking for the staircase to the basement. Sampson slipped up to the right edge of the door frame. He pinned his spine to the wall, gun ready. I pulled the door open.

The pantry. One of two doors at the rear of the kitchen revealed the laundry. When I opened the third door, we saw carpeted stairs dropping into darkness.

Easing down, guns still braced, we dissected every shadow with the powerful flashlights until we reached the floor of a massive basement. There was a small movie theater on the left and a larger game room on the right.

Beyond them, in the center of the basement was a stone wall the height of the room and about twenty feet long. Hallways ran off into the dark on both sides of the wall, which wept, water trickling down the stones into a narrow cache for the fountain.

"I'm guessing the wine cellar's behind that wall."

"Left or right hallway?"

I shone my light to the right over the cream-colored carpet, seeing where it was compressed from use and noticing a red-wine stain.

Around the right corner of the rock wall, we found a heavy whitewashed oak door with a wrought-iron thumb latch. Once again, we operated as if we were in the middle of an intense training session.

The door creaked when I pulled it, revealing a two-door wrought-iron gate with the letter *A* crafted into its face. Beyond it was a terra-cotta tile floor, a tasting table with two chairs, and four walls filled top to bottom with wine bottles.

There had to have been four thousand bottles there, maybe more. But no one was in the wine cellar that we could see, and there was no apparent exit.

Sampson drew up the rod holding the gate into the floor and pushed it open as it made a protesting creak. "This is Detective Sampson of MPD. Mr. Allison? Can you hear me? If you can, please come out."

I stepped in after John and we stood there, listening to the sounds of our breathing and nothing else for several long moments. Then we heard the distinct sounds of steel bars being thrown. A section of the back wall of the wine cellar swung slowly out about twenty degrees and threw flickering soft light into the wine cellar.

Before we saw anyone, we heard a young boy cry, "You were right, Dad! It worked perfect! He had no idea."

"I want to sleep, Mama," a little girl said, coming out from behind the secret door. She was no more than four, with curly blond hair; she was dressed in jammies, holding a blanket, and sucking her thumb.

Seeing us, she turned back against the thigh of the tall, pretty woman in a flannel nightshirt and robe. She sighed and then smiled at us. "Thank you, Detectives. I don't think I have ever been so frightened in my life. Is he still here?"

"He's not here," said a bruiser of a man in a plain white T-shirt, blue gym shorts, and flip-flops. Two identical twin boys about ten exited behind him. He put down the camping lantern he carried and thrust out his hand. "Stan Allison. My wife, Polly. He's gone, right?"

"We haven't cleared the upper floors, sir."

"He's gone," he said. "The creep found the redundant electric line that feeds the safe room and cut it, but I picked him up on a battery-powered pressure sensor leaving through the back door off the kitchen." He looked at his watch. "Nine minutes ago."

"He didn't find the safe room?" Sampson said.

"He had no clue," Allison said and chuckled. "He stood right where you are at one point, and he had zero idea we were eight feet away. I told you it was worth building, Polly."

She sighed and nodded, looking exhausted. "I'm a believer, Stanley."

"We'll get the electric company out here to get your power on," Sampson said.

"I can take care of that," Allison said and tried to bull-doze by us.

"Wait, wait a second, sir," I said. "Our dispatcher said you were watching him on camera. Did you see him?"

"See him?" Allison laughed. "We saw him a lot, recording the whole time, but he only took that hood off the once and then only for two seconds. But I got something."

He dug out his cell phone, thumbed it, and showed it to us.

Family Man was turning away from the camera, which looked diagonally down at him from high up in a kitchen corner. The camera must have caught him repositioning the hood and the night-vision goggles for comfort; he held both with gloved hands an inch above a thick shock of curly, sandy-brown hair.

You could see only an eighth of his face and even that was in considerable shadow. But the image struck me and Sampson the same way.

"Tull," we both said.

75

TWENTY MINUTES LATER, WE left the crime scene to a crew of FBI agents and forensic techs and were racing in our cars back across the Potomac to Georgetown. Sampson and I got there shortly before four a.m.

Mahoney, who had come from Baltimore, was already parked across the street from Tull's rented town house and was climbing from his car. A light shone outside the writer's green front door.

We stood in the empty street.

"Where's the Audi?" Sampson said, gesturing to the parking spot where the writer usually kept his blazing-fast coupe.

"Maybe he's been out for a race along the George Washington Parkway," I said.

"Or a time trial around Lake Barcroft," Sampson said. "Do we have a warrant?"

"It's being reviewed by a grumpy federal judge who isn't very happy with me for waking him up," Mahoney said. "But I think we'll be inside before long."

He'd no sooner uttered those words than we heard the rumble of a powerful engine coming toward us from the north. Headlights slashed the road.

"It's him," Mahoney said, and we all hurried to the other side of the street and the darkest shadows we could find.

Tull came in hot, overshot the parking space, and made a mess of parallel parking. The Audi's front right quarter panel still jutted out a considerable way into the road when he jerked open the door and climbed out.

The writer wavered on his feet a moment, then threw back his thick shock of sandy-brown hair and chortled at some recent memory.

"Someone's been drinking," Sampson said.

"He's hammered," Mahoney agreed and moved at him fast with his badge in one hand and his service pistol in the other. "Mr. Tull. We'd like to talk to you."

Tull made a jerky motion with his head before pivoting, stumbling, and almost face-planting on the street. He peered at us, then shook an index finger at us with glee.

"Gang ish all here," he slurred. "Three Stooges redux."

"Mr. Tull, how much have you had to drink?" Mahoney asked.

"Too much?"

"We're taking you into custody," Sampson said, going for his zip ties. "Turn around, hands behind your back. You know the drill."

Tull gave him a puzzled and scornful look. "Why? I'm right here. I live here. I'm not hurting anyone."

Sampson was having none of it. He spun the writer around

expertly and fitted the zip ties on him. "Drunk-driving's the least of your worries, Thomas."

When he turned the writer around, he'd sobered a little. "What is this?"

Mahoney said, "Thomas Tull, you are under arrest on suspicion of multiple mass murders, including those of the Hodges family, the Landaus, the Carpenters, the Elliotts, and the Kanes."

Sampson said, "You have the right to remain silent—"

"What? No," Tull said, shaking his head like a horse pestered by flies. "No, no, no. It's nothing like that."

John kept reading him his Miranda rights.

"I know my rights, damn it, and I did not do this!" Tull roared. He jerked free of Sampson's grasp and tried to take off. Still in restraints, he made it three feet before tripping and actually face-planting on the street.

We rushed to pick him up. Tull's nose was smashed and gushing blood. One of his upper incisors was broken. The other was gone. Blood ran from that wound.

In what had to have been some agony, the writer got belligerent.

"You beat me, threw me down," he said. "Police brutality. I want my lawyer."

76

ALEX CALLED BREE AT home around eight thirty that morning to tell her Thomas Tull was being held on suspicion of being the Family Man.

"How clear was the video still?" Bree asked, sipping her coffee.

"Like I said, it's not the straight-on or quartering-to shot you'd want ideally, but you'll see the dramatic resemblance: the chin, the cheekbones, and especially the hair."

"You sound exhausted."

"I took a long nap while we waited for Tull to sober up and for his attorney to arrive."

"You're going to interrogate?"

"Part of the team. And your day?"

"I'm going to try to relax, regroup, maybe go for a run. I'm officially done with work until Monday."

"Sounds like a nice agenda. I have the feeling I'll be home earlier than usual and facedown in bed."

"You deserve it," Bree said.

"Oh, here's Ned. Gotta go."

The call ended.

Nana Mama was sitting at the kitchen table reading the *Washington Post* and drinking coffee. She looked up. "What time did he get that call?"

"Half past two? I heard him pounding down the stairs."

"It's a wonder he stays on his feet half the time. You too."

Bree smiled. "We're both committed."

"If you take care of yourself, you'll live and stay committed longer. Look at me."

"Nana," Bree said in a teasing voice. "With all due respect, you're a legitimate freak for your age."

Alex's grandmother did not like that. "Freak?"

Bree said, "Someone who defies the norms. An outlier."

Nana Mama relaxed. "I'll take outlier."

"How's the hip?"

"It's been better. When Jannie gets up, we're going to stretch again."

"I'm going for a run," Bree said. "Clear the cobwebs."

"Keep it up and you'll be an ancient outlier like me someday."

Smiling, Bree went upstairs, changed into her running gear, and went out onto the front porch. It was a warm morning for late April, but she liked running in the heat.

After doing her routine series of stretches and ballistic drills, she bounced down the stairs and headed toward Capitol Hill. Most days, she wore earbuds and listened to music or a podcast. But Bree wanted to tune everything out and just run for a while. Like Jannie, she found that running set her free in a way few kinds of exercises did, and normally she let go of thought, absorbed in the effort.

For the first fifteen minutes or so, she ran her usual route and quickly fell into that calm state the endorphins gave her. But about thirty minutes in, as she ran on Independence Avenue along the Mall west of the hill, questions about the Duchaine investigation began to creep back in.

Could Theresa May Alcott be behind the murders at Paula Watkins's home? Was her nephew and his company involved? And what happened to his twin brother?

The idea of having to figure all this out seemed daunting, beyond her capacity and above her pay grade. *A billionaire who likes to garden and grieves for a granddaughter. A tech wizard with a company that serves federal law enforcement agencies. Could they be involved in brazen assassinations?*

Bree turned and ran toward Constitution Avenue and the far side of the Mall, readying herself for the steep climb up the hill. But when she reached Constitution, she had a thought that caused her to slow and then stop and wipe her brow. She dug out her phone from the hip holster that also held her water bottles.

She thumbed through her contacts, found who she was looking for, and hit Call.

After two rings, a familiar voice answered against the din of an active office. "Chief Stone," Detective Rosella Salazar said. "I was about to call you."

"Lucky me. What's up?"

"The assistant DA on the Watkins case would like you to come in and make a longer, more detailed statement."

"When?"

"ASAP."

"I'm not working tomorrow. I could come up on the early train."

"I'll tell her. She wants us both there. But you called me."

"I did. My rich client pulled the plug on my end. But I wanted you to know a few things before I let the entire thing slide and wait for your investigation to wrap up."

"I'm listening."

Bree told her about going to Ohio to talk with Theresa May Alcott and then seeing the name Paladin on the billionaire's desk phone and learning about her relationship to Ryan Malcomb, one of the company's founders.

"Okay…" Salazar said. "So what?"

"Paladin does work for the FBI, CIA, all the big law enforcement and national security agencies as well as big corporations. They can sort through tons of raw data looking for specific kinds of information."

"Such as?"

"Like a terrorist's cell phone. Or the links between members of an organized crime group. Or the type of person who is likely to buy one of Frances Duchaine's one-of-a-kind gowns."

"I'm still not—"

"Or the people behind a sex ring. Or the potential buyers in a sex-slave auction."

There was a long silence before Salazar said, "I would have no idea how to figure something like that out."

"Start with something simple," Bree said.

"Like what?"

"Check to see if Frances Duchaine or her company ever hired Paladin. And come to think of it, check to see if Ari Bernstein, her financier, ever worked with Paladin."

There was another long silence before Salazar came back

and said in a tight voice, "Sorry. I'm getting kicked in the ribs constantly now."

"How much longer?"

"I'm four weeks out and this kid is already a beast," the detective said, her tone softening. "Okay, Chief, I'll take a look, but I can't promise you it's at the top of my pile today. But I'll see you tomorrow."

"You will indeed."

77

THE WRITER LOOKED LIKE HELL.

Face swollen and red, his famous shock of hair a rat's nest, Thomas Tull moaned when we entered the interrogation room at the federal holding facility in Alexandria, Virginia.

"Can I please have some pain meds?" Tull said in a thick, nasal voice. "My nose is busted, I lost two teeth, and my skull feels ready to split."

His attorney, a high-dollar criminal defense lawyer named Lindy York, said, "You're just adding to the police brutality by denying him proper medication."

Ned Mahoney scowled. "The doctor denied it. His blood alcohol was three times the legal limit, and he had cocaine on board too. She said he shouldn't have anything till he sobered up."

"Which is now," Tull said.

I took pity on him, reached into my pocket, and got out a small bottle of ibuprofen I carry in case my knee acts up. I shook out four and slid them across the desk.

"That's eight hundred milligrams altogether," I said. "Prescription dose."

Tull snatched them up with his handcuffed hands, popped them in his mouth, shakily lifted the plastic cup of water in front of him, and swallowed them down. He drained the cup and said, "Tell 'em."

Lindy York said, "Mr. Tull categorically denies having anything to do with the Family Man murders beyond his interest in writing a book about them and Agent Mahoney, Detective Sampson, and, of course, Dr. Cross."

Sampson said, "We beg to differ, Counselor. We have a photograph of your client inside a house in Falls Church last night, armed and wearing the same outfit we've seen Family Man wear in other security footage."

"Produce the picture," York said.

Mahoney flipped open a file and slid a blowup of the video still across to Tull. "You shut off the main power to the house and found the auxiliary power to the safe room as well, but Mr. Allison had a third redundancy—battery packs—that got you."

York stared without expression at the picture.

Tull blinked. "Jesus, that does look like me."

"Thomas, not another word," his attorney warned.

"It's not me," the writer said. "It can't be. Where did you say this was taken?"

"In Falls Church, Virginia, not far from Lake Barcroft."

"I was nowhere near—" Tull began but he stopped when Deputy Marshal Annette Cox knocked and stuck her head in.

"Sorry to interrupt, Agent Mahoney, but there's something out here you should probably see ASAP."

"We're done here anyway," York said.

"I'm not," Tull said. "I was nowhere near Virginia last night."

Mahoney stood. "Why don't we give you a few minutes, Counselor, to consult with your client and get your stories straight?"

Mahoney gestured to Sampson and me. We followed him out the door, where Deputy Marshal Cox was standing, holding a sheaf of paper.

"Quantico did not want to e-mail you the results," Cox said. "Your office rerouted it to our secure fax."

Mahoney took the papers and scanned them. "The lab finished a preliminary mitochondrial analysis yesterday on those hairs found at the Kane murder scene—not a full DNA workup, but enough for them to feed the results into IAFIS. They got a dead-on hit this morning from U.S. military files."

He showed me and Sampson the results page.

I was, frankly, astonished.

78

WHEN WE REENTERED THE interrogation room, we had an entirely different perspective on the Family Man murders.

Lindy York, Tull's defense attorney, was drumming her manicured nails on the tabletop, slight disgust twisting her lips. Tull looked a bit less dazed. "My client wishes to tell you where he was last night," York said curtly.

Tull arched his eyebrows and shrugged. "I'm not proud of it, but I'm not going to prison for something I did not do."

"Out with it," Mahoney said impatiently.

He cleared his throat. "I was at a small get-together at a condo in Silver Spring."

"Address? Owner's name?"

The writer gave us the address but said he had no idea who owned the property. "For all I know, it was an Airbnb place or

VRBO," he said. "Anyway, I have a weakness for three things in life: good wine, good women, and good cocaine. I don't indulge often, but I binge once or twice a year, which is what I was doing last night. I rarely get in a car for at least a day afterward, but I got it in my head that I wanted to sleep in my own bed, and the ladies could not stop me."

Sampson said, "Names of the ladies and the other people at the party?"

"Lola, Heart, and Bambi. No one else."

His attorney's nostrils flared as she stared at the table.

I said, "No last names?"

"They weren't offering any," Tull said.

"How was this party organized? Who put it together?"

The writer studied me with a smile. "Exactly the question I would ask if I were you. I called someone I know in Queens, a Russian expat, who arranged for the condo, the women, the cocaine, and the wine."

"Name?"

A slight ripple of what I took to be fear flickered over his face. He said, "He will not like this."

Mahoney said, "I expect not, but you're going to need an alibi that's a hell of a lot better than three one-name hookers and a nameless Russian expat in Queens."

When the writer hesitated, his attorney said, "Tell him or we proceed to arraignment and the destruction of your good name."

Tull looked at the ceiling and said, "Dusan. Dusan Volkov."

Sampson said, "Phone number for Mr. Volkov?"

"It doesn't work like that," Tull said. "You have to go through security checks, and Volkov calls you. If he feels like it. Sometimes it takes a few days."

Mahoney cleared his throat, said, "I'm tired of this road to nowhere because we know this story's not true."

"It is true!" Tull said. "Just give the process a little time."

"I don't need to give the process a little time, and I don't think I'd trust the word of a Russian mobster anyway," Ned said, and he put the documents with the results of the mitochondrial analysis and match on the table. "We found hairs at the Kane family crime scene."

"Slam-dunk match," I said, watching as Tull and York scanned the document. "Retired U.S. Marine MP and NCIS investigator Thomas Adrian Tull."

He jerked his head up. "No! This is BS! I have never—"

York put an arm across his chest. "Not another word, Thomas. Or you're wasting the thousand dollars an hour you're paying me."

Tull glared at each of us in turn. "Utter BS," he said. "Do your job, because I will remember this when it comes time to tell the truth about this story."

Then he shut up and looked off into the distance.

79

BREE RETURNED FROM HER run and showered, and she was getting dressed when Alex phoned her.

"It's him," he said. "Tull's the Family Man. We have DNA evidence that puts him at the Kane crime scene."

"No kidding," she said. "Wow, that's…that's great, Alex. Well, we all knew you'd figure it out sooner or later. You always do!"

To Bree's surprise, she'd said this all with increasing irritation.

Alex was quiet and then said, "What's going on there?"

Bree took a deep breath, examined her emotions. "I think it's my feelings of inferiority at my inability to make the connections that I know are there," she said. "If that makes any sense."

"It does. But I've learned not to beat my head against the wall about these things. If there are connections, you'll find them. Quite honestly, it's not like we dug up the Tull connections ourselves. He made two mistakes, with the camera and with the hair."

"Big mistakes."

"He's claiming an alibi, by the way."

"Against DNA evidence and a photograph of him at the Allisons'?"

"Exactly, but I am under orders from Tull himself to do my job and check it out before rushing to judgment."

"DNA evidence and a photograph, Alex."

"Just the same, I think you might be able to help me."

"Any way I can."

"Could you get in touch with that pregnant NYPD detective for me?"

"Salazar?" she said.

"If I remember, you said she'd investigated Russian organized crime before looking at Frances Duchaine."

"The Russian mob in Queens," Bree said. "One of the leaders was killed in Paula Watkins's house. She knew all about him."

"I was hoping so," Alex said and he explained what he wanted.

"I can do that. I actually spoke with her a little while ago and I have to go up to New York tomorrow morning to talk to the district attorney assigned to the Watkins/Duchaine case. When are you coming home to sleep?"

"I was going to wait for Tull's arraignment so I could see his face when he pleaded. But the assistant U.S. attorney wants him stone-cold sober, so he won't face a judge until the morning. I'm going to take another nap, then help search his house. The warrants finally came through."

"Good," Bree said. "I'll let you know what Salazar says."

She hung up and phoned the NYPD detective for the second time that day.

"You don't quit, Chief," the detective said. "I—"

"Not that, Rosella," Bree said. "I'm calling at my husband's request."

After a pause, she said, "Dr. Cross?"

"Yes. He wants to know if you know a Russian mobster named Dusan Volkov."

"Volkov? I haven't heard that name in quite a while. But yes, I know of him. They call him Wolf because of his last name in Russian and because he's secretive, reclusive, operates deep behind the scenes."

"Do you know how Alex can get in touch with him?"

"Volkov?" she said doubtfully. "I don't know. I'd have to do some reaching out, and even then…"

"All they're looking for is corroboration of an alibi," Bree said, and she explained.

"Tull and Volkov, huh?" Salazar said. "Strange bedfellows, Chief. I'll make a few calls and see what I can—"

Bree heard a slight gasp.

"Gotta go, see you tomorrow." The detective groaned. "Big kick. Big, big kick."

80

AROUND THREE THAT AFTERNOON and finally armed with warrants, Sampson, Mahoney, and I donned blue booties, hairnets, and latex gloves while an FBI criminalist picked the lock to Thomas Tull's Georgetown rental.

The green door swung open. After the criminalist photographed the narrow front hallway, Mahoney led us inside.

The writer had done little to make the lower floor of the luxury town house his own. The furniture in the living area was all steel and black leather. There were no televisions and no pictures whatsoever.

The kitchen had top-of-the-line major appliances but was otherwise sparsely outfitted: a cheap toaster, a cheap coffee-maker, basic cooking utensils, plates, pots, and pans.

"Looks like someone bought it in one swoop at Walmart," Sampson said.

The fridge was empty save for a can of coffee, a carton of half-and-half, and leftover takeout Chinese food.

"Place is spotless," Mahoney said.

"I wonder how much time he spends here," Sampson said.

"You think he has another place in town?"

"There could be another local one, right? I mean, he's loaded. Big bestselling author."

"If he has somewhere local, we'll find it," I said, climbing the stairs to the second floor.

A door on the right revealed the master suite. The king-size bed was made military taut. Tull's clothes were crisply folded in an armoire, his shoes set in tight order below. Books were stacked on both sides of the bed.

Sampson and Mahoney went through a locker in one corner. I went through the bathroom and into the second bedroom, which was the writer's office.

It wasn't what I'd anticipated. Or was it?

I guess I'd expected a rat's nest, a disorganized mess that only Tull could make sense of. Or maybe an elaborate setup with floor-to-ceiling bookshelves and a heavy old writing desk.

Instead, the office was spartan, ordered, and efficient, a former Marine's place of work: a ladderback chair with a cushion, a long folding table, an iMac, a MacBook Pro laptop, a smaller folding table supporting a printer, and two three-drawer filing cabinets. All of it faced the far long wall of the room, which had been transformed into a visual case control, with sections of each set of victims in the Family Man's killing spree.

The murders were arranged in order of occurrence from left to right. The Hodgeses, the Landaus, the Carpenters, the Elliotts, and the Kanes.

Sampson and Mahoney found me studying the evidence that Tull had considered worthy of inclusion on the wall.

"Anything jump out at you?" Ned asked, going to the laptop and lifting the lid.

"Yes," I said, waving at the right side of the wall. "He left room for more cases. He's got strips of paper cut there on the desk just waiting for a name."

Mahoney gestured at a sticky note on the wall above the desk. "Laptop password: *FamilyMan.*"

"That right?" Sampson said, coming over.

"He's got multiple applications and files open here," Mahoney said and started working the trackpad.

I left the wall for the moment and came around behind them; I saw a Microsoft Word document labeled FAMILY MAN NOTES. Before I could scan it, Mahoney clicked on a Microsoft Excel spreadsheet.

We looked at the list of what appeared to be his monthly budget items: Car payments. Mortgage on a house in Maine. Credit cards.

Something odd caught my eye: *Cold/Cold $57.* I pointed. "What's this?"

"I don't know, but he's got an Arlington storage unit," Sampson said, gesturing to the last item on the list.

"Costs three fifty a month so it's got to be a good size," I said while Mahoney clicked on the Google Earth icon at the bottom of the screen.

We gaped when the app came up and showed that Tull had been searching in the Lake Barcroft area.

81

AFTER TAKING PHOTOGRAPHS WITH our phones of the Google Earth search and the budget spreadsheet with the name and address of the storage unit, we left the computers to the FBI criminalists, who bagged them for transport to Quantico for further analysis. We searched the rest of the house and came up with nothing.

Mahoney opted to stay on the scene when Sampson and I announced our intention to go see what Tull had hidden in Arlington.

"That storage facility is on the way to Lake Barcroft," Sampson said.

"It is," I said.

Indeed, Greenbriar Storage turned out to be just a short detour off the most direct route to Lake Barcroft and the Allison family home. Edna Martinez, the fifty-something owner, was working in the office when we entered. She remembered Thomas Tull.

"I'm in two book clubs," she said and cackled. "How could I not know him?"

"Did you hear he's under arrest?" Sampson asked.

Ms. Martinez's shock was complete. "Thomas Tull?"

"In connection with the Family Man murders," I said. "We need to get into his storage unit, please."

"Do you have a warrant?"

"Do you have a fax number? We'll get the warrant for his town house amended to add the storage unit."

The owner of the facility became more helpful, giving us her fax number and telling us she'd call the woman who cut the locks off her units.

By the time we watched the amended warrant print out on her fax machine, a forty-something woman named Lenora Sands had arrived with a special carbide saw designed to cut the curved locks that Martinez demanded clients use on each unit.

Sands led us to unit 1204 E, a six-by-ten-foot space with a red roll-down door and a stout lock that the carbide tool cut like it was butter. It fell at our feet. Sands bent down to pick it up, but I stopped her.

"Could be evidence," I said.

"Oh?" she said.

"You never know," Sampson said, putting it into a bag.

The locksmith seemed interested in seeing what we found, but we politely asked her to leave while we did our work. "Of course," she said and walked off.

I waited until she'd rounded the corner before squatting and rolling up the door. After taking a long look at the room, I turned to John and said, "I'll go get her."

Luckily, I caught up to Sands in the parking lot. "Lenora, have you ever cracked a safe?"

She closed one eye, said, "Make?"

"I think it said Liberty."

"Helps. Tumbler?"

"Digital pad."

She cocked her head in reappraisal. "That helps too."

Sands climbed into her van and soon emerged with a small black carrying case that said LIBERTY SAFE on it. "My husband and I are their certified techs in this area."

"Good to know."

"People forget their codes all the time," the locksmith said.

We returned to the storage unit. Sampson had climbed over a couch, a kitchen table, and several chairs and was rummaging through boxes stacked on the far wall.

"Anything?"

"Lot of books and knickknacks."

"Lenora says she can get us into the safe."

"I'll check the filing cabinets," he said and climbed over a credenza to four filing cabinets along the rear wall of the unit.

Sands struggled but reached the black safe at the back and soon had a notebook computer plugged into the underside of the digital keypad. She gave the computer a series of commands, then looked up and around.

"What?" I asked.

"I'm not getting a clear satellite signal through…oh, now it's talking."

"Who's it talking to?"

"A security computer at Liberty, which should generate a onetime code to override the real combination. And you are law enforcement, which we click here."

The locksmith hit Enter and looked at the safe expectantly. Several moments later, a light on the pad flashed green and heavy steel bars rolled back. Sands turned to us. "She's all yours."

"Leave us an invoice at the front counter," I said. "And thanks."

"It's what I do," the locksmith said, and she left.

I opened the safe door, revealing seven weapons. Three were bolt-action hunting rifles with Leica scopes. The other four were AR-style rifles with Aimpoint sights. Boxes of ammunition were stacked on the floor at the back.

I went through the top inner drawer and found various legal documents, including Tull's will and the title and deed to his home on Moosehead Lake in Maine. There was a Glock nine-millimeter pistol in a holster in the second drawer. The third drawer was empty.

"Find what you were looking for?" Sampson asked.

Every person who'd died in the Family Man murders had been shot with a .40-caliber pistol.

"Not today," I said, unable to hide my disappointment as I turned to face him.

"That's okay. I did," he said, grinning and holding a pen stuck through the trigger guard of a black pistol fitted with a suppressor. "Glock, forty cal. And it smells like it's been fired recently."

82

THAT EVENING ALEX CAME home exhausted but happy that they'd all but nailed Tull to the wall. The poor guy had slept less than four hours in the past two days and went to bed after dinner so he could wake up early and be there when the writer was arraigned in the morning.

Bree had to be up early too to catch the train back to New York, but she wasn't feeling tired and was uninterested in the movie Nana Mama, Ali, and Jannie were watching. She climbed up to Alex's attic office with a pair of earphones.

After closing the door, Bree sat on the couch and listened to the recording she'd made the previous day in Ohio. At first, she heard only branches scraping her jacket and the wind blowing as she ducked through the back hedge of Theresa May Alcott's estate and crossed the lawn.

Her feet crunched gravel; the door to the greenhouse creaked.

But then the big Polynesian's voice came through loud and clear: "Who are you? What are you doing here? You do not have permission to be here."

And then Alcott herself saying, "It's all right, Arthur. You have exceeded my expectations, Chief Stone. I predicted a phone call or a knock at my front door, not a barging into my greenhouse."

Bree smiled when the billionaire laughed and said, "But then I guess you are a barging-in kind of person, aren't you?"

After hearing herself say, "I guess I am. All elbows and knees," Bree paused the recording. Alcott's demeanor had been disarming. She'd liked the woman almost instantly, and when was the last time that happened?

Still, there was something about their interaction that had nagged at her most of the day. Bree fast-forwarded the recording to where she and Alcott were in the library.

She listened closely as the billionaire described her dear granddaughter's downward spiral at the hands of Paula Watkins and perhaps Frances Duchaine. Alcott then said she believed some kind of cosmic justice had been done.

Bree heard herself say, "You won't go to the journalists with the evidence I dug up?"

"Again, will that bring back my granddaughter?" Alcott replied. "The media will get its meat when Frances Duchaine goes on trial."

"She claims she's innocent."

"So did Saddam Hussein."

Listening to the recording, Bree again noted the chill in Alcott's voice. The phone on the desk rang.

"Can you hold on a moment?" the billionaire asked. "I rarely get calls on the landlines anymore."

Her footsteps were audible as she crossed to the desk. Bree heard her say, "This is Terri...Give me a minute, will you, Emma, dear? I'm with someone and I'll need to pick up in another room...I am sorry, Chief Stone. This won't take long, but it can't wait."

Bree listened to herself say, "Please. Take your time."

Bree stopped the recording, rewound it several seconds, and hit Play.

"This is Terri...Give me a minute, will you, Emma, dear?"

Bree stopped the recording again, feeling puzzled. But what about? She played that sequence again.

"This is Terri...Give me a minute, will you, Emma, dear?"

Bree had that same internal response—something was off there, but she couldn't put her finger on exactly what. The inflection of the words? The tone of voice? The emphasis on certain syllables? What was it? What was being said on that tape that she wasn't getting?

Bree listened two more times before yawning and glancing at the clock. It was nearly eleven. She needed sleep.

Climbing down the stairs, she thought, *Emma is probably some-one who works for Paladin in the investor relations office, and it's nothing more than that.*

83

AT EIGHT FORTY THE next morning, a good twenty minutes before proceedings were scheduled to start, Sampson, Mahoney, and I were in federal judge Margaret Twoomy's courtroom in Alexandria.

It was a good thing. By the time her bailiff told everyone to rise, the six benches on both sides of the main aisle were packed with journalists, attorneys, court buffs, and lookie-loos. Twoomy, a tall brunette with sharp features, took the bench and called the court to order.

"We have a full arraignment docket, so I would like to move quickly this morning," Twoomy said, peering out at the audience. "Counsel, when your client is called and the charges are read, I want a simple guilty or not guilty. Are we clear? Guilty or not guilty. You'll get a chance to tell your side of things when I consider bail." The judge looked over at her clerk. "First case, Randy?"

"United States versus Thomas Adrian Tull," Randy said. "Multiple homicide charges."

Lindy York, Tull's defense attorney, stood and carried her attaché case to the defense table as Danielle Carbone, the assistant U.S. attorney assigned to the case, said, "As many as nineteen, Your Honor."

"*Alleged* homicides, Your Honor," York said.

A U.S. deputy marshal led Tull into the courtroom.

The writer wore an orange jailhouse coverall. The handcuffs on each wrist were clamped to steel rings on either side of a padlocked leather belt. His hair was disheveled. His face was still swollen, and the area around his eyes had turned purple and dark.

"Judge, my client is obviously not being protected adequately," York said.

"Mr. Tull?" Judge Twoomy said.

"My own fault," Tull said hoarsely. "End of story."

The judge looked at the marshal. "See that he gets medical attention."

"Yes, Judge."

"Charges, then, Randy."

The court clerk read out a total of thirty-two charges ranging from first-degree murder of the members of the various families to conspiracy to commit murder in the case of the Allison family.

Judge Twoomy stared at Tull, who stood with slightly slumped shoulders beside his attorney. "How do you plead, Mr. Tull?"

The writer rolled back his shoulders and said forcefully, "Not guilty."

"So noted. Bail?"

Carbone, the prosecuting attorney, said, "We seek remand, Judge. Mr. Tull is a wealthy man and—"

Acting shocked, Tull's attorney said, "Remand? Are you kidding? Judge, my client is a world-renowned writer who specializes in describing the intricacies of law enforcement and judicial systems both here and abroad. He—"

Cutting her off, Carbone said, "Judge, the evidence against Mr. Tull is simply overwhelming. We have DNA that puts him at the scene of at least one of the family murders, video that puts him at another family's home, website searches that keyed on the Allison family, and we just learned that a pistol found in a storage unit leased by Mr. Tull has tested as a match for all the murders."

The writer looked like he'd taken a baseball bat to the gut. He bent over for a second, then straightened up, shock and disbelief all over his face. "That is wrong. That is wrong, Judge! I have never—"

Judge Twoomy banged her gavel hard and shook it at Tull. "You will end this outburst, Mr. Tull. Now."

He shook his head, looking like a prizefighter who'd been walloped.

The judge, irritated, said, "Please, in the future, let counsel speak for you, Mr. Tull. Things will go better for you."

Tull leaned over and had an intense conversation with York, who did not look happy when she said, "My client wishes to speak to Dr. Alex Cross, Detective John Sampson, and Agent Edward Mahoney. After arraignment."

"Request for remand granted, Ms. Carbone. Ms. York, your client can be visited in the holding facility here or after his transport back to the federal holding facility."

"Here," Tull said, and he looked over his shoulder at me, Sampson, and Mahoney. "Let's do this here and right now."

84

A FEW MOMENTS AFTER the marshal led the writer out of the court-room, we followed Tull's attorney into the hallway.

"I don't know what he wants to tell you, but I am against it," York said.

"Maybe he wants to confess," Sampson said.

"That's not happening," she snapped. "He would have told me that."

The marshal who'd accompanied Tull came up to us. "His transport doesn't leave for another twenty minutes if you want to talk to him here."

"I am slammed for time. I have a meeting with the director," Mahoney said, glancing at his watch. "I can wait until he's back at the federal holding facility later this afternoon."

I said, "I'd like to see why he's so insistent on talking now."

"Me too," Sampson said.

"Okay," Mahoney said, "but get it all on video."

The marshal led us through a door, down a flight of stairs, and past a series of holding cells. Tull was in the third cell on the right, waiting for us with conviction in his eyes.

His attorney went to him. "I advise you again to say nothing, Thomas."

Tull looked past her at us. "I didn't kill the Kanes. Ask Volkov."

"We tried," said Sampson, who was filming the conversation with his phone. "Volkov's a hard man to find."

"I told you that."

"Explain your relationship with him."

Tull said he had interviewed the Russian four years before when he was considering changing course in his writing career and doing an in-depth study of the world of modern organized crime.

"The book never went anywhere, but Volkov and I stayed in touch because he could help me with my...vices. That's it. Look, I'm a victim here, I'm being framed, and Volkov will corroborate that I was nowhere near the Kanes' home that night."

I couldn't help but chuckle. "Please, Thomas. DNA, video, website searches, and the smoking gun?"

He shook his head violently. "I'm telling you, I'm being framed, Dr. Cross, and I think I know by who. My research assistant. She has access to the research laptop, my DNA, all of it."

I frowned. "I didn't know you had a research assistant."

"Lisa Moore has worked with me on and off since Boston, since the electrocution murders," he said. "But we go back even farther."

"I read the acknowledgments in your books and I can't say I remember you mentioning anyone named Lisa Moore. Or a research assistant, for that matter."

Tull closed his eyes and took a deep breath. "She wanted it that way. In return for more money. Lisa cares nothing for acclaim."

"Then why would she frame you?"

He hesitated. "Revenge. Because I would not keep increasing her pay."

Sampson said, "Has she asked you for more money lately?"

"Constantly. Once on the day after I'd given her a raise. And she…uh, she recently threatened to reveal certain things about the way we work together unless I gave her a fifty percent increase in her salary. Fifty!"

His attorney said, "Thomas, you told me none of this. I advise you to—"

"I advise you to shut up or you're fired, Counselor," the writer shot back. He returned his attention to me and Sampson. "I'm not proud of this, but I used Moore in the past to…gin things up. In the stories, I mean."

My brows knit. "Give us an example of ginning things up."

He took an uncomfortable breath. "In Boston, she staged a break-in to heighten the public tension in the case. She did the same kind of thing in South Carolina during the *Doctor's Orders* murders. She's meticulous, though. Doesn't get caught. She's trained not to get caught."

"Who trained her not to get caught?" Sampson asked, sounding incredulous.

"My suspicion is either DIA or CIA. Certainly one of the alphabet agencies. When I met her, I was working for NCIS on a case that required travel to Iraq and Afghanistan. Moore was a, quote, 'private contractor' who pointed me in the right direction a couple of times in my investigation. We hit it off. A year later, in an op gone wrong, she evidently killed two civilians, a mother and a daughter, but she avoided jail by ending her contract with the U.S. government."

I said, "And going to work for you?"

"She came to visit me at Harvard and told me what had happened. I needed someone smart, someone…"

"Willing to bend and break the rules if it helped the story," Sampson said.

"That almost describes Lisa," Tull replied. "I'd actually describe her as someone who is *eager* to break the rules if it gets her to the end result that much faster."

CHAPTER

85

SHORTLY BEFORE ELEVEN SUNDAY morning, Bree watched as Newark flickered by her window. She was on the Acela bound for Penn Station, where Detective Rosella Salazar would be waiting to take her to talk with members of the Manhattan district attorney's office assigned to what the press were calling "the Paula Watkins murders."

Setting aside the newspaper, Bree called Phillip Henry Luster. She had not heard from him since the night of the murders and wondered how he was.

On the fourth ring he answered in a flat voice, "This is Phillip."

"This is Bree Stone."

"I know."

"How are you, Phillip?"

"Wanting bourbon and quaaludes," he said. "Tell me, why has it taken so long for you to call and inquire as to my condition?"

"I could say the same thing."

"Except you are a former cop and used to these sorts of unspeakable events. I can't sleep because I keep seeing the lights go out at Paula's, the flashes of the guns. I keep hearing the screams. I can't get certain things about that night out of my mind."

"I apologize for not calling sooner, Phillip," Bree said. "It was callous of me and I'm sorry. You've been such a big help. And what you're suffering from is PTSD."

"Even I can diagnose that." He sniffed. "I don't know how you do it."

"Do what?"

"Deal with all the violence," he said.

"I deal with it as little as possible and so should you. Phillip, you were caught up in things beyond your control and you lived. Be thankful."

"Oh, I am. But I fear I am more sensitive than others. I mean, look at Frances. Just plunging on as if nothing's happened."

"Plunging on in what? Business?"

"I have no idea about the business, but her social life has taken off. It's a scandal. She's actually going to attend a fundraiser I'm involved in tonight at Cipriani on Forty-Second."

"You invited her?"

"Long before the tsunami, she and I were named cohosts. Look, no one involved is happy she's coming, least of all me."

"Well, I'm in town, and I'd be happy to be a fly on the wall for that encounter," Bree said and laughed. "I'm sorry, Phillip."

"No, no," he said, then paused. "Are you free tonight?"

"I was going to head back after a meeting with the DA."

"Nonsense. You'll be my date. Your presence alone will irritate Frances no end. Do you have her gown with you?"

"No, I don't have anything like that with me."

"Well, I do," Luster said. "Come straight to my studio after your powwow with the DA is over. I promise to make you look stunning."

Bree thought about it for a moment. She really wanted to head home after the meeting, but she said, "I know you will, Phillip, and I accept. It will be fun."

"A night to remember, I'm sure," he said. "Until later."

He hung up. She realized the train was pulling into Penn Station. Looking out the window as it rolled slowly to a stop, she spotted Rosella Salazar sitting on a bench and rubbing her belly, which looked enormous.

Bree walked up to her a few moments later and said, "You're bigger every time I see you!"

Salazar grinned sourly and struggled to her feet. "He's giving me heartburn and hemorrhoids now. C'mon. The DA's expecting us at quarter to twelve."

They walked through the new Penn Station welcome hall, a stunning structure, and out onto the street, where Salazar had a car waiting. After getting in and saying hello to the officer at the wheel, Bree told the detective about her conversation with Luster and the fundraiser that evening at Cipriani on Forty-Second.

Salazar said, "You're going?"

"How could I refuse? He's putting me in one of his dresses."

The detective laughed and looked down at her belly bulging against the tent shirt she wore. "He should get me a dress. I think seeing us together would rattle Frances even more."

"I'll call Phillip back, see what he can do."

"Really?"

"Why not?"

86

Washington, DC

SAMPSON FOUND LISA MOORE right where Thomas Tull said he'd find her—in an Airbnb she'd rented in the Kalorama neighborhood. When John brought in the writer's assistant later that afternoon, I recognized Moore as the woman we'd seen putting an envelope in Tull's mail slot the same night he'd raced the Porsche up Rock Creek Parkway and the Kane family had been killed.

She almost smiled when she saw me. "Alex Cross. I know a lot about you."

"Probably more than I know about you," I said.

She smiled. "There's not a lot to know, honestly."

"That's not how Thomas Tull tells it," Mahoney said. He looked at Sampson. "Has she been read her Miranda rights?"

"At her front door," Sampson said.

The smile on Moore's face vanished. "I don't know what Thomas has been saying about me, but—"

I cut her off. "What were you before you worked for Tull? CIA? DIA?"

Moore raised her eyebrows and canted her head to the right. "I cannot answer those questions for too many reasons to count."

"You just did. Where did you go after you left Tull's house the night of April twenty-second?"

"The twenty-second?" she said and thought for a few moments. "Home. To my Airbnb."

"You were there all night?" Mahoney asked.

"All night."

"Can anyone corroborate that?"

"As a matter of fact," she said, "my lover was with me from around nine p.m. until ten the next morning. What's this about?"

Sampson said, "Who's your lover? Name, address, telephone number."

Moore took a deep breath. "I don't think she's ready to be out of the closet."

Mahoney said, "But you think you're ready for an eight-by-ten cell?"

Her eyes widened. "A cell? No."

I said, "Then give us her name."

"Keep her out of this, okay?" she said. "She's a good person and this coming out in the media would be—"

"The name," Sampson growled.

"Suzanne," Moore said finally. "Suzanne Liu. She lives in—"

"I know where she lives," I said, my mind spinning a little. "And I have her phone number. She will say that she was with you that night?"

"She will," the researcher said without hesitation.

"What about the nights the other families were murdered?" Sampson asked.

"I was in New York all those times," Moore said. "Also with Suzanne."

I asked, "How do you know that off the top of your head? The dates, I mean."

The researcher gave me a look. "Uh, I'm working on a book about the murders? I know all sorts of dates. It's kind of the job."

Sampson said, "You have access to the Family Man laptop in Tull's office?"

"I know the password and I have e-mailed things to Thomas, but I haven't been on it in at least a week."

"Convenient," Mahoney said. "Tull believes you're trying to frame him."

"Frame him?" she said. She threw back her head and laughed caustically. "I don't need to frame him. He can do that himself. Play with the truth. You do know he makes stuff up, right?"

"He admitted that he gins things up in his books," I said. "Well, he admits that he pays you to gin things up, make them more dramatic than they really are. Is that true?"

"If it is, it's not a crime."

Sampson said, "How about taking the lives of an innocent mother and daughter in the Middle East? Was that a crime?"

Moore swallowed hard. "That was investigated. I was totally exonerated."

"You can prove that?"

"It would be a challenge, given certain national secrecy laws, but yes."

"You do know Thomas Tull is in custody and has been arraigned," Sampson said.

"I'd heard that."

"But you didn't think to reach out and contact us?"

"No," she said. "I was in shock. I…I didn't know what to think or believe at first."

I said, "So what do you think now? Is Thomas Tull the Family Man killer?"

For a long time, she said nothing, just stared at the table.

"Ms. Moore?" Mahoney said.

"Little things in all the cases we worked together, you know?" she said, lifting her eyes to gaze at each of us in turn. "Little things Thomas would say or do. And the times he'd disappear for days. The facts he'd ignore or gloss over. In my heart I don't want to believe it, but I guess it's possible, Dr. Cross. Maybe more than possible."

87

AFTER SEVERAL MORE QUESTIONS, Mahoney, Sampson, and I left the interrogation room and walked down the hall.

"You believe her?" Sampson asked.

"I want to," Mahoney said. "But Tull told us she's polished, a gifted liar."

"I think eventually she'll be an excellent witness for us. Not that we need it, with all the evidence against him."

I said, "I don't buy that she hasn't accessed Tull's laptop in more than a week."

"We won't know if that's true until Quantico gets a look at his hard drive and tells us what has been accessed on that laptop and when."

Sampson said, "And what do we do with Moore in the meantime?"

Mahoney said, "Release her for now. We'll follow up with a

request for her cellular data. Just to make sure she was with Liu when she says she was."

Even with that caveat, I couldn't shake the feeling that there was something off about the triangular relationship of Thomas Tull, Suzanne Liu, and Lisa Moore. "Let's make double sure," I said. "Bree's in New York. I'll ask her to go to Liu and get her side of the story, maybe get her apartment building's security footage on the days Moore said she was there."

"Do it," Mahoney said, yawning. "I'm calling it a day."

"Right behind you," Sampson said, checking his watch. "Willow's got the dress rehearsal for her ballet recital tonight and I don't want to miss a second."

I went to the interrogation room and told Moore she could go. She seemed relieved and followed me out. On the sidewalk, the researcher thanked me, turned to leave, and stopped. "Would you talk to me about all this someday?" she asked. "When Thomas is behind bars? I think it's important for me to understand what's been going on right under my nose."

"I can do that," I said and watched her walk away. I called Bree. She answered breathlessly. "Alex?"

"Where are you?"

"Being fitted for a dress." She groaned and then explained she was staying the night to attend a gala with Detective Salazar and Phillip Henry Luster.

"You're going to end up in the society pages one of these days," I said.

"Do those still exist?" she said. She breathed deep. "God, Phillip, that's too much!"

"I'll let you go," I said.

"No, why did you call?"

"Tull's researcher claims she's the lover of Suzanne Liu."

"The book editor?"

"Correct. If you have time between galas and cotillions, could you check it out with Liu in person?"

"As long as tomorrow works."

"It does."

"Then I'd be glad to. Call you later! Gotta go!"

She hung up. The air was pleasant for late April and I decided to walk home to get some exercise and take time to think.

I'd covered no more than a block when my phone buzzed again. I didn't recognize the phone number, which had a 703 area code. Northern Virginia.

"This is Alex Cross," I said.

"Deputy Lance Conrad, sir, with Fairfax County Sheriff's Department. I was blocking the road near Lake Barcroft when you went to the Allison residence?"

"I remember, Deputy," I said. "How can I help you?"

"I apologize because it slipped my mind that I was supposed to call you with the contact info on Tim Boulter, the jogger with the Jack Russell terrier?"

"Right. Can you text it over to me?"

After a pause, he said, "I can, but I don't think it will do much good."

"Why is that?"

"I looked up him and the bakery he said he owned. Tim Boulter *is* the owner of the Sunrise Bakery. But the real Tim Boulter is no two a.m. runner. They've got lots of pictures of the real Boulter on the bakery website. He's big. Beefy. Bald. Looks nothing like our lean running guy with the dog."

That came out of nowhere, and I paused at an intersection to collect my thoughts. "Send over the contact info he gave you anyway, Deputy Conrad. And I'll take a look at that website. Thanks."

"Anytime," he said and hung up.

After looking at the Sunrise Bakery website and confirming the deputy's observations, I spent the rest of the walk home trying to figure out who the runner was and why it was so important that he impersonate a baker and his dog out for a very early-morning jog.

88

CIPRIANI ON FORTY-SECOND STREET was as opulent and grand a venue as Bree had ever seen. Were it not for the white evening dress Luster had literally sewn her into, she might have stayed longer to stare at the beauty of the Italian Renaissance architecture, the massive marble columns, the high ceilings, the inlaid floors, and the stunning chandeliers.

As it was, she grunted and said, "Even with the Spanx, I don't think I fit into this, Phillip."

Rosella Salazar laughed. "I think I fit perfectly in mine, Phillip. Thank you!"

The detective was wearing a simple but elegant full-length, flowing black gown that Luster had literally designed and made in under two hours. Looking at her move, you'd never have known she was pregnant.

"Let's hope the stitches hold in both of your dresses," Luster said, offering an arm for each of them to take. They swept into the room, where guests were already crowding the tables and the bars to either side of the front door.

"Where are we sitting?" Salazar said. "I have to get off my feet for a few."

"Table four," the fashion designer said. "I'll take you. Bree, could you get me a glass of champers? The rosé Taittinger, please?"

"I could use one of those myself," Bree said and got in line.

A well-put-together woman in her forties in front of her turned and smiled.

"I know absolutely no one here, so I'll introduce myself," she said, holding out her hand. "I'm Addie Wells."

"Bree Stone," Bree said, shaking her hand. "Nice to meet you, Addie."

"Are you in fashion?"

"A friend of a designer at Tess Jackson. How about you?"

Wells said, "I was invited by an agent who's trying to convince me to buy a book set in the fashion industry."

"You work in publishing?"

"I'm an acquisitions editor. And you?"

"Former police chief in DC and now a private detective for Bluestone Group."

The editor's eyes sparkled. "Really? How exciting. I publish a great deal of true crime and crime fiction. I'll bet you have a hundred stories to tell."

"More than a hundred," Bree said and laughed.

"Can I give you my card?"

"Why not?" Bree said, and she reached in her purse for her business cards, pushing aside the small Ruger nine-millimeter she always carried to find them.

Wells's cell buzzed after they'd exchanged cards. She looked at the phone and grimaced. "Oh, dear, it's my nanny. My kids must be on a rampage. We'll talk again?"

"I look forward to it," Bree said.

The editor walked away, finger in her left ear, cell phone pressed tight to her right.

Carrying two flutes of pink champagne, Bree found table four and Detective Salazar, who had her black sneakers up on the adjacent chair.

"Where's Phillip?" Bree asked.

"Over there, blowing air kisses with the one-percenters," Salazar said. "He's not happy with the sneakers or me putting them up on the chair. But I can't help it. My dogs are aching."

"He'll get over it," Bree said. "He was miffed at me for wearing flats, but how tall can a girl be?"

The detective laughed and looked around. "Amazing place, huh?"

"One of the most beautiful places I've ever been in."

Salazar looked longingly at the champagne. "Another time, another place, I could use four or five of those."

Bree laughed. Salazar grinned. They liked each other. A lot.

"But nothing's stopping *you*," the detective went on. "Tell you what, I'll live vicariously through you drinking four or five of…uh-oh, here comes the trouble we've been waiting for."

Bree turned to look over her shoulder, noticing that the din in the room had dropped multiple decibels. She spotted Frances Duchaine moving through the throng by the bars, flanked by the same two bodyguards who'd thrown Bree out of the fashion designer's estate.

89

IT WAS FASCINATING TO watch the crowd react as Duchaine swept deeper into the venue. Heads snapped around. Guests whispered about her presence to other guests and provoked more low murmuring and craned heads trying to spot her.

Even though the scandal had no doubt damaged her brand, the fashion designer seemed to revel in the moment. Frances was the center of attention and knew it.

Luster was suddenly standing there next to Salazar and Bree. "I can't believe it. I didn't think she'd come even after she said she would."

Bree said, "Well, it looks like she's coming right to us, Phillip."

"I am the gala's cochair," Luster said. "She has to pay her respects."

"Why?" Salazar said, taking her feet off the chair.

"Because Frances is the other cochair," Luster said as Duchaine came closer, nodding to some in the crowd and ignoring others, while the buff white bodyguard and the buffer Black bodyguard kept their eyes sweeping the crowd.

Duchaine walked right up to Luster. "Phillip, how wonderful to see you."

"Frances, dear, how are you holding up?" Luster said and blew a kiss past each cheek.

Duchaine kept up the charade, murmuring something to him, then caught sight of Bree and Salazar standing on the other side of the table. The detective had been in the news a lot with the killings at Paula Watkins's home, and Duchaine clearly recognized Bree from Greenwich. She retreated from Luster, stared at him coldly. "I can see whose side you're on now, Phillip. I wish you had told me."

"What are friends for, dear?"

Enraged, she pivoted and strode off with bodyguards in tow. They took three seats at a table two rows away.

Duchaine ate barely two bites of her entrée before murmuring to both bodyguards; they set their utensils down and rose. Bree watched her make her excuses to the other guests and start toward the front door.

Salazar leaned across Luster and said to Bree, "Let's trail her a little. Let her know she's still a target."

Luster said, "I love it. I really do. Tell me everything she does!"

Bree and the detective got up and walked across the venue and out the front door. Duchaine and her bodyguards were standing about twenty feet away, scanning the traffic on Forty-Second and Lexington. The blond guy was on his phone.

It was seven thirty in the evening in midtown Manhattan. Traffic was heavy but flowing, at least in the eastbound lane of Forty-Second Street.

The blond guy must have seen the car he was looking for because he raised his hand. Bree caught a driver about ten cars back wave in return just as a cream-colored utility van floated into the near lane and stopped.

Cars behind it began honking.

The side door to the van opened. Three men in black hoods leaped out carrying pistols; they aimed at Duchaine and her bodyguards and opened fire.

90

FRANCES DUCHAINE TOOK MULTIPLE bullets in the chest and torso at close range; she stumbled back and fell, dead before she hit the sidewalk.

The bodyguards, shot in the face and neck, were down before they got their weapons drawn. Pedestrians screamed and tried to get away.

The assassins turned and ran east on Forty-Second toward Lexington and the van they'd come in, which was still rolling. Bree and Salazar, both with years of training, took off after the assailants.

Bree had a federal firearms license and a permit to carry, and as she ran, she dug the Ruger from her purse. Salazar pulled up her gown as she half ran, half waddled, found her backup weapon in a thigh holster, and drew it.

The van crossed Lexington just as the yellow light turned

red, the gunmen in close pursuit. The detective shouted, "NYPD! Stop!"

They didn't slow. A New York taxi headed south on Lexington took off on the green light, streaked across the intersection, and intentionally hit the slowest gunman in the leg. He stumbled, hit the curb, rolled on the sidewalk, and came up shooting. Salazar and Bree fired from the middle of Lexington and hit him square in the chest.

As she ran, Salazar screamed at the pedestrians, the taxi, and the other cars stopped in the intersection, *"NYPD! Call 911! NYPD!"*

The other two gunmen were still on Forty-Second, heading east toward Third Avenue and the van, which had slowed.

"Don't let them get in it!" Salazar yelled.

Bree felt stitches in her dress burst as she lengthened her stride, trying to catch up to the two gunmen. A woman came out of a Foot Locker store and almost knocked her over.

Bree lost sight of the assassins as she struggled to keep her balance. A second later, she spotted one of them not thirty yards from the van, which moved at a crawl as it approached Third.

Where's the other shooter? Where is he?

Bree cut diagonally off the sidewalk onto Forty-Second, looking for a clear shot at the gunman who was almost to the van, when the other shooter appeared from behind a sidewalk planter about thirty feet ahead of her. He fired and hit her in the left arm; she spun around and fell on her side in the gutter.

Shocked, disoriented, she raised her gun and searched for the shooter. She saw him just as he took three steps forward and aimed his weapon at her. A gun went off.

Part of the gunman's head erupted and he died on the spot.

Bree tried to push herself up, but it was too painful; she saw

Salazar passing in that odd waddle, her gun up as she stepped over the dead man. The last shooter was at the rear bumper of the rolling van.

"NYPD!" she shouted. "Drop your weapon!"

He half turned, swinging his pistol toward her.

The detective pulled the trigger.

There was an audible click.

The gunman's pistol was almost on Salazar when Bree, ignoring the fire in her left arm, pushed herself up, pointed her pistol, got a sight picture, and shot.

The shooter doubled over like he'd been kicked by a mule, but he did not fall and he did not drop his weapon.

Bree shot him again and again, and finally he spun around, fell, and lay sprawled out in the street.

The van accelerated away.

She was aware of being dizzy, of Salazar coming toward her, and of sirens screaming far and wide.

91

THE DETECTIVE SQUATTED NEXT to her, panting. "You just saved my life, Chief."

"You saved mine first, Rosella," Bree said, becoming less confused but also more acutely aware of the agony in her arm.

"You're bleeding good," Salazar said, helping her to her feet.

Bree's vision went blurry for a moment but then cleared enough for her to see the crowd gathered and the third attacker, the one she'd shot, lying on the street, gun a few feet away. His leg moved.

"He's alive!" Bree said.

Salazar left her, did a fast waddle over, and pushed the gun away with the side of her sneaker. Bree took a few tentative steps toward the detective and heard her say, "He's wearing body armor, but you caught him good with that last shot."

The shooter moaned.

Salazar grabbed the top of his hood and yanked it off. There was blood all over the side of his face from a deep gash on the side of his head.

"I'll be damned," the detective said.

Bree felt a little nauseated. "What? You know him?"

"It's the wolf your husband was asking about," the detective said, a sudden pained expression on her face. "Dusan Volkov."

"The Russian? Tull's Russian?"

Patrol cars and ambulances were arriving on the scene. Salazar did something on her phone and got an EMT to look at Bree. Two other medics worked on Volkov in the street.

Salazar's boss, Lieutenant Ellen Larkin, arrived, saw Bree, recognized her from the massacre at Paula Watkins's home, and became furious.

"Are you telling me a civilian was blazing away with her gun in the streets of New York and you let it happen, Salazar?"

The EMTs lifted the Russian onto a gurney and moved it toward the ambulance.

The detective pointed at him. "If I hadn't, I'd be dead, and that guy? Dusan Volkov? He would have gotten away."

Larkin's attitude changed. "That's Volkov?"

"He killed Frances Duchaine," Bree said. "Right in front of us. The bodyguards too."

Salazar said, "They're back there on the sidewalk outside Cipriani."

"Jesus Christ," the lieutenant said. "Jesus H. Christ." She pulled out her radio and walked off a few feet, barking orders into it.

The EMT said the bullet had passed through Bree's arm and did not appear to have hit bone, but he wanted to take her to the ER to have it examined.

Salazar said, "After I'm done here, I'll come see how you're—"
She stopped suddenly, that pained expression on her face again.

Lieutenant Larkin walked toward her. "Rosella, the chief and
the chief of detectives want you to write up a full—"

Holding her palm up, Salazar said, "Can't. I have to go to the
hospital. Right now. With Chief Stone."

"That's a flesh wound, and you're needed here, Detective."

Salazar waddled away from her toward the rear of the ambu-
lance, thumbing something on her phone again. "Sorry, Ellen,
I'm needed somewhere else a whole lot more at the moment.
My water just broke."

CHAPTER

92

TWO MINUTES LATER, THE ambulance squealed around the corner of Lexington and headed south, lights flashing and sirens wailing.

On a gurney in the back, Salazar panted through a contraction while an EMT named Phoebe Cartwright put a fetal monitor on her belly. Bree sat on the opposite side, holding the detective's hand.

"Oh God," Salazar groaned. "There it is."

"There what is?" Bree asked.

"Just like last time."

Cartwright, the EMT, said, "Like what last time?"

"Fast." She gasped. "My labor. The contractions, they come—"

A contraction doubled her up. She squeezed Bree's hand so hard, Bree thought bones might break.

The fetal monitor beeped quicker and quicker.

From the front, the driver yelled, "How are we doing?"

Cartwright said, "This baby's coming fast. And could be in some distress. I'm seeing a nonreassuring pattern on the monitor here."

"Inbound to Mount Sinai Beth Israel. ETA six minutes."

The contraction ended. Salazar panted and then yelled, "Negative on Mount Sinai! My doc is at NYU. That's where she and my family are headed!"

Cartwright said, "I don't know if we'll get to NYU."

"We'll get there if I have to tie my legs shut," Salazar said.

"How do your doc and family know?" Bree asked.

"App on my phone. First contraction, I knew. I just pressed a button, and they were all texted and—"

Another contraction began. Salazar surfed the pain like a pro for that contraction and the six that followed as the ambulance weaved through evening traffic south and east toward NYU Medical Center.

An accident at Third and Thirty-Fourth slowed them.

Salazar moaned. "Are we there yet?"

"ETA two minutes," the driver said, finally getting around the smashed cars.

"Hold on a little longer, Rosella," Bree said.

"That's out of my control, Chief." She grunted. "Just like with his sister. Once my kids start coming, there's no stopping them."

"You're not fully dilated yet," Cartwright said.

"Gimme a minute, maybe two," Salazar said. Another contraction hit.

Just as that contraction subsided, they pulled up in front of the emergency department. Four people were standing outside the ambulance when its doors opened.

"Rosella!" cried a rugged and worried man dressed in denim.

"He's coming, Debo!" Salazar said, beaming. "Our boy is coming!"

Two nurses appeared. Bree climbed out. The nurses got in to manage the various monitors attached to the detective while the driver and Cartwright lifted Salazar and her gurney from the ambulance.

A fit older woman in yoga tights and a hoodie stepped up, fingered Salazar's gown, and looked at the sneakers. "This is how you dress to have a child, Rosella?"

"Latest birthing style, Mama," Salazar shot back.

A much younger woman in jeans, a leather jacket, and too much makeup said, "How'd you afford a dress like that? You on the take now?"

As the nurses and EMTs moved Salazar, she pointed at Bree and said, "She'll tell you, wiseass."

Then the detective moaned and the beeping of the fetal monitor quickened again. The EMTs hurried her through the double doors with her husband beside her.

"Who are you?" Too Much Makeup asked. "Cop?"

"Used to be. You're her sister?"

She nodded. "Lucinda."

"Rosella was working undercover, Lucinda. A friend of mine made the dress for her and this one for me so we'd fit in. Now I have to go see a doctor about this arm."

"What happened to you?" Salazar's mother asked.

"Gunshot wound," Bree said and walked into the hospital.

The triage nurse brought her straight back to the ER. While she waited to see a doctor, she called Alex and filled him in.

"But you're sure you're all right?" he said.

"I'm going to have a sore arm for a while, but yes, I'm

fine. Listen, Salazar identified one of the shooters. The one I wounded. He's a Russian named Volkov."

"Volkov! As in Tull's Volkov?"

"One and the same."

"But he's alive?"

"Last time I saw him, but he was in rough shape. I creased the left side of his head with a nine-millimeter round."

"Hang on," Alex said. She heard the drone of news anchors and Alex picked up the phone again. "Wow, the story's on CNN. They're calling you and Salazar heroes."

"She's my hero. She saved my life, Alex."

"I can't wait to meet her and thank her. I'm glad you're okay."

"So am I," she said and yawned. "I just want to get stitched up and out of here."

"Where are you staying?"

"I haven't figured that out yet."

"I can go online and get you a hotel room."

"I'll do it," she said. "I have my phone and nothing else to do."

"So it was some kind of Russian mob thing, huh? The hits at Paula Watkins's home and then finishing off the job with Duchaine?"

"That's what it looks like."

"But why?"

"I'm thinking it has something to do with Watkins and Duchaine elbowing in on the high-end-prostitution racket."

A doctor appeared and looked at her phone. "No cells in here."

"Sorry, doc's here and I got to go," Bree said. "Love you."

"Love you too," Alex said and hung up.

It wasn't until after Bree's arm had been stitched up and she'd been released with prescriptions for antibiotics and painkillers that she realized she still had no place to stay for the night. She figured she'd sit down with her phone somewhere and try to find something.

But when she reached the lobby, she found Phillip Henry Luster waiting.

"I was told they'd brought you here," he said. "I've got a car, and a stiff drink and a warm bed await you at my house."

"Thank you, Phillip. You're a lifesaver."

"From what I hear, it's the other way around."

CHAPTER

93

Alexandria, Virginia

AT THREE ON MONDAY afternoon, Sampson and I walked into the federal holding facility in Alexandria and met Lindy York, Thomas Tull's defense attorney, who looked more sour than usual.

Seeing a copy of that morning's *Wall Street Journal* sticking out of her leather bag, I said, "Does Tull know yet?"

"No. He's being held in isolation for his own safety. There was an attack on him last evening. Seems there are a lot of family men incarcerated here."

After we'd gone through security, we went to a room set aside for attorneys to meet with clients. Twenty minutes later, led by two corrections officers, Tull shuffled in. The writer's jaw was swollen. His right hand was in a cast.

York was horrified. She shouted at the guards, "This is outrageous! My client needs medical attention!"

"He's had it," one of the guards shot back, sitting Tull down. "All night."

"I'm aw wight," Tull said thickly. "Been through worse, and they got me on oxy."

His attorney rolled her eyes. "Not exactly the way you want to be talking to law enforcement, Thomas."

"No choice," he said. "What's happened? Why are you here?"

York and I exchanged glances. "After you, Counselor."

The attorney gave me an unhappy nod and retrieved the *Wall Street Journal* from her bag. She unfolded it and slid it across the table.

The writer looked at it, puzzled at first. Then his stare hardened on the headline.

PUBLISHER DROPS BESTSELLING AUTHOR INDICTED FOR MURDERS

"I'll sue," he growled when he looked up. "I want to talk to my agent. Now!"

"You're not exactly in a position to be making demands," Sampson said.

"They can't do this! I've done nothing wrong!"

York said, "Your new publishers say they can, Thomas. There was a morality clause in the deal memo governing your next book. They're exercising it, and they say you now owe them the four-million-dollar signing bonus they gave you."

"Not a chance! I will sue. I didn't do this! I am not the Family Man, Lindy!" he shouted. He winced and glanced at me. "Volkov. Find Volkov, Cross, and you'll know I was framed."

"We did find him," I said. "Or NYPD did. He was one of three shooters who gunned down Frances Duchaine and her two bodyguards last night. Officers on the scene returned fire, killing two and wounding the third."

"Volkov?" he said.

"Shot multiple times."

"Tell me he's alive."

Sampson said, "Your alibi's in a medically induced coma, hanging on by a thread."

The writer gaped at us for several moments as if suddenly overwhelmed by this newest twist in his predicament.

He shook his head, said, "I couldn't make this shit up if I tried."

94

Manhattan

ON MONDAY AFTERNOON, BREE climbed out of a taxi in front of NYU Medical Center. She'd slept fitfully at Phillip Henry Luster's place but had felt well enough that morning to go to Salazar's precinct and make a detailed statement about the previous evening's events to the detectives there, including Rosella's partner, Simon Thompson.

Thompson, who'd been cold to her before, had taken her aside and thanked her for saving Salazar's life. Bree was still feeling good about that when she exited the elevator on the maternity ward and asked the nurses where she could find Rosella.

Room 302, she was told. "She's having a party in there," the nurse said.

Bree went to room 302 and found Salazar in bed, an IV in her arm and a newborn in a pink blanket on her lap. She was surrounded by family: her four-year-old daughter, her husband, her sister, her mother, and two men who turned out to be the detective's brothers.

They were all bantering in Spanish when Bree knocked on the open door.

"Chief Stone," Salazar called, sounding weak but smiling. "Come in, come in."

"I'm not interrupting?"

"Never," she said. "You're family now." She introduced the people around the bed.

One of her brothers stared at Bree suspiciously and said something sharp in Spanish.

The detective's brows knit. "Because she saved my life, fool!" Salazar looked back at Bree and grinned. "Come, come see my little one."

Bree smiled as she went to the bed, and the family made room for her.

"A baby girl?"

"I'm as surprised as you are," Salazar said. "I was sure it was a boy. And you know how they were worried that the baby was in distress? Turns out that her head was in the wrong position and she almost got wedged in the birth canal."

"Wow. She's tough!"

"She is," Salazar's mother said. "With a little help from the doctors, they got her out, and she's fine now."

Salazar said, "Better than fine. Six pounds, six ounces of pure beauty."

"What's her name?"

Salazar's older daughter, Elaina, said proudly, "Analisa Bree Salazar!"

"What?" Bree said, looking at the detective in wonder. "That's so sweet."

"You saved my life."

"You saved mine first."

"I still owe you."

Bree grinned so wide it hurt. "Well, I'm honored, Rosella and Debo. When do you get out of here?"

"Tomorrow," Salazar's mother said. "Rosella was running a fever earlier and they want to make sure she and the baby are okay."

The nurse who'd directed Bree to the room entered and shook her head. "Too many people. Someone's got to go."

"I will," Bree said. "I just wanted to stop in to say hi and meet Analisa."

"When are you going back to DC?" Salazar asked.

"In a couple of hours, if I'm lucky," Bree said. "If not, tomorrow."

"Text me," Salazar said, and after saying goodbye to everyone, Bree left.

She returned to Luster's apartment and was gathering her things to head to Penn Station and the Acela train south to Washington when her cell rang. She looked at caller ID and saw a 212 area code and a number she did not recognize.

"This is Bree Stone," she said.

"Bree," a woman said. "This is Addie Wells. We met last night before…" Her voice trailed off.

"I remember you, Addie," Bree said. "How are you?"

"I'm peachy, but I heard you were part of the gunfight with the Russians after they killed Frances Duchaine."

Bree sighed. "You heard correct."

"Well, I'm thrilled you're alive."

"I'm pretty happy about it too."

Wells laughed. "You really impressed me last night, Bree. Even before the shooting started."

"I appreciate that."

There was a pause. "I'd love to talk to you about writing a book for me someday."

"Me?"

"Why not? I specialize in true crime and until yesterday I was Thomas Tull's new editor. Did I mention that?"

"I don't think so. I should tell you that my husband is working the Family Man case."

"I figured that out last night after I got home," Wells said. "Which is also part of why I called you. Does Dr. Cross know that Suzanne Liu is representing some unknown writer and shopping a book proposal about the Family Man murders and Thomas Tull?"

That came out of left field. "I doubt it. How do you know that?"

"Suzanne sent me a teaser e-mail about the project an hour ago. Claims to have the inside story. She says it's destined to be a classic and that it will *never* leave the bestseller list. The actual proposal is coming in an hour. I have thirty-six hours to decide whether to buy or not. Auction, best bid, nine a.m., day after tomorrow."

"Who's the unknown writer?"

"Uh, let me see," she said and paused. "Lisa Moore—do you know her?"

Washington, DC

WHEN BREE'S CALL CAME in, Sampson and I were driving across the Fourteenth Street Bridge reviewing our chat with Thomas Tull, who'd gone back to his cell looking as trapped as a man could be.

Over the Bluetooth connection, Bree's voice filled the car. "Did you know Lisa Moore is writing a book about the Family Man killings and Thomas Tull?"

"What? No."

Bree explained about meeting Tull's editor the evening before and then hearing from her about Moore's proposal, which was about to be submitted to publishing houses with Suzanne Liu as agent.

When she finished, I said, "Moore certainly never mentioned to us that she was writing a book. She claimed Liu was her lover and alibi, and that was pretty much it."

"I think there's more to it," Bree said. "I mean, how long ago did you arrest Tull?"

"Four days ago."

"Not a lot of time to put together a book proposal from an unknown writer."

"It is fast," Sampson said. "No doubt about it."

I said, "Any chance we can see that proposal as soon as it lands?"

"I think I can make that happen," Bree said. "I'll call you back." She hung up.

Sampson and I glanced at each other, the ramifications of the book proposal beginning to sink in.

"Tull did think Moore was framing him," John said. "And he did threaten Liu after selling his book to someone else. There could be bad, bad blood between them."

"Could be. I'm getting suspicious now."

"Highly. I feel like we should be turning around and going back to Alexandria, but Willow's ballet debut is in two hours."

"You're going to that recital," I said. "We'll look at Moore's proposal tonight and then see what Tull thinks of it in the morning."

"Sounds like a plan," John said, looking relieved.

"Willow has to come first," I said. "Always."

"Glad to be reminded, Alex."

Sampson's phone rang. He answered, listened, frowned, said, "Black Porsche? And he says we've met? I've never heard of the guy. Can you send over a photo of his driver's license? Thanks."

He hung up as we left the bridge and headed toward my house. "Some guy got arrested last night speeding in a black Porsche on the Rock Creek Parkway. He's got four outstanding warrants in Texas."

"Same guy who raced Tull?"

"Dunno, but he says he knows things we should know about Tull."

We were almost to my home on Fifth when Sampson's phone buzzed with a text.

He opened it, used two fingers to magnify the screen, stared, and, after a moment, said, "Son of a bitch."

I glanced over at a Texas driver's license with a grainy picture of a bald guy in his forties. "James Kenilworth? Who's that?"

CHAPTER

96

AFTER CALLING ADDIE WELLS and asking the editor to forward the book proposal to both her and Alex, Bree tried to convince herself it was time to head to the train station and home. But she'd had only a few hours of sleep the night before and events had been moving so fast, she was suddenly and overwhelmingly tired.

She lay down on her bed in Luster's guest room, told herself she'd nap for an hour and then regroup.

When her phone began to ring, Bree felt dragged from an almost drugged state, sure that she'd been asleep less than fifteen minutes. When she picked up the phone, however, she saw two full hours had passed.

"Hello?" she said, aware of how groggy she sounded.

"Chief Stone? This is Simon Thompson."

"Oh, hi, Detective," she said. "How are you?"

"Like I said earlier, happy my partner's alive," Thompson

said. "Listen, Rosella wanted me to call you. You asked about a company named Paladin doing work for the hedge fund that invested in Duchaine."

"Okay?"

"They did use Paladin," he said. "But, you know, turns out all sorts of companies and law enforcement agencies are using them. NYPD even has a contract."

"Does it? What about the Duchaine company itself?"

"Uh, I don't know that. Let me ask and get back to you."

"Thanks, Detective."

"Back at you, Chief."

Bree got up, put her shoes on, and freshened up in the bathroom. As she was leaving the bedroom, she heard keys jangle and dead bolts thrown down the hall.

Phillip Henry Luster came in and saw her. "Still here?"

"I'm so sorry, Phillip," she said. "I never intended to stay even overnight."

"Nonsense, I'm thrilled," he said with genuine enthusiasm. "We'll order in. Can I do the honors?"

"Please," she said, following him into the kitchen.

"Chardonnay?"

"Double please," she said. "Who was Frances Duchaine's head of marketing?"

Luster pulled the cork from a chilled bottle of chardonnay. "That would be Nellie Ray. She's an old friend of mine and she's assured me up and down that she had no idea whatsoever about the human-trafficking allegations."

"You've spoken recently?"

"A few days ago. Why?" he asked, pouring wine into their glasses.

"I'd like to talk to her."

"About?"

"A tech company outside Boston that I suspect Duchaine used."

The fashion designer pursed his lips, then dug out his phone. A few thumb taps later, he put the phone on speaker and set it between them on the counter.

"Phillip?"

"Hello, Nellie. I'd meant to call earlier."

"Didn't we all?" Ray said, her speech sounding a little slurred. "I can't count the number of people I've called since I heard. It's a nightmare!"

"It is."

"You were cochair of the gala, weren't you?"

Luster said, "I was."

After a long pause, Bree heard ice clinking in a glass. Ray said, "I know it wasn't your fault, Phillip. But I can't help thinking the security should have been better, you know?"

That annoyed Luster. "Nellie, I am standing here with one of the women who fought the Russians after they shot Frances."

Bree leaned over the phone. "Hi, Nellie. My name is Bree Stone, and I agree with you. Frances Duchaine should have had tighter security around her, given what happened at Paula Watkins's party."

"Thank you."

"But that was largely Frances's call, as I understand it," Bree said. "She had her two guards and felt comfortable with the level of security."

Luster said, "That is correct, Nellie."

"Then I need another stiff drink," Ray said. "And why not? Frances is dead. Paula is dead. And a once great company is…" She broke down crying.

Luster said, "It's going to be all right, Nellie."

"No, it's not, Phillip," she cried. "I'm forty-six. Who will hire me?"

"Tess Jackson would in a heartbeat," he said. "She'd be crazy not to."

After a snuffle and a hiccup, she said in a meek voice, "You think so, Phillip?"

"I'll talk to her in the morning," Luster promised. "But before we let you go, Bree has a question for you."

Ray sighed. "Thank you, Phillip. What's your question, Bree?"

"To your knowledge did Duchaine, the company, ever use the services of a Massachusetts firm called Paladin?"

Duchaine's director of marketing laughed. "Paladin. One of the dumber moves we made in the past few years."

"How's that?" Bree said.

Ray told her that Frances Duchaine and Paula Watkins had followed the advice of hedge-fund manager Ari Bernstein and hired Paladin to mine hard data to determine where to put new stores as the company expanded. "The demographics they came up with from their algorithms were solid on paper—proximity to wealthy towns, reasonable rent and overhead, things like that," Ray said. "But they didn't account for how devastating e-commerce was going to be for the fashion-to-wholesale-to-physical-retail business, which was our business model."

Bree said, "Should Paladin have predicted it?"

"Ryan Malcomb's supposed to be the big genius, spotter of trends, right?"

"You've met him?"

"Five or six times," she replied as Bree's own cell phone rang. "He, uh, em, uh...well, I think he uses the whole muscular dystrophy thing to his advantage."

"Hold that thought," Bree said, seeing who was calling her. She answered it as she walked from the kitchen. "Detective Thompson?"

"The docs say they're going to bring Volkov out of his coma tomorrow evening," Salazar's partner said. "But they don't think he'll be coherent enough to answer questions until the following day. If you're available, Rosella wants you there when we question him."

"I'll be there," Bree replied. "FYI? Paladin did do business with Duchaine."

"Good to know, I guess," he said with little enthusiasm. "Gotta go."

When Bree returned to the kitchen, Luster was pouring himself a second glass of wine. His phone was dark.

"Nellie had to go, unfortunately," he said. "Her mother phoned. She said you can call her back tomorrow if you need to. Another round?"

He was holding the bottle up toward her. Bree felt odd about something Nellie had said but couldn't quite put her finger on it. *What is it? Does it matter?*

"Why not?" Bree said finally, and held out her glass.

Luster gave her a generous dose. "How does organic Chinese sound?"

"Perfect," she said. Her cell phone buzzed, alerting her to a text. She thumbed the screen, saw it was from Addie Wells, and opened it. It contained an attachment titled "Write Me a True Story, Family Man."

97

Washington, DC

AT TEN MINUTES TO nine on the morning of the auction, Lisa Moore lounged on a couch, sipping espresso and watching Suzanne Liu pace back and forth across the living room of the Airbnb Moore had been renting in Kalorama.

"Are you always like this before an auction?" Moore asked calmly.

Liu looked at her as if she were mad. "Of course. Everyone is when something is hot like this."

"But you're the agent now, not the editor," Moore said, putting her coffee down.

"All the more reason to be biting my nails. This is my first time on the other side of the table, Lisa."

Getting up and walking toward Liu, Moore said, "So you should be even chiller. You said it yourself last night—we're holding an ace-high royal flush. Six different publishers said they intend to bid."

The former editor shook her head. "You don't understand, Lisa. Sometimes projects get too hot. For whatever reason, the suits start thinking the price is going to be too high for them to even bother bidding or that the writer isn't seasoned enough to execute the narrative in a bestselling manner. In that case, we could get six different no-bids in the next hour."

Moore came around behind her and started massaging her neck. "That won't happen, Suzanne. I guarantee they'll bid. How could they not? It's too juicy, too delicious, the way it takes Thomas to his knees. Everyone loves to see the big man fall, don't they? And besides, I'll have you as an editor to guide me."

Leaning back into her lover's hands, Liu said, "Everyone does adore seeing an a-hole like Thomas brought low. And you're right. You have me as a guide."

"That's my girl."

Liu's laptop dinged.

Liu pulled away from Moore, mild terror on her face as she hurried to the machine.

"You would have been terrible in combat," Moore said, sighing.

"I'd have a nervous breakdown in combat," Liu agreed and looked at an e-mail that had just come in. "Damn it!"

"What?"

Liu was trembling when she turned. "I told you it might get too rich for some people's blood."

"Which house?"

"Doesn't matter," she said, stalking away. "We need someone to believe in us here. We need someone to step forward so I can do my magic."

"You'll get it. We'll get it. We haven't gone through what we've gone through not to get the brass ring, Suzanne."

"Publishing can be a fickle, subjective business. I've told you that."

Moore gritted her teeth. "Have more faith. What's the worst that can happen? We don't get a deal and we self-publish on—"

Liu held up her hands in horror. "Don't even say it!"

Ding!

Liu ran over and was fumbling with the trackpad when—*ding!*

She opened the new e-mails, her eyes widening. She spun around, grinning wildly, and pumped her fist.

"Game on!" she cried. "Two seven-figure offers!"

The fax machine began churning out paper. Liu grabbed those pages and whooped with joy. She did a little shimmy and then jigged toward Moore. "We got ourselves a serious bidding war, lover!"

Moore took her agent in her arms, and kissed her hungrily. "Of course we do, little girl. Didn't I tell you if we paid attention to details, things would work out for us in a big, big way?"

CHAPTER

98

TWO HOURS LATER, SUZANNE LIU and Lisa Moore strode triumphantly down Water Street in DC's trendy Navy Yard district.

"I feel like we've slain Goliath," Liu said breathlessly. "I'm serious."

"You didn't think they'd go that high?" Moore asked.

"You did?"

"When four of the six were in the game, I figured we were heading right in the ballpark of where we ended up."

"Maybe you should be the agent," Liu said.

"Where would that leave you? Writing?" Moore said it a little snidely.

Liu stiffened and said, "Don't forget, that proposal would not have been in the shape it was without my guiding hand, lover."

"No doubt. And I deeply appreciate it, little girl."

They arrived at Osteria Morini, Moore's favorite lunch spot in the nation's capital. The maître d' recognized her immediately.

"Business or celebration, Ms. Moore?" he asked.

"Definitely celebration, Brian. I'd like a bottle of your finest prosecco brought to the table."

"Magnifico," Brian said, beaming.

He led them to their table along the wall, handed them two menus, and promised to have their prosecco brought right away.

"Good food here?" Liu asked.

"Brilliant cuisine," Moore said, as if Liu should have known. "The *brodetto,* an Adriatic-style fish stew, is incredible."

"Sounds a little rich for lunch. I'd have to take a nap later."

"I was actually hoping we might find our way into bed afterward."

Liu's smile turned saucy. "That does sound like a delicious dessert."

Their waiter brought over the prosecco packed in ice in a silver bucket, made a nice show of popping the cork, and poured the wine into two flutes.

"I understand a celebration is under way," he said.

Liu gestured at Moore. "I just sold her first book."

"Yes? This is fantastic!"

"Thank you," Moore said, blushing a little.

"Can I make recommendations?"

Liu said, "I heard about the *brodetto.* Sounds a little rich?"

"Then the branzino, seared Mediterranean sea bass."

"Perfect."

"That does sound good," Moore said. "Make it two."

The waiter made note of it, bowed slightly, and walked away;

Moore raised her champagne flute and said, "To many, many more of these kinds of celebrations."

"Hear, hear," Liu said, clinking her glass against Moore's. "And to many, many more books sold."

"And auctioned to Hollywood," Moore said. She drank deeply.

"Of course," her agent said and she stared into her lover's eyes as she drank from her own glass. "I have a feeling we're going to need another bottle, don't you think?"

"Mmm," the newly minted writer said. "What a grand idea!"

Liu grabbed the bottle and refilled Moore's flute. She was starting to refill her own when she noticed her companion glance up and freeze. The color drained from Moore's face.

Liu twisted in her seat and saw Dr. Alex Cross, Detective John Sampson, and FBI special agent in charge Ned Mahoney heading right to their table.

Mahoney smiled at them and said, loud enough for half the restaurant to hear, "Lisa Moore and Suzanne Liu, you're under arrest for the Family Man murders as well as multiple other crimes and conspiracies. You have the right to remain silent. You have the right to…"

Liu barely heard any of it. She was staring at Cross in disbelief. "I'm innocent," she said.

"No, you're not," Cross said.

"I didn't kill anyone!"

"Maybe you didn't," Sampson said, looking at her and then at Moore, who had gone stone-faced. "But *you* did."

"Stop talking, Suzanne," Moore hissed as Mahoney cuffed her. "Say nothing until you've spoken to a lawyer."

99

Manhattan

ON WEDNESDAY, IN AN empty hospital room in a section of the NYU Medical Center far from the maternity ward, Bree watched a screen that Rosella Salazar's partner had set up for her.

Connie Ellis, the assistant Manhattan DA overseeing the Paula Watkins investigation, stood next to her, also watching the screen.

It featured a feed from an iPhone that Detective Thompson had mounted on a tall tripod and carried to the room Dusan Volkov had been moved into after being brought out of a medically induced coma. Volkov's head was heavily bandaged, but doctors had told Thompson and Salazar that while Bree's bullet had grazed the side of his skull, he had not suffered a severe brain injury.

The Russian was certainly alert when Salazar, who'd been released from the hospital just the day before, walked slowly and gingerly into the room, followed by her partner. She ignored Volkov, who was handcuffed to the bed, and said something to the uniformed officer who'd been guarding him.

The officer left the room. Thompson turned on the sound as Salazar eased into a chair by the foot of Volkov's bed. He was watching both of them closely but said nothing until she and Thompson identified themselves.

"I know who she is," Volkov said to Thompson, gesturing at Salazar. "You? No. Does not matter, I say nothing until lawyer comes here."

"Someone from the public defender's office is on the way," Thompson said. "Not that it really matters. The evidence against you is overwhelming and it will get even more over-whelming once we execute search warrants on your home and businesses."

"What evidence? I know no evidence."

Salazar said, "Give me a break, Dusan. I saw you and two of your men kill Frances Duchaine and her bodyguards in cold blood. I shot your men. You were shot trying to kill me. I'll testify to that in court. Security footage up and down Forty-Second Street ensures that you will never see the light of day as a free man again."

The Russian said nothing.

"I wish this state still gave the needle, Dusan," Thompson said. "You deserve it."

A man who looked about seventeen knocked and entered. "I am Sergei Andreyev," he said. "I will be representing Mr. Volkov."

"You're from the public defender's office?" Thompson asked.

"No, I was hired by friends of Mr. Volkov." He said something to the mobster in Russian. Volkov smiled.

Andreyev looked at Thompson and Salazar. "I would like a moment with my client, please. And turn the camera off."

Thompson helped Salazar up and shut off the camera. A few moments later, they returned to the room Bree and Ellis were in.

Salazar groaned as she sat on the edge of the bed. "God, I hate getting up and down, and I'm going to need to pump if Junior takes a long time in there."

Thompson said, "TMI, Rosella. Anyone need coffee?"

"Bad for the baby," Salazar said.

"I'll take a small one," Bree said.

Thompson left. Salazar said, "I'm not expecting him to say much. Just doing this as a courtesy for the lieutenant before I go on serious maternity leave."

"How long?"

"Six months," she said, smiling and then yawning. "I'm going to need it."

Salazar's partner returned with coffee ten minutes later. Bree was mixing in cream and stevia when Volkov's attorney knocked on the doorjamb.

"My client has something valuable to trade," he said to the assistant DA. "In return, you take life without parole off the table."

"After he killed three people in cold blood?" Ellis laughed. "I don't think so."

Andreyev said, "You will think differently when you hear what he has to tell you."

"Can't take anything off the table unless I have some idea of what he's offering."

"How about the person behind the Paula Watkins and the Frances Duchaine killings? All of the killings."

Bree said, "He knows?"

Volkov's attorney looked at her. "Who are you?"

"It doesn't matter," Ellis said. "Answer the question."

Andreyev nodded. "He knows who hired him to kill Duchaine and he knows who tried to hire him to do the Watkins murders."

The assistant DA studied him. "This better be solid."

"He's betting his life on it."

CHAPTER

100

Washington, DC

MAHONEY DRAGGED LIU AND Moore in handcuffs into FBI headquarters and marched them through the halls to a processing unit.

"Separate rooms?" Ned asked as they were fingerprinted, had their mug shots taken, and were dressed in jailhouse jumpsuits.

"No," I said. "Together. We want them to turn on each other in real time."

"Moore has intelligence training, probably interrogation training. I say we focus on Liu. She's more likely to break."

"Agreed. She can be all over the map, and Moore's a stoic."

"You lead, then."

"You're sure?"

"This is your best game, Alex. Play it."

Sampson walked up to us, shaking his phone. "You're going to like what just came back on the Kane murder weapon."

He showed us and I smiled.

"Even better," Mahoney said.

"Game on," I said and watched Liu and Moore in prison garb being led into an interrogation room.

We walked in and sat across from them but stayed quiet.

"I want a lawyer," Moore said flatly.

Liu seemed more flustered. "We both do."

"We've notified federal defenders, but maybe you don't need them," I said. "Just answer a few questions before they arrive, and maybe this all goes away. A big mistake. Lisa? Suzanne?"

Liu said, "I've never killed anyone in my life."

Sampson said, "What about your lover? Has she?"

Moore shot John an ugly look.

"Lisa?" Liu said. "She wouldn't hurt a fly."

I said, "Did you know that during a raid in the Middle East, she killed two innocent civilians, a mother and her daughter?"

"That was investigated," Liu protested. "It was an accident. Still haunts her."

Moore said nothing.

"I bet it does. What about that book proposal you were shopping around?"

"What about it?" the former editor said, more wary than frightened now.

Moore said, "I told you to shut up, Suzanne."

"Did you have a hand in writing the proposal, Suzanne?"

Liu glanced at Moore. "Of course I did. She's a first-timer."

Moore scowled.

"Doesn't know how to put that kind of thing together?"

"Lisa's a quick learner, but yes. I helped her structure it, showed her the format. Sample chapters. Outline. Market analysis."

"And you knew whom to approach at various houses."

"I was always aware of my competition, so yes," she said, on firmer ground now.

"Did you gin it up?" Sampson said.

"What do you mean?"

"Embellish the story? Add details that might or might not be true?"

"This is nonfiction. Lisa stands by the facts in the proposal and so do I."

"One hundred percent?" Mahoney said, studying Moore.

"To the best of my knowledge, everything is true, yes," Liu said. "Why?"

I sat forward. "Because we went through the proposal and compared it to our timeline of events and then ran it all by Thomas Tull."

"Thomas?" Moore said. "Why would you do that? He's a stone-cold killer."

"He claims an ironclad alibi for the night the Kanes were killed," I said. "Says he was miles away, and yet his hair was somehow found at the scene."

"Because he was there," Moore said.

"Or someone else was. Someone involved in a frame job."

CHAPTER

101

MOORE CONTINUED TO STAY COOL. But Liu shifted uncomfortably in her seat.

I knew we'd agreed to focus on the former book editor, but I felt like it was time to turn the pressure up on both of them.

I pulled a sheaf of papers from my jacket. "This is your book proposal. Tull disputes some of these facts."

"Of course he does," Liu said.

"And there are other facts here that you could not have known about because we have not released them."

Moore's gaze was steady, but her girlfriend's eyes shifted low and to the right.

Liu said, "Like what?"

"Like the fact that the murder weapon was not found in the gun safe in Tull's storage unit but in a filing cabinet against the back wall."

"Lisa said she got that from one of the officers on the scene," Liu said.

Sampson smiled. "Except we were the only officers on the scene and neither of us saw or spoke to her about that search or any other aspect of the investigation. Isn't that right, Ms. Moore?"

"That's correct," Moore said. "I spoke with two patrolmen outside the gates of the storage facility who were there after you left and then a forensics team that was sent in to tear apart Tull's unit."

I didn't expect that. "You remember the officers' names?"

"I can get them from my notes," Moore said. "What else?"

"How about James Kenilworth?"

Moore's face went several shades lighter.

Liu's brows knit. "James who?"

"Kenilworth," Sampson said.

"Never heard of James Kenilworth."

I said, "Funny. He's heard a whole lot about you. From Ms. Moore."

"What?"

Mahoney said, "Turns out, Kenilworth is a two-time felon with warrants out on breaking-and-entering charges in Fort Worth. He was more than willing to tell us he'd ginned things up for Tull in the past—hired by Ms. Moore, of course. For the past three months, he's been working solely for Moore. And, in effect, for you, Ms. Liu."

"No," Liu said, then looked at Moore, who was expressionless.

"Oh, yes. Mr. Kenilworth has admitted to being the intruder at the Allison home. He's confessed to using the toupee your girlfriend gave him so he would look like Tull."

Mahoney slid a picture of Kenilworth's driver's license and the still from the Allisons' security recordings across the table.

"He's bald in real life. He's also a runner and owns a little Jack Russell terrier named Sparkle. He does look a heck of a lot like Thomas Tull with the toupee on, doesn't he?"

Liu looked at the pictures and then at Moore. "Lisa?"

"Shut up, Suzanne," Moore said. "For once, shut up."

I nodded to Sampson, telling him I was setting him up for the kill.

Then I turned back to Moore. "You went on the laptop in Tull's office and called up Google Earth and the Allisons' house and the Kanes', then left the app running."

Tull's researcher said nothing.

Sampson opened a large manila envelope he'd brought in with him. "While my colleagues were placing you both under arrest, I was executing a search warrant on your Airbnb apartment. And look what we found on a shelf in one of the closets."

He drew out an evidence bag containing a baggie holding several locks of sandy-brown hair.

"We haven't tested them yet, but they are the right color," I said. "And they sure look about the same length as the hairs we found at the Kane crime scene and later identified as Tull's."

Liu stared at the hair, then at Moore, then at Sampson. "Which bedroom?"

Mahoney pointed at Moore and said, "It gets worse."

Sampson picked up his phone and showed the screen to them. "That's a report from the crime lab on the forty-caliber Glock we found in the storage unit. Not only has it been confirmed as the murder weapon in every one of the Family Man killings, but partial fingerprints were discovered, one on the clip and one on a cartridge that was still in the clip."

I said, "We ran them through IAFIS, the fingerprint database, and got a hit."

"Thomas?" Liu said.

"Your girlfriend," he told her.

Moore's mouth went slack, and her eyes widened with disbelief. "No. That's not true."

"But it is," Mahoney said.

She turned angry, shaking her head, and glared at me. "Look, I ginned the excitement up a little, hired Kenilworth to invade the Allisons' place. If it was necessary, he was going to go into another house in Northwest DC, the Pan family. I learned from Thomas how to ratchet up the tension in a case."

"Why did you drop the hair at the Kanes'?" Mahoney asked.

"I didn't," Moore said. "I honestly had never been near that house until after the family was murdered."

I said, "How do you explain Tull's hair in your room and your prints on the gun that killed more than eighteen people?"

"I…" She looked lost. "I can't. I—"

A knock came at the door. An FBI agent leaned his head in and informed Mahoney that the two federal defenders were on their way up.

"We'll leave you now," I said, standing. "But it's over for the both of you. You'll spend the rest of your lives behind bars, and rightfully so."

Liu's destruction was complete. She stared at the table and sobbed.

We headed for the door.

Moore shouted, "Wait!"

102

Manhattan

ON THE SCREEN, BREE watched the assistant district attorney and Detectives Thompson and Salazar return to the hospital room where Dusan Volkov and his boyish-looking lawyer Sergei Andreyev were waiting to hear the Russian mobster's fate.

"They agree?" Volkov asked. "No life in prison?"

"We haven't agreed yet," ADA Ellis said.

Andreyev protested. "My client's going to be straight with you about many things. You should take life in prison off the table."

"He does minimum twenty-five or no deal whatsoever," Ellis said. "And this information has to be solid as concrete."

Andreyev started to counter, but Volkov waved him off. "I start," he said. "When you think you hear enough, you take these things off the table, yes? And fifteen years minimum, because I know many, many things about many, many people."

The ADA folded her arms, said, "I'm listening."

The Russian said, "One day—I have the date somewhere, but I don't remember now, maybe six months ago?—I get text on private cell phone and e-mail in private, secure e-mail. Same message saying Duchaine and Watkins are taking over high-end prostitution in Manhattan."

"Who sent the message?" Ellis pressed.

"He calls himself Maestro and M."

Bree's heart started to pound. She sat forward, riveted, and started filming the screen with her phone to show Alex later.

"Who is he?"

"I told you," Volkov replied. "Maestro and M. That's it. He uses burn phone and messages through Tor. You know this Tor?"

Ellis sounded irritated when she said, "An anonymous messaging system."

"Yes, but you are government, you can look at pictures I took of every message he sends me. FBI traces him."

Arms crossed, Salazar asked, "How do you know this Maestro is behind the killings at Paula Watkins's house?"

"Because he tries to hire me to do the killings at Watkins's and I refuse. You will see from pictures."

"Why did you refuse?"

"Too risky. I mean, eleven people at one time?"

"Who did M hire for that?"

"I have no idea."

Thompson said, "But you agreed to kill Duchaine for M?"

"After he said money was no object, that he had someone with deep, deep pockets who wanted to make sure Duchaine never corrupted anyone ever again, and then proved it, yes."

"How much?"

"Twenty million in Bitcoin. Half up front. Half on finish."

Sergei Andreyev said, "This is enough?"

Ellis shook her head. "Not until I know if Maestro even exists."

"He doesn't," Salazar's partner said. "It's bull."

"I agree," Salazar said. "And I'm out of here."

"No deal," the assistant district attorney said.

"I'm telling you the truth!" Volkov cried.

"I don't care what you call it, life in prison is what we're seeking," Ellis said and she left the room while the two Russians shouted at each other.

Thompson shut off the feed. Bree turned off the camera on her phone, ran into the hallway, and intercepted Ellis, Salazar, and Thompson, who shut Volkov's door to muffle the shouting.

"Can you believe that nonsense?" Salazar asked Bree.

"Actually, I can," Bree said.

"What?" Ellis said.

"Maestro exists," Bree said quietly. "It's a vigilante group run by someone who calls himself M."

"C'mon," Thompson said.

"It's real," Bree insisted. "M sent men in helicopters to kill my husband and his partner last year deep in the Montana wilderness. They'd gotten too close to Maestro operators who were assassinating corrupt federal and local law enforcement agents and destroying the Alejandro drug cartel."

Ellis said, "I remember reading about those killings and the cartel, but I don't recall any reference to an M or Maestro."

"The government wanted to keep it quiet," Bree said. "They didn't want to glorify a vigilante group, figuring it would bring out the crazies."

"Especially when they're killing law enforcement," Salazar said. "Corrupt or not."

"Exactly."

"Well," Ellis said. "Even if M and Maestro exist, I certainly don't have enough to give Mr. Volkov the slightest leniency. And I do have other things to do. We'll let him stew, see if he remembers more in a few days."

"C'mon," Salazar said to Bree. "We'll go find you a ride to Penn Station and me a ride home to my baby."

Bree was about to agree when she remembered something Alex had asked her to do while she was in New York.

"Can I go ask Volkov a question for my husband first? It's about the Family Man murders in DC."

Ellis shrugged. "Fine by me. If he'll talk."

103

Alexandria, Virginia

ON THE SIDEWALK OUTSIDE the federal detention facility, I kneaded the knotted muscles in my neck with one hand and held my phone tight to my ear with the other. "You're sure that's what Volkov said?"

"Hundred percent," Bree replied. "I recorded it."

"Volkov know you were recording?"

"He did."

"Send me a copy?"

"Of course. Guess who Volkov said hired him to kill Duchaine."

"No clue."

"M."

"What?"

"I'm serious. M offered him twenty million in Bitcoin to do it."

"Does Volkov know who M is?"

"No. He was always contacted through Tor encrypted messages, just like you. And he said M tried to hire him to kill the people at Paula Watkins's place, but he refused."

M was behind the Duchaine killings. How had that happened?

I was about to ask that when Bree said something, but her voice faded in and out like it was coming in over a shortwave. "Say that again, Bree."

But the reception was even worse.

"One of us is having phone issues. I'll see you at Union Station at seven thirty."

"Love you" was all I understood before she broke the connection.

I pocketed my phone and looked up to see Mahoney and Sampson waiting. "Anything yet?" I asked.

Ned said, "Agents went into Haps Premium ten—"

His phone buzzed with a text; he looked at it, then nodded at us. "Cold/cold."

We were soon in one of the rooms the detention facility set aside for law enforcement and attorneys to meet with prisoners.

Tull came strolling in wearing irons and a smirk on his face, which was less swollen but still black-and-blue.

"I saw on the news they were arrested," he said, his words sounding clearer than the last time we'd spoken. "I told you they were framing me, and you're finally coming to your senses, Dr. Cross. Finally seeing the light."

He said it all with such satisfaction that I let him revel in it for several moments.

"I've always been a little slow on the uptake," I said eventually. "I'm curious. Is that how you'll write it? That Moore and Liu framed you to hide their roles in the murders?"

"Their roles?" he said with condescension. "Lisa's a stone-cold killer. And Suzanne would stab her own mother in the back if it suited her purposes."

"Moore admits she called up Google Earth on your computer and pinned the position of the Allisons' house and the Kanes'."

"Did she? What about the murder weapon?"

"What about it?"

"I read that they found Lisa's fingerprints on it."

"Partials."

Tull laughed scornfully. "Some serial killer. Doesn't even know to wipe her weapon down before she plants it in my storage unit."

We said nothing.

His smug smile returned. "When am I getting out? I've got a book to write."

I leaned forward, said, "I'm thinking you'll have plenty of time to write that book."

The writer blinked and retreated slightly. Good. I wanted him off balance.

Then the smile returned. He tilted his head. "When can I get out?"

"Just a couple of loose ends to take care of and you're free as a bird, Thomas."

"Let's knot them up, then."

I sat back. "There's another explanation for why your hair was at the Kanes' crime scene. Something other than that Lisa Moore planted the hair before she went on a killing spree in order to frame you and send you to prison."

He raised his eyebrows.

"You planted it," Sampson said. "You planted your own hair."

104

THERE WAS A LONG pause as the writer looked at us with increasing incredulity. After a moment, he threw back his head and howled with laughter, tears streaming down his cheeks. We watched him until he composed himself.

"You're killing me." Tull chuckled. "Why in God's name would I ever do that?"

Sampson said, "You discovered that Lisa had joined forces with Suzanne and that they were trying to gin up the case for you being the killer. The fact that you are the killer, Thomas, left you with only one recourse. You had to frame them instead."

Before he could reply, I said, "It's quite a bold move. I mean, incriminating yourself in the short run to be free in the long run. And it's deft too. You could have overplayed your hand and left Lisa's hair at the Kanes'. Instead, you played their game against them, subtly depicting them as framers and killers, planting your own hair at their apartment. And then your master stroke: Lisa's smudged partial fingerprints, one on the clip, the other on one of the bullets, suggesting that she'd tried to rub down the gun but had botched it, a killer who up to that point had been flawless."

Tull's smile never wavered. "Nice theory, Dr. Cross. Except fingerprints don't lie. I've never seen that gun before in my life."

"Except you have. Lisa remembers you having a Glock when you both went shooting up in Pennsylvania."

"A nine-millimeter," he said.

"That's what she said you'd say. But it wasn't the nine-millimeter that day, was it? You had the forty that day and called it a nine-millimeter."

He chuckled again. "Why would I do that?"

"So you could take one of her forty-caliber clips and replace it with your own when she was off in the woods taking a pee."

"Ridiculous," he said.

"Yes," I said. "Except that some serial killer you are, Mr. Tull. You forgot to wipe your own prints off the clip you put in her pistol."

He said nothing for several seconds, as if searching his memory. "Nonsense," he said finally. "You're bluffing, fishing."

Now I chuckled. "You got me. It's just a theory. By the way, we caught up to your alibi, Volkov."

The tension fell from Tull's shoulders. His smile broadened. "I knew you would. He put me in that condo with his girls, right?"

I put my phone on the desk and hit Play. Bree had told me where to start it.

"Thomas Tull?" Volkov said on the recording. I hit Pause.

The writer looked at me, puzzled.

I said, "Oh, did I tell you that Volkov is under arrest for the murder of Frances Duchaine and her bodyguards? And he's trying to get life imprisonment off the table."

Before Tull could answer, I hit Play again.

Volkov said, "I know Tull. He has nasty habits that I feed from time to time."

Tull smiled smugly. "Told you."

"What about that night?" Bree asked on the recording. "Did you set him up with three hookers, a condo, and cocaine?"

"This is important to you, yes?"

"Very," Bree said.

Another man with a Russian accent said, "Get the ADA back in here, then."

After a moment, a woman said, "This is Manhattan assistant district attorney Connie Ellis witnessing. Go ahead, Mr. Volkov. Answer the question."

"Tull is very bad man. He knows things about me and my business," Volkov said.

"Answer," Ellis said.

"He asks me to give him alibi for that night in return for two hundred grand," Volkov said. "There were no girls. No coke. Nothing."

Bree said, "Why would he do that?"

"Because Tull is killer, like me. But he is different. Tull, he *likes* to kill."

Across the table in the interrogation room, Tull snarled, "This is bullshit. I've—"

I said, "Wait for it."

"How do you know that?" Ellis said.

Volkov cleared his throat. "Because he kills two of my girls, one last year, one the year before, and pays me to keep quiet."

Bree asked, "Why do you think Tull needed an alibi from you that night?"

"Not difficult to see. He was killing someone that night, taking pleasure in it."

"An entire family," Bree said.

"I say it again. Thomas Tull, he likes to kill people."

105

I SHUT THE RECORDING off and gazed at Tull.

The smug smile was gone. "You put Volkov up to saying that. And I've never killed any of his girls."

I leaned across the table. "He says you did and we believe him, you cold, evil bastard. Did you kill every one of the victims in your books?"

"Never."

"We think you did. We think you murdered most if not all of them. We think you framed the men in prison just so you could lay down the stories of your homicidal fantasies the way you wanted them told and make sure you never faced justice."

"This is all nonsense and hearsay and you know it," Tull snarled. "Show me one concrete thing that ties me to the Family Man murders that isn't linked to Lisa Moore. Just one thing."

Sampson smiled. So did Mahoney. And so did I.

Ned held up his cell phone. "We have agents out in Gaithersburg inside Haps Premium Meats and Cold Cold Storage. They've opened the meat locker you rent there, the one Lisa Moore figured out you had."

The writer blinked, frowned, and stared into the distance as if trying to revise a sentence or a plot point in his mind.

Before he could spin the story another way, I said, "But there wasn't meat inside your locker, Thomas, was there?"

Mahoney turned his cell phone to show Tull a picture of two anodized black boxes, each about the size of a small microwave oven. "These were in your locker, Thomas."

Sampson said, "State-of-the-art jamming equipment stolen from the U.S. military and repackaged like this."

"Funny thing about these jammers," I said. "They eat a lot of power and they like to be kept cold. The colder the better, especially if you're trying to jam the entire area around one of your kill sites. Or keep your home in a total blackout."

Tull said nothing although his lips were moving, as if he were mouthing words, trying to put them in the correct order.

"Why did you have to kill whole families?" I said.

The writer did not reply.

"I know why. It's because no one cares about yet another series of people dying in some gruesome manner anymore. Every book has to be bigger, more lurid, more sensational or it won't make the bestseller list. Isn't that true, Thomas?"

Tull finally focused on me. He snorted. "Of course it's true, Dr. Cross. That's the way publishing works these days."

106

ON THE AMTRAK TRAIN bound for Washington, DC, Bree drifted in and out of sleep. In that buzzy state between consciousness and dreaming, she relived Volkov's destruction of Tull's alibi and his earlier insistence that M and Maestro were behind the assassinations of Frances Duchaine and the others involved in the sex-trafficking ring.

In the odd way of dreams, those memories were soon replaced by others. She relived two evenings before when she and Phillip Henry Luster had been in his kitchen, hovering over his phone, listening to Nellie Ray, Duchaine's former marketing director:

"Ryan Malcomb's supposed to be the big genius, spotter of trends, right?"

"You've met him?" Bree heard herself say.

"Five or six times. He, uh, em, uh…well, I think he uses the whole muscular dystrophy thing to his advantage."

Bree woke up then, her conscious mind straining to know why that was interesting enough to bubble up from her subconscious. Then, as the train approached Baltimore, she understood. She grabbed her phone and listened once again to the recording she'd made of Theresa May Alcott in the library when the billionaire got the call from Paladin.

"This is Terri…Give me a minute, will you, Emma, dear? I'm with someone and I'll need to pick up in another room…I am sorry, Chief Stone. This won't take long, but it can't wait."

Bree began to breathe faster. She rewound it and listened again, and this time she heard it slightly differently.

Was that right?

She played it a third time and heard it the same way. Then she searched her phone for Nellie Ray's number and called it.

She got the woman's voice mail and was starting to leave a message when her phone buzzed. Ray was calling her back. "Hi, this is Bree Stone."

"I saw you called. How are you?"

"Good, Nellie. Listen, when we were on the phone the other night, you were saying that you thought Ryan Malcomb played up his muscular dystrophy."

"Well, I'd be canceled if I said that on social media," Ray said. "But yes, I think he takes advantage of it."

"Okay. On another note, does he have a nickname, by any chance?"

"A nickname? Uh, yeah, I guess. Why?"

107

AT SEVEN THIRTY THAT evening I stood in the grand hall of Union Station watching travelers exit the tunnel from the Acela tracks. I spotted Bree, her arm in a sling.

We hadn't seen each other in four days, and I grinned until I realized she wasn't smiling back at me. My poor wife looked dazed and confused.

"Are you all right?" I said, giving her a hug. I took her bag.

"I don't know, Alex," she said in a quiet voice. "I just…"

"Just what?" I said, growing concerned. This was not like Bree at all.

"Nothing physical. It's complicated. Hard to explain. And I don't know if I'm right."

"Give it a try."

We started walking to the Massachusetts Avenue exit. When

we got outside, dusk was falling and the air was thicker, the first hint of the summer heat and humidity to come.

"Get an Uber?"

"Let's walk," Bree said, still pensive. "Remember Volkov said M hired him to kill Frances Duchaine?"

"How could I forget?" I said as we crossed Massachusetts and began to climb toward the Senate side of Capitol Hill.

"Stop a sec. I want you to listen to something I recorded at Theresa May Alcott's the other day."

Bree played the section of the recording she'd made in the billionaire's library: "This is Terri…Give me a minute, will you, Emma, dear?"

"Who's Emma?"

"She's not saying 'Emma,'" Bree said. "Listen again. She's saying 'em, uh.'"

She played it once more.

"I hear it now," I said. "But I don't get the significance."

"She's on the phone with Paladin," Bree said. "She's talking to Ryan Malcomb."

"Malcomb? Are you sure?"

"Positive," Bree said. "Theresa May Alcott's his aunt, and she was guardian to him and his twin brother after their parents' death."

"Still," I said. "I'm not getting where this is—"

My wife cut me off, insistent. "Malcomb has a nickname, Alex. People close to him call him M."

I stared at her in the gloaming. "Is that true?"

"A woman who used to work for Frances Duchaine and has been to Paladin's headquarters many times says it's absolutely true. Think about it, Alex. You always said M had to be incredibly wealthy. Malcomb is rich in his own right and might have his aunt's billions at his disposal. And think about this: Sampson has always said that M had to be someone affiliated with the NSA, someone who could listen in on devices."

I said, "But Malcomb can't. Paladin only has authorization to mine the data it is given by law enforcement or intelligence groups."

Bree raised an eyebrow. "Who told you that?"

I thought about it. "Ryan Malcomb."

"And M was sure as hell listening in on you and John last year before you went to Montana. He was anticipating your moves. Remember?"

I nodded and looked at our phones, which we changed constantly because of our concern about being hacked. Now, once again, I felt weirdly violated.

"You don't think Malcomb's listening to us right now, do you?"

108

Haverhill, Massachusetts

IN THE SECRET DEEP operations center below Paladin's headquarters, Ryan Malcomb stared at the huge screen in the front of the amphitheater where a fuzzy feed from a Washington, DC, CCTV camera showed Alex Cross and Bree Stone standing on a sidewalk in Lower Senate Park at the base of Capitol Hill.

Malcomb and everyone else in the room heard Cross say, "You don't think Malcomb's listening to us right now, do you?"

Stone said, "He sure could be, Alex."

Cross tapped his phone and said, "Well, if he is…if you are M, Mr. Malcomb, and you are listening, here's a heads-up: We are going to come for you and everyone else in Maestro. You will face justice for what you've done."

Malcomb's features hardened. He felt the attention of everyone in the room on him and knew he was now facing the biggest threat of his life and theirs.

He smiled at his comrades and said, "No worries, Maestro. We've prepared for this moment, haven't we?"

Edith Walton, Malcomb's longtime deep ops director, nodded. "We have, M," she said. "In fine detail."

Malcomb looked over at his partner, Steve Vance, who'd gone ashen and grim.

"Your call," Vance said.

The founder of Paladin took a long, deep breath, let it out, and said, "Initiate bugout procedures, Maestro. Erase everything. Take this op to the ground where no one can find it."

Without hesitation, Vance, Walton, and the other people in the deep ops center turned to their consoles and keyboards and began typing.

Malcomb waited until the feed on the big screen died and turned his wheelchair toward the door. "I have things to attend to in my office, Edith."

"Go to it, M," Walton said.

Malcomb wheeled himself through the door and let it shut behind him before stopping to lock the chair in place. Then he pushed himself to his feet and strode confidently toward the elevator and a new and more dangerous life.

Discover the next exciting instalment
in the Alex Cross series . . .

CROSS
Out

PUBLISHING OCTOBER 2023

Read on for an exclusive extract . . .

CHAPTER

1

South Camp Springs, Maryland

ON THAT MID-NOVEMBER MONDAY morning, after nearly three years of careful planning, the forty-eight-year-old man donned latex gloves and scanned the rental-car agreement one last time.

His eyes paused on the flowing signature *Marion Davis* before he stuffed the agreement into an aluminum clipboard storage box, the kind construction estimators use. He set it on plastic sheeting on the credenza in a dingy motel room not far from Joint Base Andrews.

Davis had been there the past three days; he'd told the young woman at the front desk that he was holing up to finish his first movie script. His claim seemed to impress her enough that she agreed to keep housekeeping away, which was good, because how could he have explained the thin plastic sheeting covering every bit of furniture and taped over the floors and walls? Or, even harder to explain, the four large plastic storage bins he'd bought at Walmart and filled with bleach, hydrogen peroxide, and distilled water?

The acrid chemical scent irritated Davis's eyes and nose, but he didn't dare open the windows for ventilation. Instead, he'd kept the air conditioner going nonstop and wore goggles and a KN95 mask. He left the room only in the dead of night, when it was safe to ferry supplies. Now Davis crouched by the closest storage bin, reached with gloved hands into the chemical solution, and pulled out a long belt of .50-caliber bullets bought two years before on the blackest of black markets, this one at a remote ranch in northern Colorado.

He knew from training and experience that a soldier could adjust his aim at a moving target by using this ammunition belt. Every fourth cartridge fired a tracer round that glowed hot orange as it sped through the air.

However, the tracers also revealed the position of the shooter. Davis left in the first four tracer rounds but removed the remaining ones and replaced them with live rounds from a second bleached ammunition belt.

When he was done, he sank the first belt back in the chemicals and went into the bathroom. There, Davis stripped off his clothes and put them in a plastic garbage bag that he closed and sealed with duct tape.

Next, he stepped into the shower stall—all but the drain covered in plastic sheeting—turned on the hot water, picked up a razor, and shaved every inch of skin he could reach, from his already shaved head to the insteps of his feet.

He poured two cups of bleach down the drain when he was finished shaving, turned off the water, and retrieved a large tube of Airassi hair remover. Davis used a sponge on a long handle to smear the stuff on the skin he'd just shaved and all over his back. His eyebrows, eyelids, and ear canals were also dabbed. The cream burned, especially on his testicles, but he waited nearly fifteen minutes before rinsing it off. It was worth the pain to ensure that no FBI crime scene tech would find his hair anywhere.

Davis stepped out of the shower, stood and waited for his body to dry, then applied copious amounts of CeraVe moisturizer, again head to toe, to keep flecks of his skin from shedding. Only then did he step into a white disposable hazmat suit. He pulled the hood over his head and zipped it to his neck.

With the goggles and respirator on, Davis lugged the storage bins into the bathroom and drained them, leaving the various components of his weapon and custom tripod in them. He used two blow-dryers to remove the rest of the moisture and lubricated the parts with oil and graphite.

When he was satisfied, Davis put lids on the bins, tore down the plastic sheeting, gathered everything he had used in the past seventy-two hours, and stuffed it all into four lawn-and-leaf bags. These he sealed with duct tape and put next to the motel room's door.

He pushed back the curtains and saw the rear of the tan utility van. No one else was in the parking lot. But why would anyone be? It was a weekday morning. The kids who lived at the motel were all in school, and their mothers were working or sleeping it off.

Davis opened another bag, retrieved a new Baltimore Ravens hoodie, and put it on over the hazmat suit. A new brown coverall with the logo of the National Park Service went on next. He finished with a pair of glasses with heavy black frames and clear lenses. He added a respirator to cover his face, checked his look, then tugged the mask down around his neck.

All of this had taken several hours. Davis had a great deal of confidence in his preparation, but his heart still raced when he finally opened the motel door. He quickly moved the storage bins and bulging plastic bags into the rear of the van, near a mountain bike and two blue fifty-five-gallon drums, one strapped to each wall. A laptop computer, purchased the year before from a pawnshop in Kentucky, went in the front seat.

Davis left the key to the spotless room on a chair by the door and drove out of the parking lot a few minutes after two p.m. He felt fully in control of his fate and pleased about the impact he was about to have.

Davis allowed himself a smile, thinking: *Isn't that the way you want to be when you're about to commit mass murder for a righteous cause?*

Have you read them all?

ALONG CAME A SPIDER

Alex Cross is working on the high-profile disappearance
of two rich kids. But is he facing someone much more
dangerous than a callous kidnapper?

KISS THE GIRLS

Cross comes home to discover his niece Naomi is missing. And
she's not the only one. Finding the kidnapper won't be easy,
especially if he's not working alone . . .

JACK AND JILL

A pair of ice-cold killers are picking off Washington's
rich and famous. And they have the ultimate target
in their sights.

CAT AND MOUSE

An old enemy is back and wants revenge. Will Alex
Cross escape unharmed, or will this be the
final showdown?

POP GOES THE WEASEL

Alex Cross faces his most fearsome opponent yet. He calls
himself Death. And there are three other 'Horsemen' who
compete in his twisted game.

ROSES ARE RED

After a series of fatal bank robberies, Cross must take
the ultimate risk when faced with a criminal known
as the Mastermind.

VIOLETS ARE BLUE

As Alex Cross edges ever closer to the awful truth about
the Mastermind, he comes dangerously close to defeat.

FOUR BLIND MICE

Preparing to resign from the Washington police force, Alex Cross is looking forward to a peaceful life. But he can't stay away for long . . .

THE BIG BAD WOLF

There is a mysterious new mobster in organised crime. The FBI are stumped. Luckily for them, they now have Alex Cross on their team.

LONDON BRIDGES

The stakes have never been higher as Cross pursues two old enemies in an explosive worldwide chase.

MARY, MARY

Hollywood's A-list are being violently killed, one-by-one. Only Alex Cross can put together the clues of this twisted case.

CROSS

Haunted by the murder of his wife thirteen years ago, Cross will stop at nothing to finally avenge her death.

DOUBLE CROSS

Alex Cross is starting to settle down – until he encounters a maniac killer who likes an audience.

CROSS COUNTRY

When an old friend becomes the latest victim of the Tiger, Cross journeys to Africa to stop a terrifying and dangerous warlord.

ALEX CROSS'S TRIAL
(with Richard DiLallo)

In a family story recounted here by Alex Cross, his great-uncle Abraham faces persecution, murder and conspiracy in the era of the Ku Klux Klan.

I, ALEX CROSS

Investigating the violent murder of his niece Caroline,
Alex Cross discovers an unimaginable secret that could
rock the entire world.

CROSS FIRE

Alex Cross is planning his wedding to Bree,
but his nemesis returns to exact revenge.

KILL ALEX CROSS

The President's children have been kidnapped,
and DC is hit by a terrorist attack. Cross must
make a desperate decision that goes against
everything he believes in.

MERRY CHRISTMAS, ALEX CROSS

Robbery, hostages, terrorism – will Alex Cross make it
home in time for Christmas . . . alive?

ALEX CROSS, RUN

With his personal life in turmoil, Alex Cross
can't afford to let his guard down.
Especially with three blood-thirsty
killers on the rampage.

CROSS MY HEART

When a dangerous enemy targets Cross and his family,
Alex finds himself playing a whole new game of
life and death.

HOPE TO DIE

Cross's family are missing, presumed dead. But Alex Cross
will not give up hope. In a race against time, he must find his
wife, children and grandmother – no matter what it takes.

CROSS JUSTICE

Returning to his North Carolina hometown for the first time
in over three decades, Cross unearths a family secret that
forces him to question everything he's ever known.

CROSS THE LINE

Cross steps in to investigate a wave of murders
erupting across Washington, DC. The victims have
one thing in common – they are all criminals.

THE PEOPLE VS. ALEX CROSS

Charged with gunning down followers of his nemesis
Gary Soneji in cold blood, Cross must fight for his
freedom in the trial of the century.

TARGET: ALEX CROSS

Cross is called on to lead the FBI investigation to find
America's most wanted criminal. But what follows will plunge
the country into chaos, and draw Cross into the most
important case of his life.

CRISS CROSS

When notes signed by 'M' start appearing at homicide scenes
across the state, Cross fears he is chasing a ghost.

DEADLY CROSS

A shocking double homicide dominates tabloid headlines.
Among the victims is Kay, a glamorous socialite and Cross's
former patient – and maybe more. But who would want
her dead, and why?

FEAR NO EVIL

Alex Cross ventures into the rugged Montana wilderness
where he's attacked by two rival teams of assassins,
controlled by the same mastermind who has stalked Alex
and his family for years.

Also By James Patterson

ALEX CROSS NOVELS

Along Came a Spider • Kiss the Girls • Jack and Jill • Cat and Mouse • Pop Goes the Weasel • Roses are Red • Violets are Blue • Four Blind Mice • The Big Bad Wolf • London Bridges • Mary, Mary • Cross • Double Cross • Cross Country • Alex Cross's Trial (*with Richard DiLallo*) • I, Alex Cross • Cross Fire • Kill Alex Cross • Merry Christmas, Alex Cross • Alex Cross, Run • Cross My Heart • Hope to Die • Cross Justice • Cross the Line • The People vs. Alex Cross • Target: Alex Cross • Criss Cross • Deadly Cross • Fear No Evil • Triple Cross

THE WOMEN'S MURDER CLUB SERIES

1st to Die (*with Andrew Gross*) • 2nd Chance (*with Andrew Gross*) • 3rd Degree (*with Andrew Gross*) • 4th of July (*with Maxine Paetro*) • The 5th Horseman (*with Maxine Paetro*) • The 6th Target (*with Maxine Paetro*) • 7th Heaven (*with Maxine Paetro*) • 8th Confession (*with Maxine Paetro*) • 9th Judgement (*with Maxine Paetro*) • 10th Anniversary (*with Maxine Paetro*) • 11th Hour (*with Maxine Paetro*) • 12th of Never (*with Maxine Paetro*) • Unlucky 13 (*with Maxine Paetro*) • 14th Deadly Sin (*with Maxine Paetro*) • 15th Affair (*with Maxine Paetro*) • 16th Seduction (*with Maxine Paetro*) • 17th Suspect (*with Maxine Paetro*) • 18th Abduction (*with Maxine Paetro*) • 19th Christmas (*with Maxine Paetro*) • 20th Victim (*with Maxine Paetro*) • 21st Birthday (*with Maxine Paetro*) • 22 Seconds (*with Maxine Paetro*) • 23rd Midnight (*with Maxine Paetro*)

DETECTIVE MICHAEL BENNETT SERIES

Step on a Crack (*with Michael Ledwidge*) • Run for Your Life (*with Michael Ledwidge*) • Worst Case (*with Michael Ledwidge*) • Tick Tock (*with Michael Ledwidge*) • I, Michael Bennett (*with Michael Ledwidge*) • Gone (*with Michael Ledwidge*) • Burn (*with Michael Ledwidge*) • Alert (*with Michael Ledwidge*) • Bullseye (*with Michael Ledwidge*) • Haunted (*with James O. Born*) • Ambush (*with James O. Born*) • Blindside (*with James O. Born*) • The Russian (*with James O. Born*) • Shattered (*with James O. Born*)

PRIVATE NOVELS

Private (*with Maxine Paetro*) • Private London (*with Mark Pearson*) • Private Games (*with Mark Sullivan*) • Private: No. 1 Suspect (*with Maxine Paetro*) • Private Berlin (*with Mark Sullivan*) • Private Down Under (*with Michael White*) • Private L.A. (*with Mark Sullivan*) • Private India (*with Ashwin Sanghi*) • Private Vegas (*with Maxine Paetro*) • Private Sydney (*with Kathryn Fox*) • Private Paris (*with Mark Sullivan*) • The Games (*with Mark Sullivan*) • Private Delhi (*with Ashwin Sanghi*) • Private Princess (*with Rees Jones*) • Private Moscow (*with Adam Hamdy*) • Private Rogue (*with Adam Hamdy*) • Private Beijing (*with Adam Hamdy*)

NYPD RED SERIES

NYPD Red (*with Marshall Karp*) • NYPD Red 2 (*with Marshall Karp*) • NYPD Red 3 (*with Marshall Karp*) • NYPD Red 4 (*with Marshall Karp*) • NYPD Red 5 (*with Marshall Karp*) • NYPD Red 6 (*with Marshall Karp*)

DETECTIVE HARRIET BLUE SERIES

Never Never (*with Candice Fox*) • Fifty Fifty (*with Candice Fox*) • Liar Liar (*with Candice Fox*) • Hush Hush (*with Candice Fox*)

INSTINCT SERIES

Instinct (*with Howard Roughan, previously published as Murder Games*) • Killer Instinct (*with Howard Roughan*) • Steal (*with Howard Roughan*)

THE BLACK BOOK SERIES

The Black Book (*with David Ellis*) • The Red Book (*with David Ellis*) • Escape (*with David Ellis*)

STAND-ALONE THRILLERS

The Thomas Berryman Number • Hide and Seek • Black Market • The Midnight Club • Sail (*with Howard Roughan*) • Swimsuit (*with Maxine Paetro*) • Don't Blink (*with Howard Roughan*) • Postcard Killers (*with Liza Marklund*) • Toys (*with Neil McMahon*) • Now You See Her (*with Michael Ledwidge*) • Kill Me If You Can (*with Marshall Karp*) • Guilty Wives (*with David Ellis*) • Zoo (*with Michael Ledwidge*) • Second Honeymoon (*with Howard Roughan*) • Mistress (*with David Ellis*) • Invisible (*with David Ellis*) • Truth or Die (*with Howard Roughan*) • Murder House (*with David Ellis*) • The Store (*with Richard DiLallo*) • Texas Ranger (*with Andrew Bourelle*) • The President is Missing (*with Bill Clinton*) • Revenge (*with Andrew Holmes*) • Juror No. 3 (*with Nancy Allen*) • The First Lady (*with Brendan DuBois*) • The Chef (*with Max DiLallo*) • Out of Sight (*with Brendan DuBois*) • Unsolved (*with David Ellis*) • The Inn (*with Candice Fox*) • Lost (*with James O. Born*) • Texas Outlaw (*with Andrew Bourelle*) • The Summer House (*with Brendan DuBois*) • 1st Case (*with Chris Tebbetts*) • Cajun Justice (*with Tucker Axum*)• The Midwife Murders (*with Richard DiLallo*) • The Coast-to-Coast Murders (*with J.D. Barker*) • Three Women Disappear (*with Shan Serafin*) • The President's Daughter (*with Bill Clinton*) • The Shadow (*with Brian Sitts*) • The Noise (*with J.D. Barker*) •

2 Sisters Detective Agency (*with Candice Fox*) • Jailhouse Lawyer (*with Nancy Allen*) • The Horsewoman (*with Mike Lupica*) • Run Rose Run (*with Dolly Parton*) • Death of the Black Widow (*with J.D. Barker*) • The Ninth Month (*with Richard DiLallo*) • The Girl in the Castle (*with Emily Raymond*) • Blowback (*with Brendan DuBois*) • The Twelve Topsy-Turvy, Very Messy Days of Christmas (*with Tad Safran*) • The Perfect Assassin (*with Brian Sitts*) • House of Wolves (*with Mike Lupica*) • Countdown (*with Brendan DuBois*)

NON-FICTION

Torn Apart (*with Hal and Cory Friedman*) • The Murder of King Tut (*with Martin Dugard*) • All-American Murder (*with Alex Abramovich and Mike Harvkey*) • The Kennedy Curse (*with Cynthia Fagen*) • The Last Days of John Lennon (*with Casey Sherman and Dave Wedge*) • Walk in My Combat Boots (*with Matt Eversmann and Chris Mooney*) • ER Nurses (*with Matt Eversmann*) • James Patterson by James Patterson: The Stories of My Life • Diana, William and Harry (*with Chris Mooney*) • American Cops (*with Matt Eversmann*)

MURDER IS FOREVER TRUE CRIME

Murder, Interrupted (*with Alex Abramovich and Christopher Charles*) • Home Sweet Murder (*with Andrew Bourelle and Scott Slaven*) • Murder Beyond the Grave (*with Andrew Bourelle and Christopher Charles*) • Murder Thy Neighbour (*with Andrew Bourelle and Max DiLallo*) • Murder of Innocence (*with Max DiLallo and Andrew Bourelle*) • Till Murder Do Us Part (*with Andrew Bourelle and Max DiLallo*)

COLLECTIONS

Triple Threat (*with Max DiLallo and Andrew Bourelle*) •
Kill or Be Killed (*with Maxine Paetro, Rees Jones, Shan Serafin
and Emily Raymond*) • The Moores are Missing
(*with Loren D. Estleman, Sam Hawken and Ed Chatterton*) • The
Family Lawyer (*with Robert Rotstein, Christopher Charles and
Rachel Howzell Hall*) • Murder in Paradise
(*with Doug Allyn, Connor Hyde and Duane Swierczynski*) • The
House Next Door (*with Susan
DiLallo, Max DiLallo and Brendan DuBois*) •
13-Minute Murder (*with Shan Serafin, Christopher Farnsworth
and Scott Slaven*) • The River Murders
(*with James O. Born*) • The Palm Beach
Murders (*with James O. Born, Duane Swierczynski
and Tim Arnold*) • Paris Detective • 3 Days to Live

For more information about James Patterson's novels,
visit www.penguin.co.uk.